THE QUEST OF THE
SULTANA

THE QUEST OF THE
SULTANA

J. L. Rothdiener

NAVIGATOR BOOKS

SAN DIEGO, CALIFORNIA

THE QUEST OF THE SULTANA

Copyright © 2015 by J. L. Rothdiener

Navigator Books

www.navigator-books.com

ISBN-13: 978-1-940397-50-4

Printed in the United States of America

Dedication

I dedicate this book to my grandchildren, Kaylie, Braden, Kaiden, and Maddox. May their generation never forget America's history and the price that was paid by the soldiers of both the North and the South during the battles of the Civil War, the prison camps, and the sinking of the S.S. *Sultana*. On the ill-fated morning of April 27, 1865, more than seventeen hundred men and women lost their lives in America's worst maritime disaster. May we always remember!

Acknowledgements

In writing this book, I am indebted to...

Sara Gonzalez and Ensembles of the Past for her beautiful reenactment photo used on the cover. Sara was also the costume designer for Brooke's lovely antebellum gown, and posed as Brooke in the cover cameo.

Veda Gonzalez Photography for her cover photo of 'Brooke.'

Holmes Brigade USV, Inc. for allowing their reenactment photo to be used on the cover.

Company E, 4th Missouri Infantry Regiment, CSA for their input.

Chris Warwick for his help in gathering information on the Civil War.

City of Marion, Arkansas, and the Sultana Exhibit.

National Prisoner of War Museum located at Andersonville, Georgia.

Henry Repeating Arms Company and its President, Anthony Imperato, for their input and support.

Paul Murdock, composer, musician of *The Sultana*, which I listened to over a thousand times as I wrote this novel.

My wife Joy for her encouragement and help in editing this book.

Burt and Sylvia Murdock for their hundreds of hours in editing this book.

My publishers Jeff and Maria Edwards for their hard work in getting this project out.

Thomas W. Bankes for his great photo used on the cover. The last picture of The S.S. *Sultana* taken on April 26, 1865, at Helena, Arkansas hours before she sunk.

Prologue

April 27, 1865
2:20 AM
On the Mississippi River, North of Memphis

He floated to the surface. His head felt like it was going to burst. Being pulled rapidly downstream by the frigid water made it almost impossible for him to catch his breath.

The semiconscious man squinted to see the men in the fishing boats who had just tried to rescue him. He caught a glimpse of a man holding the baby. A couple men in the other boat were pulling the woman to safety.

He took a shallow breath and went under again. How much time passed, he had no way of knowing.

Thank God, he again surfaced, gasping for air.

He saw a man reaching over the water, holding a lantern and barely heard his muffled voice, "Sir… where are you? You saved these two people, help us save you, mister. Please say something!"

The victim in the water tried to speak, but his voice wouldn't come. His head was throbbing. He knew time was running out.

In the distance, he saw what was left of the wooden hull—flames shooting skyward. After colliding with the muddy banks of the Mississippi, the burning steamship was slowly sinking.

He could hear the screams of the men still trapped inside: men who—only hours before—had been laughing and singing, celebrating their newfound freedom. The returnees were headed home to their families—no more war, no more prison camps.

Dead bodies floated around him.

As he began to slip under the water one more time, his eyes tracked again to the remains of the sinking paddleboat. He could scarcely make out the word on the side—*Sultana*.

His life flashed in front of him—his concerts, the Civil War, his time as a prisoner in Andersonville.

The pain in his head was intense and details were fuzzy.

How did I get here?

It was as if God answered his question when the face of a beautiful woman appeared through the mist.

His eyes closed as water began to fill his lungs.

When he thought his life was over, he saw her face. The love of his life, come into view again. He could hear her calling his name…

"Barrett… Barrett… come *home* to me!"

Somehow, he managed to struggle back to the surface, gulping down the cold air.

There was only enough strength in him to whisper one word. "*Brooke*."

He was in the grip of death now. As he began to sink into the dark abyss, his thoughts slid back to the day he met her...

Chapter One

Sunday, October 16, 1859
Harpers Ferry, Virginia

The sun had disappeared below the horizon, but its scattered rays created a spectacular afterglow of pinks and purples—a perfect backdrop for an artist.

There was an eerie quality to the darkened street when the proud rider, sitting tall in the saddle of his spirited horse, strutted through the center of town. His bearded face showed the seriousness of a man fixed on bringing to the forefront a wrong that had to be made right.

Following him were almost twenty riders—some old, some young, some white, some black. Not a word was spoken among them. They were men on a mission, and their stern faces showed it.

The lead rider nodded and tipped his hat to a young lady who was walking briskly across the dusty, rutted road.

Ignoring the horsemen, a slightly gray-haired black man walking with the attractive young woman, muttered, "Miss Brooke, you sure this the way?"

At twenty-three, Brooke Fortner, with her black flowing hair, caught the attention of every man who passed. Her low-neck, blue three-tiered gown, elegant bonnet, and lace-trimmed gloves were proof that she came from a well-to-do family. A white shawl graced her shoulders.

She proudly claimed Savannah, Georgia as her birthplace. Years ago, her great-grandparents had settled there from Germany, and her family had lived on the same estate since then.

Many men had eyes for the young lady, not only because of her beauty, but also because of the social status of her family. However, she believed marriage was not in her near future. The one special man she longed to spend her life with certainly had not yet crossed her path.

Feeling a little uneasy, but not wanting to display any hint of fear, she politely smiled and nodded her head, acknowledging the man leading the other riders.

"Best be getting off the street, ma'am. A young lady should not be out alone this time of night," the man on the horse cautioned in a deep voice.

Turning on her usual charm, she responded cheerfully, "I am going to a piano concert tonight, sir."

"Ah… is Gottschalk performing here? I saw him once in New York." He stopped his horse, obviously interested.

"No, sir, he is a concert pianist named Barrett von Weber."

The rider thought aloud. "A German… von Weber… oh, yes, the Hymnist."

"Yes, we sing many of his songs in church. I have heard he will be one of the greats."

A rough-looking, young man in the group rode up alongside the older man. "Is this your slave?" he queried the woman, all the time glaring at the black man accompanying her.

"I am nobody's slave," the black man answered gruffly, protectively stepping in front of the woman.

The rider neared the black man. "I ain't talkin' to you. I was talkin' to the lady."

Trembling, Brooke stepped closer to her servant. "I am here with my brother on family business. He took sick, so I decided to attend the concert by myself. William here is my escort."

"Please excuse my son for his rudeness. My boys are quite protective of me," the bearded leader laughed.

Just then, a tall, dark figure emerged from the shadows, cautiously edging toward the unnerved woman. "Good evening, gentlemen." Eyeing the young lady, he tipped his hat. "Good evening, ma'am. Did I hear you say you're going to the concert?"

Looking directly into the handsome, well-dressed man's blue eyes, she responded nervously, "Yes, sir, are you going as well?"

"As a matter of fact, I am. I would be happy to accompany you, and the gentleman with you, to the theater. You must be careful where you walk at night. No telling what kind of riff-raff you may run into." He glared at the two men on horseback.

"Why sir, that would be mighty considerate of you." The woman's rich Southern accent added to her charm. "Have you heard von Weber perform before?"

He smiled. "Many times. I don't think he is as great as some think he is. On the other hand, I understand he is a humble man."

Another rider from the group rode his horse near the bearded leader. Anxiously, he shouted, "Pa, shall we take 'em?"

Brooke took a couple steps closer to the protection of the tall stranger with the well-trimmed goatee.

The bearded man on horseback introduced himself. "Name is Isaac Smith and these are my two boys."

The well-dressed man, suspicious of the riders, opened his coat deliberately revealing a shoulder pistol.

Smith noticed the weapon and motioned for his sons to stand back. "Interestin' firearm ya have there, sir." He bent over in his saddle to get a closer look.

"It's a Colt. Not even on the market yet. Holds five bullets and can hit a fly at fifty feet." The well-dressed man's eyes showed how serious he considered the situation.

"I see. Question is, can you hit a fly at fifty feet?" the bearded man challenged, emphasizing "you."

"No, sir! I can hit three flies at fifty feet." He moved his hand closer to his impressive weapon.

Smith cracked a smile, realizing that the stranger was referring to him and his sons. "Bet you can." He paused. "I did not get your name."

"I never gave it," he answered curtly.

Smith nodded agreeably, shoulders hunched slightly. "I best be on my way. I wish you the best, ma'am. I suggest you move with heaven's speed to that concert. Don't leave 'til it's over. The streets out here could be dangerous." He tipped his hat.

The tall stranger shot the rider a questioning look and offered the lady his arm. Neither one of them questioned Smith's intentions, nor his warning.

As the woman linked her arm in his, her heart unexpectedly quickened. She wasn't sure if it was because of the encounter with Smith, or the closeness of the sandy-haired, broad-shouldered man who towered over her. Whatever it was, she felt relief.

Continuing toward the concert hall, she glanced back at the gang of riders.

The kind man whispered, "Don't look back, just keep walking."

"I don't understand, sir," she protested.

"I've seen that look before. That man's eyes were wild. He's a man on a mission," The stranger knew it was not a good sign in a country on the brink of a civil war.

They walked a short distance before he spoke. "What brings you to Harpers Ferry, Miss…?" he asked, searching for her name.

"My name is Brooke, and I am here on official business! My father is trying to sell his goods in this area. My brother and I are here meeting the local businessmen. Since I have always wanted to see the Hymnist, this seemed like the perfect opportunity. I am glad William agreed to be my escort."

"William," he repeated. Stopping abruptly, he faced the middle-aged black man and introduced himself. "Hello, William. Some people call me 'Bear.'" He extended his hand in a friendly greeting.

William stared at the outstretched hand. After a lengthy pause, he reached his hand out in response and shook it weakly.

"Let me give you some friendly advice, William. When you greet someone with a handshake, you should always shake with a solid grip. Never greet someone with a weak handshake." He grabbed the black man's hand again. "You don't have to squeeze hard, just hold firm. Your handshake and your word are the most important tools a man can have, especially in the business world." He looked at the young lady remembering the reason she was in town and added, "Or a woman." He smiled. "Seriously, you can learn a lot about another person from a handshake. Try it again!"

The black man squeezed his hand a little firmer.

"Very good!" The younger man chuckled. "Now, next time someone offers you a hand, shake it like that. Show them that you care… you are concerned… you are interested, yet strong."

William nodded timidly.

The trio began walking again.

"That was very nice of you. Why did you do it?" Brooke cast him a questioning look.

"Do what?"

"Well, I never know how people will treat William, or me—a woman in the business world—for that matter. I have had him, I mean, William has been in my father's employ all my life. He and his wife helped care for me since my birth."

"His wife?"

"Yes, they could never have children of their own, but they both have been loyal to my family. Delilah died about four years ago."

"I'm sorry to hear that."

"William has protected me many times from animals, both four legged and two legged, if you know what I mean."

"Judging by your beauty, I do. Believe me, I do." He stole another quick glance at Brooke. "Would William like to go to the concert? I can make arrangements for him to get in."

"No, I would not want to see you get in trouble. You are most kind for escorting us to the concert hall."

"Oh, it's no problem. I am concerned about a young lady being out after dark in a strange city, far from home. Like I said, you never know what kind of trouble you will run into."

"Should I be afraid of you...? Bear... what kind of name is that anyway?" She blinked her long lashes at him.

"As I said, that is what some of my friends call me. And, no ma'am, I am pretty harmless."

Since the darkness had crept over them, a chill took over the air. They were thankful for the light of the almost-full moon illuminating the road as they walked.

Brooke shivered and wrapped her cloak tighter.

By the time they arrived at the theater, a group of people had already congregated.

"Well, here we are," the man announced, facing Brooke.

She smiled and offered her hand to him. "Thank you, sir, you are truly a gentleman." Remembering what he had told William about the handshake, she took the opportunity to hold his hand tighter.

"The honor was mine." He grinned, realizing she was still holding his hand. He raised her hand upward, snapped his heels, and then kissed the back of her gloved hand.

"Oh, my, I guess chivalry is not dead. You do not see this much in the North any more. Will I be seeing you again, Bear?"

"That is true for Northerners. They are more interested in business than remaining gentlemanly. As for seeing you again, Brooke, I am sure of it. Now, if you will excuse me, I must go. Perhaps I will see you at intermission."

"Perhaps so." Brooke's heart skipped a beat.

She studied the fascinating man as he walked away.

William interrupted her thoughts. "Miss Brooke, I know it's not my place, but Massa Rory would not be happy if he saw you carrying on with that stranger."

"Stranger? William, he came to our rescue when we were in danger. I do not need to tell you those men on the street frightened me. I think Bear is a perfect gentleman." She exhaled.

"I was scared too, Miss Brooke, but I don't believe his name is Bear. He did not even give you his real name."

"True… but he did say he may see me during intermission." She searched his face for a second. "William, would you like to attend the concert? I am not sure how they would treat you in this establishment, but we could try."

"No need to worry 'bout me, Miss Brooke. I will sit across the street with the horses. I be all right." He took a couple steps across the street and then turned around. "I see you after the concert, Missy. You go enjoy the music. I mean it, don't be worryin' yourself 'bout me."

She watched as he crossed the street and sat on the curb next to a few carriages. *Oh William, I wish things were different.*

Brooke walked to the booth to purchase her ticket. As she waited in line, she noticed a small poster of a man sitting at the piano. She studied it:

Sunday, October 16, 1859
7 PM
One performance only
The Hymnist, Barrett von Weber

Behind her, an older woman in her church-going dress began to ramble on. "He is much too young to be appearing here. However, I love to listen to the piano. Our preacher let us out of church early tonight, so we could attend the concert. I hope he is good. Some are saying he is better than Gottschalk."

"Have you ever seen Gottschalk?" Brooke asked.

"Twice in New York. He is the greatest."

Brooke's eyes returned to the poster. "Well, we sing von Weber's music in church all the time. I would suspect he is every bit as good as Gottschalk."

"Perhaps you are right," the woman sighed.

"The main thing is to enjoy what he has to offer."

"Yes. Enjoy the night. Enjoy the music."

When Brooke reached the booth, she said, "One," as she offered the cashier payment.

The ticket man ignored her outstretched hand holding the money.

"Ticket for one please," she voiced again.

"A gentleman has already paid for your ticket. He said it was for the black haired young lady with the blue dress and white shawl. That matches your description."

Before she could argue, the ticket man summoned a young boy standing outside the booth. "Jonathan!"

"Yes, sir."

"Please escort the lady to her seat."

"Yes, sir." Jonathan looked at the ticket and smiled. "Please follow me." He led her to a seat in the first row, directly in front of the piano.

"Thank you, sir. But, why here?" Her voice held a quiet joy.

"I don't know ma'am. I only do what I am told. You have the best seat in the house. Enjoy the concert."

She let her eyes grow accustomed to the murky, smoke-laden light in the theater. The noise and the chatter were typical for a small town concert hall. Her stomach churned at the reek of sour beer and cigar smoke.

The woman next to her asked, "Is this your first time here?"

"Why, yes it is. Everyone is dressed so elegantly."

"We don't get many concerts here, especially religious ones. It's mostly loose women dancing with their skirts held high. Disgusting!"

"Did you come alone tonight?"

"My husband is the banker in town and I insisted he come with me."

"Where is your husband now?" Brooke looked around.

"Where he always is when we go out." She nodded her head toward the left of the stage where four men stood talking, all dressed in fancy suits. "Drumming up business. Since the government moved all those arms to the city, he's been trying to get in on some of the action."

"Arms? What do you mean arms?"

The white-haired, stout woman moved closer to Brooke and whispered, "Rumor has it that thousands of weapons were moved into the old armory. They say the weapons are going to be used against Virginia if it secedes from the Union. Some folks say there may even be two Virginias." She shook her head, dismayed.

Brooke sat taller in her seat. "Why would Virginia secede or split?"

The talkative woman never answered the question, only made another comment. "Traitors! If you ask me every one of them should be hanged on the nearest gallows."

Brooke was shocked at what she was hearing, but was hoping it didn't show on her face.

Before she could respond, a man strutted to the center of the stage.

"Ladies and gentlemen, please be seated. The concert is about to begin." The rustling of footsteps grew loud as everyone took his or her seat, and the aroma of cigar and pipe smoke became stronger.

The announcer continued, "As mayor of this fine town, I am proud to introduce tonight's guest. This is the first time Barrett von Weber has appeared in Harpers Ferry. In fact, this is the first time this fair town has had someone of his caliber grace this establishment. I hope it is not the last. Tonight's entertainment promises to be much better than we usually have here." He chuckled. "Please give a warm welcome to Barrett von Weber... the Hymnist."

The audience clapped and shouted, roaring with approval.

On the dimly lit stage, the dusty curtain rose slowly. In the spotlight, a shadow emerged. As he neared the front of the platform, a grin spread across Brooke's face as she recognized the man—he was the gentleman who escorted her to the theater.

He stopped in front of the aged piano and bowed slightly to the delighted audience.

Immediately his eyes tracked to Brooke, and a smile encompassed his face; a smile that made her head spin. She blushed and could feel the heat in her cheeks.

The audience continued to applaud as he turned his attention to them and bowed again. He sat on the piano bench with an air of confidence. His fingers rippled over the ivory keys as he effortlessly played several of his well-known hymns.

At intermission, the entertainer stepped off the stage and greeted the people who approached him.

After a few moments, he politely excused himself and stepped over to Brooke. He gently took her hand, clicked his heels, and bowed in the traditional German greeting. "I am sorry if you think I misled you, Miss. It is important that you know me as myself... not as a concert pianist." He gestured toward the stage.

"But, you are not just a concert pianist. You are the 'Hymnist,' one of the greatest musicians in the world."

"That is kind of you, but still, I wanted you and William to know me as me. I was afraid you would act different if you thought I was someone famous."

"Oh, you need not be afraid of that. I was honored to have met you and even more so now," she said with a slight giggle.

"May I play something tonight in your honor?"

"You have already played my favorite hymns." Her throat sounded dry.

"Well, in that case, I have been working on a new piece. I have not named it yet, but since I met you, I decided to name it... *Brooke*."

"Sir, I am honored." Her brown eyes sparkled with delight.

"Please call me Barrett."

"Barrett? But I thought your friends called you 'Bear'."

"They do. Barrett means *Bear* in German. I am called that because of one of my past exploits. But, you, my dear, please call me Barrett."

"Okay. Barrett it is."

"I must finish the show. May I walk you home after the concert?"

"Yes, I would like that very much."

He kissed her hand. As he returned to the piano, his face displayed a boyish grin.

The Hymnist continued playing more of his popular music, ending the concert with a haunting melody, *Brooke.*

The audience rose in ovation, appreciating the musician's talent, but especially the closing piece.

The song had barely finished when a frantic man ran into the theater yelling. "Help! They seized the armory. People have been killed."

Panic spread throughout the concert hall. People jumped up and began running in all directions trying to escape the wild uproar. Some folks headed to the safety of their homes; others to the armory to battle whoever had taken over the military building.

Frightened, Brooke stood still, unsure what to do.

As strangers fleeing the turmoil shoved her, Barrett's gentle hand reached out and grasped her arm. "Come, follow me!" He pulled her quickly up the stairs of the stage. They ran to the dressing room in the back of the building and slammed the door shut.

"Thank you, sir. I was quite frightened." Her terrified eyes fixed on the man who captivated her.

He pulled out a chair and motioned for her to be seated. He sat next to her, wiping the perspiration off his brow with a towel.

"What do you suppose that was all about?" Her voice sounded breathy.

"Politics, I would suspect. This nation is headed toward war and it's not going to be pretty."

"I pray not, sir. I mean Barrett," she replied, her large, dark eyes wide with wonder.

"I still have not learned your full name."

"My name is Brooke Fortner."

"Fortner! My father once did business with a Fortner from Georgia. I believe he sold textiles–Alton Fortner, I recall."

"That would be my father." A grin spread across her flawless face.

"What a small world. How is your father doing?"

"He is fine. He still runs the textile business, but does not travel as much as he once did. He leaves most of that to his children. We still make garments from the cotton grown in the area."

Her Southern accent as well as her beauty charmed him. "I believe I was about fifteen when my father took me to visit your mill. I still remember a pretty Spanish girl on a beautiful horse greeting us."

She smiled, blushing. "That was me and my horse, Spirit. I loved riding... still do."

"At the time, I did not know which was more beautiful, the horse or the girl. Now that you have grown up, I have no doubt that it was the girl." He angled his head, staring into her piercing, dark eyes.

Brooke stared nervously at the floor, hoping to hide her embarrassment. "I was eleven and Mr. von Weber... I mean, Barrett, you sure know how to sweet talk a lady." She batted her long lashes flirtingly.

"I was just telling the truth. May I walk you home now?"

"I would be honored. We should find William first. He must be worried sick about me."

Barrett offered her his hand and led her out the back door.

"How serious do you think this armory thing is?" she asked.

"I don't know. I am just visiting like you. What have you heard?"

"Well, the lady I was sitting next to at the theater told me that thousands of rifles were brought here a few weeks ago."

"There is an armory here, so why would that be suspicious?" He scratched his well-trimmed beard.

"She said something about building up weapons to prepare for war in Virginia. The rumor is that Virginia may split and become two states. Do you think it was Southerners that attacked the armory?"

"I find that highly unlikely. They would have had to bring up a small army to do so. Most likely, it was those rowdy characters we met on the street tonight. What did the man on the horse say his name was...? Isaac Smith?"

"Yes, he did say he was Isaac Smith."

"Might be a fictitious name."

As they paced down the road, they could see the town bustling with activity.

Brooke noticed William frantically peering around, obviously searching for her. As soon as he spied her, he started to cross the street in front of a group of soldiers on horseback. The lead rider spotted William and pulled back on the reins. The spirited horse reared. In response, the angry rider slammed his whip across William's back. "Get out of the way," he shouted. The whip sliced down again.

Immediately, von Weber sprang into action. He grabbed the whip, yanking the soldier off the horse. The stunned soldier slammed to the hard ground.

The soldier scrambled to his feet, pulling his gun out of its holster. "Why you... how dare you interfere with the United States military. You just earned yourself a piece of lead," the arrogant officer roared.

In one swift motion, Barrett kicked the gun away. Grabbing the man's arm, he flung him to the ground and pressed his foot against his throat. In a split-second, Barrett pulled his gun and pushed the barrel of it to the downed officer's face.

Two soldiers began to dismount in an attempt to help their leader.

Barrett turned in their direction. "Do you want to continue this?" he bellowed, pointing his pistol at them.

A white-bearded rider in civilian clothes rode over to them and barked a command to the men who were still on horseback. "Get a move on now!"

Fuming, he shouted at the officer on the ground, "Lieutenant Gibbons, get back on your horse and leave the local people alone. They are not the enemy!"

"But, Colonel, this man just...."

"I am well aware of what this man did. I saw the whole thing. You are lucky he didn't break your neck and I would not have blamed him. Now get on your horse and act like a Marine, not like a hooligan."

Barrett shifted his pistol back to Gibbons, still on the ground.

The angry lieutenant scowled at von Weber, his left eye nervously twitching.

Without a word, Barrett released his hold on the Marine and returned his weapon slowly to its holster, inside his jacket.

"Where did you get a weapon like that?" Gibbons asked, standing up brushing the dust off his uniform.

Von Weber remained silent, watching the Marine retrieve his hat and mount his horse.

Barrett picked up the lieutenant's gun, removed the shells, and tossed it back to him.

"We'll meet again," Gibbons scoffed.

"I'm counting on it," Barrett replied calmly.

The lieutenant rode off, leaving nothing behind him but a cloud of dust.

"Young man, I apologize for my lieutenant. He is trying to make captain, but he is going about it the wrong way."

"Thank you, sir, for coming to his rescue. It could have gotten ugly... for him."

The dignified-looking officer nodded his head in agreement, smiling. "I got called to duty and didn't have time to change into military attire." He pointed to von Weber's jacket. "You know, I saw a gun like yours a few weeks ago at the academy, but this is the first time I have ever seen anyone carrying one."

"It is the weapon of the future." Barrett picked up William's hat, brushed it off, and handed it to the black man.

"I wish I could convince my superiors of that. They are still stuck in the ball and bayonet mindset."

Barrett chuckled. "I know what you mean. It's hard to bring the future to men who are stuck in the past."

The middle-aged colonel grinned. "Very well put." He paused for a moment eyeing the Hymnist. "I suggest you escort your beautiful young lady to her destination, where she will be safe. I would not want either of you to get hurt."

"Yes, sir, I'll do that."

As the colonel rode off, Barrett faced Brooke. "Do you know who that was?"

"Oh, yes. Everyone knows who Robert E. Lee is." Her voice held a degree of awe.

They watched as the man rode away.

"So that was Lee… seems like an honorable man."

"Oh, that he is. My father has met him many times. A good Southern gentleman."

"I wonder what side of an insurrection he will end up being on."

"Miss Brooke, I'm sorry I caused all this." William placed his hat on his head.

"It wasn't your fault, William." She patted his arm.

As Barrett escorted Brooke to her aunt's home, they chatted along the way.

Her brother, Rory, met them at the door. An anxious look clouded his face.

"Get in here. There is a battle brewing out there. Some Northerners tried to capture the armory. They want to give all the guns to the slaves."

"That's interesting. The town's people are saying Southerners have taken over the armory to steal weapons," Barrett responded.

"Who is this?" Rory asked Brooke, frowning at von Weber.

"This is Barrett von Weber."

"The piano player you're always talking about? Couldn't you find a real man to walk you home?"

"How dare you," Brooke shot back, glaring at her brother.

"What do you think Father would say? You need to be courted by a prominent Southern gentleman, not some Yankee piano player."

She turned to Barrett and took his hand. "I'm sorry for my brother's harsh words. He sometimes speaks before he thinks."

"No problem. I think he needs to be taken out behind the building and given a whipping. He reeks of liquor." Barrett cast a concerned look.

"You think you're man enough to do that?" Rory challenged, stepping closer to him.

Barrett simply looked at the much-shorter man and shook his head. A grin crept across his face.

He kissed Brooke's hand, tipped his hat, and whispered, "I hope to see you again."

"My sister will not see you again, you Bluebelly coward."

"This man is not a coward. He saved our lives tonight," William spoke up.

Rory scowled at the black man. "Sometimes you forget where your place is!"

Brooke immediately admonished him. "Don't you ever talk to William like that!"

She turned to Barrett. "Again, I am sorry. My brother is on the spirits fighting a sickness." She took a step back. "I am sure Father would be pleased to see you again."

"Again?" her brother questioned.

"Yes. Barrett's father was a good friend of our father."

"Still, I do not want you to see this man again. Understood? And you…." he grabbed Barrett's arm in a menacing way, "…leave my sister alone, or I'll take care of you myself."

"Sir, you will remove your hand from me immediately!" His blue eyes were clear, intense.

"Or what? You German…."

Barrett pushed the angry man's hand away and shoved his head against the wall. "You need to be more polite to people you don't know. Now listen closely, I am only going to tell you once. I am not one to be insulted or threatened. If I want to see your sister again, I will. She is the one who will decide. It is between her and me… not you! One more thing, if you continue to harass me, I can and will make your life miserable." He released his grip on Rory.

Barrett shifted his focus back to Brooke. "I'm sorry, miss. I pray we meet again."

"No apology needed. You will see me again, in spite of what my brother says. I make my own decisions."

He nodded and turned to go. "William, take care of Brooke and remember what I taught you."

William nodded with a broad smile.

Rory slammed the door shut. He yelled, face red with rage, "You will not see that German again! Am I clear?"

Brooke slapped her brother's face hard. "Don't you dare tell me who I can see! I am not your slave. Father would tan your hide if he had seen the performance you put on tonight." She stormed toward her room.

Later that night while she prepared for bed, she could not stop thinking about the intriguing man she had met earlier. *He is thoughtful—he offered his hand to help me across the street. He is brilliant and talented—he composes and plays beautiful, inspiring music. Yet, he is strong and courageous—he stands up and fights for what he believes.* As she ran the brush through her thick, black hair, staring at her image in the mirror, she uttered softly, "I want to get to know Barrett von Weber better. I don't care what you say, Rory!"

Chapter Two

Harpers Ferry was typically tranquil, but this night had been anything but normal. Gunshots sounded in the distance; people were scurrying around frantically. The townspeople either tried to hide from the chaos, or searched for answers to the frightening events occurring around them. Rumors spread rampant. Confusion reigned.

By mid-morning, the military unexpectedly forced an evacuation of the area.

Rory decided that for security reasons it would be best to catch the first train out of town. He also wanted to get his sister far away from that German who infatuated her. The look in her eyes the previous night was something he had never seen. He didn't like it one bit!

Unknown to Rory, Brooke had already left the house. She wanted to see the handsome pianist again before she left. To be safe, she had William take her to the theater.

Upon her arrival at the theater, she was informed that the pianist had already left. Her disappointment was noticeable as she wiped a stray tear, feeling somewhat betrayed. *I guess he was just a man of empty words, like so many others.*

"I'm sorry, missy. I know how much you wanted to see him again." William tried to cheer her up. Through the years, he had learned how to read Miss Brooke. She had always treated him as if he was a member of the family.

"Why would he leave? He said he wanted to see me again." She couldn't hide the pain in her voice.

"Don't be sad, Miss Brooke, maybe Massa Barrett's plans changed, like ours. There been gunfire though the night and I heard say that a number of men have already been killed, including the mayor. I heard say a black man at the train station was gunned down—never had a gun or nothin'—they just up and killed him."

Disheartened, she began walking slowly back to the guesthouse where she was staying.

A familiar voice caught her attention and made her heart quicken. "Brooke, oh, Brooke, where art thou, Brooke?"

She spun around and saw Barrett holding a single, red rose in his right hand, his hat tucked under his left arm.

He handed the fragrant gift to her. "This was the only rose I could find. I think it fitting to give it to the most beautiful lady in this town... Brooke Fortner."

"Why sir, you are making me blush." Reaching for the flower, she deliberately swept her hand across his. "I was afraid you had left town without saying goodbye. The battle in town is about to begin. Rory found out that the Marines are going to storm the armory. It's frightening!"

"Yes, it is! I have to leave for another engagement in Washington. I am to play before President Buchanan next week."

"What an honor!" She smiled. "We're heading to Washington, also. We received news this morning that my father would be traveling there on business. He hopes to sign a contract with a major textile factory. They want to buy all the cotton fabric we can produce. We are thrilled with the prospect."

Barrett's face clouded, displaying a hint of doubt. He did not want to tell her that the contract and the sale would more than likely be short lived. He believed war was inevitable.

He finally shifted his gaze and noticed William standing nearby. "William, how are you this morning?" His demeanor changed and a smile replaced the look of doubt.

"Fine, suh," William mustered a slight smile.

Barrett turned again to face Brooke, trying to capture her beauty, somehow etching her flawless features into his memory.

Brooke's words tumbled forth more rushed than usual. "Will I be able to see you in Washington, and maybe reintroduce you to my father?"

"I was hoping to see you again, and yes, I would love to visit with your father."

Their attention shifted to a wagon noisily dragging a cannon down the dusty road.

"Sure looks like they mean business," Brooke commented nervously.

"Yes, it seems the man we met in the street last night, Isaac Smith, is the ringleader. He and his cohorts have locked themselves in the firehouse at the armory. Smith is bent on freeing the slaves in the South. They have already killed a number of people and kidnapped others, including George Washington's great-grandson. Thank God they did not grab you last night." He reached for her hand.

Brooke sighed. "I suppose they might have taken me if it wasn't for you coming to my rescue. That leader was quite impressed with that pistol you carry. Do you know any more about what's going on?"

"That is all the information that has been released. That man we talked to yesterday, Colonel Robert E. Lee, is the man in charge of the military operation."

"Any idea what Smith plans to do with the guns in the armory?"

"Rumor has it he is going to arm the slaves in the South."

Brooke searched Barrett's eyes, uncertain what to say. She thought about her own family, knowing they had what some folks would call slaves. She was unsure how Barrett would react when he found out about it.

"I better get back to the guesthouse. Rory will be looking for us."

"May I walk with you?"

"Please do. I feel much safer with you by my side."

As they walked, the couple continued their conversation.

William followed close behind, protectively.

Barrett queried, "Has there been any talk of a war in Savannah?"

She hesitated. "Yes, but my father does not believe it will happen. He would be against it, but I fear two of my three brothers would be for it— maybe all three. I am not sure about Samuel."

"I assumed Rory would be all for going to war." Barrett rolled his eyes, a look that definitely showed his displeasure with her brother.

"Oh, he wants nothing more than to see the Yankee Northerners put in their place."

For a few moments, they walked in silence.

Brooke sniffed the sweet fragrance of the delicate rose she was holding. "May I ask you something?" She looked directly into the tall, handsome German's eyes as they continued their slow walk.

"Sure."

"If we do go to war, what do you think will happen? I mean… how do you think it will end up?"

"No war is ever good. Many decent men will die. This war will pit brother against brother, father against son. Many relatives will be on opposite sides. It's bound to be a bloody, heartbreaking, possibly very long war."

"What do you think the outcome will be? I mean, who will win?"

"Honestly?"

"Yes."

They stopped walking when a dozen soldiers rushed by on horseback.

He paused, trying to find the best way to frame his thoughts. "The North has all the steel mills, the gun suppliers, the superior rail system. The South has the food supply and the materials for clothing, like cotton. But, just the strength of the North will prevail, unless...."

"Unless what?" Brooke's eyes widened.

"Unless the South gets an ally like France, England, or Spain."

"Do you think that could happen?"

They resumed walking.

Barrett explained, "I have read that the South has already sent envoys to those three nations and others, like Prussia, and even Germany. Truthfully, no, I do not think any other country will join them. They have their own problems. And quite honestly, the South has little to offer—like cotton, and maybe a little gold. But, what happens if the North destroys the cotton fields? I do not think any nation will support the South and risk losing favor with the North. They may aid with humanitarian things like food and medicine, but nothing more. And that will be at a cost. Nothing will be free. Nothing ever is."

"I hope and pray it does not come down to war." Sadness colored her words.

They reached her guesthouse and found the coach loaded, ready to go.

Barrett cupped Brooke's hand in his. "I pray that the two sides can find some common ground. Maybe we can elect a President who can prevent war." He tried to sound hopeful for Brooke's sake. He looked at the ground and then fixed his gaze on her dark, brown eyes.

"Will I see you in Washington?" she asked, hoping with every ounce of her being.

"You can count on it." Barrett smiled, squeezing her hand tighter.

She moved a step closer and gave him a quick kiss on his cheek, very close to his lips.

He raised his hand to touch the spot she had kissed. His thoughts swirled. *Who is this woman who makes me feel things I've never felt before?*

Without another word, the Hymnist turned to help her step up into the carriage.

Suddenly, an uneasy feeling overcame Barrett. Sensing someone behind him, he spun around and ducked instinctively when a fist came at him, grazing his shoulder. He gripped the man's arm and thrust him to the ground with a loud thud.

"Rory!" Brooke screamed, "What are you doing?"

Barrett stood over her brother like a champion boxer in a fighting ring who had landed the knockout punch.

Fear was written all over Rory's face; calmness remained on Barrett's.

Brooke touched her new friend's shoulder. "Please, let him go."

Barrett looked directly into Rory's panicky eyes, reluctantly releasing his grip.

Still shaking, Brooke's brother struggled to his feet and brushed himself off. Not backing down, he ordered, "Leave my sister alone!" Rubbing his sore arm, he scowled at Barrett.

"You are not in any position to tell him that. Now go! Go, Rory! I'll meet you at the train station," Brooke demanded, her voice growing louder with each word.

Rory stormed off in a huff

Turning to Brooke, the pianist explained, "I'm sorry. I didn't want to hurt him. I hope you are not upset with me."

"No apology needed. He attacked you. He thought he was defending my honor, but I am the one who kissed you. I apologize for my brother's actions. He was certainly not a Southern gentleman!"

"I will cherish your kiss until we meet again."

She smiled, keeping her eyes on Barrett's handsomely rugged face. "May I ask you another question?"

"Ah, a woman with many questions. Certainly, you can ask me anything."

"I know there is a lot I don't know about you, but I am most curious about one thing."

He raised his brow, a trait she had noticed before and found extremely attractive.

Brooke cleared her throat. She was uncertain how much she dared ask this fascinating man, so proceeded cautiously. "How did you learn to fight like that? I have never seen anything like it."

"Oh, that. My parents were missionaries and we traveled all over the world. We spent six years in the Orient. I became good friends with a couple Chinese boys whose father was an instructor of an ancient fighting technique in the Chinese military. It's called Kung Fu. Over the course of five years, he taught us what he knew. We learned to use our hands, feet, and entire body to fight. He taught the proper use of knives, swords, and bows. He would tell us, 'Learn to fight, so you don't have to fight.' I didn't understand what he meant until I got older. There were always those who challenged me. I did not flaunt it, but when people discovered my ability to defend myself, they quickly realized I was a better friend than enemy. My parents taught me how to live a holy life. Ku Siam, taught me about survival."

"Your reflexes are amazing… so quick and precise. It is almost as though you knew you were about to be attacked by my obnoxious brother." She rolled her eyes.

"I did feel it coming. It is like a sixth sense and an essential part of the training. It is ninety percent mental—knowing where you are at all times and being ready to defend yourself at any moment. However, I must admit that your kiss caused me to be vulnerable for a second." He grinned, "But it was worth it."

"I am embarrassed and at the same time, impressed. Is there anything else I should know about you, Mr. von Weber?" she drawled, her Southern accent sounding even stronger than usual.

"I guess time will tell. I know one thing… I'm looking forward to getting to know you better. So far, there's only one thing I do not like about you—that is your brother! Should I have to worry about your other two brothers and father?"

She let out a long sigh. "Definitely not my father. Now… my other brothers… well, they are protective of me, but I think they will like you."

He suppressed a chuckle. "I hope so."

Just then a round of gunfire sounded nearby, a reminder of the tumultuous times.

Brooke shuddered at the thought of how her life could change if a war between the states broke out.

The bright sun overhead was bearing down on them. She wiped her hand across her forehead and pulled on her bonnet to better shade her face.

Brooke continued, "Judging by what you did with that soldier's pistol yesterday, you know about guns, too. You are certainly a fascinating man!"

He laughed. "I spent part of my life in New Haven, Connecticut. I attended church with Cornelius Hall. He has worked for firearm dealers all his life, and is good friends with Benjamin Henry and Oliver Winchester. My father became close friends with both Hall and Henry. They taught me all about guns. I was honored to be a champion marksman three years in a row when I was in my teens—both rifle and pistol."

"If you are trying to impress me, you are doing a good job." Her voice was ripe with teasing.

"God has blessed me abundantly." He gave her an easy smile.

"Where are your parents now?"

Sadness clouded his face, but before he could respond, William interrupted, "Miss Brooke, I'm sorry to have to say this, but we gotta go. Can't miss our train!"

"Oh yes! Thank you for reminding me, William." Turning back to Barrett she asked, "Will I see you in Washington?"

"Like I said, I'm counting on it." He clicked his heels, kissed her hand, and then helped her into the carriage. Already missing her, he watched them fade out of sight.

Brooke's mind reeled with the events of the last couple days.

"Miss Brooke?" William interrupted her thoughts. "That man... do you believe everything he says? I mean, I overheard much of what he said, and it sure seems hard to believe, ma'am."

"Yes, I do believe him, William. You saw how he overpowered that soldier last night. And today with Rory—that was quite impressive." Her eyes sparkled with delight.

The black man smiled broadly. "Miss Brooke, I do believe you are smitten."

"William, I do believe you are right." She laid her head on the back of the seat, returning to her thoughts of a man who certainly caused her heart to race.

Chapter Three

November 3, 1859
Washington, D.C.

The city was bustling with activity. Neatly dressed men and women were rushing from place to place, meeting to meeting, crowding the roads and sidewalks. Horse drawn carriages lined the streets waiting for their busy occupants.

Most visitors were unaware that there was a battle underway in the Halls of Congress as talk of a looming war escalated among the politicians.

Two weeks had passed since she met that exciting man who had swept her off her feet. He was brave, yet cautious; rugged, yet kind; strong, yet tender. Intrigued by his knowledge of the problems facing the nation, she also couldn't get her mind off his strong physique, and ruggedly handsome face, to say nothing of his God given talents. Just thinking of him made her heart quicken.

One chilly afternoon, Brooke accompanied her brother, Rory, to an upscale restaurant for lunch with a number of high political officials.

The conversation started cordially.

The men talked politics, a topic occupying most of their thoughts lately. Being from the South, all were in agreement on key issues and seemed confident that the North would not decide their livelihood, or change it in any way.

At one end of the table, Brooke chatted softly with a couple of the politician's wives. She knew the men would not welcome her participation in "business talk," even though she held a large interest in her father's textile operation.

At the same time, she tried to keep an ear open to what Rory and the men at the other end of the table were discussing. Her brother had been acting strange lately; it was as if he was looking for a fight over anything. Granted, these were stressful times, but he treated anyone from the North as open prey. Maybe that was why he hated Barrett so much—at least that's the only reason Brooke could come up with.

One of the elderly men lit his cigar. "I see Colonel Lee and his Marines took care of those scoundrels at Harpers Ferry."

"Lee did a great job, but if you ask me, they should have all been taken out and hanged immediately. They don't deserve a trial," Rory stated cynically. "Mr. Fulbright, since you are the cotton king, and one of the largest slave owners in Georgia, what is your opinion?"

"Oh, they'll all hang. Especially their leader... what is his name? Oh yes, John Brown... that slave lover," Gerard Fulbright boasted. "What say you, Senator?"

"I'm sure Senator Toombs stands with us. He always has," Rory interrupted.

Fulbright chided, "I'm certain the senator can speak for himself."

The senator leaned closer. "Everyone knows where I stand on slavery. They need a quick, but fair trial. If we do not give them justice, we go against the principles that this great country was founded upon. The result can be nothing less than the gallows for Brown and all his cohorts. I find it interesting that the first person they killed was a slave... a little irony there, no doubt."

There was silence for a moment as everyone pondered the words of the well-known senator from Georgia.

Gerard Fulbright's wife spoke. "Brooke, dear, I heard some gossip the other day. Someone told me that you met those slave lovers while walking to a concert in Harpers Ferry the night John Brown attacked the armory."

Dressed in a dark green gown, Brooke looked stunning. Her pearl necklace complimented the lace trim down the front.

The women could tell Brooke's mind wasn't focused on the table talk.

"Excuse me. My head must have been elsewhere." Brooke took a lengthy breath, wishing she were elsewhere.

"I said, I heard you encountered that scoundrel, John Brown, when you were at Harpers Ferry the other day." Mrs. Fulbright repeated herself, louder.

Brooke's mind shifted to that night and a smile appeared. "Yes, I did meet him. Isaac Smith, he called himself."

"What was he like? That dreadful man... did he threaten you?" Mrs. Fulbright questioned further.

"No. In fact, he was rather polite. I was with William."

"Your slave was with you?" Senator Toombs probed, obviously disturbed. "What on earth would a slave be doing at a concert?" Most everyone at the table began laughing.

"William is not a slave. He is a free man... a servant." Brooke realized her tone sounded agitated.

"Servant, slave, property... they are all the same," Fulbright laughed robustly.

Brooke glared at him, her displeasure mounting.

"Don't pay attention to them, honey. Tell us your story." Mrs. Toombs angled her head from one side to the other.

"Yes, it sounds exciting. I want to know more," Mrs. Fulbright commented as she leaned closer to the table, anxious to hear all the juicy details of the encounter.

Brooke took a deep breath. "William and I were headed to a concert that night when we were approached by a tall, bearded man leading about twenty riders."

"Were you scared?" the senator's wife asked.

"Not really. William grabbed my arm to shelter me."

"Lot of help he would be," Fulbright joked, followed by a roar of laughter from the others.

"William would die for me. He would have protected me if I needed it."

Rory shook his head, disgusted with his sister's comment.

"Go on, dear. What did he say to you?" Mrs. Toombs persisted.

"He asked me where I was going at that late hour and reminded me that a lady should not be walking the streets at night. I told him I was going to a piano concert."

"Oh, that's right, you went to see the Hymnist when you were at Harpers Ferry." Mrs. Toombs added, "He played before the president just last week."

Brooke gave a weak smile.

Rory rolled his eyes. "Gentlemen, enough of this. Let's talk about the important matters at hand."

"Let the young lady finish. I want to know what she thought about the murdering traitor." Mrs. Toombs leaned forward cupping her hands together.

"Murderer... traitor... that remains to be seen," Brooke struggled to keep her voice even. "He didn't hurt me. Although now, as I look back at it, he seemed like he was a man on a mission. He was leaving town, heading across the bridge."

"To the gallows, that's where he's headed now… him and his boys, and the rest of his gang." Rory took a drink of water, proud of his comment.

"Shh! Let your sister continue. I feel there is more to the story." Mrs. Toombs crossed her arms waiting, growing more impatient with Rory by the minute.

"Nothing that would interest you. She never should have gone to that worthless concert that night. She could have been killed," Rory blurted angrily.

An awkward silence crept over the table.

Toombs finally spoke, "Right. Now, getting back to the politics at hand, I see no real candidate running for president. Certainly, there is someone better than Douglas."

"I'm sure we can forget about Lincoln," Fulbright stated definitively.

Senator Toombs added, "He is neither a strong enough candidate, nor on our side."

They all shook their heads, murmuring in agreement.

Suddenly a voice from behind caught everyone by surprise. "Don't be so sure of that!"

Brooke was stunned when she turned around to see Barrett von Weber standing by their table. An older man, dressed fashionably, stood next to him.

Her face instantly lit up, and it was apparent to the other women at the table that the smile she wore was more than just a casual greeting.

The talkative women gawked as Brooke's and Barrett's eyes were instantly drawn to each other.

Barrett tucked his hat neatly under his arm, clicked his heels, and nodded his head. "Brooke, you are not a dream. You are as real and beautiful as I remember."

"Why, thank you, sir. You are much too kind." She felt her heart rate quicken.

Rory jumped up; his face red with rage. "I thought I told you not to see my sister again."

"Mr. Fortner… if I remember right, the last time I saw you, you were not in any position to tell me anything. Maybe we should leave it at that," Barrett replied, composed.

Immediately, Senator Toombs stood and took charge, "I don't know what this is all about, but we need to be civil inside this fine establishment."

Toombs anxiously shifted his attention to the man standing next to Barrett, and asked, "Rory, do you know who this gentleman is?"

"No, but I know who this man is," he pointed to Barrett. Rory's cold, dark eyes showed his disgust.

Choosing to ignore Rory, the senator introduced the honored guest. "This is Cornelius Hall. He is one of the salesmen for a rifle company called, New Haven Arms." Toombs explained further, "We have invited him to dine with us today, to talk business. Cornelius, it's good to see you again." He greeted the man warmly, shaking his hand.

"Senator, thank you for this opportunity."

Rory interrupted rudely, "Well, I can understand why you invited him, but why is this piano player here?"

Cornelius Hall stepped forward, extending his hand to Rory. "And who may I ask are you?"

"I am Rory Fortner, from Savannah, Georgia."

"Fortner?" Hall asked with raised eyebrows.

"Yes!"

"You must be Alton's son."

"That is correct, I am his youngest."

"Well, Mr. Fortner, it is obvious you have no idea who this man is." He motioned toward von Weber who still had his eyes on Brooke. "I have known Barrett since he was a child. I asked him to join us because he is a weapons expert. He knows my products better than I do." He chuckled.

"I have always been impressed with his marksmanship. His keen eye and calm nerves are uncanny. At the age of ten, he won shooting matches, beating men who spent their lives as sharpshooters. Matter of fact, he has never lost a contest! He knows all about the guns our company makes. That is why he is here, not just as a friend, but as a professional expert and advisor."

"He's just a piano player," Rory snidely mumbled.

"No! He is a concert pianist, one of the greatest in the world, and the writer of many of the hymns we sing in church," Hall was quick to add. "And he is certainly not a man to be trifled with!"

"Barrett von Weber— the Hymnist?" Senator Toombs queried.

Toombs placed his hand on Barrett's shoulder. "I am honored to meet you. We sing your hymns in church frequently. I was disappointed to miss your concert last week at the White House."

Mrs. Fulbright stood and extended her hand to the famous pianist. "The Hymnist! I can't believe I'm meeting you. Your words are so... so... so inspiring." She let out a nervous giggle.

"Thank you, ma'am. My hymns are meant to be inspirational. The music stirs your soul, but it's the lyrics that can bring you closer to God."

"Enough of this nonsense, let's talk about the important issues." Rory folded his arms and sat down, his expression hard.

"Please, be seated. Let us enjoy this delicious meal before we excuse the women and talk business," Toombs announced, feeling the tension in the room.

Barrett and Cornelius sat across the table from Brooke.

Small talk continued as they enjoyed their main course.

Oblivious to the clanging of the dishes, the wafting aromas from the kitchen, or even the busy chatter at the table, Brooke and Barrett were involved in their own wordless conversation. For a short time, they were in a world of their own, filled with flirtatious eyes, daring smiles, and racing pulses.

"Mr. von Weber, I understand you are a personal friend of the King of Germany," Toombs interjected, jarring Barrett back to the conversation at hand.

"There are many leaders in Germany. I don't believe you can say I'm a personal friend of any of them. However, I have had the honor of performing for some of them."

"The article I read reported that you had dined with them."

"I have dined with a few, as I am dining with you at this moment. I have even gone on hunting trips with a few, but that does not make me a personal friend, only an acquaintance."

"Do you have to bow to the king when you meet him?" Fulbright chuckled.

"I bow to no man!" Barrett stated emphatically.

Toombs shot him a look of confusion. "Are you not required to bow to a king or a nation's leader?"

"Do you bow to President Buchanan?"

"No, of course not."

"Then why would I bow to a leader of another country?"

Toombs shrugged his shoulders. "Out of respect for the office?"

Barrett sat back in his chair and folded his arms. "I wrote a hymn called, *Is This My King?* The lyrics go like this... *Is this my King upon the cross, Whose blood flowed freely for the lost? He gave His life to set me free; that is why I bend on knee.*"

The guests all sat quietly, reflecting on the words from the Hymnist's song.

"Senator, show me a leader... a king... an emperor who would do this for his people, and I would unashamedly follow him, but still, I would never bow to him. The fact is, there is only one King."

Brooke studied Barrett. The admiration and respect, the growing feelings she had for him, all were evident by the sparkle in her eye, the radiant smile on her face.

They enjoyed the rest of their lunch with interesting conversation, mostly about von Weber and his world travels.

By the time the table was cleared, Rory's patience had grown thin. *I have had enough of this German being the center of attention*! He exhaled and tried once again to get the conversation directed the way he thought it should go. "Let's get down to business, the reason we gathered today. Ladies, if you will excuse us, the men have some important issues to discuss."

Mrs. Fulbright stood. "I know when it's time to disperse. It's cigar talking time." She laughed lightheartedly.

Brooke boldly stepped in. "No. I'm curious. Why should the women have to leave?"

Mr. Fulbright responded, "The men need to talk business. You will only be bored."

A couple of the men laughed.

"Well, bore me away, Mr. Fulbright. I own one-fourth of Fortner Textiles. Anything you want to say to my brother, you can say to me." Her eyes held a fire that Barrett hadn't seen before.

"I would prefer you leave, my dear sister," Rory said scathingly, not looking at her, twirling his finger around the rim of his coffee cup.

"My dear brother," she sliced him with a glare, "anything that needs to be said about father's business can be said in front of me." She had a determined look on her face, begging Rory to accept the challenge of taking her on.

"Suit yourself," her brother grumbled through gritted teeth.

Turning to the gun salesman, Rory continued, "Mr. Hall, the reason we asked you here today was because we want to order some rifles and small arms from you."

Cornelius sat taller in his seat. "That's what I am in business for, selling rifles. New Haven Arms makes the finest weapons in the world. However, I represent other companies also. I have many different types— the old flint, which is still popular, or the latest rimfire rifle. How many are we talking about?" he asked, taking a sip from his water glass.

Rory glanced at each man, one at a time. His hardened face made him look much older than his twenty-two years. He sighed heavily. "Say fifty thousand rifles and five thousand pistols."

Brooke's jaw dropped, and her eyes widened twice their normal size. *What is he talking about?*

"Fifty thousand!" Hall gasped, almost spewing water from his mouth.

Patrons at the nearby tables looked in their direction.

Hall lowered his voice and leaned closer. "What do you need fifty thousand rifles for, unless... unless you plan on equipping an entire army?" He set his glass back on the table. Folding his arms, he waited for an answer.

There was a contemplative silence.

"Rory, does Father know about this?" Brooke interrupted the quiet.

"You stay out of this! This is between the men," Rory shouted. He was furious with his sister.

"Rory, keep your voice down," Toombs demanded, trying to gain control of the heated conversation.

"Between you and the men!" Brooke spoke loudly. "I am involved as well. I thought you were here to sell our textiles, not buy guns. Father doesn't know this, does he? Answer me, Rory!"

"No, Father does not know what is happening. He does not understand how serious the times are. He is in his own little world believing that everything is going to turn out all right. The man's living in the past—that's why he puts flowers on our dead mother's grave every morning while the North is preparing to invade us. I am doing this to protect what our family has spent years accumulating. If we do not do something, the Northerners will take it all. They will destroy everything our family has built. I'm not about to stand by and watch that happen."

Barrett sat quietly, listening. He wasn't prepared for the flash of fire shining in the young woman's eyes, or the intensely serious expression settling over her features.

Brooke added, "Mr. Hall is right. That is your plan. You want to equip an army, don't you?"

Cornelius took his handkerchief from his pocket and wiped the heavy sweat from his brow.

"Cornelius, let me assure you, it is for peace only. Georgia needs to defend itself from outside intervention." Toombs claim sounded rehearsed.

"Just name your price," Rory blurted. "We can pay you in gold if you like."

Senator Toombs scowled at Rory and whispered, "Let me take care of this, young man!"

Rory continued undeterred. "Let them know the terms... these men are business people. When someone is offered a high price for their commodities, they always take the deal." He looked directly at Hall. "What do you think, sir? We will pay you top dollar... in gold."

Hall wiped his mouth with his cloth napkin and stood. "There is more to life than the mighty dollar. I've had enough! If you'll excuse me, I must take my business elsewhere. Barrett, it is time for us to leave!"

Von Weber immediately took his place next to his friend.

"Elsewhere?" Rory argued. "We are offering you gold… lots of it!"

"Sir, what you are offering is to buy my products to kill men you consider your enemy. That quite possibly could be my friends, my family, your family, or me, for that matter. I will not have any part of that for two reasons. First, because I am an American who supports the Constitution of this great country. Second, if I were to sell you my wares, I would either be locked up in chains and sent to prison for treason, or taken out and hanged at the nearest tree. That would be after my employer fired me." He tipped his hat. "Excuse me, gentlemen… ladies."

Toombs scowled at Rory. "Why did you not let me take care of this? You have to be more diplomatic."

"I'm not going to be intimidated by Northerners," Rory huffed.

"You just ruined our chances of getting arms."

"Then we will buy them from Europe. They have better guns anyhow."

"You just don't get it, do you young man?" Toombs shook his head.

Barrett bent slightly over the table. "Miss Brooke, if you are not doing anything this evening, could we meet for dinner?"

"Why yes, I...."

"No, she will not!" Rory exploded.

Angrily, she shouted, "You are not my father. You cannot and will not order me around. Father will be here this afternoon, and he will set you straight."

"No, he won't! He is not coming!" Rory's tone was belligerent.

"Not coming?"

"No. I wired him and told him everything was already taken care of." His face was smug.

"What do you mean taken care of? We have not talked to anyone about textiles." As Brooke said those words, it dawned on her that the possible textile contract was a ploy, a lie. As the sad truth settled in, her voice quivered, "There never was a buyer, was there?"

Rory's voice sounded cold, dry. "You catch on quickly, sister. We are here to buy, not sell. The future of Georgia depends on it. You're a woman, you wouldn't understand."

"I understand you lied to our father. Do our brothers know about this?"

He remained quiet, staring into space.

Brooke realized that something bigger was going on. "They do know! Well, let me assure you, my dear brother, I know more about Father's business than all of you put together. I'm part owner of this company. We will not spend our money on weapons. Not now, not ever! Not if I have anything to say about it." She pushed back her chair from the table, ready to stand.

"Well, you don't! Not anymore," Rory blurted out.

"What do you mean?" She shifted her attention to the man sitting next to Rory. "Mr. Cradle, you are one of our family attorneys, enlighten me." Up to this point, the lawyer had not said a word.

The attorney's voice was soft, but direct. "I'm sorry, Brooke. You were taken off all contractual accounts. It is best that a woman not be in charge of such important documents, especially a young woman, like yourself."

"Like myself? What does that mean? Does Father know about this?" She could feel tears starting to sting her eyes, but wouldn't give her brother the satisfaction of thinking he won.

"He knows what he needs to know," Rory affirmed. "It was for the interest of the family business that you were cut out as a partner. Father agreed in part with it. Since you are of legal age, you could have sold your portion, or brought in by marriage an outsider who could have destroyed the company. Therefore, we changed that! He also put in a provision regarding you being involved in the business... your decisions now must go through a Board of Directors."

"Board of Directors?" She glared at Rory and then turned her attention to Harrison Cradle.

The attorney nervously looked away, unable to make eye contact.

The pieces of the puzzle were beginning to fit, as she realized what her brothers had done. "I am beginning to understand." She took a deep breath, struggling to stay composed. "Charles must be in charge of the textile operation at home. Samuel most likely is in charge of the outside holdings. And you, Rory, have to be the one in charge of the financial decisions of Fortner Textiles." Brooke let out a long, loud breath.

The confidence of victory showed clearly as the corners of his lip turned upwards, smugly. "This is what you fall for, my dear sister." Rory pointed at Barrett. "If you were to marry this man, and you never will, he could come in and dismantle our operation for some stupid reason. He would probably give away our money to some slave's tribe in Africa. That cannot happen now. We protected ourselves; since you let your feeble female emotions get in the way. You can't always see straight, sister."

Cornelius jumped in. "Mr. Fortner... I would suggest you refrain from such language toward this distinguished gentleman."

"Or what, sir? Who are you to tell me what I can and cannot do? If you won't do business with us, we will find someone who will. There are other gun companies. There are plants in England and Europe who will gladly take our gold. It's your loss."

"Good luck with that! Gentlemen, I'm leaving... good day." Cornelius turned to leave.

Brooke threw her napkin down, stood up, and rushed toward the door.

"Brooke, wait!" Barrett chased after her.

"Leave my sister alone," Rory ordered. "Or, she will be cut off from all family matters."

Barrett turned and looked directly into Rory's cold eyes. "Mr. Fortner, there will come a time when you will regret everything you have done here." He spun around and rushed off with Cornelius Hall.

Hall showed his frustration. "Barrett, you know they are committing suicide, don't you. Not only physical, but also financial. They will lose everything."

"I know." Barrett was concerned with only one thing now. "Brooke, wait for me!"

Hearing his voice was like a ray of sunshine after a thunderstorm. Relief flooded her soul. She was a strong woman, but the betrayal by her family was almost more than she could bear.

Standing near the door of the restaurant, Barrett grabbed Brooke's hand and held it lightly. "I'm sorry they hurt you like this."

She looked past him. "How could Father allow this? Why?"

"He is being misled by his greedy sons," Cornelius added.

Barrett stroked her hand, trying to calm her.

Sick at heart, she grabbed Barrett around the neck, and pulled him close. She sobbed in his strong arms; nothing could calm her broken heart.

After a short time, Cornelius whispered, "Miss Fortner, if we don't convince your father to stop your brothers, his business will be destroyed. If not now, then a few months down the road. You need to know that I have the responsibility to inform the government of what took place here today. They will look at this act as treason."

With her head still resting in the comfort of Barrett's muscular shoulders, her tears finally began to subside.

Suddenly, a commotion caught her attention. Looking through teary eyes, she saw her brother charging toward them brandishing a knife. She screamed, "Rory!"

Barrett instinctively released his grip on Brooke, pushing her toward Hall. The pianist stepped aside as the knife pierced the air, narrowly missing him. His quick hands grabbed Rory's extended arm, forcing the knife to drop. In one smooth action, Barrett flipped him to the ground and pressed his foot on the man's throat, stopping just short of crushing his larynx.

Cradle and Fulbright rushed over to assist Rory.

Barrett yanked his pistol from his holster. "I suggest you stop right there." He pointed the weapon toward the attorney's head. "I never miss!"

The patrons in the restaurant froze, all eyes glued on the unsettling scene before them.

Barrett shoved his gun back in its holster, glaring at the man who had just tried to stab him. "I'm not sure what to do next... turn you over to the police, or put an end to this right now. It would only take a little pressure from the heel of my boot to crush your throat—that would be the simplest thing. It would put an end to this stupidity, jealousy, and hatred. However, the fact remains... I intend to see more of your sister. And since you have foolishly taken her out of the family business, she would have nothing to lose when I do."

Rory was in no position to reply.

Just then, two police officers rushed into the restaurant. Looking at the downed man, one questioned, "What is going on here?"

Barrett peered at Brooke, who was being comforted by Hall.

He nodded his head toward Rory. "This gentleman bet me I could not arm wrestle him to the ground... as you can see, he lost." Barrett released his hold on the angry brother.

Brooke flew into von Weber's arms.

"Sir!" one of the policemen asked. "Is that what happened?"

Cradle helped Rory to his feet. He staggered, massaging his throat. "Yes, it is. I need to be more careful who I challenge."

One of the officers recognized Toombs. "Is that what happened, Senator?"

He paused briefly. "It's just as the man said... let them go."

"Next time, do your fighting outside, or I will toss both of you in a cell," one of the policemen threatened.

As Rory watched his sister walk away with Barrett's arm around her, he mumbled soft enough that only a couple of his friends could hear him, "I'm going to kill you some day, von Weber!"

Chapter Four

Late November 1859

In the days ahead, Barrett and Brooke spent much time together, in spite of Rory's persistent disapproval. Occasionally it was dinner at an upscale restaurant, followed by the theater; other times they took a long walk in the park. Sometimes they just sat on the veranda and talked for hours over a cup of tea.

Before long, the couple became the talk of Washington, D.C. Pictures and articles surfaced on the front page of the newspaper, with the headline—*The Hymnist Courts Southern Belle Textile Heiress.*

While many citizens believed the two seemed an unlikely pair, they agreed on one fact—Brooke Fortner certainly looked radiant clinging to the arm of the well-known musician.

If the town's gossipers weren't chatting about the probability of war, they were discussing that unique relationship. After all, it was no secret how much Brooke's brother hated Barrett von Weber. Everyone seemed to have a guess why, but no one actually knew the reason for his animosity.

At the same time, the men in Rory's circle of friends began to realize the power and influence von Weber had. Barrett knew many people in high-ranking positions. Senator Toombs and Gerard Fulbright, the outspoken slave owner of Georgia, thought he may be helpful to their cause in the future, especially if his relationship with Brooke grew more serious.

The Hymnist performed at the White House for the annual Thanksgiving Day festivities. When he walked into the elaborate banquet room hand-in-hand with Brooke, everyone could tell that their relationship had deepened.

Trying to be inconspicuous, President Buchanan's wife whispered to the president, "It looks like the Hymnist has found his perfect match. They look simply divine!"

It was a tearful goodbye at the train station the next day; an ache settled in Brooke's heart. As the approaching train sounded in the distance, Barrett stared into her eyes. They studied each other for a minute, a comfortable silence between them, then Barrett bent down and kissed her in a way that left no doubt of his intentions. He wanted to be with her and planned to find a way for them to be together. But for now, they must part ways. He had engagements in New York and Pittsburgh. She would return home to confront her father—she needed answers!

Savannah, Georgia
December 1859

Rory stepped out of the carriage first and offered his arm to help Brooke, but she just glared at him, waiting for William's assistance. The hurt in her eyes was evident, almost to the point of disdain.

Alton Fortner hurried out of the house to welcome his family when he heard the carriage arrive. His German Shepherd, Arminius, named after a famous German tribal leader, followed him wagging his tail in a friendly greeting.

Rory filed past him with only, "Hello, Father."

Confused by the cool greeting, Alton watched his son enter the Fortner mansion. He turned and faced his downcast daughter.

Unable to ignore the tension between his children, Brooke's father confronted her. "I sense a problem between you and Rory. Is it simply a brother and sister spat or more than that?"

Brooke half-heartedly hugged her father and gave him a kiss on the cheek. "Father, we need to go to the study."

"The study? This must be serious," he joked as he watched her rush up the wide marble stairs and into the house.

The Fortner study was the place business decisions were made. Father had a rule in his family that business was never talked about around the dinner table, or anywhere else, only in the study.

As he closed the study door, he noticed his daughter was standing in front of a portrait of her mother. The resemblance was uncanny. His dear wife had been killed two years prior in a horse riding accident. How he missed her!

Alton walked behind his desk and sat down. He folded his arms, indicating it was time to get down to business.

Brooke wasted no time in getting to the point. She looked directly into her father's concerned eyes. "How could you? How could you do such a thing?"

"Let me see." He scratched his temple. "Tell me what I did and I will explain my actions."

Brooke always believed the direct approach was best; there was no sense in dragging things out. Boldly, she blurted, "How could you cut me out of our family business? I am as much a part of Fortner Textiles as any of my brothers. They spent their lives playing games, while I spent time with you and mother learning all about the business."

He sighed, wondering how to calm her down. "So that's what this is all about. My dear, you were not taken out of the business. We felt it necessary to make a stipulation to prevent some outsider from taking advantage of you. We were afraid that some shrewd character would say he was marrying you for love, when what he really wanted was to take control of the business."

She swallowed the lump in her throat. "Oh, Father! That's not what happened. It isn't at all like that!"

"What do you mean?" He raised a questioning brow.

As Brooke tried to form her words, the door flew open. Rory and his brothers burst into the room.

"I'm in a meeting here," Alton barked. "You know when that door is closed no one is allowed to enter. Now turn around and get out!" He pointed to the door.

"Sorry, Father, but any conversation with Brooke must be discussed with the rest of the family," Rory insisted.

Arminius growled, reacting to his master's elevated voice.

Alton stood, obviously angered by his son's lack of respect. "I'm not asking… I am ordering you to get out now! I'm talking to your sister."

Charles, the oldest brother, stepped forward. "Father, you don't understand. Brooke is no longer part of the business. She also has been taken out of your will."

"What? I never agreed to that." Alton's anger doubled.

Rory felt the heat rising in his cheeks. "Sorry, Father, but you did."

"What are you talking about?"

Rory placed a folder marked *Fortner Textiles* in front of his confused father. He opened the file and pointed to Alton's signature. "You agreed to this, and you signed it with the rest of us. We were afraid with the political turmoil in this country that Brooke could not make the emotional decisions that need to be made. And you agreed to it!"

Alton scowled, lips tight. "My intent was never to take your sister out of the business and definitely not out of my will! Your sister should receive twenty-five percent of my estate and the business. She is the one I want in control of Fortner Textiles... she has better business sense than any of you!"

Rory rolled his eyes. "You would change your opinion if you had seen her gallivanting around Washington with some Northern Yankee."

"What are you talking about?" Father groaned.

Rory slammed a newspaper on the desk in front of his father. The headlines were circled. "Here is proof that we did the right thing when we took her out of your will. And frankly, Father, I am growing weary of you standing up for her all the time. She is nothing but a fast trick and is an embarrassment to our family name. Our reputation is at stake here."

Alton glared at Rory and snapped, "Mind your tongue boy! You don't talk about your sister that way. I'll take you out back and give you a lashing. And I can and will do it!"

The bold letters on the front page stood out as Alton peered at the article on his desk.

Hymnist and Textile Heiress—Talk of the Town

Instantly, her father felt like the wind was knocked out of him. He took a deep breath and shifted his attention to his only daughter. Sternly, he asked, "What is the meaning of this? Explain it, young lady."

Rory interrupted, "It is what it says. Newspapers don't lie!"

Alton picked up the article and studied it. His face displayed no visible sign of emotion.

Brooke, however, was a different story. She struggled to contain the sob that threatened to choke her. A hot tear slipped down one cheek and then the other.

Her youngest brother smirked as if the victory was his.

The room was hushed; time seemed to stand still.

When he finished reading, Alton faced Brooke. Waving the paper in the air, he voiced, "Barrett von Weber has been courting you?"

"Daddy, you don't know the whole story. Barrett came to my rescue. He probably saved William's life and mine. And Father, trust me, it's not at all like my precious little brother is trying to portray." She sneered at Rory.

"Barrett! You are on a first name basis with this man?" Alton spoke, shaking the newspaper.

Silence reigned for a time; all eyes focused on the patriarch of the family. A huge unexpected smile encompassed his face. "The Hymnist has been courting you?"

"See, Father, she has embarrassed our family. We are a joke in Washington," Rory persisted.

"My little girl is being courted by Barrett von Weber. I feel most honored," Alton chuckled.

Confused, all three brothers stared blankly at each other.

"I knew his father well. He was a good, honest man. I am delighted for you, my child." He rose and walked around the large mahogany desk and took her hand. Still chuckling, he gave her a fatherly hug.

"You see, Father, this is exactly what I was afraid of. This man is trying to get your money," Rory pointed out, his voice escalating with each word.

The father burst out laughing.

"Where is the humor in this?" Rory shouted, his face crimson with rage.

"What you said is humorous... that Barrett von Weber is after my money."

"He is," Rory roared. "I know it! My sister needs to be courted by a Southerner, a well-to-do man—Tennyson Garrison, for example. His parents own half the city of Atlanta."

"That dolt! He looks like a leftover from the revolution, with brains of an orangutan," Brooke griped. "Besides, he's twice my age."

Her father continued to laugh, partially because he was relieved, partially because the irony of it all. After all, he could not have chosen a more honorable man for his daughter.

The blood drained from Rory's face. "You see, Father... that is just what I'm talking about. She should not be able to pick and choose whom she will marry. She needs to marry up, into a family of importance. Our name is at stake."

"Like Mildred Harris did?" Brooke shouted sarcastically.

"Yes, like Mildred Harris." Rory turned, confronting her.

"She's the unhappiest woman I have ever met. She regrets the day she ever became a Harris. She hates her father for arranging that marriage, and she hates the dimwit that she married. She confessed to me that he beats her."

"Some women need to be beaten! They need to be taught where their place is in the home and in this world," Rory shouted angrily.

"How dare you say that!" Brooke shot back. "If a man ever raised a hand against me, I would defend myself with whatever means I could."

Pointing his finger directly in Rory's face, Alton threatened, "If I ever found out that a man hurt Brooke, I would beat him within a breath of his life." He didn't blink. "And if I ever found out you were treating your wife like that, I would whip you so hard it would be a month of Sundays until you could sit down. I don't care how old you are!"

A smile turned up the corners of Brooke's mouth. "Father, I think we should arrange a marriage for Rory," she stated, her voice finally calm.

"Do you have any one in mind?" Father played along.

"As a matter of fact, I do. Gertrude Farris."

The other two brothers snickered.

"I'll see what I can arrange," the father offered, grinning from ear-ear.

"That girl looks like the butt end of a horse," Rory contested.

"And just as big, too." Charles laughed.

"Make a joke," Rory replied, his face red from both embarrassment and anger.

"Oh, it's not a joke. It can go both ways. If a marriage can be arranged for me, then one can be for you." Brooke did not back down.

"Okay, enough of this bickering. The fact is you have no idea who Barrett von Weber is, do you, son?" Alton returned to the chair behind his desk.

"He's just a piano player." Rory muttered cynically.

"A concert pianist by choice; his father was Baron Omar von Weber," Alton leaned back against his chair, arms crossed over his chest.

"Who's that?" Charles asked.

Without missing a beat, Alton filled in his rebellious sons. "He comes from a good family. In fact, his grandfather was at one time a military commander for the German army. His mother and father were missionaries. Sadly, they were both killed when their ship sank off the coast of Africa. They were going to spend five years among an African tribe. Terrible accident. Some believe pirates sank the ship, but nobody knew for sure. Their bodies were never found. Barrett was their only child. He inherited their entire fortune."

"Fortune? How can missionaries have a fortune?" Charles asked.

Alton cleared his throat. He looked off in the distance as he remembered the details. "As I recall, the family owned a large winery in southern Germany. Not just any property, but prime land in Germany— known as The von Weber Winery. Upon their death, everything was left to their only son. In short, Barrett von Weber certainly is not after my fortune. In fact, he could buy me out with his pocket change."

The jaws of his sons dropped.

Alton frowned at them and his demeanor changed. Slamming his fist on the desk, he shouted, "I want my will changed back to read that each of my children shares the estate equally. In fact, I may give Brooke twenty-eight percent of the business, and give each of you twenty-four percent. That would give her major control."

"But Father!" All three sons voiced their opposition in unison.

"Don't question me! Did my attorney, Miles Hendrick, know what you were doing?"

"No, sir, it was set up by his new partner, Harrison Cradle," Charles confessed.

"Brother, your mouth is getting too big. Know where your place is," Rory threatened his older brother.

Alton yelled for his trusted servant. "William, please come here!"

"Yes, suh, Massa Alton," William replied, rushing into the room.

"Take the buggy to town immediately and bring Miles Hendrick back with you. Tell him to review my will and see if he thinks the wording is accurate."

"Yes, suh, Massa Alton." William hurried to the barn to get the wagon.

Shaking a finger at his sons, the infuriated father ordered, "I want this entire affair settled by this afternoon. You do realize that what you did is illegal and I could have you sent to jail."

"Father... I was just following Rory's orders," Charles cowered.

"Yes. It was his idea." Samuel said, pointing to his younger brother.

Rory glared at his two brothers.

"It doesn't matter whose idea it was. You all knew what you were doing when you signed it. Now leave this room before I cut all three of you out of my will," he demanded, "And don't ever cross me again!"

Alton watched his grown sons stomp out of the room.

Alone with Brooke, a smile returned to his face. "I'm sorry, my dear." He walked over to her, took her hand, and stared into her dark eyes.

"What?" she blushed.

"I see your mother in you. You have her same beautiful black hair, the same dimples, and her piercing Spanish eyes. You will make a fine wife for the man who captures your heart. Please understand that I would never intentionally hurt you." He looked toward the door where his boys had exited. "What made them do that? And what on earth made them think they could get away with it," he wondered aloud.

"Thanks for defending me, Daddy." She squeezed his hand.

Brooke was anxious to hear her father's thoughts on the political unrest. She carefully posed the question. "Are you worried about… about… well, do you think we will go to war?"

"Are you concerned about that?" The words churned in his mind.

"Yes, I am. In Washington we heard a lot of talk from both sides."

"Be more specific." His curiosity, prompted him to ask for details.

"People are talking of a possible secession of the Southern states."

Her father gave a sad shrug. "I don't believe there will be a war… so put your mind at ease. If we elect a leader who understands the South, then there will be no secession and definitely no war." He paused for a second and smiled at his daughter, trying to calm her fears. "Ultimately, God is in control."

She shook her head, thankful that her father had a way of calming her hurting heart.

Alton took a deep breath. "Please tell me about your trip, and tell me about von Weber. I remember about twelve years ago when he came here with his family that I was impressed with the young lad." He noticed a certain sparkle in her eye at the mention of his name, a look he had never seen before.

Brooke's thoughts were racing. *Could Daddy really not know what is happening? Was Rory right about that? I have seen a different side of Rory the last few months… and it isn't good! I don't know what to believe.* She closed her eyes and whispered a quick, silent prayer for wisdom and strength.

Brooke drew a deep breath and blurted, "Father, in Washington, Rory and some of his friends were trying to buy guns."

"Guns? Why on earth would they want to buy guns?" he shot back as he sat down again.

"Fifty thousand of them!" Brooke exclaimed.

"Fifty thousand guns!" his voice raised. "Where would they get the money to buy that many guns?"

Alton paused for a moment pondering his son's bizarre behavior. He straightened in his chair as the truth began to dawn on him. "So that's what this is all about. They want control of our business, so they can use Fortner Textile's money and influence to purchase weapons. That is why Rory telegraphed me saying everything was going as planned, my presence was not needed. Brooke, I don't have enough money to buy that many weapons."

Brooke cleared her throat, and continued, "I think they know a lot of people and have the backing. They had a meeting with Cornelius Hall from some rifle company."

"I know the man. Nice fellow."

"I was surprised to see him at our luncheon because I thought we were there to sell textiles."

"So did I." Alton frowned.

"Hall came with Barrett... Mr. von Weber." Brooke grinned, dimples showing.

"I can see why. Von Weber is an expert with guns. He can hit a target dead center from eight hundred yards. I saw him do it when he was here visiting as a youngster. And he's surely only improved as he matured."

Alton could tell by the look on her face, there was more to the story. She was never good at hiding her feelings from him. "What's going on? You never had a good poker face. That is why the boys always beat you at cards." He smiled. "I can tell from your eyes how much you care about this young man. Should I be prepared for an announcement, or a surprise visit?"

She grinned. "I hope so, but, Father, Rory despises him." She walked to the window and gazed out at the rolling hills, wondering how much she should reveal.

"Mighty strong words about your brother."

"Father, he picked a fight with Barrett twice, and tried to... to... he tried to stab him."

"What? Why?"

"I don't know Rory anymore. He thinks he is saving me from him."

"Let me ask you this. Was he hurt?"

"No, Barrett was not hurt. He disarmed Rory."

"I wasn't talking about Barrett. I was talking about Rory. Did Barrett hurt Rory?"

"No. What made you ask that?"

"Like I said, I know von Weber. Barrett is nobody to fool with, especially one-on-one."

She nodded, smiling. "No, he did not hurt Rory. Scared him though!"

He scratched his chin. Looking around, he sighed. "I may be sitting behind this desk too much. I have had my eyes closed to what's going on."

"What do you mean, Father?"

"I mean, my own sons tried to cut you, and me, for that matter, out of my own business. They planned to use my money and influence to buy guns to equip an entire army. If they had succeeded, I could have been arrested and tried for treason. I can hardly believe it!"

"Oh, Father, are you all right? I hated to tell you about Rory, but you had to know."

"Don't worry about me." Alton shook his head, disheartened.

After a few moments of pondering the situation, he began to feel the weight of his responsibility. "Tell me, who else was at that meeting?"

"Senator Toombs, Gerald Fulbright, and Harrison Cradle, along with some of their wives."

"Cradle, oh yes, he's the young lawyer that works for Miles. I suspect he was the one who changed the will." Alton pulled a blank piece of paper from a drawer and began scribbling on it—*Toombs and Fulbright*. He peered at his daughter. "Really? Toombs that old scoundrel... and Gerald Fulbright, the cotton king?"

"Yes."

"Interesting."

"Why would Fulbright be there?" Brooke questioned.

"What does he have to gain?" Alton thought for a second. "Oh, my word! The money is in the slaves."

"What do you mean?"

"I have always believed that the argument is that the South does not want the North to mingle in our business. You know, 'states' rights.' In reality, the issue is slavery."

"Slavery? Father, we do not have any slaves... you freed them. You pay everyone a fair wage when they work."

"There are those who say I own slaves. After all, I do have a piece of paper stating that I own them."

Brooke nodded, understanding.

Alton continued, "But, Fulbright has one of the largest populations of slaves in Georgia. He could lose a lot if the North calls for an anti-slavery bill."

"Can they do that?" Brooke raised a questioning brow.

"They can and have. It did not pass, but each time they bring it up they gain votes."

"How do they gain votes?"

"That's how things work in Washington. Unfortunately, votes can be bought with favors. You know if you keep running a horse in a circle, it will eventually wear down and do what the owner says. Same in politics. Just keep bringing something up for a vote until the opposition wears down and gives up the fight."

"Seems to be the wrong way to do things." She shrugged sadly.

"Depends on what side of the issue you are on."

Brooke nodded. "I guess you have a point."

Alton began to massage his forehead. "Dear, we know where Rory stands, so we need to be cautious of him. But, Charles and Samuel... we'll have to watch them."

"Father, I'm scared." Brooke's tone was subdued.

"Of what?"

"Barrett said that war is inevitable and it will pit brother against brother, father against son. I can see that it has already begun between you and Rory, and also me and my brothers. It's frightening, heartbreaking."

"I pray that it does not come down to that. Now go, but be on the lookout. Be alert at all times. We have no idea what other schemes Rory has up his sleeve. What am I going to do with that boy? Ever since I can remember, he has caused trouble. Mother must be rolling over in her grave."

Brooke walked behind the desk and gave her father a quick hug.

Alton watched her leave, slowly closing the door behind her.

In the quiet of the study, his thoughts took over. He looked at Arminius, sprawled out next to him, and spoke aloud, "I adore Brooke, but I'm afraid what her future holds... what the future holds for all of us. I'm certain trouble is brewing." He stroked his pet's head.

Alton looked up at the painting of his wife and uttered, "Since your death, I have buried myself in my business. I have been blind to what has been happening in my own family for far too long. One thing I am certain of, now my eyes have been opened. I can see clearly for the first time in a long while."

Later that day, Alton sat on the veranda in the chilly breeze, drinking a cup of orange tea, his dog next to him.

A carriage barreling down the long lane disrupted the quiet.

William had returned with Alton's lawyer, Miles Hendrick.

The attorney jumped out of the wagon apologizing energetically. The last thing he wanted was to lose an influential client like Fortner. "I'm sorry, Alton. I was unaware of their shenanigans."

He hurried up the steps, and was greeted by the protective dog. "Hi, Arminius!" He put the dog at ease, stroking under his chin a couple times. The dog settled back down, his job done.

Hendrick faced Alton and began his explanation, "I had my new assistant, Mr. Cradle, draw up those papers. I barely scanned over them and did not realize what your boys had done. I take full responsibility. My associate has been dealt with and this will not happen again."

"Let's continue this in my study."

Alton closed the door behind them. "I want my will and all business documents to be rewritten." Fortner sat down looking Miles straight in the eyes. "I want Brook to have twenty-eight percent of my entire estate."

The attorney stared at Fortner in disbelief. "That gives her the majority. Charles is your oldest son. I don't need to tell you that giving a woman the majority is almost unheard of." The attorney cautioned, "The boys will protest."

"Do you want to take care of my legal affairs or not?" Alton snapped.

"Yes, sir! I was just giving you some legal advice. I don't want you to be caught unaware—your sons could get a lawyer and challenge it."

"This estate is mine, I will distribute it to whomever, and however, whenever I want." His eyes held a fire showing he was a force to be reckoned with.

"Sir, consider it done. I will file all documents immediately. Some will have to be sent to Atlanta. I will bring everything back to you for your signature when it is complete. Is there anything else?"

Alton stood. "No, Miles. Just get this taken care of and pay attention to my affairs. I am your biggest client and I deserve your loyalty."

Miles shook his hand. "I understand, sir."

As the men walked to the door, Alton asked, "Miles, have you heard any political news that I should know about?"

"What do you mean?"

"Have you heard anything about Georgia starting a militia, or arming men to fight?"

The attorney stopped and looked at Alton. "Fight what?"

"You tell me." Alton studied the man's eyes to see if he was hiding anything.

Miles moved closer to Alton and lowered his voice, "All I have heard is someone tried to buy a number of rifles to equip an army for Georgia. The talk is that if we do not get a pro-slavery president, Georgia, and a number of other southern states, will secede from the Union. If need be, they will start a new nation more in line with the South's way of life."

"Would they really do that? Secede from the United States?" Alton sounded dubious.

"Can and will."

"What then?" Alton pushed further.

"This nation could get locked in a civil war." Miles' frown darkened.

For a long moment, the old friends looked at each other trying to comprehend what a civil war for their nation would mean.

"Let's just hope that never happens," Miles declared.

"No, Miles, we must pray that never happens."

Alton put his arm around his attorney and walked with him to his carriage.

Chapter Five

The silence of the stately Fortner Mansion shattered when a booming knock on the large mahogany door reverberated through the halls.

William pulled open the heavy door.

"Good afternoon, William," the pleasant young man standing at the entrance announced, smiling broadly.

"Good afternoon, suh."

"Are you ready for Christmas and the new year?"

"It's just another year," William replied, matter-of-factly.

"Not just another year, it will be a new decade—1860." The deliveryman handed him a stack of envelopes from the post office in Savannah. "If I don't see you before Christmas, have a Merry Christmas, William."

"Thank you, suh."

"When am I going to get you to stop calling me sir? My name is Paul. My parents named me after the Apostle Paul."

"I know what your name is. You tell me every time. Have a good day, suh." The servant's answer was curt.

"You too, William. I'll see you later, Lord willing." The man darted down the front steps.

William closed the door, glancing at the large amount of mail in his hand. He strode over to the study and knocked, waiting for a response.

"Enter," a voice sounded.

"Here is today's mail, suh." William neared the oversized desk where Alton's head was buried in paperwork.

"Thank you. And William, will you have Sylvia bring me some tea? I'm rather thirsty and I need to get this paperwork in order."

"Yes, suh, I will tell her."

Alton shuffled some papers on his desk, barely looking up. He had been having a hard time concentrating. Between his troubled family and the disturbing situation facing America, he found it difficult to settle down to the work that demanded his attention.

He picked up the letters, scanning through them quickly, and began organizing them in orderly piles, according to their importance. A bewildered look covered his face as he held up a cream-colored envelope and studied it more closely.

"William?" He spoke loudly, summoning his manservant.

"Yes, suh?"

"Is Brooke in the house?" Without waiting for an answer, he mumbled, "Strange symbol. I wonder who sent this."

"I believe she is upstairs, Massa Alton. She has been in her room all morning, upset after the conflict with her brothers."

"Send her down. She has a letter that looks important." He placed it aside and continued his sorting.

"Yes, suh." William hastily left.

Minutes later Brooke rushed in. "You want to see me, Father?"

"Yes, you have a letter that arrived today." He handed the mysterious piece of mail to her, carefully watching her expression.

"A letter for me? Who would write a letter to…?" She stopped speaking when she noticed the initials in the upper, left corner.

"Who is it from?" Alton raised a questioning brow.

"It's from Barrett." A smile lit up her face.

"How can you tell that?"

"The symbol is actually his initials. Big B and big W, with the little v right in the middle. Look! " She handed the envelope back to her father, waiting for his reaction.

As he studied it, he commented, "Yes. I see it now… Barrett von Weber… BvW. You just got home from your trip. How could this letter come so soon?"

Anxiously, she removed the letter and noted the date it was written. "He wrote this on November 7th." She recalled the memorable evening. "That was the day he took me to dinner and the theater."

"Why would he write you after your date, knowing that you would not read it until you got back home?" the father asked his smitten daughter.

Brooke never acknowledged her father's words. She left his study and quickly scooted out the back door. In the large greenhouse where Alton grew his flowers all year long, she sat on a decorative stone bench enjoying the fragrant roses, and clutching the newly acquired prized possession close to her heart. With eyes closed, her mind drifted to the events of the evening the letter was written. Smiling, she began to read it aloud:

My Dear Brooke,

If you are reading this letter, you must be home. I did not want a day to go by that you did not hear from me. Therefore, I am sending you a letter every day. Oh, how you have changed my life! I once had music running through my head, but now the image of your lovely face is all I see. As I sit here under the dim lamp, I see nothing but the radiance of your beauty. Moreover, I envision your sweet smile, which could make a beggar rich and royalty bow. I cannot wait to see you again...

She clung to every word of the three-page letter and read it over and over again, noting that it ended with the words, *Sincerely, Barrett*. When finished, she held it close, visualizing the handsome face of the writer. She remembered with fondness every memory that he mentioned.

Anxious to share her thoughts with him, she ran up to her bedroom, and immediately began writing him back.

This started a pattern. Barrett never missed a day. Every day Brooke received another letter detailing the highlights of their evening together.

He wrote his letters in the same way he did his hymns—each word full of meaning. She noticed the greeting progressed from *My Dear Brooke*, to *Dearest Brooke*. The latest letter began with, *My Darling Brooke,* and ended with *Love, Barrett.*

One afternoon, Brooke hurried back from her daily ride, anxious to see if that day's letter had been delivered.

William met her in the hallway. "Miss Brooke, you have a letter. I put it in your room."

"Oh, thank you, William." Brooke dashed upstairs, excitedly.

When she opened the door, she stood face-to-face with Rory!

"What are you doing in my room?" she cried out.

Mockingly, he read from the letter. *My Darling, Brooke. It has been seven days since you left my arms and returned home. I miss you with every breath....*

She tried to snatch the letter from him, but her brother spun around, keeping it out of her grasp.

"Rory put that down and get out of my room! Now!" The rage inside her was suffocating. Tears burned her eyes. She noticed all of her love letters scattered on the bed, some crumpled on the floor. "I cannot believe that you have stooped this low and have been reading my personal mail!"

Ignoring her outburst, he continued to read... *The days are dark and the nights are cold as I think about your warm embrace.* Suddenly, Rory's joking changed and his sarcasm shifted to anger. He began tearing the letters up, shouting, "You're nothing but a whore."

"Give that back to me!" she yelled, unsuccessfully reaching for the remnants of the letter he was destroying.

"You're a tramp… a whore. How dare you insult our family name?"

"It's my life, not yours. Put my mail down and get out of my room! Now!"

Hearing the ruckus, William ran into Brooke's room.

"You stay out of this, old man." Rory didn't hesitate to insult William.

"Massa Rory, please…." William pled with the angry, out-of-control brother.

Brooke reached again for the torn letter, but a stinging slap to the face caused her to fall back on the bed. "You need to be taught a lesson, woman!" He threw the paper down and took a step closer to his terrified sister.

William protectively stepped between them. "Massa Rory, you no treat Miss Brooke like that!"

The enraged brother pushed the servant with such force that it knocked him into a desk, gashing his head, and sending him crumpling to the floor.

"William!" Brooke cried, kneeling next to her protector's motionless body.

A couple other servants had gathered by the door. One of them ran downstairs to get help.

Hearing the commotion, Charles rushed in. "Rory! What on earth are you doing?"

Rory pointed his finger in Charles' face, menacingly. "You stay out of this, big brother. This does not concern you!"

Charles immediately backed down. Experience told him that when Rory was this angry he could not be reasoned with.

Rory was not finished with his sister. He reached down and grabbed a fistful of Brooke's long hair, forcing her to stand. Pulling her to within an inch of his face, he bellowed, "Our sister here needs to be taught a lesson and put in her place." He directed his comment to Charles, who stood watching, cowardly.

Just as their shaken father ran into the room, Rory raised his fist in a fit of rage.

At the same moment, Brooke spun around, grabbed Rory under the arm, and flipped him to the floor. She stood motionless staring at him, shocked by her own actions.

Alton, Charles, and the servants were also stunned. A couple of them couldn't help but smile; they all adored Miss Brooke.

Rory, face down on the ground, tried to gather his bearings, uncertain of what had hit him. Finally, he struggled to his feet. Still determined to knock some sense into his lovesick sister's head, he again raised his fist.

Instinctively, his father shoved him against the wall, which knocked a picture down, shattering it. "What's the matter with you, boy?" Alton yelled. "How dare you even think of striking your sister!"

"She's a tramp... a whore! Read the letters for yourself, Father. Stop standing up for her, she's not worth it!"

Trembling with rage, Alton raised his hand to strike his son. He paused to take a deep breath. Lowering his voice, he spoke, "If I ever hear you call your sister a name like that again, or if you ever put your hand on her, I will disinherit you from everything. No questions asked! Do you hear me?" Everyone in the room knew Alton Fortner meant what he said.

Rory's lips clamped shut.

Alton pressed his arm against his son's throat to reinforce his message. "I'm not kidding. Don't you ever put a hand on your sister again! Understand? Do you hear me?"

Reluctantly, Rory nodded his head.

"Say it!"

"Yes."

"Yes, what?"

"Yes, sir, I hear you."

Alton released him, and Rory stormed out of the room in a huff.

The hurting father knelt next to his daughter, who was picking up pieces of the letter Barrett had written, tears streaming down her cheeks. "I'm sorry, Brooke."

"Oh, Father," she sobbed. "Why is Rory doing this? I have done nothing wrong. Since Barrett has been courting me, he has been the perfect gentleman. I assure you I have done nothing to embarrass the family name. Barrett is the kindest, most gentle man I have ever met. Why does Rory despise him?" Still on their knees, she melted in her father's arms.

Alton's voice was barely audible over her sobs. "I don't know why your brother is acting this way. I know you have done nothing to shame the Fortner name. Rory is the one who is hurting our reputation."

"What am I going to do? Father, I love Barrett so much. It hurts me when people insult and threaten him."

"Brooke, dear, I will do everything in my power to talk some sense into Rory. When he has calmed down, I will try to reason with him."

Alton helped his daughter to her feet and a weak smile came to his face. "Where did you learn to do that… that… well, how on earth did you knock Rory to the ground the way you did?"

"Oh, Barrett has taught me a few things… ways to defend myself," she chuckled.

"He certainly did a good job." Alton shook his head. "I'm sorry about the letter, but you should be able to at least read it." He planted a quick kiss on the top of her head.

Alton glanced at the gash on William's forehead. "Let's go downstairs and get that cut cleaned up."

"You need not worry about that, Massa Alton. I can care for it."

"Nonsense. I can help. Let's go!"

"Miss Brooke? Can I be of any help?" her chambermaid, Prisse, asked, reaching for Brooke's hand.

"No, thank you. I would like to be left alone for now."

"If you need anything, let me know."

Heartbroken, Brooke sat on her bed holding the torn letter. A light smile came to her face as she pieced it together and began reading it.

In the following days, Brooke did everything she could to avoid Rory. Disgusted with his behavior, she wanted nothing to do with him.

Alton was surprised to learn how close Brooke and Barrett had become emotionally, even though the miles separated them physically. He had the highest respect for the von Weber family and was certain the young man inherited his parents' values. Many men had unsuccessfully tried to steal his daughter's heart through the years. A few families attempted to arrange a marriage, but Alton would have none of that! He had hurt several business relationships by refusing to accept arranged marriages to Brooke by influential families. He always believed a couple should marry for love. No other reason would suffice! And why not? His marriage was the perfect example of love and devotion.

Chapter Six

March 1860
Fortner Mansion

The pink and white flowers that lined the long pathway at the Fortner Mansion brightened the landscape and announced the coming of an early spring.

Brooke never grew tired of seeing the rosy-pink blossoms on the Eastern Red Bud trees that were abundant during the month of March in Savannah. All part of the area's natural splendor.

She had just awakened and was sitting at a small table on her balcony enjoying the cool, brisk morning air. William served her a cup of steaming tea while her chambermaid, Prisse, brushed her thick, jet-black hair.

Still sleepy, Brooke opened a book that she had purchased on her Washington trip. Quickly, she lost herself in the exciting novel.

Spotting a lone rider coming down the lane, William walked close to the porch railing and watched in silence. With each stride of the rider's horse, the image became clearer. The magnificent white horse captured his interest. Then he shifted his attention to the man in the saddle.

The rider waved to a few servants who were busy working in the gardens. He stopped his horse and chatted with a couple of the children who were playing near their parents. Two of the youngsters ran up to the stranger, their excitement evident as they began petting his snow-white, stately horse.

Watching from a distance, William noticed that the amazing animal had a tail that nearly touched the ground. He was certain that it was not an ordinary horse; it had genuine character.

The rider reached into his saddlebag and pulled out some small objects. He handed the mysterious items to the curious children. The youngsters studied their gifts, and then cautiously put them into their mouths. An immediate smile spread across their faces indicating their joy.

He must have given them sugar candy, William thought.

The stranger gave a soft laugh, which was barely heard from where William stood, almost like an echo.

The approaching horseman continued down the path toward the elaborate house, the children running beside him.

William continued to gaze at the rider. When he recognized him, a huge smile came to his face. "Well, I be," he muttered. Still watching the rider, he called out, "Miss Brooke, don't you think it's time you get dressed?"

She glanced at him with a puzzled look. "Why, William, what on earth would make you say that? I'm enjoying my book."

"Just in case of unexpected company." He watched the rider dismount and tie his horse to the hitching post in front of the house.

The maid, unable to see what captured William's attention, continued to brush Brooke's long hair.

Brooke started to pick up her cup of tea, still engrossed in the book, when a familiar voice from below startled her. "Good morning, William. Is the lady of the house in?"

Recognizing the voice, Brooke shrieked. She jumped up, pulling the tablecloth, and spilling the tea all over the balcony floor. "Oh my goodness, I am still in my nightclothes!" she whispered to Prisse. Embarrassed, she stepped toward the door, pulling the maid with her, brush still tangled in her hair.

"Why, Miss Fortner... I have never seen you looking so radiant." The handsome visitor gave her a sassy grin when he spotted her on the balcony above.

She had been caught like a fly in a spider's web. Blushing, she replied, "You're too kind, Mr. von Weber. I just awoke... obviously."

"If this is how you look when you awaken, the man you marry will have a lot to look forward to in the morning. In fact, he might not want to go to sleep. I know I wouldn't." He tipped his hat, smiling.

The mansion door opened.

Rory glared in disbelief at the unwelcomed visitor and wasted no time in pulling a pistol from the rack inside the house. "Grab a gun," he yelled to his brothers as he stormed to the edge of the veranda and aimed the weapon directly at Barrett's chest. "Turn that horse around and get off my property. I have every right to shoot you where you stand. You are trespassing!"

"Rory! What on earth are you doing?" Charles' mouth was tight with irritation as he grabbed a rifle and followed him.

"You stay out of this, brother!" Rory bellowed.

Samuel picked up a pistol, ready for action.

Hearing the commotion below, Brooke screamed, "Rory!" She spun around, ran through her bedroom, and bounded down the stairs

"Put that gun down, Rory," Charles ordered. "He is a guest."

Ignoring Charles, the angry brother cocked the hammer on his 44. "I will not tell you again. Get out of here—now!"

Without a word, Barrett dove to the ground. Tumbling, he pulled his gun from his holster, ready to defend himself.

At the same moment, someone from behind jerked Rory's arm upward, causing his gun to discharge. The bullet blasted through the ceiling, narrowly missing Prisse, who was standing on the balcony above.

Rory barely got a glimpse of his father as Alton yanked the gun from his hand, and pushed him down the porch steps. "What's the matter with you, boy? This man has come in peace." The father scurried down the steps.

Barrett stood, gun still drawn.

"Put your guns away, boys!" their father thundered. "Now!"

Stunned, they cast a doubtful look at their father, then at Barrett.

"I said, put your guns away! This is not what I call Southern hospitality. What are we... savages? We do not know this man to be our enemy."

Barrett made the first move, shoving his gun back in its holster, and brushing himself off.

Brooke ran out of the house, down the steps, throwing herself into Barrett's arms. "Are you all right?"

Holding her tight, his words comforted Brooke. "I like this welcome better than the one I got from your brothers." He smiled his boyish, charming grin.

Rory sat on the ground, rubbing his arm, and scowling at Barrett. For once, he was silent.

"You must be Barrett von Weber." Alton emptied the bullets from Rory's pistol and stuffed them into his own coat pocket. He tossed the unloaded weapon to the ground.

"Yes, sir."

"Well, young man, I am sorry for the way my youngest has welcomed you to our home. Forgive his rude behavior." The father shot a look of displeasure at his son. "Please come enjoy a hearty breakfast with my family."

Still embracing Brooke, Barrett responded, "I would love to, but do I have to sit next to the little brother?" He smiled, eyes sparkling.

Alton chuckled. "I'll see that you do not. In fact, we have a custom in our house that a guest sits at the head of the table. But judging from the enamored look on my daughter's face, you are more than that."

"Time will tell." Von Weber crossed his arms, grinning.

Brooke blushed.

"Come… breakfast is getting cold, and I hate cold eggs." Alton gestured for him to follow.

"I agree, sir." Barrett reached for Brooke's hand and a bright smile came to her face.

An energetic youngster, who looked to be in his mid-teens, ran over and grabbed the reins of Barrett's stallion. "Suh, you have a beautiful horse."

"Thank you. His name is Annapurna."

"Anna… purna," the boy repeated the name slowly.

"That's correct. His mother was a gift from an Arabian prince I know."

"But, suh, Anna's a girl's name."

"True. Anna is a girl's name, but Annapurna is the name of a mountain range in Nepal, next to India."

"That's a beautiful name, suh. I will take special care of him."

"What's your name, young man?"

"Titus… named after a book in the Bible."

"Oh yes, Titus… the legitimate son in the faith."

The boy's face brightened. "You know about Titus?"

"Yes, I write hymns. I consider myself a minister of the gospel."

"But you carry a gun... preachers don't carry guns." Titus frowned.

Barrett looked directly into the young boy's eyes. "I carry a gun for protection. There are times when I need to use it to protect myself, or someone I care about, from four legged animals… or two legged." He winked at Brooke.

"I wish I could have a gun so I could protect myself."

Barrett cast a questioning eye to Alton.

Brooke's father explained. "He was born small and has been picked on much of his life."

"How old are you?" Barrett asked.

"Sixteen."

"I see. Let me tell you, there are other ways to defend yourself, and if we have time, I will show you a few."

"Would you do that?" the lad said with a big grin.

"I would love to. But just remember… you learn to fight, so you don't have to."

"What does that mean?"

"I will tell you later." Barrett patted the boy's shoulder. "Will you see to it that Annapurna is wiped down, watered, and fed? It's been a long ride. And don't make fun of his name… he's the most loyal, and one of the fastest horses alive." He smiled.

Barrett reached in his pocket, took out a coin, and flipped it to the young boy.

The lad caught it midair; his eyes grew large. He glanced at Alton seeking his approval to keep the coin. When Alton nodded his head, a big smile came to the lad. "I will take good care of Annapurna." He took the reins and led the impressive stallion to the stables.

Hand-in-hand Barrett and Brooke walked toward the steps.

Alton strode next to them. "So you are Barrett von Weber... the son of Baron Omar von Weber."

"Yes, sir."

"I have been looking forward to meeting the gentleman who stole my daughter's heart."

"I look at it more like she is the woman that stole mine." Barrett extended his hand to Brooke's father for a hearty handshake.

Rory stood, muttering a few choice words under his breath. Angrily, he kicked the dirt.

Brooke paced over to her brother. Not saying a word, she slapped him across his face so hard that he almost fell backwards.

Calmly, she took Barrett's hand. Without looking back, they walked up the steps.

Alton glowered at Rory. "I was going to do more than that. Hope you learned a lesson. You can eat with us if you remain civil. If not, you can eat in your room, or out in the barn since you are acting like an animal." The father stomped away.

Stunned, Rory rubbed the red mark on his cheek, his ego as bruised as his face.

In the spacious dining room, the large table was elegantly displayed with linen and fine china. The scent of bacon lingered in the air.

Before anyone was seated, Alton formally introduced Barrett to Charles, Samuel, and their families.

The father spoke with authority. "As I said, it is a custom in my home that the guest is seated at the head of the table." He pointed to the chair at the end. "I believe my wife took your mother and you to Savannah to see the sites the day your family visited here. Your father dined with us and sat in that very chair. Please have a seat."

For a short time, Barrett stared at the chair, realizing its significance, and reeling in the fact that his own beloved father sat there years before.

After he was seated, Brooke wasted no time taking her place next to him.

The kitchen staff served a hearty breakfast.

The bountiful array of breakfast foods satisfied every appetite.

"Von Weber... I remember your parents well." Alton spread a large, blue linen napkin across his lap. "Met them on a few occasions. I remember twelve or thirteen years ago when they came for a visit, your father and I went for a long ride." He reached for a large bowl of scrambled eggs and passed them to Barrett.

Barrett took a hearty amount, realizing he had worked up quite an appetite.

A petite black woman handed Alton a platter of warm, fluffy biscuits. "Thank you, Tonya. They look wonderful. Please start them with our guest."

Alton continued, "I was surprised to hear your father say he was going to Africa." He paused. "I was heartbroken when I heard of their passing."

"Yes, sir, but they were serving the Lord when the accident happened."

"Well, it seems you have followed in their footsteps."

"I'm not so sure writing hymns is the same as being a missionary. They had a hard life, but they knew God had called them."

"Don't sell yourself short. The hearts you have touched with your music can never be traced. Your hymns are used in most church services these days."

"I guess you're right," the musician humbly agreed.

"Shall we say grace?" Alton extended his hands.

Everyone around the table joined hands and bowed their heads, while the staff stood motionless, also praying.

Lord, we are grateful for this wonderful meal. We acknowledge that everything we have is because of Your goodness to us. Thank You for bringing Mr. von Weber safely into our home. Lord, continue to protect us. Now, let this food be nourishment and give us strength. In Your Holy name, we give thanks.

They all gave a hearty *Amen.*

Barrett took a couple biscuits, smothered them with gravy, and took a few bites. "Very good... I need to get the recipe."

"Good luck with that. Sylvia has been cooking for me since I was a little boy. She will not tell anyone her secret recipes."

"Wait till you taste her orange tea," Brooke chimed in.

Barrett grinned. "Well, my compliments to the chef." He took a sip of coffee. "I remember the time I came here as a child. I know my father was impressed with your business, your values. Thank you for making my parents feel at home and for supporting their missionary work."

"The pleasure was mine."

Conversation about his parents continued.

Finally, Charles stepped in. "Mr. von Weber, I understand your parents were worth a sizable fortune."

Alton let out a noticeable sigh of disapproval.

Barrett smiled slightly, uncertain how to react to the somewhat rude statement. "Well, yes and no. The holdings belong to the von Weber Trust Fund. My parents put all their assets in that trust when they went to serve the Lord on the mission field. I have done the same. I do quite well with my hymns and concerts. The money is available if I need it, but I have never tapped into it, nor do I ever plan to."

"Don't say never, sir," Charles responded quickly. "You don't know when you may need the money. With the world changing so fast, it may be necessary to withdraw your funds."

"Even with what is happening in the world today, it would be hard to change my mind. I believe a business is only as good as the government that's in control."

"Would you like to elaborate on that?" Charles asked with keen interest.

Rory finally entered the dining room, head down. He sat, sullen, not saying a word.

Barrett continued, "Ponder this thought. My family's winery has been in business for over a hundred years. The German government has changed a number of times. I sometimes think of it as a revolving door. It has gone through many kings and dictators. Let us suppose that one day the government took by force everything my family owned–the winery, the workers, even the land. If that happened, I would be powerless to stop it, and I would be left with nothing. All my money and earthly possessions would be gone! However, there is one thing that could never be taken from me—my music! My music makes me content; it is in my soul, my heart. Even the highly respected composer, Beethoven, was deaf, but still had his music. You don't need money to be happy."

"You just need your music to be contented?" Alton teased.

"Well… there may be one other thing." Barrett smiled at Brooke.

"You talk about kings and leaders, we need a good leader. One who knows what the people need," Samuel interjected, changing the topic from Germany to America.

"That creates a problem. Which people do you speak of... the poor, the rich, the young, the old? No leader can solve that dilemma. There has only been one perfect leader, one perfect king throughout history... and we hung Him on a cross."

There was silence for a long moment.

Von Weber finally continued, "When you come right down to it, where did our leaders and kings get their power? By plundering those who labor. Almost every king, emperor, or dictator that has ever lived became rich by taking from the poor. Our American president is the exception, because the people elect him and can vote him out if need be."

The small talk continued without Rory.

"What about the threat of secession and possible war?" Charles asked.

"Charles, what kind of question is that?" Alton asked, giving his eldest a cross look.

"It's a legitimate question," Barrett interjected. "May I have another serving of biscuits and gravy, please? It is delicious."

"Eat all you want. We have plenty." Alton passed the biscuits to his guest. Barrett took another one and covered it with more of the tasty sausage gravy. "Please do not get angry with me, but consider what I have to say. I like to look at all sides of an issue before making a decision. Have you considered what may happen if Georgia does secede from the Union?"

"No, I have not." Alton leaned back in his chair.

"I have," Charles replied swiftly.

Puzzled, Alton peered at him. "Charles?"

"Pardon me, Father, but my brothers and I have discussed this matter at length. We have gone over all the possibilities of what would happen to us, as well as to the textile business."

"And what do you think will happen?" Barrett inquired, eyebrows raised.

"That is the reason Rory wanted to buy the guns. We must be prepared."

Barrett put down his fork and looked directly into Charles' serious eyes. "Let me be direct. I do not want to insult those who have fed me, but I must be truthful. There is never a winner in war. I have been many places and seen the battle scars. If Georgia and other states do secede, a war will certainly break out. When that happens, people like your father will lose the most in the end. His business, his land, possibly one or all of you will lose your life." He hesitated. "He may even lose his precious daughter." He shook his head in sorrow.

"I beg to differ with you," Samuel rebutted. "And I know Rory would completely agree with me. We can and will defend our state from the likes of the Northern states who are trying to force their beliefs, their ways, on us."

"I do not question your ability to defend yourself. I only say what I know to be true. If Georgia does secede, it is only a matter of time before war breaks out."

"Then we will fight," Charles, answered emphatically, eyeing his brothers.

"You will fight, and you will fight valiantly, but you will lose." It gave Barrett no satisfaction in saying those words, but he knew there would be no winner in war!

"Lose? No way! It is the North who will lose." Charles leaned in closer to the table.

Barrett drew a loud breath. "They believe as strong in where they stand as you do. That is why there is an impasse. I agree with you on the battle for states' rights, but in the end, it is not a question of states' rights. It is a question of human rights." He cast a sad look at Brooke.

"Meaning exactly what, Mr. von Weber?" Charles asked.

"I have been many places and seen many things. As a young boy, I watched the slaughter of men during the Schleswig War. I saw the nonstop brutal fighting in China, the massacres in Africa." A shudder ran through him. "I have seen slave ships from Africa and the slave trade of women of all races in Egypt. We do not have a corner on inhumanity in this country."

"We treat our slaves well," Charles added.

Alton scooted his chair away from the table. He countered, "We have no slaves. Any of them could leave at any time. They all get paid a fair wage for their work."

"If you have papers on them they are considered your property. Therefore, they are still considered slaves. In order to be truly free, the only paper a man should have is a birth certificate, and later in life, a degree from a university, if possible." Barrett leaned back.

"Blacks have neither," Charles spoke sharply.

"Right! Their name is only on a bill of sale." Barrett sipped his coffee.

Increasingly more uncomfortable with the political talk, Brooke interrupted. "Father, I find this talk boring. May I be excused? I would like to freshen up a little."

"Yes, go ahead. Why not take Mr. von Weber on a horseback ride around our estate?"

Barrett nodded. "Yes, I would like that."

"How long do you plan to be around?" Alton asked.

"Just long enough to take care of a little business."

"If you need any help in that business, please feel free to ask me. I know most everyone in this area." Alton cleared his throat. "In fact, you are quite popular around here. I know I could set up a concert for you in Savannah, if you wish."

"I would be happy to entertain in this fine town. Any time I can promote the gospel message, I will." Barrett smiled. "However, there is one thing I would like to ask."

"Is it business?"

"In a way it is."

"I have a custom in my home… no business is discussed around the table, only in my study. Gentlemen, please excuse us."

Barrett stood and pushed his chair in. "First, I need to retrieve a package."

"William will get it for you." Alton nodded to William.

"It's on the back of the saddle, wrapped in white cloth," Barrett added.

"I will bring it to the study, suh."

Barrett followed Alton.

Charles and Samuel glanced at Rory, who was still silent. They were curious what von Weber had up his sleeve. The older brothers did not dislike the German, but they would not go against what Rory wanted. He may be the youngest, but he always led the way… right or wrong.

As the men stepped into the study, Alton stated, "Please have a seat, and talk to me about the urgent business on your mind." He pointed to one of the comfortable chairs in front of his desk.

"I think, sir, it would be better for you to sit."

There was a knock on the door.

"Enter," Alton's tone was businesslike.

William walked over and handed Barrett the package.

"Thank you, William," Barrett smiled.

William nodded his head and left.

Fortner eyed the German with a questionable, yet polite stare. He reluctantly sat in his usual chair behind the desk.

Barrett took a deep breath and began his story. "Sir, about six months ago I was minding my own business, content with my life, happy doing concerts, and writing hymns. Then one evening, I was walking to one of my concerts and came upon a young, beautiful, dark-haired damsel in distress. That encounter changed my life. It was at the moment our eyes met, that I realized there was something I loved more than my music."

"And what may I ask was that?"

"Not what, but who? That would be your beautiful daughter."

"I see. What has that got to do with me?"

Barrett looked at Alton and then at the package he was holding. "Sir, I am an adviser for the New Haven Arms Company in Connecticut and test many of the products they manufacture. I would like to give this to you as a gift." Barrett handed the package to him.

"A gift... for me?" Carefully, Alton unwrapped it. His eyes showed astonishment. "What is this? I mean I know it is a rifle, but...." He held the gold plated rifle up and studied it carefully.

"It is a Henry repeating rifle," Barrett proudly stated.

"Repeating rifle?"

"Yes. One of the first made. You don't add gunpowder and a ball. It holds sixteen shells. You pull down on the lever and the next shell loads. Maybe later I can show you how it works."

"I would like that." He looked at the rifle, amused. "I don't know what to say. Thank you." Alton put the rifle on the desk and smiled slyly. "Young man... what do you want to ask me?"

"Sir, you know I have been courting your daughter. I believe it is proper to ask the father of the woman you love for her hand in marriage." Barrett stood at attention, clicked his heels, and nodded his head. "Sir, I love your daughter, and I would like to ask you for her hand in marriage."

Fortner stood. He began rubbing his chin with his hand, something he often did when he was deep in thought. Looking von Weber directly in the eyes, he spoke from his heart. "I see. You come to my house on a beautiful white stallion named Annapurna, that you claim was a gift from an Arabian Prince, named after a mountain range. You get into a fight with my youngest son, cause strife between his sister and her other brothers, and tell stories that many people find hard to believe. You even bring me a gift... a rifle, which sounds too good to be true. Then you ask me if it is all right to marry my daughter. Mr. von Weber, I do not know who you think I am, but such things do not easily impress me. Furthermore, in the South, many marriages are arranged by parents."

Barrett felt himself tense up, wondering what was coming next. His expression fell and thoughts bombarded him. *Maybe it's too soon. Perhaps they have another man chosen for Brooke. She could have any man she*

*wanted, so why would she spend her life with someone so opinionated,
someone her brother loathes?*

Alton grinned, finally deciding to let the young man off the hook.
"Barrett, seriously, if you want Brooke's hand in marriage, go and ask her.
It will be her decision, not mine, and certainly not her brothers'. If she says
yes, then I will gladly give you my blessing. My daughter's happiness
means everything to me."

Tears welled up in the proud father's eyes as he grabbed von Weber's
hand firmly. "I would be honored to have you as my son-in-law. And
furthermore, my daughter will have the most beautiful wedding any girl in
the state of Georgia has ever had."

A loud knock on the door interrupted them.

"Daddy? Is Barrett still in there with you?"

He gestured for Barrett to leave. "Now go! Come back with her answer.
I will be waiting... and praying."

"Yes, sir, and thank you." As he opened the door, Barrett looked back
and saw a big smile covering the father's face.

Brooke greeted Barrett with a broad grin. She looked radiant in her
riding clothes and feathered hat, holding her quirt.

"What have you two been talking about behind closed doors?" Brooke
shyly asked, batting her long lashes in a way that made Barrett's heart pick
up speed.

"Your father has agreed to back my next project."

"Really? Are you planning on starting a business here in Savannah?"

"It's not really a business."

Alton stepped in. "Brooke, please show Mr. von Weber to our guest
quarters."

"Really, sir, I already have a place to stay in Savannah." Barrett
politely declined.

"Nonsense. You came all this way to visit; I insist you stay here. As
you can see, we have plenty of room. This will keep you from having to
travel back and forth. That way you two can spend more time together.
And me... well, I can keep a closer eye on the two of you." He laughed.

"Daddy!" Brooke rolled her eyes.

"Now go. I have paperwork to finish."

Brooke linked her arm in Barrett's. "Come on. Let me show you your
room, and then I will show you Annalise."

"I have been looking forward to it. You have talked so much about this
place."

She gave him a quick, unexpected kiss on the cheek.

As he pulled her into a warm embrace, she seemed to be lost in a trance. *Nothing would make me happier than to share my life with you. But what about Rory's hatred of you? He will stop at nothing to destroy our relationship.* Brooke shuddered, partially from excitement of what could be, partially from fear of the unknown.

The couple ascended the large staircase and ambled down the hallway.

"How many rooms are there in this house? It's more like a hotel." Barrett chuckled.

"Father is a big family man. He enjoys having his children and grandchildren nearby. There are eight bedrooms upstairs. My room is right here." She pointed to a closed door. Father's room is next to mine. Charles' family is at one end of the hall; Samuel's is at the other."

"Their children are well-behaved. I never heard a word from them at breakfast," von Weber commented.

"Father demands obedience in his house. If you live under his roof, you obey his rules. Children are never permitted to speak at the table, except to quote Scripture from the Bible. And business is not allowed to be discussed at the table."

"And politics? Was I out of line, or too strong in what I said?" Barrett wove his fingers through his thick hair, waiting for her response.

"No, it was fine. The children can learn from such talk. You are permitted to disagree with Father, but arguing, yelling, insulting, or being disrespectful of each other is never tolerated."

She stopped at a door. "I'm sorry to tell you this, but this is your room."

"Why are you sorry?"

"Because Rory's room is next to yours." She opened the door and stepped into the spacious guestroom. A quilted bed skirt attractively decorated the canopy bed. A cherry wood desk tastefully sat in the corner. A glass door opened to the veranda that encircled the entire house.

"It's lovely. I will be comfortable here."

"How long do you intend to stay?"

"That depends on when I get some answers."

A young maidservant walking into the room interrupted their talk. "I'm sorry, Miss Brooke. I was told to bring these towels up to the guest room."

"It's all right, Haley. Have you met Mr. Barrett von Weber?"

"Barrett von Weber?" Instantly her voice filled with excitement, "the Hymnist?"

"As a matter of fact he is," Brooke replied proudly.

The young black girl grinned from ear-to-ear. "May I shake his hand, Miss Brooke?"

"Why of course you can. He doesn't bite."

Haley moved closer to him and curtsied. "Pleasure to meet you, suh."

Barrett held out his hand to greet the anxious woman. "The pleasure is mine."

"Massa Alton gave our church a few hymnals a while back, and I seen your music in 'em. I love 'em words. Sang solo once." The young woman stopped, realizing she was getting close to rambling.

"Really? Which one did you sing?"

"The Power of Almighty God."

He smiled, trying to ease her nerves. "That's one of my favorites. I wrote that while overlooking the majestic Niagara Falls."

"I heard of 'em... you seen Niagara Falls?" Haley's eyes were wide with curiosity.

"Several times. That particular day I was invited to lunch with my friend, Johann August Röbling, a close associate of my father. He was the man who built the famous London Bridge. At the time, he was building a bridge over Niagara Falls. As I sat under a tree marveling at his work, I realized that as amazing as it was, it could not compare to the power or marvelous works of our almighty God." He shifted his eyes heavenward.

Brooke relished the moment, silently taking in Barrett's words, his godly wisdom.

The Hymnist added, "I would love to hear you sing that song while I am here... maybe at your church?"

"Would you, suh? Honestly?" Her heart swelled.

"Yes. I would be honored."

"Will you play for me, suh?"

He reached for the young girl's trembling hand. "I would be honored to accompany you."

"Thank you, suh," Haley squealed excitedly. She took a deep breath. "Shall I shut the door, Miss Brooke?"

"No, Haley. You know Mr. Fortner's rule about a room with a boy and girl in it."

"Yes, ma'am. Leave the door open, so all can see." As she backed out of the room, a slight giggle sounded.

Brooke snickered.

Haley continued to talk to herself as she walked away. "I can't believe this is happenin'. Praise Jesus, praise Jesus." Strolling down the hallway, she sang Barrett's hymn loud enough for the couple to hear.

The power of Almighty God, the power of His love,
The power of His forgiveness, a gift from above.

Cannot be measured in earthly terms, or in any human way,
Yes, the power of our loving God in your heart is here to stay.

"My, she has a lovely voice," Barrett commented.

"Looks like you met your biggest fan." Brooke moved closer to Barrett. "Did you mean it?" she asked, walking to the door.

"Mean what?"

"You would accompany her at church?"

"Of course I did. I would be honored."

"Their church is different than most… it is loud and lively."

"Loud and lively is good. After all, the Good Book tells us to make a joyful noise unto the Lord." He gave a fun wink.

For a short time, Brooke watched Barrett. Her mind whirled. *The wonderful man that I am growing so fond of continues to amaze me. His humility, his humor, his kindness… the list of his positive attributes seems endless.*

She finally spoke aloud, "I'll meet you downstairs in thirty minutes."

Brooke slipped away, quietly closing the door behind her. Leaning on the other side of the doorway, she rested her head on the door. *Barrett von Weber is too good to be true. Will I awake and find this all is nothing but a dream?* She let out a long sigh.

Chapter Seven

The sky was cloudless and a deep cobalt blue. Brooke sat in the rocking chair on the front porch enjoying the warm breeze.

Patience was not necessarily Brooke's strongest attribute and this time was no exception. She was excited to see Barrett and waiting for him to come down from his room seemed like it was taking an eternity.

She watched Titus bring the horses from the stable to the front hitching post.

"Miss Brooke, Annapurna is some horse. I never seen one so gentle, yet high-spirited. I think he run faster than the wind." Titus stroked the beautiful stallion's neck as he spoke, "He's so big... I wonder why."

Brooke walked down to where Titus was standing and took a closer look at the large, sleek horse. "I don't know about that. He weighs much more than our thoroughbreds."

"Yes, but look at his length, the giant strides he can take while running. Oh, how I would love to see him race in Savannah!"

"Did you rub him down real good?" she asked running her fingers through the horse's thick mane.

"You know me, Miss Brooke. Horses are my life."

Brooke smiled at him as she placed her foot in the stirrup and gracefully flung her other leg over the back of her horse. She settled comfortably, yet modestly, in the saddle. Even though she was raised in a household of boys, she always tried to act like a lady.

Barrett bounded out of the house and down the steps.

Brooke smiled flirtingly. "If you catch me... I will give you a kiss."

Barrett grinned as he watched her take off. He was up to the challenge. He jumped on his horse and sped after her at a full gallop.

Titus stood in awe, watching Barrett's horse. *Wow! Look at Annapurna run.*

It took a few minutes, but the challenger finally caught up to Brooke.

A look of surprise covered her face. "I can't believe you actually caught me!"

"I have never seen a horse that could beat Annapurna in a race," he stated emphatically.

"My father owns three of the fastest horses in the state, maybe in the entire South. This is one of them, Selma." She reached down and patted the animal on her neck.

"Selma... that is Spanish for *peace*."

"Very good. Father named her after his grandmother."

"How old is she?"

"His grandmother?"

"No, your horse. I know better than to ask a woman's age."

They broke out in laughter.

"I know. I was just giving you a hard time." Brooke let out another giggle. "She is eight. About four years ago she gave birth to Annalise."

"Impressive," Barrett replied honestly.

"Annalise has never been beaten in a race."

"Sounds like Annalise is an amazing animal."

"She is. She was sired by Dark Shadow."

"Dark Shadow?" Barrett repeated, noticeably interested.

"Yes. He is the only horse that might be able to beat her. However, Father refuses to let the two race against each other. He believes it is unfair for a sire to compete with his foal, and certainly not a mare. If you stay around long enough you may get to see one of them race."

"That would be interesting. Annalise? Isn't that what your plantation is called?"

"Yes. However, it is not actually a plantation. Besides the textile business, Father raises cattle, fruit, vegetables, and flowers... oh, and racehorses."

"He's a busy man."

As they rode side-by-side, they continued to chat.

"May I ask you a question?" The hint of a sparkle appeared in Brooke's eyes.

"Sure. You can ask me anything."

"What were you and Father talking about earlier?" Brooke cleared her throat nervously.

Barrett gave a crooked grin. "I will talk to you about it later. Right now, show me this place you call Annalise."

As they rode, Brooke pointed out different landmarks.

The long, winding lane curved like a snake. The gentle slope of the land made it difficult to notice that they were actually climbing a good-sized hill. When they reached the top, Barrett noticed an enormous oak tree. Tombstones encircled the mighty oak.

They came to a halt and dismounted.

"This is Annalise." Brooke motioned with her hands. "From here, everything you see belongs to my father." She moved in a circle, arms spread wide. "You can barely make out the house through the foliage. To the left are the mills." She pointed to a cluster of large buildings. "Right across the road from the house are the livery stables and barns for our livestock and prize horses. Do you see the large greenhouse behind our house? That's where Father raises flowers and vegetables all year long. To the north about a half-mile is a large barn which is seldom used anymore except for hay storage." She paused, "This is Annalise... this is where I was born and raised."

Barrett could see that her radiant face expressed the pride she had for Annalise. It was clear that it was more than a home—it was her heritage, a life she loved.

She continued, "The place was named after my great grandfather's daughter who died at a young age. They emigrated from Germany. She was the only girl of six siblings. In fact, there have only been two girls born in the Fortner family in four generations—Annalise and myself."

"You're kidding," Barrett snickered.

"No, two girls and twenty-seven boys." She let loose a lengthy sigh.

"Twenty-seven boys. Amazing!"

The couple stood next to each other for a moment not saying a word, taking in the breathtaking view.

The pianist finally broke the silence. "Annalise! What a beautiful name for the estate. How old was its namesake when she died?"

"She was only nine. Her and my father were actually cousins. The story is that she caught malaria and lived just long enough to see this place. Annalise is buried close to here, but not in this cemetery. My other relatives are buried here, including my mother."

They led their horses closer to the small cemetery.

Barrett looked up at the enormous oak tree towering over them. "Why do the graves circle the tree? Most cemeteries are laid out in a straight line." He cast a questioning look.

"That was Grandfather's idea. He was a family man. We always ate meals around the table and held hands while we prayed. In fact, he had everyone recite Scripture while we ate and asked us how it related to our lives. Daddy often does the same thing at supper." The dark haired beauty took a deep breath. "Even in death, Grandfather felt that the family had to stick together. He made the cemetery circular, as if the family was holding hands around the table. I can still hear him say," Brooke lowered her voice imitating her grandfather, "'Our cemetery will be a circle because lining graves up in a straight line is like putting your family in military formation.'"

Barrett laughed at her impression.

She added, "Grandfather believed the tree was the center of the property. He used to say that it represented the Fortner's heart, and that the circle symbolized the fact that our family ties would never be broken, nor would the property be taken from us. Any of us would die defending Annalise. Most people who work for us would do the same."

"I thought a buried person is supposed to face eastward, so they can meet Jesus face-to-face when He returns," Barrett commented.

"Oh, Grandfather had an answer to that also." She lowered her voice again. "'If the Lord can raise you up, He can certainly turn you around.'"

Barrett broke out laughing. He stared at her for a long moment. *I love the fire in her eyes, the resolve. She speaks of her loved ones with such passion and conviction. In reality, I love everything about this woman. She is intelligent, beautiful, humorous, and she fears God. What more could I want in a wife?*

His eyes wandered to some fresh flowers on a gravesite. He read aloud the words inscribed on the rock. *"Isadora Theresia Ambrosia Fortner. Born: June 3, 1815. Died: June 7, 1857."*

He turned to Brooke with questioning eyes. "This is my mother's grave."

"Fresh flowers? From you?"

"No, from my father. His horse is awaiting him every morning at six when he comes out of the greenhouse with a bouquet of flowers. He rides here and lays it on her grave. He has never missed a day since her death—rain or shine. He loved her so much!"

She glanced at Barrett who seemed to be staring through her. He quickly shifted his gaze back to the gravesite. "Hmm... name sounds familiar. She's not from Spain, is she?"

"Yes. Mother married my father when she was eighteen. She came from an aristocratic family in Spain."

"That's where I heard the name." He shook his head slowly, staring at the tombstone. "He must have loved your mother very much."

"Oh yes, he still loves her... although she is only a memory now. I know that the man I wed will have to be remarkable. Father will not let just anyone marry me. That's one of the conflicts between my brothers and me."

"What do you mean by that?" he asked, raising a questioning eyebrow as they started down the hill on foot, leading their horses.

"There have been men knocking at my door in the past. Some parents have tried to set up the marriage, you know as they often do. My brothers, especially Rory, have tried to marry me off… usually to some old coot." She giggled.

As they walked, she continued the conversation, "My older brothers' marriages were both arranged by the bride's parents. Charles married Ashley, a Georgia politician's daughter. Samuel married Reba, a cotton grower's daughter. Both came from wealthy, influential families. They seem to be happy. Of course, Rory is still single. His temper and underhanded dealings keep anyone from wanting to marry him." Brooke rolled her eyes.

"I can understand that." He gave her a wide grin.

"Father will not have shenanigans like that for me. He is more interested in my happiness. He will not force me into a marriage, even for business reasons. I once had a prince show up at the front door in a fancy carriage surrounded by a dozen knights."

"Like medieval knights?"

"Yes, can you believe that? They were dressed in steel armor and everything. It was really somewhat comical. I think he was trying to impress me. He walked up to the front door and knocked. When I opened the door, he immediately got down on one knee, held up a ring with a walnut-size diamond, and in broken English asked for my hand in marriage. He was from some country in Europe that I never heard of before."

"What did you say to him?"

"I was only sixteen and my father was in Atlanta on business. I thanked the prince, but firmly declined his offer. He had brought six thoroughbred racehorses from his homeland. Rory and Charles said I was reacting too quickly and tried to push me into saying yes. After all, it is not every day a girl is asked by a prince to marry him. They told me that our father would be furious with me for sending the man away." She snickered. "I really think I did hurt the young man's feelings."

"Was he good looking?"

"As a matter of fact, he was." She gave him a sassy look.

"What did your father say when he returned home?"

"He went chasing after Rory and Charles with a whip, yelling at the top of his lungs, 'How dare you try to get rid of your sister!'" She was laughing so hard by the time she finished her story, tears were streaming down her cheeks.

Barrett joined in the laughter. "Don't tell me, that's how you ended up with the horses."

"Actually, he said that I could have all the horses if I married him. He went home broken-hearted and left the horses here. He said it would cost too much to take them back. Eventually, Father located the prince and paid him a fair price for the horses."

Barrett stopped walking and listened. "What is that noise?"

"Oh, that is *Annalise's Lair*. When Annalise saw it, she thought it was the most beautiful place she had ever seen."

As they neared the haunting sound, the foliage grew denser. "Oh my, whoever found this place?"

"Grandfather and Annalise found it. Back then, the opening was only large enough for a person to squeeze through. Over time, my family enlarged it so a horse could ride through it."

Brooke led the way through a small opening covered with vines and branches.

Not sure what to expect, Barrett followed close behind. He pushed aside some low hanging vines and made his way through the dark opening. When his eyes adjusted to the light, the scene astounded him. Speechless, he looked around, trying to take in the sights and sounds. A short distance away, nestled between the cliffs, a beautiful waterfall cascaded into a large, crystal-clear pool. Although it was loud, somehow it was tranquil, soothing. A startled deer drinking from the cool water ran off into the trees when the visitors made their appearance. An abundance of birds and wildflowers had made the cozy glen their home.

Brooke didn't say a word, giving Barrett time to take it all in.

Finally, he let out a sigh. "Oh, my goodness… Annalise was right… it is spectacular. God's work at its finest!"

"When I was a little girl, I would ride my horse up here and swim in that pool. It was ice cold, but refreshing. Brrr."

He ambled closer to a giant boulder next to the waterfall and noticed a large cross engraved on it. Closer examination revealed an inscription. He read it aloud. *"Here lies my precious daughter, Annalise. She was my angel on earth. Born January 3, 1806. Went home to be with Jesus on April 17, 1815."*

Confusion covered Barrett's face. "This is all rock. How did he bury her?"

"What is amazing is that Grandfather Ludwig did it all by himself. Grandfather knew how much his only daughter loved it here, so when

Annalise was near death, he carried her to this spot. He kissed her on the forehead and whispered a prayer for her. He told us, 'This is the place my little girl loved, this is the place she died, and this is the place she will be buried.' I heard that Annalise stared at the waterfall, and then closed her eyes with a peaceful smile on her face. Then she was in the presence of Jesus. When it came time to bury her, Grandfather refused help from anyone, even though he had six sons. My father told me he took nothing but a pickaxe and shovel. When he returned two days later, his hands were a bloody mess from all the digging he had done."

Barrett looked off into the distance. "What an amazing love story! The love of a father doing what seems impossible for his child. That is unconditional love."

Realizing he was deep in thought, Brooke questioned, "What are you thinking?"

"About God's love for us." He smiled. "Your great grandfather's love for his child was so strong, but the love of God for His children is even stronger."

Brooke nodded in agreement.

In the stillness, they relived in their minds what occurred in that location nearly forty years before.

Barrett finally spoke. "When my father was a young boy, he saw Beethoven conduct his Ninth Symphony in one of the greatest performances ever by an orchestra and choir. My father said the entire crowd was awestruck by the unbelievable performance. One summer, when I was eight or nine, Father took me to Stuttgart, Germany, so I could also experience the thrill of hearing the same masterpiece. I was mesmerized that night."

Barrett stooped, picked up a flat pebble, and skipped it across the calm pond. "I hope to write a symphony someday. I pray that it will be a smidgen as good as Beethoven's Ninth."

Brooke listened closely, grateful for the opportunity to know this man better.

The Hymnist stared directly into Brooke's big, brown eyes. "Oh, the love that was expressed here over forty years ago!" He turned and looked at her with moist eyes. "Perhaps this is the best place for me to do this."

He released the reins of Annapurna. The horse whinnied and walked over to the cool pond to get a lengthy drink. Brooke allowed her horse to join him.

Noticeably nervous, Barrett fumbled for something in his pocket. He exhaled through pursed lips.

Brooke tilted her head to the side, wondering what was happening.

Barrett glanced around, and then led her by the hand to a bed of spring flowers blooming near the water. The sunlight shining on the mist from the waterfall created a rainbow. Birds chirped in the warm air.

This is the perfect setting. Barrett took both of her hands and held them tightly.

The smile that lit his face made her head go light.

Gazing deep into her brown, Spanish eyes, he spoke loud enough to be heard over the roar of the waterfall.

"My sweet Brooke, I am twenty-seven years of age and have lived a life that many men would envy. I have seen some of the most beautiful sights God has created on this planet, such as the place we are standing right now. Yet, none of them can compare to the beauty of the woman who stands before me."

He hesitated and took a long, deep breath, slowly releasing the air. "Brooke Fortner... I would like to behold your beauty for the rest of my life. I would like to go to bed at night knowing that when I awake, I will be looking into the eyes of the most beautiful woman in the world, my wife, Brooke von Weber." He dropped to one knee and held up an exquisite diamond ring.

Her heart jumped to her throat as an immediate procession of tears rolled down her cheeks.

"This ring was my mother's. My father presented it to her when he asked for her hand in marriage. She gave it to me just before they left on that ill-fated voyage. She had a premonition that she would never return." He paused in an effort to keep his composure. "She told me, 'When the woman of your dreams appears, you will know it. Give this ring to her with my love and my blessing.' My darling, I know you are that woman, and I love you with my whole heart. Brooke, will you be my wife?"

Brooke finally stammered out the words, "What will my father say?"

Barrett grinned. "I already asked him and he gives his blessing if you agree. He awaits your answer... and so do I."

For a moment, her head was spinning. "Then we must give Daddy an answer." Her eyes danced with excitement. "Oh, yes. Yes, I would be honored to marry you, Barrett von Weber. Nothing in this world would make me happier than being your wife."

He wrapped his strong arms around Brooke and pulled her closer, kissing her with such passion that it left no doubt of his feelings.

His kiss left her breathless.

An excited giggle surfaced from deep within her. "Hurry... I want to tell Daddy... and the whole world!"

They hurried back to the mansion, anxious to share their news.

Alton was sitting in his rocker on the front porch, waiting for the couple to return. He wanted to catch his daughter's expression; one he hoped would be joy.

Brooke did not disappoint him—the excitement on her face was undeniable.

Her father jumped up and sprinted down the wide steps when he saw them approaching.

Their horses had barely come to a halt when Brooke dismounted directly into the protective arms of her father. "Daddy!" she squealed. "Barrett asked me to marry him and I accepted. Do we have your blessing?"

He gently stroked his daughter's hair. "Yes, my child, you have my full blessing."

Alton called his sons, "Boys, come out here!"

All of her brothers and their wives came running out of the house to see what the commotion was.

"Father... what is it?" Charles questioned.

"Mr. von Weber and your sister are betrothed. They have my blessing."

The three straight-faced brothers stayed on the porch, while the rest of the family gathered around the couple, offering their congratulations and looking at the huge diamond ring on her finger.

Charles asked the youngest brother, "Now what do we do?"

Rory retorted with disdain, "If he is as rich as Father says, maybe we can use this to our advantage." Evil tainted his words.

"Boys!" Alton shouted. "Come down here and congratulate your sister. There will be no more hostility toward my future son-in-law." Alton directly faced his three sons. "If there is, it will be you who will be out in the cold. Understood?" He spoke with authority. They all knew he was a man of truth—he meant what he said. Always!

Before they could respond a carriage came barreling down the long lane. In it was Alton's lawyer—Miles Hendrick.

The attorney jumped out of the wagon. "I hope I am not interrupting anything Alton, but I have all the documents ready for your signature." Looking around, Miles noticed the boys' troubled expressions. "I am disrupting something, aren't I? I'm sorry, but I knew you would want to take care of this immediately."

"No problem, Miles. Have you met Barrett von Weber?"

"Barrett von Weber... you mean, the famous Hymnist?"

"The one and only."

The attorney eyed the man who had his arm around Brooke.

"He just proposed to my daughter, and they will be married soon."

Miles took a step backwards "Married... the Hymnist... How did she meet him?" The attorney snickered, "My wife will be envious."

Alton proudly introduced his future son-in-law. "Miles Hendrick, meet Barrett von Weber."

The pianist clicked his heels and nodded his head. He grasped the hand of Alton's lawyer in a vigorous handshake.

"This is an honor, sir," the lawyer stated, unaware that he was still shaking hands. "My wife is the church organist and she plays all your music. Before we moved here, my father was a constable in one of the towns close to where your family used to reside in Germany. He had some business dealings with your family."

"All pleasant I hope."

"Certainly. As a matter of fact, he had the highest respect for the way your family treated their workers. He told me that one Christmas your father gave two chickens and a bottle of wine to every family in the village. Must have cost your family a fortune. When asked why he did it, Baron von Weber replied that he was just giving back to the people who had helped him."

"Thank you for your kind comments about my father. My parents were special people."

"So, you are going to marry Brooke."

"Yes, sir, I asked and she accepted." Barrett smiled proudly.

"Congratulations. Will the wedding be here?"

"I'm counting on that." Barrett crossed his arms.

"Great. I hope I will be invited."

"You're on my list," Alton acknowledged. "Now, let's get to the item at hand in my study."

Brooke's father turned to von Weber. "Barrett, I will let you get back to your beautiful fiancée."

"Thank you, sir."

Alton and his attorney chatted as they made their way to the study.

Miles patted his leather briefcase. "Like I said, I have everything here. Sorry it took so long, but I had to pull a lot of strings to keep your sons from being indicted."

"Thank you, Miles. And you have everything corrected?"

"Yes. It just awaits your signature."

As they entered the study, Alton closed the door. After they were comfortably seated, he spoke, "Miles, I have another change to make."

"What's that, Alton?"

"I want the designated percentage changed," he lowered his voice.

"Changed? In what way?"

"I want Brooke to get fifty-one percent of the business. Her bothers will split the other forty-nine."

"That gives her the majority." Miles raised his brow.

"That is correct. I felt if something were to happen to me, even with the twenty-eight percent she owns, the three boys could unite and oust her. I want to prevent that from ever happening. I trust Brooke with Annalise, but sadly, I don't trust my sons anymore."

"I understand. I will make that change, but we will need a couple of signatures to make it legal."

"I can get William to do it."

"I'm sorry, sir, but because of the circumstances I suggest you get someone else. William is still considered by many to be a slave, his signature will never hold up in a court of law... at least not in Georgia. Maybe von Weber can do it."

He called the servant, "William!"

"Yes, suh."

"Please bring Barrett to my study."

"Yes, suh. I get him now."

"Let's get this over with... I have a wedding to plan." Alton slapped his attorney on the back.

Chapter Eight

May 7, 1860
Ten Broeck Race Course

The news of the approaching wedding spread quickly throughout Georgia. Gossip ran rampant. Citizens predicted whether it would be the wedding of the year.

Brooke was highly respected in the community. Many eligible bachelors felt a sense of loss. No man had been able to win her love… not for lack of trying. Until now.

Since she was a young girl, Brooke had dreamed of a June wedding. The weather should be lovely—not too hot. The flowers would be abundant, especially the roses. And an abundance of produce would be in season to add to the many creative dishes for the reception. June should be the perfect month for the perfect wedding!

The bride would need assistance with many details since time was short. Alton suggested his two daughters-in-law help plan the event. Brooke welcomed the idea. Ashley and Reba were both eager to assist and were assured upfront that no expense was too much!

While the wedding plans were underway, Barrett stayed at the estate. He frequented the church the Fortner's attended, playing the piano on several occasions. He also kept his promise and accompanied Haley at the small church on the Fortner Estate. As Brooke had warned… it was indeed a lively church.

The people in the community had been familiar with von Weber's music, but now they were getting to know him as a person. Most people liked what they saw. Not only was he a man of faith and integrity, but he was compassionate, kind, and generous. Most of the people in Savannah understood why Brooke Fortner was enamored with him.

The Hymnist performed a concert in Savannah and met many influential people; some were well-known politicians, others were military personnel.

During their time alone, Barrett and Brooke rode the trails surrounding the large estate. Often they would have a picnic lunch and talk for hours.

Barrett became friendlier with Charles and Samuel, but Rory still kept him at arm's length. The youngest brother was civil for the most part; he knew his father was serious about cutting him out of the will. However, he still detested von Weber, and nobody knew why.

The sky was gray and overcast, further affecting Brooke's mood on the day the family went to the races at Ten Broeck Race Course in Savannah.

"I hate this place," Brooke announced upon arrival.

"The racetrack? Why?" Barrett raised an eyebrow, puzzled by her reaction.

"Last year it was turned into a spectacle."

"What happened?"

She walked over and pointed to a couple old sale bills crudely nailed to the side of the stands, as if to remind people what Georgia believed.

Barrett quietly read the notice:

SALE OF 440 NEGROES!

PERSONS DESIRING TO INSPECT THESE NEGROES WILL FIND THEM AT THE RACE COURSE, WHERE THEY CAN BE SEEN FROM 10 A.M. to 2 P.M. UNTIL DAY OF SALE

J. BRYAN

Staring at the sale bill, Barrett finally spoke up, "I am not really familiar with the slave industry. It is no secret that I do not agree with it. Still, four hundred and forty sounds like a lot of people. Did a plantation shut down? Was it Bryan's?"

She shook her head. "No! Bryan is a slave trader who works on commission. A man named Pierce Butler owned the actual plantation. Rumor has it that he sold everything to pay off his gambling debts." Sadness clouded her eyes.

"Pierce Butler? That name sounds familiar. Isn't he one of the wealthiest men in the country?"

"That was his father, who was also a signer of the Declaration of Independence."

"How ironic... becoming one of the richest men in this country and ending up losing so much." Barrett sighed.

Brooke shook her head sadly. "Selling people like they were animals. You can't get any more demeaning than to do it at a horse racetrack."

"Were these families or individuals?"

"Families, even little children. They were supposed to be sold together, as families, but many were not. Politicians and news reporters came from everywhere to publicize the sale. Even the famous newspaper writer, Horace Greeley, came to report it. It was billed as the biggest slave sale ever." She sniffed and reached for a handkerchief in her reticule.

"Barrett could see how distraught Brooke was. He reached over to hold her hand and changed the subject. "Let's make our way closer to the track. I am excited to see your family's horses race."

Brooke nodded in agreement.

The couple wove their way through the enthusiastic crowd to join Brooke's three brothers, who had opted to stand against the fence to have a better view of their animals.

Brooke hoped things would change between her youngest brother and her fiancé after they spent time together that day.

After they had watched several races, Samuel asked haughtily, "Well, Barrett, what do you think of our horses?"

"Your horses are fast. I'm impressed. Fine looking animals." Barrett kept his eyes on the track.

"Our Spanish thoroughbreds are the fastest horses in the world," Rory boasted, leaning on the fence, staring at Barrett.

"It's true. They are the fastest. Since we have been racing here, they have seldom lost," Samuel reinforced his brother's words—something Barrett noticed that he often did.

"They are good, strong racehorses, but winning is not just in a breed," Barrett cleared his throat before he continued. "It has a lot to do with the individual horse. Take Annapurna for example...."

Interrupting, Charles teased, "I still say that's a girl's name. Probably runs like a girl, too." He laughed, amused by his own comment.

Rory sarcastically added, "Who in their right mind names a male horse a girl's name?"

Charles and Samuel laughed robustly.

In return, Brooke frowned at her brothers.

Barrett felt himself tense up. "I assure you, sir, Annapurna is not a horse to poke fun at. The mountain range he was named after is the roughest in the world and has never been beaten... much like him." He held Rory's glare for a full minute. "He is an Arabian stallion—extremely fast and resilient. He is tall, and strong. He has an unusually long stride—your horse would have to take three strides to equal two of his. I find it hard to believe that any of your horses could beat Annapurna." Barrett folded his arms across his chest.

Unwilling to let the matter drop, Rory continued the bantering. "Oh, come now, I will admit that your horse is a fine specimen, but I am certain that he cannot hold a candle to any of our Spanish thoroughbreds. The best European horse breeders in the world raised them. I would be willing to bet that my horse can beat your horse in any race, any day of the week." Rory's face looked smug, arrogant.

"Lucky for you, I'm not a betting man." Barrett took Brooke's hand and the couple turned to walk away.

"Oh, come now, von Weber. You mean to tell me you would not wager a friendly bet on a race. It would appear that you are scared of losing. Almost... cowardly," Rory egged him on. "Is that what it is... are you afraid of losing?"

Barrett whipped around, facing Rory. He felt the heat rising in his cheeks. "Not at all. I'm certainly not afraid of losing, but I will not be goaded into racing."

Rory ran his fingers through his hair. "How about a friendly race—just between you and me? I mean, we are almost family." A mean-spirited chuckle rumbled through him.

"You and me?" Barrett could tell that his future brother-in-law was not going to give up.

"Right. I know we have been at odds with each other. Maybe this is a chance we can get together," Rory baited.

Barrett stood a good head taller than Rory, so when he looked at him, he looked down into his cold, angry eyes. "We have not been at odds with each other; you have been at odds with me. And I might remind you, for no apparent reason."

"Oh, I have my reasons. I don't like Northerners, plain and simple." He lifted his chin and glared at him.

"That's your gripe... you hate me because I am a Northerner. My ancestors and yours came from Germany. Near the same area, I believe. Does that hold any weight?"

"No. Afraid not. I left my German roots where they belong—in Germany. I have adopted my mother's Spanish aristocratic side, not my father's German gardening side. However, I am a proud Southerner through and through—a Georgian Southerner. You can't beat that!"

Rory's brothers laughed at the youngest Fortner, egging him on more.

Barrett cleared his throat and continued, "Most of my life I have competed on the gun range, in Chinese fighting arenas, and also in piano competitions. And, I have even raced Annapurna a few times for fun. My competitive nature would love to race you. Problem is I'm afraid after my horse wins, you will hate me even more. For the sake of your sister, I must decline."

"Rory, please stop," Brooke pleaded with her brother as she watched her father approach them.

Rory responded with a hearty laugh. "No way, little sister. Can't do it! He made the statement that his horse is faster than ours. I want him to prove it."

"If you remember correctly, I said that I find it hard to believe that there is any horse faster than Annapurna."

Rory put his arm around his brother's neck. "Charles, my brother, does that not sound like a challenge to you?"

Charles was quick to respond, "Sounds like one to me."

Brooke was fuming. "Father, Rory's trying to force Barrett into a horserace."

"Okay, boys, you have had your fun," their father admonished sternly. A frown creased the older man's brow.

"This is just a friendly wager," Rory insisted.

"Rory, if the man doesn't want to race, drop it. He probably does not want to gamble." Alton blew out a deep breath.

"Who said anything about gambling? Just braggin' rights, that's all I want. I'll even give your horse a five second head start." He turned back to Barrett, eagerly awaiting his response.

"Rory, I won't tell you again," Alton snapped.

"All right!" Barrett had enough. "I'll race! I won't bet, and there will be no money exchanged between the two of us. And there certainly will be no five second head start." He gestured toward the racetrack. "You said any race, any day of the week, right?"

"Any race, any day of the week." Rory's face was smug.

"All right then. We'll race twelve furlongs, starting from the other side of the track and ending in front of the stands."

"Okay, I accept the terms." Rory appeared confused by the change of mind Barrett had, but he wasn't going to question it.

"That way we can give the crowd a show by racing in front of them twice. Let's give the people something to cheer about… a mile and a half race." Barrett's eyes indicated his earnestness.

"One and a half times around the track... a mile and a half," Rory repeated, looking at the track.

"Right! If you win, you get your bragging rights. However, when I win, in fact, even if I lose, you have to be civil to your sister and me until the wedding is over. One more thing, you must jockey your horse, and I will ride mine."

Rory spit in his hand and reached it out. "Deal!" His dark eyes gleamed with triumph.

Brooke moved close to Barrett, doubts surfacing. "Darling, you don't have to do this."

"If it will make him treat you better, I am happy to oblige." He smiled broadly.

She faced her obnoxious youngest brother, looking straight into his eyes. "Rory, why do you do this? What is your game?"

"Do what, little sister?" He lit up a cigar and arrogantly puffed smoke in her face.

"I'm not your little sister... I am older than you."

"Taller, too." Samuel said, grinning.

Rory glared at him, but decided to ignore his remark.

Brooke stared at him as though she was reading his mind. "You're going to ride Dark Shadow, aren't you?"

"Well, how did you ever know that?"

Brooke faced Alton. "Father, do something. The race is rigged."

"I'm sorry, honey. There is nothing I can do... they have already sealed it with a handshake."

"Brooke, don't worry. It's only a race." Barrett struggled to keep his voice calm.

"No, it's not. Daddy, I know Rory is up to something. He cannot be trusted. He will stop at nothing to hurt Barrett. You know that Dark Shadow has never lost a race. Never!"

"When is this race going to take place?" Barrett probed.

"I will clear it with the owner of the track. Let's say in two weeks. That is the biggest racing day of the year. There will be scores of people here... a lot of money will be wagered."

"I sense that you think you will make a lot of money that day."

"I know I will. Everyone will bet on me! Problem is... who will bet on you?" Cocky, Rory strutted away laughing. He already tasted victory.

Charles and Samuel followed like puppets behind their brother, chuckling all the way.

Barrett realized the stakes might be high if he won. It could put Rory up against a wall and he may fight even harder. On the other hand, losing… that word was not in von Weber's vocabulary.

Chapter Nine

Alton and his soon-to-be son-in-law watched Titus gallop Annapurna around the small practice track near the Fortner Estate. The thundering hooves of the splendid animal as he ran would make anyone take notice. His long, white mane flew in the air like feathers dancing in the breeze.

"He's one beautiful horse. This is the first time I have ever seen an Arabian," Alton admitted.

"I raised him since he was a colt. My father was close friends with an Arabian prince who raised prize-winning horses. The prince gave me a bred mare. Annapurna was one of the first Arabian horses born in America."

"Where does he get his size? He's so large; I thought Arabians were smaller."

"They usually are. The prince had been doing some crossbreeding of his horses. I believe Annapurna has some Friesian blood in him."

"Friesian? I have never heard of that breed." Alton angled his head.

"They are a breed from Belgium and the Netherlands."

"Are Friesians fast? Do they make good race horses?"

"Yes, they do. They are not as fast as an American thoroughbred, but horsemen do race them—and win."

Alton's face grew serious. "Son, I wanted to tell you that you don't have to follow through with this race against Rory. No one will think of you as a coward if you back out."

Barrett liked the way Alton already treated him like a member of the family. It made him feel special when he called him 'Son.' Barrett smiled. "It has nothing to do with me being brave. It has to do with your daughter being treated like a lady."

"I understand." Alton didn't blink. "You do know you will lose," his tone expressed certainty.

Barrett looked at Brooke's father with skepticism. "I see that you do not know me very well, and you certainly do not know Annapurna."

"Well, your odds are not good. Someone could make a fortune if you win."

"You mean, when I win."

Alton eyed Barrett. "Very few people around here will bet against Dark Shadow. They all know that he can't be beaten."

"We'll see." Von Weber spoke with confidence, not arrogance.

Brooke rushed up to the two men.

Charles followed close behind her.

"Good morning, darling," Barrett greeted her enthusiastically.

She kissed Barrett on the lips and threw her arms around his neck.

Brooke turned to her father, ready to speak, when Charles interrupted, "Father, I need to talk with you privately." His manner conveyed the urgency of his request.

Alton turned an eye to Charles. "Anything you have to say to me, you can say in front of Barrett."

"No, sir, I cannot. It has to do with the race." Charles's face registered concern.

"Don't worry about me." Barrett looked over at Titus working with the horse. "I am going to spend some time working with Annapurna. Brooke, my dear, would you like to join me?"

"In just a moment. I'll be there as soon as I finish talking with Father."

Barrett smiled and gave her a kiss on the cheek.

When he was out of hearing range, Brooke began talking. "Daddy, I didn't want to tell you this, but Rory... Rory has bet Dark Shadow on the race."

"Dark Shadow... to whom?" A quick spark of what appeared to be irritation flashed in the man's eyes.

Charles jumped in, speaking fast. "Some European shipping tycoon. The guy bet twenty thousand dollars that Annapurna would win. Rory did not have that much money, so he put up Shadow as collateral. Then he and Samuel added five thousand cash on Shadow."

"I didn't think Rory was going to bet." Brooke's heart sank.

"You know that boy has a mind of his own. He is going to do what he wants." The disappointed father shrugged his shoulders.

"He is so sure he is going to win," Brooke replied.

"Well, I think he is, too. And we were just discussing who would bet against Dark Shadow," Alton quipped.

"I don't know, but somebody did. Father, if by some chance Rory does lose…." Charles, sensing the urgency of the situation, turned to his sister, "You need to tell Barrett to throw the race."

"What? I will do no such thing." Brooke felt a sick feeling in her stomach.

"Think about it… if Barrett happens to win, Rory loses everything… including Dark Shadow."

"Charles, you have no right to ask your sister to do that." Alton's answer was quick.

A brisk breeze arose, but it couldn't blow the seriousness of the moment away. The mood was somber as the trio pondered the situation.

Charles interrupted the silence. "Father! Please think about it! That horse is worth a fortune and is partly mine. If he loses, Rory will lose everything he owns. You have to do something!"

"That is his choice, not yours, or mine. As for ownership of the horse, that will be between you boys. You can tell Rory this—I will not bankroll his stupidity. As for Shadow, well, the horses belong to you boys. It was the three of you who developed them into what they are today. It's something to be proud of."

Brooke chimed in, "Father, are you forgetting those horses were originally given to me?" A frown accompanied the question.

"You showed no interest in them, and remember, Father bought them outright," Charles chided.

"I'm just saying I should have a say in this, too." Brooke continued to stand her ground.

Alton leaned forward cupping his hands together. "Brooke, I am afraid not. The fact is, while the boys were working with the horses, you were busy learning how to run the business. In the end, you will come out ahead. Besides, Rory made the deal, and you can't change it."

Brooke glanced at her fiancé stroking his horse's neck, a short distance away. "I have had enough of this talk. Excuse me." She stormed off.

"Remember what I asked you, Brooke. Rory could lose everything, he may even get killed," Charles hollered, watching her go.

"Not my concern," she quietly snapped with her back to them, waving her hands in frustration.

Even still, they heard her.

Barrett immediately noticed Brooke's distress. "What did they say that brought that look to your sweet face?"

"Rory bet Dark Shadow and another five thousand that he will win the race."

"He bet Dark Shadow against me?" Von Weber thought for a moment. "He is the favorite, but who would bet against him?"

"That is what everyone is saying, but it seems some European shipping tycoon has bet against him." Brooke sighed. "Honey, we can't lose Dark Shadow. He is the future of our racehorses."

"I see." Barrett grew rigid and took a step back, fully understanding the dire situation. "Are you asking me to throw the race?" he questioned cautiously.

Her lower lip trembled. "I would never ask you to do that."

"But others have, right?"

She looked toward her father and Charles, still deep in discussion. "Yes. However, Father did not go along with it."

Barrett pulled his fiancée close and stared into her dark eyes. "My father taught me to do my best in everything I do and never yield to any man. But, what do you want me to do?"

"You're already a winner in my eyes." She mustered a small, but sincere smile.

"I didn't ask that. I asked what you want me to do. Should I throw the race?"

She looked at him and suddenly realized the importance of what he was asking. It was a test of her loyalty.

She stood taller, and with determination, vowed, "No! I want you to win. I want you to go out there and do the best you can. If Rory loses everything, then so be it. Don't sacrifice your respect and your honor for the likes of my brother."

"I was hoping you would say that." He gave her a heartfelt hug.

"Massa Barrett, suh?" Titus interrupted the tender moment.

"I want you to call me Barrett."

"I can't do that Massa Barrett."

"Yes, you can. We are in this together." He put his hands on Titus's shoulders. "We need to get Annapurna ready for the race. You are in charge, so please call me Barrett."

"Yes, suh, Barrett."

"There, that's better. Brooke, if you will excuse Titus and me, we have a horse to prepare for a worthy opponent."

"Don't be too hard on him." She winked.

He turned and smiled, and they walked away, Titus leading Annapurna.

"Has he ever raced before Massa Barrett? I mean Barrett, suh."

"Many times."

Titus continued, "I see Annapurna is fast, but no horse is faster than Dark Shadow."

"Do you think Annapurna has a chance?" He searched the boy's face for an answer.

The lad looked over the lengthy horse and then over at the barn that housed Dark Shadow. "No, suh, I don't."

Barrett put his arm around the boy and calmly replied, "I guess we will have to show the good people of Savannah just who Annapurna is."

Von Weber's mind was churning. He realized he was in a bad situation. *If I win, how will Rory react? Brooke's brother may possibly lose everything he owns. If Annapurna loses, Rory will have bragging rights and could win a lot of money. In the end, will Rory's hatred continue towards me?*

Losing was not an option as far as Barrett was concerned. *Let the hand be dealt! I will race to win. Even if I lose, I will have done the best I could. I still will have the love and respect of Brooke—that is the most important thing to me.*

Chapter Ten

May 19, 1860
Ten Broeck Race Track

Clouds covered the sun allowing for slightly cooler than average temperatures on the late spring morning.

Distinct smells and sounds added to the excitement and anticipation building inside the horse racing fans. A visitor could not easily identify the smells, but a racing enthusiast would describe it as a mixture of leather from the saddles and the sweat of the horses.

Various sounds echoed through the stands—the crowd roaring with enjoyment, the blast of the starting gun, the commands of the riders, the cracks of the whips on the horses, and the familiar pounding of the hooves beating on the well-maintained dirt track.

However, for most people, it was about the betting—watching with baited breath to see if the horse they had wagered on would be a winner. There would be no greater thrill to many racing fanatics.

The racetrack owners were excited about the event and expected the Hymnist would draw a big crowd.

He and his much-talked-about horse did just that.

Droves of people had gathered. Rory knew what he was talking about when he predicted the place would be packed. Saturday's races were always crowded, but this day there was standing room only.

Rory had been exploiting the race in any way he could. He had posters placed throughout the city. The headlines read:

The South's undefeated racehorse champion, Dark Shadow, to face off against the Hymnist's Arabian champ

Barrett, Brooke, and Titus spent the day preparing Annapurna—trying to keep him cool and calm. Occasionally, they would walk him, trying to keep his muscles from tightening up.

Titus had seen a drawing of an Arabian horse with braids. With the help of an older black woman from the estate, they braided Annapurna's mane to give him that Arabian look. They fluffed his lengthy tail and brushed him numerous times.

Hundreds of fans filed by the Arabian horse's stall hoping to catch a glimpse of the animal that so many folks were talking about. People in the crowd were murmuring that just the sight of the magnificent horse was worth the price of admission.

As for the bets, Annapurna was heavily the underdog, as predicted.

Nevertheless, beauty was not going to win this race, and despite Annapurna's growing popularity, everyone knew about Dark Shadow. He was invincible. The last two times he raced he won by over ten horse lengths.

The wagers were coming in strong in favor of Rory's horse—four hundred to one.

Barrett realized if he won today, there would be many unhappy Georgians. One, in particular, would lose a lot of money and a very expensive, famous horse.

The first race began at ten in the morning.

Their race would be the final one—in the heat of the day, three in the afternoon.

Walking around the stands, Brooke and her father introduced von Weber to many people in the crowd. During the pleasantries, somehow the topic often came back to Georgia seceding from the Union. Some people even seemed to look forward to a war. When that happened, Alton was quick to change the subject, or walk away.

The last preliminary competition had finished forty-five minutes before the main race—the big one!

The racing officials intended to get all the publicity they could out of the matchup between Dark Shadow and Annapurna. The longer the wait, the more anticipation would mount, the more people would spend at the concessions, and the more bets would be made. The name of the game was money!

Rory had the experience of raising and training his horses, but even for as small in stature as he was, he was too heavy to compete at a professional level. Still, he was capable and had great confidence since he had trained Dark Shadow.

Barrett had two big disadvantages. He was eight inches taller than his opponent and thirty pounds heavier.

Most fans believed there would be no records broken, since neither Rory nor Barrett were professional jockeys.

The race would not only depend on the strength of the horse, but also on the capability of the rider. Pure speed alone wouldn't win the race. The first horse to cross the finish line would also be the strongest, the smartest, with the most determined rider. The race was sure to be grueling.

When the time came to bring the two horses to the track for the spectators' approval, the crowd roared with delight.

First, the youngest Fortner and his stable boy brought out the hometown favorite, Dark Shadow. The high-spirited, jet-black horse had red-dun stockings on his rear legs, mane, and tail. He snorted and reared up, but Rory managed to calm him down. No doubt, Dark Shadow was ready for a race.

When Barrett and Titus stepped out with Annapurna, a hush fell over the crowd.

The stallion walked proudly with his tail high, making him look even longer and taller than he was. His snow-white color, brighter than the clouds of heaven, captivated the audience. His strut was more like a prance. His legs rose high with pronounced energy, exposing his beauty and poise, along with his power.

Just the sight of the Arabian stallion caused some folks to run to the betting windows to change their bets.

Brooke and Titus strode around the track next to Barrett, who looked like a natural on the back of his beloved horse. It was important to Brooke that people understood her loyalty for her future husband.

Even though the odds had dropped when the people saw Annapurna for the first time, they were still heavily in Dark Shadow's favor. People in the area knew Rory was a capable rider. More importantly, they knew Dark Shadow.

As the horses approached the starting line, the betting windows closed.

The spectators took their seats, or stood where they could get the best view of the highly publicized event.

Barrett leaned down from his horse and gave Brooke a quick kiss.

"Win or lose, I still love you," she said, smiling at her fiancé.

Brooke paced over to Rory on his horse. She was about to wish him luck when he snarled, "Well, sister, we are about to see how your friend likes to lose."

"Rory, I don't know why you hate Barrett so much, but I love him. Win or lose, your hate must stop here… today!" She swallowed hard, trying to keep her composure.

Rory looked at her with no expression. "We'll see." He gave an uneasy chuckle.

Bile rose in her throat. "Rory, you made a deal."

"I made a deal that I would be civil to him through the wedding, but I do not have to like him! However, my sister, I do know one thing for certain.…"

"What is that?"

"I'm about to become a very rich man, thanks to your foolish German fiancé." He turned his head and looked straight ahead, ignoring her pleas.

A disheartened Brooke, and Titus, turned and headed toward the bleachers.

"Miss Brooke… the race startin' here?" Titus asked, looking back at the horses.

"Yes, it's a mile and a half race—twelve furlongs. Didn't Barrett tell you that?"

"No, ma'am, he just said it was a race. So it not startin' at the normal gate?"

"That's right."

"Did Massa Rory know this?" Titus blinked his big, brown eyes.

"Yes, of course he did. Why do you ask?"

A huge smile took over his face. "I wish I could bet."

Brooke looked at the boy with skepticism. *Why would he want to bet?*

The boy's smile spread even wider as he and Brooke stepped into a roped off area reserved for the owners.

She spotted her father and two brothers and walked hastily to join them

"Barrett is as ready as he can be!" Brooke said, excitedly.

"He's still gonna lose," Samuel crowed.

Just then an angry voice from the crowd hollered, "Get that slave boy out of here. He doesn't belong here!"

Brooke glared at the man, and without hesitation retorted, "Titus stays. If you don't like it, you can leave!"

When the man made a hostile move toward Brooke, her father and brothers protectively stepped between them. Without another word, the rude man stormed off.

After the Fortners and Titus found their seats on the bleachers, Brooke again noticed the boy's big grin. "What are you smiling about? Do you know something I don't know?"

Titus could hardly contain his excitement. "Massa Alton, do you have any money on your horse?"

"No, I'm not a betting man."

"We do," Charles said matter-of-factly. "Rory bet the horse and five thousand bucks."

"He bet Dark Shadow?" Titus exhaled hard.

"Yes… and he's about to become a rich man."

Titus angled his head. "Scuse me, Massa Charles, but I think he gonna lose."

"No horse can beat Shadow… no horse!" Charles was adamant.

"In a normal race, maybe. But this ain't no normal race."

"What do you mean, boy?"

"Massa Barrett told me 'bout the difference 'tween an Arabian and a thoroughbred. He told me thoroughbreds like Dark Shadow make fast starts, but wear down quickly. Arabians don't take off so quick, but they have somethin' Massa Barrett calls endurance. They keep goin' faster and last longer."

"You are saying what, boy? You're not making sense," Charles grumbled.

"It's a mile and a half race. Shadow will tire at the one-mile mark, that's where he be used to runnin'… but Annapurna will be just gettin' goin'. That's when he starts winnin'."

"Boy, you're out of your mind," Samuel scoffed. "That horse will never beat Rory. Not a chance!"

"Oh yes, he can, and I think he will. You see!"

"I'll tell you what, Titus. If Barrett wins, I will muck the stables for a week." Samuel smiled smugly. "But when Shadow wins, you have to remove that big stump by the old barn on your own time." The middle brother folded his arms arrogantly.

"Samuel, that stump will take weeks to dig out," Brooke stepped in.

"So be it," Samuel maintained.

Titus spit on his hand and reached out to Samuel, "Deal!"

Brooke closed her eyes and whispered a silent prayer.

Titus noticed her concern. "Don't worry, Miss Brooke. I know Annapurna will win. I take good care of him. He win… you see. Massa Rory's horse can't hold up to Annapurna in the long stretch. That why Massa Barrett said twelve furlongs."

Brooke stared at the boy for a few seconds. *Does Titus know what he's talking about? Was Rory beaten at his own game?*

Her thoughts were interrupted by a voice bellowing, "On the count of three. One… two… three. The sound of the starting gun had barely penetrated the air when both horses launched forward.

Dark Shadow was quick to spring off and take the lead as Titus predicted.

Rory wanted to gain a sizeable lead at the start; he planned to embarrass the German any way he could.

Halfway around the track Dark Shadow was a full four horse lengths ahead of his opponent.

Yet, the beauty of Annapurna, the solid white animal, gracefully circling the racetrack, awed the crowd. It seemed like the Arabian was suspended in air, riding on a cloud of dust.

When the two horses raced past the packed grandstand, everyone went wild.

There was private betting going on between some of the horse enthusiasts in the stands. How many horse lengths will Rory win by? Can Annapurna hold up the entire race? Any part of the race they could bet on, they did. Everyone wanted a piece of the action.

When the horses finished the first lap, Rory was ahead by eight lengths. It appeared he could not lose.

"At this rate, Shadow will win by ten lengths," Samuel gloated. He leaned closer to his sister. "Looks like your fiancé's horse isn't all he said he was."

Brooke ignored his comment, her hands folded in front of her face as if she were praying.

The air was heavy and still, offering no relief from the hot afternoon sun, yet the people in the stands were so excited they barely noticed the rising temperature.

The horses were dripping with sweat, and so were the riders.

The roar of the crowd was deafening.

The stride of the powerful Arabian was not only magnificent, but also relentless.

When Barrett gave his stallion the entire reins he had been asking for, the initial blast of acceleration was exhilarating. Annapurna's stride quickened, as if the horse realized what was at stake.

Brooke was impressed with Barrett's gentle manner, the way he handled Annapurna by goading him, rather than beating him. *Another one of his fine qualities!*

Rory looked under his arm to get a better look at the white stallion behind him. He was shocked to see his big lead cut in half and dwindling.

Like a shot from a cannon, Annapurna's speed accelerated even more. He caught up to Dark Shadow with only a quarter of a lap to go, continuing his quest toward the finish line.

Coming in to the home stretch, Annapurna seemed to be gliding. His quickness and long strides pushed him in front of the thoroughbred.

"Faster, faster!" Rory whipped his horse to get him to accelerate.

The mass of people continued to cheer for Dark Shadow. Without his victory, a lot of money would be lost. The hometown favorite could not lose. Rory could not lose.

However, the man with the flag was only seconds away.

Rory hit Shadow harder and harder, so hard he cut the horse's side with the whip. Even that could not make the horse catch the Arabian stallion. As the flag came down, Annapurna was a full two horse lengths ahead.

Silence fell over the crowd at the Ten Broeck Race Course.

Brooke smiled at Titus, who was jumping up and down excitedly. "See, Miss Brooke, I told you he do it!"

Some in the stands started to cheer because they had witnessed something they had never seen. Others remained in stunned silence, shaking their heads in disbelief, realizing how much money they had lost.

Brooke, Titus, and her father gathered around Barrett and his champion horse, congratulating them. Winners and losers crowded around them, anxious to get a closer look at the amazing stallion and his owner.

Rory's reception was different. Men cursed him for losing the race.

"The race was fixed," one man shouted.

Another one yelled, "You lost it on purpose because von Weber is going to be your brother-in-law."

Rory ignored the remarks, even though his instinct was to punch the hecklers in the face. His body was too weak from the grueling race, and he was too dazed with the outcome. He realized that not only had he and his brothers lost a small fortune, but he also lost his prize horse—a horse that was worth ten times the cash he lost. Now someone else would have the rights to all of Dark Shadow's offspring.

Only a few people had picked Annapurna to win, and they made out extremely well. In fact, some were instantly wealthy.

A mustached man, dressed in a suit and tie, carrying a gold cane approached Rory—it was time to claim Dark Shadow! Speaking in a strong European accent, he spurted, "I really do not need a race horse. Would you like to buy him back?"

Rory handed the reins of his prize horse to the gentleman, shaking his head sadly. "Can't... I lost all my money betting on him. I should have won. It was a sure thing! Everyone told me that an Arabian could never beat Shadow in a race."

"Sir... that is one of the stupidest things I have ever heard. A thoroughbred could never beat an Arabian stallion the caliber of Annapurna in the mile and a half. A mile, yes, but not twelve furlongs. The quickness of a thoroughbred cannot beat the endurance of an Arabian—especially in the heat of the day."

Rory looked at the horse that had beaten him and its rider. "You mean... it was fixed?" His blood began to boil.

"No! I mean you said yourself you had a sure thing. Only problem is, you bet on the wrong horse. I'll take my horse now." The man took the reins and led Dark Shadow away.

"Father is going to kill you," Samuel snapped.

"I'm going to kill that man!" He fixed his gaze on Barrett; hatred consumed him.

"You will do no such thing!" His father's voice boomed from behind him.

Rory turned with his fist clinched. "He cheated—he fixed the race!"

"No, he didn't. You said 'any race, any day.' He only set the rules, but you foolishly agreed to them. You could have denied the terms, but your ego was too big."

"I lost everything because of him," his irate son shouted.

"You still have your life. I'd tan your hide, except I know you are already beating yourself up. Let it go! Stop the vendetta you have against Barrett. You have no reason to despise him. He is a good and decent man and will soon be my son-in-law, your brother-in-law. I will not tolerate any more hatred from you."

The father shifted his glare to Charles and Samuel. "That means from any of you. Let this be an expensive lesson for all of you." He took a deep breath. "You still have Selma, Annalise, and the other horses... if I were you, I would have Annapurna breed with a couple of them. Imagine their offspring."

Alton looked over at the large white stallion. "Sure was impressive the way that horse sped up. I never saw anything like it." He shook his head, grinning.

None of his sons knew what to say, so they remained silent, heads down.

"Now, if you will excuse me. I am going to the winner's circle with my daughter and future son-in-law. Rory, take seriously what I have said to you." Alton hurried off.

Rory stood alone, seething. He looked over at Barrett and Brooke, surrounded by dozens of well-wishers. With fists clenched so tight his knuckles were white, he muttered under his breath, "Go ahead and enjoy the victory, Mr. von Weber. But, you're a dead man… you just don't know it!"

Chapter Eleven

June 1, 1860
Fortner Estate

The sun had not yet risen when Barrett and Alton stepped out of the Fortner Mansion, eager to start their day. Birds chirped a happy song welcoming the warm June morning. Excitement filled the air.

"Good morning, Titus," Alton greeted the dependable stable boy, smiling.

"Morning, Massa Alton. I have your horses ready, suh."

"Thank you, Titus." Alton walked into his greenhouse, his daily routine.

"Morning, suh." Titus shifted his gaze to Barrett.

"Hello, Titus." Barrett grabbed the reins of his horse.

As the two waited for Alton to return, they chatted about Titus and his love of horses.

Within a couple minutes, Alton returned.

"Beautiful flowers you have this morning, suh," Titus commented.

"Isadora will love these zinnias that I added to the usual rose." Alton referred to his deceased wife as if she was still alive.

As Barrett and Alton rode away from the greenhouse, the soon-to-be-groom stared at the large wedding tent near the house. Thoughts of his bride flooded his mind. *By the end of this day, I will be married to the most beautiful girl in the world. The good Lord has blessed me abundantly.* He felt inner peace, joy, contentment.

Within minutes, they were at the cemetery. Alton dismounted his horse and strode over to his wife's burial place. He took his hat off and tenderly placed the flowers on her grave. After bowing his head for a moment, he replaced his hat, and returned to his horse. It was the same ritual every day.

Barrett interrupted the quiet. "Sir, I know it is not my business, but wouldn't it be more convenient to plant flowers by your wife's grave?"

"This gives me an excuse to visit her every day... to keep her close. It helps keep me going." Alton paused to watch the red sun slowly creep above the horizon. "I am blessed to see a new sunrise every morning."

"Coming here, visiting my wife's grave, and seeing this," he turned in a circle with his arms outstretched. "This place we call Annalise... it was our dream."

Barrett stared at the man he had grown to admire and respect. "I believe your daughter and I will have a special love like yours."

Alton smiled, "You are a blessed man. Love like we had is rare."

"Yes, I am. I will treasure her."

Fortner mounted his horse. "Well, enough of the chit-chat. We have some fish to catch."

With a knock on the door, Prisse burst into the bedroom. She pulled the curtains apart allowing the sun's beams to shine in Brooke's eyes. "Don't sleep away the day, Miss Brooke. It is June first and it's six-o-clock in the mornin'. There's rumors that there is a wedding here at eleven." The chambermaid laughed heartily.

With her eyes partially closed, Brooke stretched; a giant smile covered her face. "Prisse, can you believe in just a few short hours, I will be the wife of the Hymnist, Barrett von Weber?"

"Not if you don't get a move on, you won't!" The servant girl handed her a robe.

"I poured your bath water, and Melba, your hairdresser from Savannah, is here to fix your hair. Now, Miss Brooke, you have a lot to do. This is the biggest day of your life!"

"Is my dress here?"

"It be here by eight, they promised."

"I pray they are not late." Brooke shuddered at the thought.

"I saw Massa Barrett and your daddy leaving early this mornin' for a ride."

"Oh, dear," Brooke sighed. Sitting up, hanging her legs over the side of the bed, she yawned. "I hope Father does not give Barrett the speech— 'Brooke is my only daughter and she means the world to me. If you don't take care of her, I will tan your hide,'" she lowered her voice, imitating her father.

"I reckon he never say that. Massa Alton and your intended have a good relationship. I think them men went a fishin'. They most likely talkin' 'bout the best way to care for you. That man's head over heels in love with you."

"Fishing?" Brooke stood. "How can a man fish on the most important day of his life?"

"I think menfolk do it to relax. I reckon both of 'em be plum scared. They both gonna have big changes in their lives. One is gonna give away someone he adores. The other 'bout to have the job of carin' for two folks... you know, two mouths to feed 'stead of one in these scary times."

"I never thought of it like that."

"Hurry, let's get your bath over with, so we can get your hair fixed, or both 'em men will get after me." Prisse took hold of Brooke's hand, pulling her into the washroom.

There was not even a ripple on the surface of the pond. The morning air was exceptionally still and the dew heavier than usual.

Before long, Barrett pulled out a catfish.

"Nice catch, son," Alton complimented, taking a closer look at the fish.

Barrett grabbed the line, watching the fish flop around trying to escape the hook in its mouth. Releasing the fish from the thin hook, he swiftly threw it back into the water. "Sir, you loved your wife very much, didn't you?"

There was silence for a moment as Alton struggled to frame his thoughts. "Still do. Many times, I wake up at night, roll over in bed, and reach for her."

"Forgive me for my boldness, but do you think you will ever marry again? I mean, you are young enough, could you ever find love in the arms of another?" Barrett cast his line back into the water.

Alton's face showed he was searching for an answer. "I know many men do fall in love again and remarry. As for me, I think I can honestly say that I don't see that in my future."

"Don't you ever get lonely for female companionship?"

"Yes, I do, but I stay busy."

"I noticed that. You spend a lot of time in your study. Could it be because you are lonely?"

Alton looked at his future son-in-law. "You may have a point. I will have to ponder that. You see, I loved with all my heart. My beloved wife gave up everything for me. You may not know, son, but she was royalty in line to the throne." He stared at the water; his voice sounded like he was thinking aloud. "My sweet Brooke is the spitting image of her mother. Giving her away today will be one of the hardest things I have ever done."

Without hesitation, Barrett replied, "Sir, I want you to know that I love Brooke with my whole heart, and I will care for her and defend her life with my own."

"I know you will. You are everything a father would want for his daughter. I have never seen Brooke happier."

"Speaking of your daughter, I think we had better return to the house, we have to get ready for a wedding."

"Yes, I agree."

"May I ask one more question?" Barrett queried, as they gathered their fishing gear and began walking to their horses.

"You may talk to me about anything, anytime."

Barrett cleared his throat. "Sir, did your wife ever regret her decision?"

"You mean choosing me over the throne?"

"Yes, sir."

"I asked her many times about that, but she always said she had no regrets. Honestly, our life was hard, especially in the beginning. Sometimes I would see her staring off into the distance and wonder what she was thinking. The truth of the matter is, when she made the decision to marry me, her family disinherited her. They considered her dead. I think that is what hurt her most."

"Where did you meet her?"

Alton smiled. "I met her in Savannah and it was love at first sight. She was there for only a brief visit, and three days later we were married."

"Three days! No one told me that. How old were you?" Barrett raised a questioning eyebrow.

"I was twenty, and she was just eighteen. Her parents tried to take her back by force, but she refused to go. Almost started a war because of it." He chuckled.

"Did her parents ever forgive her?"

Standing next to their horses, Alton continued his story. "I am not certain. Something strange happened about four months after my Isadora was laid to rest. Titus told me he saw an unfamiliar carriage at the cemetery."

"A carriage?"

"Yes. I did not think much about it, but the next morning when I went up there for my usual visit, I saw fresh flowers on her gravesite... and I hadn't put them there."

"That is interesting."

"Yes. A few days later when I went into town, I asked around about the flowers. It seemed an older man and woman with a Spanish accent bought them."

"Any idea who it was?"

"Not for certain. I always wondered if her family came back to say goodbye to her. I only wish they would have stopped by and talked to me about her. I will never know for sure, but it eases my mind to think they may have still cared about their daughter."

Barrett remained silent, contemplating the older man's words.

Alton seemed to have something else on his mind. "I don't doubt that you will care for my daughter, but I see a problem in the near future." His face showed his concern as deep wrinkles etched his forehead.

"And what might that be?"

"I now believe our country is going to war. The life of every living soul in this country will be changed forever. You and I will have major decisions to make that will affect the lives of our loved ones. I believe that many of those decisions will have life-altering consequences."

A chill ran down Barrett's arms. Quietly, he mounted his horse, staring at Brooke's father. "My prayer, sir, is that God directs those decisions."

"Prayer may be the only thing that can save this country," Alton replied, his voice dropping almost to a whisper.

Barrett nodded in silent agreement; no additional words seemed fitting.

Consumed in thought, they allowed their horses to trot back to the estate.

Brooke was in her room getting her hair prepared and having last minute alterations made to her exquisite wedding dress.

She watched out the window as Barrett and her father returned from their ride. *I'm so happy that Barrett and Daddy are close. I wish Rory would see him for the fine man he is.* She sighed.

Barrett glanced up at her window, but Melba quickly stepped in front of the bride-to-be. "It is bad luck for the groom to see the bride on her wedding day."

"Can I see him?" Brooke kidded, trying to peek around the hairdresser.

Melba smiled, watching Barrett lead Annapurna into the stable. "I can see why you want to look at him."

They both laughed.

For a couple years, Melba had routinely cared for Brooke's hair. She always felt she could talk to Brooke openly, more like a friend. As she put the jewel band in her hair, she inquired, "Miss Brooke, is it true the governor of Georgia is attending the wedding?"

"So I've been told, as well as many other politicians. I hope they behave themselves and do not argue about the current state of things."

Melba snickered. "That is wishful thinking... I think politics is in a man's blood. I think it's even worse than fishing and hunting."

Brooke nodded definitively.

The beautician probed further, "Who did you say was standing up for Barrett?"

"Cornelius Hall... he's from Connecticut."

"He sure is coming a long distance for the wedding. Is he a school friend?"

"No, actually he is more of a father figure. They have known each other since Barrett was a young boy. He works for New Haven Arms—a big rifle manufacturer up North. I think there is something in the past that ties the two together, but I do not know what it is, and I have not asked. I think Barrett will tell me when he is ready."

"Miss Brooke, there is nothing more to be done with your hair. The ringlets are perfect and you are absolutely beautiful." Melba stepped aside smiling, satisfied with her handiwork.

Brooke's handmaiden, Prisse, stepped up to tighten the laces of the bride's corset. By the time she was finished tugging, Brooke wondered whether she would be able to breathe during the ceremony. However, she didn't complain; she wanted to look her best.

Melba inched closer. "Are all your brothers standing up with him?"

"Yes. That is a miracle in itself." Brooke rolled her eyes.

Prisse put her hands on her hips. "How did you ever convince Massa Rory to do that?"

"I think Father ordered him to. I just hope Rory's antics do not ruin my wedding. He has been acting strange lately."

"What do you mean lately?" Melba chuckled.

"You're right, he is acting normal." Brooke laughed with her.

Melba changed the subject. "I saw where the ceremony is going to be, and it's lovely. The arch leading to the garden... I must say, I love going out there to see that flower garden of yours. The hummingbirds and butterflies were out in numbers. It is a little heaven on earth."

"The garden actually is a replica of the one at the Ludwigsburg Castle." A big smile took over Brooke's face. "Barrett is taking me to Europe in the near future. In fact, he will be performing a concert for the king in the main ballroom there." The thought made her heart flutter.

Prisse opened a fan and waved it in front of Brooke. "Oh, Miss Brooke, I reckon there will never be a dull moment with that handsome husband of yours at your side."

The Fortner Estate was bustling as staff finished the last minute details for the garden wedding and reception.

Dozens of carriages arrived early and parked in the designated area on the estate lawn.

Alton dressed hurriedly. Aware that time was getting short, he rushed downstairs to take one more look around and make sure everything was ready.

As he walked onto the back veranda, he noticed a dozen men gathered around his sons.

"If we secede, so be it," Rory exclaimed loudly.

"We can walk into Washington and take over. Them Northerners will run with their tails between their legs. We should kill every last one of 'em!" an elderly man smoking a pipe added.

Alton stormed over to the group. Pointing his finger at Rory, but looking at all the men, he barked, "I am going to remind all of you, in no uncertain terms, this is my daughter's wedding. There will be no talk of secession, war, or politics. In addition, Rory, Charles, and Samuel, you know better than to talk about such things outside the study. Now everyone disperse. Feel free to talk about honorable things... or you may leave these premises." No one dared to question Alton.

The crowd immediately scattered, leaving the Fortners standing by themselves.

"Father, we have to be prepared," Rory implored.

"I will have nothing ruin your sister's wedding."

As Rory turned in a huff, his father grabbed his arm. "You listen closely, Son. You had better be civil to Barrett and your sister, or I will...."

The vein in Rory's neck showed the rising of his temper. "You will what, Father... take me out behind the shed and tan my hide? Don't make me laugh. I will be who I am, and talk about what I want to talk about.

Remove your hand from my arm." He had never talked to his father with such disrespect.

Stunned, Alton released his grip.

Charles and Samuel gasped.

Some of the arriving guests noticed the commotion, but Alton was not going to let his rebellious son have the last word. He inched closer to Rory's face and folded his arms, his expression hard. Through gritted teeth, he said, "You think you hold all the cards. Let me tell you this, young man. I can and will replace you in my business, and if need be, cut you out of any inheritance... no questions asked!" He did not break eye contact, not even a blink.

Rory scowled at Alton. He could tell his father had reached his limit. The youngest son stormed off and bumped into Prisse with such force that he almost knocked her off her feet. He sneered, "Get out of my way!"

Not being deterred, Prisse announced, "Massa Alton, the wedding start soon. Miss Brooke waitin' for you to walk her down, but she wanna talk with you first."

"Where is she?"

"She in her room, and Massa Alton, she sure is purdy."

Alton walked to the bottom of the stairs and slowly ascended. *This is my little girl's special day and I will not let Rory or anyone else ruin it for her.*

Outside her bedroom door, he stopped and took a deep breath. "Will I have the strength to let her go?" he whispered.

He knocked.

Brooke spoke softly, "Come in."

He slowly opened the door and saw the back of a white dress. Her long, black curly hair contrasted with the gown.

Looking from the balcony door, she turned, smiling. "Oh, Daddy, this is the day I have dreamed of all my life."

"You are stunning! You look... you look just like your mother. Is that her wedding dress?" His voice cracked with emotion.

She embraced him. "Yes, Daddy. Mother gave it to me years ago. She dreamed of me wearing it at my wedding."

"It's beautiful."

"I wish she could be here. Daddy, I miss her so much."

The moment was cut short by a knock on the door.

Prisse peeked in, "Brooke, honey... time to come down. Everyone wants to see the bride. And oh my, you have a handsome young man waitin' for you!"

Alton backed up to catch another glimpse of the gorgeous bride. "I hope I don't step on that lengthy gown. I stepped on your mother's." He chuckled, relieving the tenseness of the moment.

"It's called a train, Father. Just stay close to my side and you'll be fine. Oh, and hold my arm tight, Daddy. I am so nervous I could faint."

"Are you feeling all right, or is it just the wedding jitters," her father asked, concerned.

"I am so happy… just nervous. Father, I am marrying the Hymnist, one of the most eligible bachelors in the world, and he chose me to spend his life with. I never knew my heart could be filled with this much love."

"Barrett is an honorable man, a godly man."

"Oh, yes, he is. God has blessed me abundantly."

Alton reached over and kissed his daughter gently on the forehead. "Let us not keep the groom waiting."

She slipped her arm through her father's arm. As they strolled to the edge of the wide Victorian staircase, her pulse was racing, her heart overflowing.

Some of the family gathered below, watching the bride glide gracefully down the steps, with her loving father by her side. Her stylish gown displayed lace, layered over white silk. Sprays of orange blossoms adorned the veil, worn low on her forehead. She was truly a picture of elegance and grace.

They stopped at the bottom of the staircase and Prisse straightened the veil.

Brooke noticed a teary-eyed William waiting for them. "Miss Brooke, you are the most beautiful bride I ever saw."

She gave William a heartfelt hug. "Thank you, William, for always being there for me."

He lightly put his arms around her. "It was my pleasure, Miss Brooke."

She again locked arms with her father and they began the walk out the back door to the arch, where the man of her dreams was waiting.

The large grandfather clock in the living room chimed, signifying the eleventh hour, as the bride and her father stepped out through the large French doors to the waiting guests.

Marcia Hendrick, the wife of Alton's lawyer, was playing a special tune on the grand piano.

"That's a beautiful melody, Daddy. Do you know if Barrett wrote it?" Brooke questioned her father.

"A fellow German composer named Wagner wrote it. It is known as *The Bridal Chorus*. Barrett told me that it was first performed at the wedding of the daughter of the Queen of England." He whispered, "He knew you would like it."

"I am honored."

In that instant, Brooke's eyes caught Barrett's. Her heart quickened and dozens of butterflies fluttered in her stomach.

His face was beaming, his eyes glistening as he stared at the woman of his dreams. There was an entire future in that smile—a world of hope and the promise of unspeakable joy.

She made her way next to him, and he whispered, "You are beautiful."

Uncontrolled tears slid down her face.

She did not notice anyone else—not her brothers standing next to Barrett, her brothers' wives who were standing with her, or any guests. Her focus was on the man she had waited for all her life.

The ceremony, the vows, all went flawless. Even the weather was perfect.

The guests laughed when Samuel's youngest daughter, serving as the flower girl, dumped all the rose petals in a single pile near the front.

When the preacher told Barrett to kiss the bride, he didn't hesitate. Since he caught the first glimpse of her in her wedding gown, he looked forward to that moment.

The kiss left both of them breathless, wanting more.

At the reception, some guests filled their plates with food that had been elegantly arranged on long narrow tables. Others stood in small groups chatting and enjoying liquid refreshment.

The music from a grand piano and a stringed ensemble entertained the guests who were mingling under the tent.

When a certain familiar tune began to play, Barrett stood, offering his hand to his wife. "I believe this is your song." His radiant smile shone. "Mrs. von Weber, may I have this dance?"

"This is the song you dedicated to me at the concert the night we met... the day that my life changed forever." She curtsied. "I would be honored to dance with you, Mr. von Weber."

Many of the guests were misty-eyed while they watched the bride and groom dance—it was a dance filled with romance, passion, and grace.

Barrett wondered if life could be any better, if he could be any happier. The joy and fulfillment he felt could not be expressed in words. There was no doubt that Brooke was the woman God had chosen for him.

Standing close to a table laden with dozens of pies, Rory and his brothers were sipping a glass of Sylvia's famous orange tea. Occasionally, a friend would make his way over to chat with them.

Looking around, Rory recognized the face of a man visiting with the governor and a couple other politicians. "Charles, isn't that the man who bet against me at the race?"

Charles eyed the man and nodded. "It certainly is. Who invited him?"

Rory glanced over at Barrett and Brooke, still dancing. "My hunch was right—the race was rigged."

"If it was, it was set up by you," Charles chuckled.

Rory strode over to the man who was conversing with Governor Joe Brown and Senator Robert Toombs. In his typically blunt way, he interrupted what appeared to be an intense conversation, "Sir, may I ask you why you are at my sister's wedding?"

"Good afternoon." The man nodded his head in an attempt to be friendly.

"You did not answer my question," Rory blurted.

The governor frowned. "Mr. Fortner, this is Jacob Reinhart, from France. He owns a lucrative shipping business. I would suggest you speak to him in a more civil tone."

Rory shot back, "I do not care who he is. I know him only as the man who stole my money and horse. Now oddly, he shows up at my sister's wedding. I smell a rat. I feel that the entire race was a setup. Sir, did you know that I was going to lose that race?" he challenged Reinhart, with his chest puffed out.

Governor Brown stepped closer to Rory, but Jacob held his arm in front of him indicating he would handle the situation himself.

Reinhart stood face-to-face with Rory, not backing down. "Sir, I guarantee the race was not rigged. Barrett von Weber doesn't play by those rules. He is a man of integrity. You believed that your horse could win. He might have been able to if you had agreed to race a normal race, but your ego caused you to think that your horse could win anytime, anywhere. Your pride interfered with your good sense."

Rory glared at him, removing his gloves from his pocket.

Reinhart noticed the movement and questioned, "Are you challenging me to a duel?"

The youngest Fortner raised his hand, ready to slap the guest across the face with the gloves, a tradition the European was all too familiar with.

Suddenly, a hand came out of nowhere, grabbing Rory's arm.

He found himself looking directly into the stern eyes of Barrett. Struggling to free his hand, Rory shouted, "You will let go of me now, or I will quickly make my sister a widow."

"Your temper and bad judgment is going to get you in a lot of trouble one of these days," Barrett scowled.

Hearing the commotion, Alton rushed over.

Barrett released his grip, and pushed Rory away from Reinhart. Then he straightened his cummerbund and frock jacket.

Brooke hurried over and grasped his hand. *Why would Rory cause problems at my wedding? Will he stop at nothing to destroy my husband?* She had a nagging feeling that things would only get worse, but she was determined Rory would not spoil this day.

Barrett drew a loud breath. "This is my friend Jacob Reinhart, from France. His family originally came from Germany. Jacob is one of Europe's most prominent shipping industrialists. He is here to set up shipping ports throughout the South. I had met him in Savannah and told him about the race."

He shifted his gaze and his words to Rory. "Yes, he wisely did bet against you."

"He stole my money and my horse," Rory pouted.

"No, son," Alton added sadly, "you lost them in a fair bet."

"They knew I would lose." He pointed to Barrett and the European, each word growing louder.

"William?" Barrett's voice sounded composed.

"Yes, suh."

"Will you tell Titus to bring forth Rory's wedding gift from me?"

"Yes, suh," William responded readily.

Barrett spoke loud enough that all the guests could hear. "It is customary for the groom to give the men who stand up with him a wedding gift. I was going to do this later, but circumstances have forced me to change my plans."

Cornelius brought two packages over and handed them to Barrett.

Barrett handed Charles and Samuel each one.

When the brothers opened the packages, their eyes lit up. Each of them took the item out of the case and studied it.

Charles inquired, "Is this a Colt revolver?"

"Indeed it is." Barrett replied. "Newly designed, specifically for the Army."

Charles shook Barrett's hand. "I don't know what to say… thank You."

Samuel did the same.

The youngest brother stood back with a confused look on his face.

"Where is mine?" Rory demanded, sounding more like a spoiled child than a grown man.

"I didn't think I could trust you with a pistol." He chuckled. "Besides, I had already procured your special gift."

"And what may that be?" he remarked snidely.

"William, please wave Titus in."

The room was hushed, all watching the turn of events, excitement mounting.

Within minutes, Titus stepped into the tent with a horse—not just any horse, but Dark Shadow.

Rory's mouth dropped as he stared at the stallion he had lost the month before. "Dark Shadow… what is he doing back here?"

"To be perfectly honest, Rory, he never left," Barrett confessed.

"What?"

"It was common knowledge that you were betting all your money on that race. It was even rumored that you were considering wagering Dark Shadow. It put me in a precarious position—I win the race and you lose everything, or I lose the race. I have never been a man who likes to lose, so that was not an option. I ran into Jacob at a restaurant in Savannah. I had not seen him for over a year. We discussed the upcoming race, and he was shocked that anyone would even consider racing against Annapurna. I told him the problem I was facing and he suggested a solution. The plan from the beginning was to return your horse if you were foolish enough to bet him, and lose the race. So here he is—a gift from your sister and me." Barrett smiled, reaching his hand out as a gesture to put the past behind them. "Let's start anew."

Rory stared at Barrett's outstretched hand.

His father and sister smiled, believing this kind act by Barrett would be the turning point in their relationship.

Slowly, Rory's look of astonishment turned to an evil smirk. "I get it. You really think that this… this… kind act, as you claim, would make me change my mind about you. Do you take me for a fool? In reality, it is for your own ego."

Rory spoke loudly, almost as if he was preaching. "The great Hymnist… the great Barrett von Weber. He can do no wrong… he is Mister Perfect. Well, Mister Barrett von Weber, keep the horse. I do not want your pity, and certainly do not want a gift from you. I just want you out of my life!"

Rory stormed off in a huff, leaving everyone staring at him in stunned silence.

"Barrett," Alton put a hand on his new son-in-law's-shoulder, "that was an honorable effort, despite the way Rory acted."

Brooke glanced up at her new husband. "Honey, you are so kind. I did not realize you had done that."

"I was hoping it would help Rory get rid of his ridiculous, unfounded hatred of me. I truly wanted him to be able to put the past behind him. So sad." He shook his head, dismayed.

Reinhart leaned close to Barrett's ear and whispered in German, "That boy is trouble and it's going to end badly for him."

Barrett nodded.

"Can I have the horse?" Samuel asked.

In disbelief, his father shook his head. "Take the horse back to the stable, Titus."

Alton motioned for the musicians to resume playing. *I will not allow my spoiled son to ruin this day for my daughter. I will not!*

The governor walked over to congratulate the bride and groom, and then faced Alton. Shaking his hand, he stated, "I was hoping to get a chance to talk with you about what is happening in Washington, but you obviously have been busy." He looked in the direction where Rory disappeared. "Please stop by my office the next time you are in Atlanta... we need to talk. We need to know that you are with us if Georgia secedes from the Union."

The governor's words shocked Alton. Yet, he remained silent, and nodded his head, still shaken and embarrassed by Rory's childish behavior. He was putting on a front on the outside, but inside he was fuming.

Chapter Twelve

1860
New Haven, Connecticut

Although he always had enjoyed meeting new people, traveling had never been Barrett von Weber's favorite thing. However, it came with the life of a concert pianist.

During the six weeks following the wedding, the young couple visited other Southern states. Then they returned to Annalise to spend a few days with Brooke's family.

Finally, they headed north to what would be Brooke's new home in New Haven, Connecticut. By the time they reached their final destination, it was almost September.

When they approached the house, Brooke wasn't surprised to find it modest and inviting. *It's not a mansion, but it's perfect for us.* Although her husband was considered wealthy, he did not flaunt it.

As he helped Brooke out of the carriage, he apologized, "I know this is not what you are used to. It is not Annalise, but it is home. I think you will find it comfortable."

"I love it," she stated, her voice earnest.

"There is a room for William downstairs. Prisse can have one of the extra rooms upstairs. Titus can stay in the living quarters above the stable. The house overlooks the lake... let me show you the incredible view." Barrett took her hand and eagerly led her to the best spot to take in the scenery.

"It is beautiful," Brooke acknowledged, looking around. "Who takes care of it when you're gone?"

"It just so happens that my friend, Cornelius Hall, is also my neighbor. He sends his housekeeper over twice a week to dust and check things out.

116

His stable boy helps with the horses, but with Annapurna here, I knew I would need an extra hand, that's why I hired Titus. I believe I can trust the lad to take good care of him since we can't take the horse to Germany with us."

"Titus is still pretty young. Are you sure he can do it?"

"He will do fine. This will give him experience and if he needs help, Cornelius is nearby."

"When are we leaving?"

"We're leaving after the election. The weather in the Atlantic may cause the seas to be rough, but I thought it would be splendid to spend time at my old home in Germany next spring. It's beautiful that time of year, when the grapevines come to life!"

Barrett noticed concern in her eyes. "Is it the election? Are you worried about it?"

"Not as much about the election as to what might happen afterwards." She was silent for a second and then blurted out the question that was on the mind of every Southerner. "Barrett, do you really think Georgia and other states will secede from the Union?"

"Yes, I do. I don't think the people want to, but the leaders do, and the leaders make the decisions." A frown creased his forehead.

"Charles thinks each state should have the right to decide its own future."

"I believe that too, I'm a big states' rights advocate, but in this case we are talking about human life. The black man should not be enslaved, nor should the Indian, or Oriental. Some of the greatest words ever written are in our Declaration of Independence. *We hold these truths to be self-evident, that all men are created equal, that they are endowed by their Creator with certain unalienable Rights, that among these are Life, Liberty and the pursuit of Happiness.* I believe every man should have the same rights!"

Brooke was silent, mesmerized by her husband's wisdom, his perceptive words.

She knew he was right, but she was also afraid of what the future would bring to this great nation. The threat of war terrified her.

News of the election of Abraham Lincoln did not come as a surprise to Barrett. What did surprise him was receiving an invitation to perform in Washington D.C.

Loyal supporters had planned an extravagant ball to celebrate Lincoln's victory. The guests of honor would be the newly elected president and his wife.

Before their lengthy trip, Barrett went down to the stable to spend some time with Annapurna. He pulled some sugar cubes out of his pocket and fed them to his horse, talking to him as he would a friend. "I'm going to miss you, big fellow, but you are in good hands."

Titus overheard the comment and moved closer. "Massa Barrett, are you sure you want me takin' care a this place for you? I jus' seventeen."

Barrett placed his hands on Titus's shoulders. "You are more mature than most young men your age. You have a good head on your shoulders. Winters are harsh, but you have plenty of wood, food, and water, for both you and the horses. You even have a variety of good books to read. Keep learning, and one day you could be a lawyer or a doctor."

"I'd love to be doctorin' people… or animals."

"I believe you can do anything you want to do."

The boy smiled at the thought of it.

"If you need help with anything, remember, Mr. Hall lives next door. Even when he is traveling, he will have someone stop by. Just remember, you are always to be a gentleman."

"Gentleman, suh?" His voice showed confusion.

"I've seen how you look at Mr. Hall's servant's daughter, Milly," Barrett teased.

"Suh, she is only fourteen." Embarrassed, Titus stared at the floor.

"Remember… treat her like a lady, like a Southern gentleman should."

Titus chuckled nervously. "Yes, suh."

Barrett reached out to shake his hand.

The boy vigorously returned the handshake. "Thank you, suh, for givin' me this chance. I won't let you down."

Brooke and William stood a short distance away, smiling.

"William?" Barrett called.

"Yes, suh, Massa Barrett." William looked ready to move on command.

"Are you ready to meet the President of the United States?"

"Yes, suh," he said, excited.

"Then let's get moving… we have a celebration to attend, then a ship to catch."

Titus watched as the carriage disappeared from view. For a short time, fear threatened to overcome him as he realized the enormity of the responsibility on his shoulders. Then he did what he often saw Barrett do, he prayed. "Lord, help me do good."

Washington D.C.

Cooler fall temperatures had settled over Washington D.C. The visitors noticed the chill as soon as they stepped off the train.

Cornelius Hall was at the train station to greet them.

With a wide smile Barrett inquired, "Cornelius, old friend, don't you ever spend time at home anymore? Seems like you are always here."

"Times are changing, Barrett. Because of our newly elected president, states are already preparing to secede from the Union."

"Why not give the man a chance?" Barrett exhaled loudly.

"His election was the final straw for many states. South Carolina is expected to announce secession as early as December, even before Lincoln officially takes office. Alabama, Florida, and Georgia are expected to follow... just to name a few."

"Georgia?" Brooke was stunned. Even though she knew it was a possibility, hearing the words sent a shiver down her spine.

"Yes. I am here to sell weapons to the army."

"To the army?" Brooke's eyes widened.

"Yes. I'm afraid so."

"God help us all," Barrett uttered.

Cornelius sighed. "Let's get you to the hotel, so you can get ready for tonight's celebration. There will be many bigwigs attending."

Barrett crossed his arms and gripped his elbows. "I pray that they will be able to focus on the message of peace my hymns offer."

"I hope so. You will like Mr. Lincoln. He is a godly man."

"Yes, I heard he starts each morning off in prayer. I met him once before in Springfield, Illinois. He seems to be a wise man, and he will need that wisdom during his term in office."

Silence overtook them as they pondered their role in the uncertain future of the nation.

The celebration was a spectacular event.

Most of the men were dressed in a dark tailcoat and trousers, white linen shirt, black bow tie, and tall top hat.

The women looked glamorous in their flounced skirts and colorful evening gowns.

Brooke looked stunning in her new tailored green outfit, perfect for the occasion. Her lavishly trimmed bonnet completed her apparel.

"Look at all these gorgeous women," Brooke whispered, walking hand-in-hand with Barrett.

"None can hold a candle to you, my love." Barrett squeezed his wife's hand. "You look exceptionally beautiful tonight."

Brooke snuggled closer to her husband.

"Ah, there is Cornelius. Great! His wife, Margaret, is with him." Barrett waved to his friend.

"At least I know someone here," she mumbled, smiling. Linking arms with Barrett, they sauntered over to them.

"Cornelius, you didn't tell me you had your wife with you."

"Are you kidding? This is what she lives for." He smiled at Margaret.

Sensing Brooke's uneasiness, Margaret reached for her hands.

"I am so nervous," Brooke whispered.

"Don't worry, you will do just fine. You are a natural. Come… let me introduce you to Mrs. Lincoln. We will let the men talk politics."

The men watched their wives cross the room. After they were out of hearing distance, Barrett probed Cornelius for answers. "Any more news on the states seceding?"

Cornelius glanced around making sure he could speak privately. He whispered, "News is that seven states will secede before the inauguration. After that… well, it does not look good."

Barrett studied him, contemplating his words.

"Ah, I see the newly elected president, let me introduce you." Cornelius pointed to a cluster of men.

Meanwhile, Margaret led Brooke by the hand to the president's wife who was visiting with a number of women.

Mrs. Lincoln's face brightened when she spotted Mrs. Hall. "Margaret, I am delighted to see you, my dear." She hugged her old friend.

The president-elect's wife noticed Brooke. "My, who is this elegant young lady with you?"

"Mary, I am proud to introduce you to Brooke von Weber."

"Oh, so you are the Hymnist's wife. I look forward to hearing your husband entertain us." After giving Brooke a quick hug, Mrs. Lincoln stepped back with her hands on Brooke's shoulders. "You are one beautiful woman. With your black hair and bronze skin, my guess is you may be of Spanish descent."

Before Brooke could respond, Margaret spoke up, "Yes, her father is Alton Fortner—the textile king of the South. Her mother was Isadora Theresia Ambrosia Fortner, related to the Queen of Spain."

"So, my dear, you come from royal linage?" Mrs. Lincoln asked.

"Well, it was pretty far down the line," Brooke stated humbly. "I resemble my father's family side more. They were gardeners."

Mary smiled. "Flowers or vegetables?"

"Flowers. When my father first saw my mother, he presented her with a bouquet of flowers. She was impressed... even more so, when she found out a couple days later that he had been arrested for picking them." Brooke giggled.

"Your father was arrested for picking flowers?" Mrs. Lincoln's eyes grew wide.

"Yes, he picked them from the governor's mansion. It seems the governor's wife did not like the idea of her flowers disappearing."

"How romantic," Mary stated. "Margaret, I'm going to like this sweet gal." She reached for Brooke's hand. "Please sit with me at the head table. Your husband will be playing soon, and I want you to tell me all about him." Mrs. Lincoln winked, smiling broadly.

Barrett typically was the tallest man in a room, but at six feet four, Abraham Lincoln beat him by two inches.

"Mr. President," Cornelius greeted.

"Cornelius, my old friend, how is your employer, Mr. Winchester, doing? And, it is Mr. Lincoln for now... I have not been sworn in yet," he said loud enough that everyone could hear.

"He is doing fine, sir. He sends you his regards."

Lincoln eyed Barrett and reached his hand out to greet him. "You, sir, I have seen before. You are Barrett von Weber."

"Yes, sir."

"We met about two years ago in Springfield, Illinois. I attended your concert there."

"You have a good memory, sir.

"The concert was the best I ever attended. We visited a bit that night. Let me see if I can remember exactly what you said regarding a poor person." The president-elect scratched his chin, thinking. "I believe it was, 'Give a man a fish and he can eat for a day. Give a man a fishing pole, and he can eat forever.'" He added, "Or something along those lines."

"That's exactly what I said, but I believe I had heard those words before. In fact, I think they came from one of your speeches."

Lincoln laughed. "They just might have, they just might have."

When the laughter subsided, Cornelius handed Lincoln a long package. "Mr. Lincoln, I have a gift for you."

"Now what am I to do with this?" Lincoln joked, holding the package.

"Open it, sir. It is a gift from Mr. Winchester. I think you will find it fascinating."

Abraham opened the box and stared inside it. "Oh my word, that's one of the most impressive pieces of equipment I have ever seen!" He removed the item to get a closer look.

"It's a Henry lever action .44 rimfire rifle... the newest and best rifle in the world," Cornelius boasted.

Lincoln studied the weapon checking out the unique craftsmanship.

"The handle is made out of walnut; the barrel and sides are gold plated," Cornelius pointed out.

Within seconds, dozens of men surrounded the president, and he delighted in showing off his new gift.

"I hope it's not loaded." Lincoln aimed at a flower vase.

"It is empty, sir."

"Good. I do not want to be tempted... there are people here that I am not too fond of." He grinned. "Oh, to have one of these when I was young. I might have been able to catch wild game, and thus not be as thin as I am now."

Everyone roared with laughter.

"What size pellet does it take?" one of the generals asked.

"It takes a .44 rimfire," Cornelius was quick to respond.

"Rimfire? What on earth is that?" another man griped.

This was his chance to do his job—sell the weapon, so Cornelius spoke loud enough that all the men in the crowd would take notice. "That means it's a shell. You do not put a ball and powder in the muzzle. A man can fire ten to twenty rounds in the time it takes an average soldier to reload his rifle. And the best part is that you never have to worry about the powder getting wet."

"You are kidding," one of the officers commented.

Cornelius opened a box of ammunition and passed some shells around for the men to inspect.

"Bet it's not cost effective," a man in the background complained.

"That shouldn't matter. The object is to get the best equipment in the hands of our military—that's how you create a strong army, so you can defeat your foe the quickest way possible," another army officer interjected.

"I've seen these before, they fire fast, but the accuracy is not very good and they blow up in your face. Give me a long barrel Springfield any day," another officer stated, holding a drink in one hand, rocking back and forth on his heels.

"The accuracy of a rifle is as good as the man firing it," Cornelius insisted. "That's why proper training is necessary."

"That is something that remains to be seen," the same man responded.

"Right. You'll have to prove that to me," another officer joined in.

"Gentlemen, gentlemen, I believe we can settle this quickly," Mr. Lincoln offered. "Cornelius, shall we go fire a few rounds?"

"Well, I guess so. We really are not dressed to go to the shooting range, or go on a hunt."

"We do not have to go anywhere. I thought we could step out onto the back porch and partake in a little target practice." Lincoln's eye had a glint.

"Sir," his aide said protectively, moving closer to him. "I don't mean to intrude, but it's been years since you fired a rifle."

"Oh, for land sakes, I wasn't talking about me doing the shooting," Lincoln replied, laughing. "I want to see von Weber shoot. I heard he was world champion three times." He looked directly into Barrett's eyes offering the challenge.

"Well, it wasn't world champion." Barrett's face turned crimson.

"Bets are on," someone in the crowd yelled.

"No bets," von Weber responded.

"You can't have a shooting challenge without bets."

"No bets," Barrett reiterated, without a hint of a smile.

Cornelius leaned over and whispered to Barrett, "This is a chance of a lifetime to sell this rifle. President Lincoln and his generals are here to see this."

Barrett listened attentively and agreed.

Without further chatter, the men strode out back, and grouped in a half-circle.

Lincoln handed his new rifle to Barrett. "Mr. von Weber, how far away do you think that fencepost is?"

Barrett scanned the field and saw an old fence in the distance. "I would say some two hundred and twenty yards."

A general sitting alone on the porch with his feet propped up on another chair, offered, "I concur." He took a sip of whiskey, while holding a fat cigar in his other hand.

Barrett glanced at him and nodded.

In return, the man raised his drink in a toast.

"You can't hit that post. It's impossible," another general insisted.

"I think he can," the officer with the cigar replied, a grin took over his face.

"I think he can, too," Lincoln agreed.

"Hall, what do you think?" another bystander questioned.

Cornelius shook his head. "The sight has been calibrated, but not for Barrett. He would need at least three shots to calibrate it correctly."

"I will give him three shots," shouted one of the men in the growing crowd. "One hundred greenbacks says he cannot hit the post in three shots."

"I will match that," the senator from Ohio shouted.

"We have two hundred dollars that says he cannot hit the target. Anyone want to take him up on the bet?"

A female's voice took everyone by surprise. "I will take that bet." They all turned to see Brooke standing next to Mary Lincoln.

The men blankly looked around at each other. "We cannot take money from a woman," some of them whispered.

"You are not taking money from me... I will be taking money from you. Besides, I'm not just a woman... I'm this man's wife." Brooke didn't even blink as she linked arms with her husband.

Barrett couldn't help but smile at his wife's boldness. Her confidence in his ability delighted him.

"That does not change the fact that the fence post is some two hundred yards away, give or take a few yards. Look at the sun... it is almost down. Dusk can play tricks with your eyes and make things look different in the distance," a colonel added.

The politician from Ohio interjected, "Mr. President, what will you give the Hymnist if he does hit it?"

Lincoln smiled. "Umm, let me see." He scratched his newly grown beard. "I will give him the state of Maine."

There was a hush for a second, and then an outburst of laughter raced through the crowd.

"Mr. Lincoln, Maine is a beautiful state, but you can keep it." Barrett loaded three shells.

Everyone stepped back.

Silent anticipation enveloped the crowd.

Von Weber knelt down, set his rifle on the railing, and aimed.

An officer ran out with a retractable spyglass and handed it to Lincoln.

"Thank you, sir," the soon-to-be president focused it on the fence post.

"No... not Maine... I want Connecticut," Barrett smiled.

In the tense quiet, Barrett slowly pulled the trigger.

With the sun lowering behind the fencepost, it was difficult to see clearly. Yet, everyone could see the top of the fence post explode as the silence was shattered. The first bullet had found its mark.

"Well, I'll be," one of the men who bet against him stepped forward.

Barrett stood up, emptied the rifle, and handed it back to Lincoln. "Just package Connecticut up for me. I will take it with me when I leave."

There was complete silence as the expert marksman took Brooke's hand and led her away. Cornelius followed close behind.

On their way into the house, she yanked two hundred dollars from the betting soldier's hand. "Thank you, gentlemen," Brooke drawled.

"He is joking about the state of Connecticut, isn't he?" a worried politician from that state shouted.

Lincoln and the rest of the men broke out laughing.

On the porch, they passed the lone officer who was puffing on a cigar.

Barrett nodded to him, and then whispered to Cornelius, "Who is that man?"

"That there is one sorry excuse for an officer, although, he is good when he is sober. His name is Ulysses S. Grant."

"I will have to remember him." Barrett took one last glimpse of the man who had aroused his curiosity.

Brooke accepted the invitation to join Mary Lincoln at her table for the elaborate five-course dinner. They chatted and laughed about their lives and their husbands—both had remarkable stories to share.

Following their meal, the Hymnist stepped to the piano to entertain the distinguished guests. While Barrett's long fingers effortlessly glided over the keys, no one spoke a word. The crowd was enthralled by the music.

When the evening was over, Barrett and Brooke said their goodbyes.

"Mr. President, thank you for the invitation," von Weber spoke. "We are honored."

"No, no... the honor is ours. It has been an interesting evening, to say the least. I had heard rumors of your exploits, and when Cornelius handed me that rifle, I simply had to see for myself."

Mary embraced Brooke. "Take care of that husband of yours. If there is ever anything you need, come see us," Mrs. Lincoln said warmly.

"I will. Thank you for your hospitality. It was a lovely evening."

"Yes, it's something I really still don't feel comfortable with. Abraham came from a humble background... he would rather fish, or cut down a tree with an axe than host one of these functions." Mary laughed.

"It comes with the territory," Abraham countered. "Speaking of territory, Mr. von Weber, you do know I was just kidding about Maine and Connecticut?"

Barrett laughed loudly. "Yes, I do, but we really had everyone going, didn't we?"

"I still can't believe you hit that fence post." Lincoln looked at Barrett, studying him. "Tell me the truth, lad. Were you aiming for the top of the fence, or was it a lucky shot?"

Barrett's face grew distant for a moment. "I learned a long time ago, always go for the head. If it is a case of life and death, and you only have one shot," he turned to face Lincoln, "you better make it count."

"Good point. Stop in and say hello when you return. Maybe you will write that masterpiece while you're in Germany."

"Maybe I will, but I may not have time." He smiled looking at Brooke.

Lincoln winked. "I understand. How long will you be gone?"

"About two years. I have concerts set up throughout Europe. I hope Brooke likes traveling because we will be doing a lot of it."

"Well, have a safe trip. If you ever need anything… the door is always open."

"Thank you, sir. Good luck in leading this nation. I will pray for you daily."

"Do you have any suggestions on how I can lead effectively?" Lincoln inquired.

Barrett pondered the best way to phrase his answer. The words of a great man came to mind. "Mr. President, while attending school in Connecticut, I had an assignment to recite a speech by a statesmen of this great land. It went something like this: *I have lived, Sir, a long time, and the longer I live, the more convincing proofs I see of this truth—that God governs in the affairs of men. And if a sparrow cannot fall to the ground without his notice, is it probable that an empire can rise without his aid?*

"Ah, yes, one of my favorite statesmen… Mr. Ben Franklin." Lincoln nodded.

Barrett took the president's hand and shook it firmly. "Mr. President, I humbly suggest to lead this nation successfully, you do so on your knees."

Lincoln looked directly at von Weber as those words soaked in. "Great advice that I will heed."

The Hymnist took his wife's hand and turned to leave.

The Lincolns watched as the von Webers and William climbed aboard their carriage.

"Delightful couple, aren't they, Abraham?" Mary snuggled her head to her husband's side.

"Ah yes, delightful."

They continued to watch until the carriage disappeared down the lane.

"I pray they stay in Europe for a long time; they may not like what they come home to in this country." As the president-elect thought about the country he loved, and the tremendous load on his shoulders, his heart grew heavy.

Abraham took his wife's hand and together they walked slowly into the house.

Chapter Thirteen

1861
Germany

The Atlantic Ocean was known to be frigid and rough the month of January—this year was no exception. At times, the howling wind and huge waves tossed the ship violently from side to side.

Brooke had never sailed the high seas before. It didn't take long before she realized it was going to be a long, grueling trip to the von Weber's ancestral home.

Barrett prayed that seasickness wouldn't overcome his wife as it had many of the other passengers. He tried to get her mind off the choppy waters by keeping her busy. Sometimes they strolled the deck, other times he enjoyed reacquainting Brooke with the German language, and a bit of French.

English was the main language at Annalise, although her family had come from Germany. Grandfather had always preached, "We live in America now; we must speak the language spoken here and adopt the customs of this land," so Spanish and German became almost non-existent in her home.

After weeks on the sometimes-treacherous water, the honeymooning couple finally arrived in France. Once there, they traveled by coach and train to Paris where the Hymnist had a number of concerts scheduled.

The countryside of France was beautiful with its green hills and valleys, but the city of Paris was dirty, dark, and uninviting. Homeless people lined the streets. It pained the couple to see children dressed in rags, begging for food.

Occasionally, when they were dining at a fine-eating establishment, children would push their faces to the windows, staring at them, hoping for a handout. Even when they frequented a sidewalk cafe, the youngsters would crowd as close to the table as they could, watching every bite they ate. The people who operated the restaurants would shoo the begging children away with a broomstick.

A number of times Brooke deliberately left food on her plate. Under the watchful eye of her loving husband, she later gave it to the hungry, grateful children.

Barrett would smile with approval.

After almost a month in Paris, they continued on their journey to Germany, Barrett's native land. Most of the time they traveled the winding roads by carriage; sometimes they rode the train. The hilly roads were challenging and the weather sometimes stormy as spring was trying to make its entrance.

The couple did much sightseeing in their free time, exploring places Barrett wanted his bride to see.

Throughout Europe, the Hymnist performed many concerts. Barrett's popularity soared among the wealthy, as well as the peasants.

A cousin, Hans Rothschild, met them at the train station in Stuttgart, Germany.

"Hans, my cousin, you are looking good." Barrett greeted him with a hug.

"Not as good looking as you. And I see you have become quite famous." Hans punched Barrett's arm lightly.

"And quite married," Barrett teased. Grabbing Brooke's hand, he pulled her close. A radiant smile revealed her dimples.

"Yes, seems like I heard something about that." Hans eyed Brooke. "So, this is the young lady who captured your heart?"

"Hans, meet my lovely wife, Brooke."

The cousin gave the typical German greeting, clicking his heels and bowing, and then kissing her gloved hand. "The honor is mine."

Brooke felt a certain ease about the man. "Enough of that! Barrett has done nothing but talk about you since we crossed into Germany. Seems like you two have quite the past." She lovingly wrapped her arms around Hans and pulled him into a warm embrace. "This is how we greet someone we care about in America."

"I like this greeting better! Maybe we should adopt this custom here in Germany." He winked with approval at Barrett.

Von Weber laughed. "Okay, okay, that's enough of the formalities. Oh, Hans, there are two more members of our family I want you to meet. This is William, and this is Brooke's chambermaid, Prisse."

Hans clicked his heels and bowed, giving them both a warm welcome. "Do you speak German?" he asked, focusing his eyes on Prisse, then William.

"Only what we learned on our voyage," William replied.

"Well, much of the staff knows how to speak English, even though we rarely have English speaking guests anymore."

Hans faced Barrett. "Cousin, I understand churches across Europe are playing your music. I often get invitations for you to play at a church or concert hall. If you want to stay here permanently, you could have plenty of work." Hans grinned, revealing his near perfect white teeth.

Barrett didn't comment as he helped Brooke into the large, covered carriage drawn by six beautiful horses.

There was silence for a time while Brooke gazed at the sights—the hills and valleys, ornate castles, and small villages. Shepherds walking down the narrow roads guiding a small herd of sheep, or oxen pulling a cart, especially amused her. Usually, the herdsman waved as the carriage rode by, as if an old friend was inside.

Brooke would smile and wave back.

As they traveled to the von Weber estate, they passed field after field of grapevines, just now developing a tinge of green.

Hans pointed to a field of grapes and explained, "Most of this belongs to the von Weber family. We have one of the largest wineries in the country."

"How many people do you have working for you?" Brooke inquired.

"Right now only about a hundred and most of them are family members. But shortly, we will have almost a thousand—from the planting, to the picking, crushing, bottling, and finally, the shipping process. Practically everyone from miles around works in some capacity for the winery, once the harvest begins."

"I didn't realize it was that large."

"You will see for yourself. We will tour the winery once you have rested. I know it has been a long trip." Changing the subject, he asked, "May I ask what your family does in America?"

"They operate a large textile business." Her stomach churned, suddenly feeling a twinge of homesickness.

"Maybe you and my wife, Sonya, can go into town one day and do some shopping and see if your goods have made their way to Stuttgart. If you're anything like my wife... she loves to shop." His face beamed with joy when he talked about his wife.

Brooke laughed. "That would be delightful. Do you have any children?"

"For some reason children have not been in God's plan for our lives."

"I'm sorry to hear that."

"Well, we had hopes and dreams for children and we still do, but in the meantime, we pour our lives into the business."

Hans cleared his throat and changed the subject. "In a few weeks these hillsides will be bursting with clusters of green flowers on the vines, and the air will be filled with their delicate fragrance. Springtime is so beautiful in this area."

As the coach rounded the hill, Hans yelled to the driver, "Gunter, stop here."

The carriage came to a halt.

Hans reached over and opened the door. "I want you to see this."

Barrett helped Brooke out of the carriage. Her eyes immediately were drawn to the hills that were laden with grapevines.

In the middle of the valley was a cluster of large buildings. Nearby, a towering castle dominated the landscape.

Brooke gasped at the breathtaking view.

She noticed a potent odor. "What is that smell?" Brooke inquired.

Hans laughed. "You will get used to it. It is the smell of over one hundred years of hard work—from the raising of the plants, picking of the grapes, crushing of the fruit, to the fermenting of the wine."

Brooke thought for a moment and then finally asked, "How do you crush the fruit?"

"That is an ancient art... a very beautiful art," Hans responded with a hearty laugh, eyeing Barrett. "It is done by the bare feet of young maidens."

"What?" She stood taller, her face showing surprise.

Hans straightened his hat. "I will show you that later. Making wine is a process that takes many steps, and I do mean steps."

The men laughed harder.

"It's going to be an exciting spring with the two of you in the house," Hans spoke truthfully.

As they drew closer to his home, the silhouettes of the buildings were growing more defined.

"This was your home?" she asked Barrett, a hint of wonder in her voice.

"For the first eight years of my life. After that, I was here occasionally."

Brooke eyed the three story stone structure. "How many rooms is in this... this castle?" she asked, sounding somewhat giddy with excitement.

Hans replied, "It has twenty-seven rooms, including a ballroom. Barrett, your grand piano is still located in the music room your parents designed for you."

"Well, of course it is. How on earth would you get the instrument out? It took ten men and a thick rope to hoist it up there." Barrett laughed. "My room is the one with the veranda on the top floor. See it?" He pointed to the room. "My parents said I needed seclusion to practice the piano."

"Truthfully, I don't think they wanted to hear you banging those ivory keys day and night." Hans turned to Brooke. "Of course it did not really matter because there are other pianos throughout the castle."

"Yes, but that one was all mine," Barrett teased.

Brooke stared at the former home of her husband. Finally, she spoke, "Is there something you are not telling me? I mean was your father a king or something?"

"He was a baron, not a king, but still significant. I believe the wine business is what made him so important. My family always made sure the kings and their families had access to the best wines. I am sure that helped in their business, and it also helped protect us during times of conflict. You see, Europeans like their wines. During war, both sides made sure their wine producers were safe. This area has been unscathed by war for years. In fact, there has only been one battle fought here in over a hundred years. It set a precedent that has held to this day. I will tell you that story later."

When they reached the mansion, two men and a woman rushed out to greet them and quickly stood at attention. One of the men opened the carriage door and helped Brooke out.

Hans introduced Brooke to each of them. "I have instructed the staff to do their best to speak English during your stay. This is Otto. He is the house manager; he is in charge of the staff."

The tall, sandy-blonde haired, older German greeted the guests, bowing his head.

Hans continued the introductions. "This is Brahms, the butler. Anything you want or need, ask him, and he will take care of it."

The shorter man clicked his heels and bowed.

"And this is Mrs. Gilda Schmidt, the head housekeeper." Hans motioned toward the younger woman.

"Gilda?" Barrett reached for her hand and kissed it. "Are you the same Gilda I remember from my childhood?"

She curtsied, smiling. "Yes, sir, the same one."

"My, you have grown up! I remember when we explored this entire property together as kids."

"Fond memories, sir."

"Remember the time we crawled into that hole under the tree." Barrett snickered.

"That certainly was the surprise of my life," Gilda replied, blushing.

"What happened?" Brooke asked eagerly, her curiosity heightened.

"Uh…." Barrett hesitated as he glanced back at Gilda.

"Don't look at me, you brought it up. I would like to have forgotten it," the servant smiled sheepishly.

"Now I am most curious," Brooke countered.

Barrett's eyes returned to his wife. "We came face-to-face with an entire family of skunks. Needless to say what happened after that was humiliating for both of us."

Embarrassed, Gilda quickly changed the subject. "It's nice seeing you again, Mr. von Weber. Did you ever finish your masterpiece?"

"You can call me, Barrett. This is my wife, Brooke. And no, I have not finished, or even started my masterpiece."

Gilda was still beet red as she curtsied to Brooke. "Welcome, madam. You are beautiful. Mr. von Weber is a fine man and a perfect gentleman, I may add."

"Thank you for the compliment, and thank you for your observation about my husband. I couldn't agree more."

"Gilda, what fine gentleman captured your heart?" Barrett asked.

She eyed the man next to her. "I married Brahms four years ago. We have a two-year-old daughter." Gilda wrapped her arm through her husband's arm, smiling proudly.

"Congratulations. We look forward to meeting your little girl."

Hans stepped in, "We have a staff of fourteen, but if there is anything you need, any of these three will take care of you. Come let us show you your rooms. After you are settled, we will give you a tour of the estate."

Brooke snuggled close to her husband. "Why on earth did you ever leave this home?"

"That's what missionaries do. They go where God tells them to go, and that's what my parents did. I do not regret one moment of my life… except of course, my parents' death."

"I'm sorry… I would love to have known them."

"They would have loved you." He squeezed her tighter. "So, you could get used to living here, right?" He grinned.

"Oh, yes."

During the ride, William had been quiet, listening. When they arrived at their destination, he grabbed a bag.

Brahms reached for the same piece of luggage. "Let me get that for you, sir."

William was stunned, uncertain how to react. Holding tight to the handle on the bag, his face remained stern.

"Sir, let me take that for you. I will show you to your room," Brahms reinforced.

"Thank you, but I can get this for myself," William said through gritted teeth, not backing down.

Barrett and Brooke watched the confrontation from a short distance away, curious about the outcome.

"No, sir, it is my job. I am happy to do it for you," Brahms insisted.

"I said, I will get these, and stop calling me suh." William sighed loudly showing his frustration.

Brahms backed off, looking dejected.

Noticing Brahms's reaction, William stated, "Please, call me William."

"As you wish, sir. Please follow me." Brahms was noticeably upset.

"William does not know how to act. He has spent his life serving, and now someone is trying to serve him." Brooke's mouth tipped up at one corner.

Barrett nodded. "It will be interesting to see how Prisse and William react to all this attention. They do not realize it yet, but they are no longer servants, but welcomed guests who will be treated accordingly."

"I hope they can adapt." Brooke folded her arms. "I am pretty sure Prisse will, but William, I'm not so sure."

"Within a couple days they will be having fun in the kitchen playing cards and chess all hours of the night with the other workers," Barrett snickered.

"That should be interesting to see."

As they walked toward the front door, Brooke probed her husband, "By the way, I am pretty good at reading other women. Do you and Gilda have a past? And, what is the story about the skunks? I have a feeling there is more to it."

He smiled and whispered in her ear, "She is the first girl I ever kissed."

"Should I be concerned?"

He laughed. "Not unless you think two twelve-year-olds having their first kiss means that much. Yes, she was my first love, but that ended abruptly when I moved. We were both heartbroken." He glanced back at Gilda. "I'm glad she found happiness."

"And you?"

"Me? I found the love of my life and couldn't be happier. Don't ever forget that." Unexpectedly, he reached down and planted a quick kiss on Brooke's forehead.

"What about the skunks?" she kidded.

"Well… those skunks sprayed us with a vengeance. We got out of that hole faster than you can imagine. And we… we did the first thing that came to our minds."

"Which was?"

"We shed our stinky clothes in no time flat. Before we knew it, we were standing there in our undergarments, red-faced, unsure what to do next."

"What did you do?" Brooke tried not to laugh.

"My, you are relentless."

"I have heard of the exploits of Barrett von Weber. This is one I never heard before… I do want to know what happened."

He chuckled. "Well, we put our clothes back on just as fast as we took them off and ran home. We couldn't face each other for almost a week. Just too embarrassed. Eventually things returned to normal. Not long after that, my family moved to China. That was the last time I saw her." Barrett glanced back at Gilda who was carrying a piece of luggage into the house. "When we came back a few years later, she and her folks had left to work in Stuttgart."

Barrett led Brooke through the giant wooden door of the castle. He spread his arms out, "Welcome to my family home."

Brooke stood in awe, gazing around the huge entryway. The first thing she noticed was the giant crystal chandelier hanging from the tall ceiling. When the sunlight hit it, colorful prisms bounced off the wall.

She wondered about the tasteful décor. *There must be fascinating history behind these magnificent art pieces.*

Her eyes traveled up the wide marble staircase to the second floor. For a short time, she closed her eyes and imagined what living there would be like. *Yes, I think we will be happy here.*

As they followed Hans up the stairs to their room, Brooke inquired, "Gilda knew about your masterpiece way back then?"

"Yes, Gilda and I did everything together as children. One day my parents took us to a performance of Beethoven's Ninth Symphony in Stuttgart. That night I told her, 'One day I will write a masterpiece as good as this.' She said that she was going to sing lead in the opera. For months after that, Gilda walked around singing in an operatic voice, and I banged the piano in a senseless manner."

Brooke laughed at the thought, and then grew serious. "I am sure you can do it... I mean, write that masterpiece."

"Yes, but I need the inspiration."

They paused at the top of the stairway. "What was Beethoven's inspiration?" Brooke asked, looking into his deep blue eyes.

"I read that it was because he believed that God told him to."

"Well then, when the time comes for you to do it, God will tell you."

He smiled. "You know, I am really going to enjoy my life with you. Maybe you will be my inspiration."

They walked down a long hallway, finally stopping at a door.

Entering the bedroom, Hans walked over, and opened the bright-blue silk drapes. "This will be your room," he motioned with his hand.

A large canopied bed caught her immediate attention and reminded her how weary she was from her journey.

Brooke's mouth dropped as she walked over to peer out the picture window. Grapevines covered the hills as far as she could see.

She noticed about a dozen horses near a barn happily cropping the fresh spring grass. Some colts close by them frolicked in the sunshine.

For the next few minutes, the couple watched the horses grazing in the pasture.

Realizing the couple's need for rest, Hans commented, "I will let you two have some time to yourself. Oh, before I forget, they are performing Beethoven's Ninth Symphony in Venice in late spring. Would you like me to get you some tickets? I am sure there will be no problem getting some for you. In fact, I have a request for you to perform a couple concerts there. Would you be willing?"

"Yes, of course, that would be splendid," Barrett, replied. "We have no date set to return to America."

"Consider it done, now get some rest." Hans left and closed the door.

Now that the couple was alone, Brooke fell flat on the bed, laughing aloud. "I cannot believe this. I thought my father's house was big. Who all lives here?"

Barrett plopped down next to her. "Hans and his family live here, along with all the household staff and their families." After a moment he added, "There are five guest houses. There is even an old battle castle. Remember, it's a twenty-five thousand acre spread."

"Battle castle?"

"Yes, actually, it's the remains of a castle, complete with a moat. Built in the early 1700s. Everyone in the area would run there for safety when an enemy approached. There was even a time when we even had our own little army. Germany is more sophisticated now… the king provides the protection."

"Remains?" Brooke's eyes doubled in size.

"Yes. My ancestors were tending their crops when they were brutally attacked by a tribe of nomads. They were all murdered before they could reach the safety of the castle, which was ransacked and destroyed."

"Murdered?"

"Yes, their bodies were found stripped and strung up."

"Did they ever catch the men who did it?"

"Oh, yes. Three of the sons survived because they were away. When they discovered the horror, they went on their own quest for justice. A few weeks later, they caught up to the killers camped by a river, about seventy of them."

"What happened?"

Barrett was quiet for a moment. "Evidently, the nomads had wandered up from the Middle East, leaving a lengthy trail of death and destruction. They were found with horses, gold, and other possessions that belonged to my relatives and others in the area. Everyone in that tribe was killed. The bodies were tossed in a ravine and burned. It was quick justice. Pitiful in a way, but at the same time…." he stared at the ceiling as he spoke. "…it was justice. Our family never had to be afraid of anyone after that."

Barrett picked up one of the pillows and patted it, making his head more comfortable. His mood had changed, almost as if he was living that part of history himself.

Brooke remained silent, giving him time to gather his thoughts.

Finally, he shifted his gaze to her. "Perhaps I will take you there sometime."

Brooke could see that it was a sad part of the von Weber history. If her husband ever needed to discuss it further, she would be there for him, but now, nothing more was said about it.

Chapter Fourteen

1861
Von Weber Castle

Brooke awakened one morning to the delightful sound of piano music. She reached over to hug her husband, but his side of the bed was empty. She slipped into her warm robe, since the castle was cool in the morning, and followed the sweet sound of the music. Quietly, she climbed the stone stairs to the upper loft and sat on the steps, watching through the doorway, listening. A warm fireplace near the piano heated the room, making it feel cozy.

She had heard Barrett play in many concert halls, but because of their hectic schedules, she had rarely seen him like this—it was different. In the solitude of the morning hour, he sat at the piano, lost in his music. He was not entertaining thousands, but appeared to have an audience of One. Alone with God, it was a time of worship for her husband. She almost felt she was intruding. He played tunes that she had never heard, his hands swiftly gliding over the keys. Even more amazing, he was playing the beautiful melodies by ear. *Perhaps he is writing his masterpiece.* She smiled at the thought.

When she thought he was almost finished, she quietly returned to their bedroom to wait for him.

This scenario would occur many times over the next few months.

The couple made a few side trips around Germany visiting places Barrett remembered from his childhood.

They spent much of their spare time riding horses around the von Weber property. They would talk for endless hours. It fascinated her that Barrett, not yet thirty years of age, had been around the world and met many important people in his short life.

Early one misty morning, their tranquility was interrupted when a rider approached the von Weber castle. He dismounted, rushed toward the large doors, and pounded on them with both fists.

Brahms opened the heavy door.

An impatient courier shouted in German, "I have an urgent message from America. I need to talk with Barrett von Weber." The man was out-of-breath and his facial expression showed the intensity of his mission.

Barrett and Brooke were finishing breakfast when they heard the commotion. They hurried out of the dining room, followed by Hans.

When the visitor spotted Barrett, he rushed over to him. "Sir, I have an urgent message for you." Standing at attention, he handed him an envelope. "It is from Cornelius Hall."

"Why would Cornelius be contacting me?" Barrett questioned in English, as he took the envelope from the man's outstretched hand. He carefully opened the letter and began reading silently. The more he read, the more his shoulders slumped. Sadness crept into his eyes.

Watching his reaction, Brooke felt a wave of panic. "Honey, what is it?"

His voice sounded flat. "The South attacked Fort Sumter."

"Attacked? What do you mean?"

Barrett shuffled from one foot to the other. He glanced at Brook before he started reading aloud:

My Dear Friend,

I am writing to tell you the grave news that hostilities between the North and the South have taken an ugly turn. You may not be aware that since the election of President Lincoln seven states have seceded from the Union. On April 12, 1861, a well-armed Southern militia, calling itself the Confederate Army, fired upon Fort Sumter, a key fort held by Union troops in South Carolina. President Lincoln has ordered an army to be established in an effort to retake it. Meanwhile, four border slave states joined the Confederacy, bringing the total to eleven. The scuttlebutt is the Union intends to crush the Rebels before they have a chance to prepare a great army. In my humble opinion, there is no end in sight. Barrett, please stay where you are. You and your bride are safe there. What you feared all along has happened. I am afraid it will be a long and bloody fight. Union forces have commandeered the weapon-manufacturing plants in the North. No contract that any Confederate state has with New Haven Arms will be honored. I will keep you informed as events develop. God be with us in this time of trial.

Your Friend,

Cornelius Hall

Barrett stared at the letter in his hands for a long moment and then peered at his wife solemnly. "If Rory would have succeeded in obtaining that contract, your family would have lost a fortune."

Not saying a word, she wrapped her loving arms around her husband's strong neck. *I wish I could stay safe in his arms forever.*

"They may still lose everything," Barrett whispered, running his fingers through her thick hair.

"Barrett, you need to stay here where it is safe. This is your home now," Hans emphasized the contents of the letter.

The Hymnist glanced down again. "This letter was dated April 15th."

"That was two months ago," Brooke acknowledged, searching his eyes for answers.

"That's how long it takes for a message to get here from America. No telling what has happened since," his voice quivered.

"Maybe they found a peaceful solution," Brooke said optimistically, trying to encourage him.

"Not likely. People like your brother, Rory, are leading the South. Even your other brothers blindly support it. Very few people in the South agree with your father. No, I do not believe that a peaceful resolution has been found, nor will be. I fear the worst."

There was silence as everyone gave Barrett time to absorb the news.

Slowly stepping away from his wife, he uttered, "We need to think about what to do next. Let's go on our morning ride and discuss our options."

He looked into Brooke's big brown eyes and noticed her concern. "And I do mean our options." He emphasized the word "our," reassuring his wife that no matter what happened, they would face it together.

"Whatever decision you make, honey, I will support you." She kissed him on the cheek.

"Me too, cousin," Hans chimed in. "However, I sure could use your help around here. And just think, you could sit by the hour in your studio of this great castle and write your masterpiece."

Barrett mustered a small smile and put his hand on Hans' arm. "That is tempting... very tempting."

Hans could see distress in Barrett's eyes. A civil war, which had happened many times in Europe, had begun in America. He knew his cousin's heart must be heavy and dreaded to hear what his ultimate decision would be.

Barrett stared at the letter. "Hans, instead of our usual ride, I want to show Brooke the battle castle. We will spend the night at our southern guesthouse."

"I will have Brahms and Gilda gather what supplies you need," Hans offered. "The horses are already saddled and ready to go."

Within a few minutes, they were on their way.

As they rode, Brooke's mind traveled across the sea to her home—Annalise. *Will we ever get back there, and if we do, what will we find now that war has begun?*

The ride was slow, not as lively as usual. The horses seemed to sense the uneasiness of their riders.

After quite a distance, Brooke halted her horse, interrupting the tenseness. "Where are we? We have never gone this far."

"Remember the story I told you about the battle castle?"

"Yes, I am curious about that."

"It is right over that hill," Barrett said, nodding his head toward a large grove of trees.

"I am anxious to see it."

Soon they reached the crest of the hill and gazed over a large valley. Their attention was drawn to what was left of a dilapidated structure, surrounded by a moat.

When they arrived at the ruins, Barrett helped Brooke off her horse. They dropped the reins, knowing their trusted animals would not stray far.

"So this is the castle you told me about?" Brooke raised a questioning brow.

"Yes. I have not been here for many years."

She studied the scene before them. "Oh, my! It was huge, almost like a fort."

"Come with me." Barrett took his wife's hand and led her to an old rundown cemetery. Somberly he stated, "Here are the remains of the men, women, and children who died defending this castle over a hundred years ago."

They stopped in front of a grave with a large tombstone. They stared at the faded inscription—Ludwig v*on Weber.*

"This is the grave of the patriarch of the von Weber family. He died defending his home from an evil enemy. I understand he was a good man."

Brooke stared at the grave and then shifted her focus to Barrett. As she thought about their uncertain future, and wondered how the war in America would affect them, tears began to well up. "Please promise me you will seek God's guidance before making the decision to return to America." She removed the hanky from her reticule and wiped her eyes. "As much as I miss home, I want to be with you. We can build a life here if that's what you think is best."

Barrett pulled her into an embrace. "I will wait to hear again from Cornelius. I pray this entire thing can be resolved peacefully. However, Americans are not only resourceful, they are stubborn—bullheaded. Only time will tell."

Their evening together at the southern guesthouse offered the couple the solitude they needed. It was a time to soul search and share their intimate feelings. It was a night neither of them would ever forget.

Chapter Fifteen

Barrett had accepted an invitation to play for His Majesty King William of Württemberg at an afternoon luncheon in late July.

The afternoon was a scorcher.

When they arrived at the palace, Brooke could hardly contain herself. "Father will be delighted when I tell him I saw the gardens that Grandpa helped plant." Her excited eyes gleamed as she looked around.

They entered the exotic ballroom and took their place in the back of the growing line of guests.

Barrett spoke softly, "My understanding is that the king seldom comes here anymore; he spends most of his time at the palace in Stuttgart."

"Such a waste of a beautiful building." Brooke glanced around the ballroom. "I feel I am underdressed," Brooke whispered.

"Nonsense… you are the most beautiful woman here."

"But look at the lavish gowns some of these women are wearing."

"None can compare to your beauty."

She smiled. "You always know the right things to say, darling." Her Southern drawl seemed even more apparent than usual. "Look at that extravagant food they are serving."

"Yes, looks quite delicious."

Peering in a different direction, Brooke remarked in a bubbly voice, "Oh my, Barrett, is that the king?"

"Yes, and his wife… his third, I may add."

"He doesn't look like I expected a king to look."

"You should have seen his father."

"His father?"

"Yes, Frederick. He ruled Germany with a heavy thumb."

"Really?" Her eyes widened.

"Yes, he weighed over four hundred and fifty pounds."

It took a second, but Brooke finally caught the joke. "Oh, Barrett, you are so cruel."

She leaned closer and whispered, "Did he really weigh that much?"

"Yes, he did." Barrett chuckled.

"I hope my German is understandable."

"You'll do fine... I will help you."

When it was their turn, Barrett handed their invitation to a well-dressed man. The man read it and snapped to attention. "Welcome." Then the attendant faced the king, who was talking to other guests in line, and loudly announced their arrival in German. "Your Majesty... from the United States of America... Barrett von Weber and his wife, Brooke."

Silence engulfed the room.

The king shifted his attention to them.

Then the whispering among the guests began.

"There he is... the Hymnist."

"He is quite debonair."

"His wife is stunning. Is she Spanish?"

The king extended his hand to Barrett. "Ah, the famous Hymnist, Barrett von Weber."

Barrett shook the king's hand, slightly nodding his head. "Your Highness, thank you for the invitation."

"The honor is mine. The queen loves your music. When she heard you were visiting our great country, she told me, 'We must host a ball and invite the Hymnist to entertain.' I dare not question the queen."

The queen smiled and said, "It is true. I enjoy your music immensely."

Barrett gave his German salute and kissed her gloved hand. "I hope I don't disappoint you."

"I am quite certain that you won't."

"We have a gift for you, your highness... a bottle of our finest wine." Barrett handed the bottle to the king.

The king read the label aloud, "von Weber Wine, 1821." He bent over and whispered, "Thank you. I will save this refreshment for later." The king laughed heartily.

Barrett joined in the laughter. Then he gently reached out to Brooke, pulling her closer. "Permit me to introduce my wife, Brooke."

The king examined her closely, eyeing her from head to toe and back up again. "Oh, my... you, young lady, are one beautiful woman."

Brooke smiled, curtsied, and offered her white-gloved hand to the king.

He kissed her hand, but kept holding it.

Barrett's voice sounded casual. "Her family lives in America, but at one time her grandfather was a servant on these grounds."

"He was, was he?"

"Yes, he was caretaker of the beautiful garden when it was in its prime."

"Oh, the garden, how quaint. What was his name?" He finally released her hand.

"Ludwig Fortner."

"Fortner," he repeated. "I do not recall a Fortner, but then again, I have many people coming and going."

"Are you a gardener, too, Mrs. von Weber?"

"I ahh...."

Barrett stepped in. "Her grandfather settled the family in Georgia and started a textile operation. They own thousands of acres and have done quite well."

"A success story from one of my subjects, how thrilling."

"Her mother was related to the Queen of Spain," Barrett added.

The king's eyes grew wide. "Really? A mere peasant gardener marrying royalty?" His face showed his confusion.

Barrett eyed a man dressed in full military uniform standing close to the king.

The king noticed von Weber staring at the man. "Have you met Otto Bismarck?"

"General Bismarck!" Barrett's voice filled with surprise.

The general gave the German salute and bowed.

Von Weber acknowledged the greeting. "I have read much about you. You, sir, are a legend."

"And I have read much about you. The bear story intrigues me most... is it true?" Bismarck's handlebar mustache quivered when he talked.

"Oh, the bear story," Barrett blushed. "I would like to put that one behind me, but yes, I must confess, it is true."

"You actually shot a bear from two thousand yards? That was an amazing feat. I could use a fusilier like you in my army."

A dark scowl replaced Barrett's usual smile. "I consider a sniper... fusilier... as you call it, just another word for a cold-blooded killer and should have no place in battle."

The remark confused Bismarck. Cocking his head, he studied Barrett, trying to understand what his harsh words meant. "Why would an excellent sharpshooter like you say something like that? Would it not be better for the common good of your country to do away with the enemy in any way possible?"

"To shoot at a man firing at you is one thing, but to kill an unarmed soldier sitting on a horse is quite another." Barrett's voice elevated.

"You still would have killed the enemy. Isn't that what war is all about?"

"Depends on where you are sitting." Barrett's answer came swift.

"Please elaborate."

"Are you the one behind the rifle, or the one sitting on the horse? It's a moral decision. A good soldier would never shoot an unarmed man."

"Ahh… I understand now. Well, still, I would love to have you in my army," Bismarck insisted.

"Thank you, sir, but I am proud to be an American now." Barrett put his arm around Brooke's shoulders.

"Once a German always a German," Bismarck noted.

Barrett let the reply slide.

The conversation continued in German. "I have heard rumors that you have a civil war brewing in your country," the general spoke smugly.

"Much like the one here," Barrett shot back.

"Nonsense! We do not have a civil war brewing. It will be a war uniting the smaller countries into one large country, which will be easier to govern and defend."

"Sounds like a civil war to me."

"It is for the good of Germany, sir." Bismarck didn't blink. "As I said, it is easier to govern one country than thirty, which we do now. It will also be easier to defend against the larger countries, such as Russia and France. It will be similar to America's states."

"The problem I see is the government forcing states to act contrary to the beliefs of the people in those states." Barrett took a step back.

"Interesting," Bismarck replied. "Perhaps we can get together before you head back to America and discuss this further."

"I would like that. Now if you will excuse me, I must get ready to perform."

"And I have to make my way to my seat." Bismarck saluted him.

The couple sauntered through the ballroom hand-in-hand.

Brooke passed a white handkerchief across her forehead before speaking. "Your German was impressive. What was that all about?"

"My understanding is that he wants to unite the surrounding small countries into one Germany."

"Do you think that will happen?"

Barrett glanced back at Bismarck without even a hint of a smile, "Yes, I do."

"Does that mean a war is coming?"

"Yes, but war is nothing new for Europe. However, he does have a point... it would make Germany a stronger nation. He is an extremely brilliant, yet shrewd politician."

"I thought he was a general." Brooke asked with an inquisitive look.

Barrett smiled as he looked at her. "I think the uniform is more for show. He is really a politician, an ambassador for Germany." Barrett glanced back at Bismarck. "But he is a great leader. I just hope he leads the people in the right direction."

Barrett gave his wife a quick kiss on the top of her head. "Now, my dear, I must make my way to the piano and you must find your seat."

The guests noticed the Hymnist nearing the instrument and made their way to their chairs, anxious to hear the famous pianist.

Within minutes, Barrett sat at the piano, his blonde hair gleaming, and his usual smile of confidence covering his face. His fingers swift and sure, he made the piano come to life in a way that only he could.

After a few minutes, Barrett glanced around the ballroom. He was grateful the audience seemed to be as captivated by his music as he was.

Brooke beamed with pride; her husband surely was a master of the ivories. He would never cease to amaze her. God had blessed him with an extraordinary gift. She soaked in every note, every melody he played.

When the final piece was finished, the crowd applauded enthusiastically, showing their approval and wanting more.

After the concert, Barrett took Brooke on a tour of the palace.

"It is so big, so elaborate. Where are the gardens?"

"We will get there... be patient, my dear. First, here is a painting of Frederick, William's father." He pointed to a framed portrait hanging on the wall.

"Oh my, he was a sizable man."

"Yes. He had to have a special throne made so he could fit in it... and a special bed."

A few minutes later, Barrett opened the back door.

Flowers of every color imaginable captured Brooke's immediate attention. "Oh my goodness, I have never seen such a beautiful garden." Caught in the moment, she held her skirt up so she wouldn't trip, and ran to the sweet scented flowers, leaving Barrett several steps behind.

She bent down and sniffed a gorgeous red rose. "Oh, how fragrant!" Her face shone radiantly as she walked around trying to take in the sights and sounds, submitting them to her memory. "I can't wait to tell Daddy I was here. Thank you for the unforgettable day."

Chapter Sixteen

August 1861
Von Weber Winery

By the end of summer, hundreds of people from surrounding towns came to assist in harvesting luscious grapes from the loaded vines.

One morning during breakfast, Brooke asked the question she had been most curious about. "Honey, when are you going to show me how they make wine?"

Barrett smiled, speaking to his cousin. "Are the grapes ready to crush, Hans?"

"The picking has begun. I'm sure we have enough to begin crushing this afternoon, if you wish." He grinned. "I think Gilda can help with it."

"Can Prisse be part of it?" Brooke asked.

"I see no reason why not. It will be fun," Barrett acknowledged.

"As well as entertaining," Hans added.

Brooke had seen the large vats where the grapes were crushed, but had never seen how it was done.

That afternoon the three anxious women appeared at the winery in lightweight dresses and a scarf covering their hair. They walked up the steps in their bare feet, and then down into a giant vat.

Since Gilda was experienced, she entered the tub of squishy, purple grapes first. She was delighted to show Prisse and Brooke exactly what to do.

Brooke moved carefully, afraid she was going to slip and fall, but Gilda grasped her elbow to steady her.

"Are you sure this is all right for us to do? I mean should a lady be doing this?" Brooke asked, wide-eyed.

The men had been watching from the sidelines, amused by the antics of the girls.

Barrett flashed a flirting smile at his wife. "You are quite ladylike, and by the way, you look gorgeous."

"Miss Brooke, are you sure you want me doing this?" Prisse said, reaching her hand out to Gilda. "You know... me being colored and all."

Barrett assured her, "Prisse, do not worry about a thing. This is how wine has been processed for thousands of years."

Brahms grabbed an old ukulele from a nearby storage room and began playing an old, familiar German tune.

Hans and Barrett joined in by clapping their hands and singing loudly, off key.

The three women laughed as they joined hands in a circle and danced, crushing the grapes and causing the juice to squeeze through holes into a container below.

"Oh my, it feels so strange," Brooke acknowledged. "Will we smell like wine?"

"It tickles my toes," Prisse exclaimed.

"Look at our purple feet... how long will they stay like this?" Brooke wondered.

"I reckon I do not have to worry 'bout that," Prisse giggled.

Everyone joined in the laughter, enjoying the lighthearted chatter.

Brooke's focus turned from crushing grapes to flirting with her husband for a short time. She was jolted back to reality when she slipped, taking Gilda and Prisse down with her. An eruption of laughter burst from the men when the trio tumbled into the purple pulp. At first, the young ladies were embarrassed by the fall, but as they envisioned what a sight they must be, the women began to laugh so hard tears streamed down their purple faces.

The sound of an equestrian riding into the castle courtyard interrupted their laughter. A man who looked familiar quickly dismounted and walked briskly toward the building they were in.

Hans and Barrett hurriedly helped the women out of the vat, and then turned to greet the visitor outside the door.

Brahms handed each woman a wet cloth, and they began cleaning the purple stain from their faces and legs.

Brooke stood a short distance away, watching the man snap to attention, and hand her husband a letter. She was certain who it was from, but uncertain what it said. The look on Barrett's face confirmed her concern.

Hans handed the deliveryman a tip, and he left as quickly as he came.

Barrett trudged back to Brooke.

"It's a message from Cornelius, right?" Her heart quickened.

"Yes." He kicked the ground.

"What does it say?"

Barrett began reading softly, so only Brooke could hear him.

My Dear Friend Barrett,

I am sorry to inform you that the first major land battle between the North and the South has resulted in major causalities, some predict as high as eight to ten thousand men. This battle was at Manassas, just south of the capital. The Union soldiers were overrun. The future of Washington is in jeopardy right now. Fortunately, for us, the Southern military leaders did not know how vulnerable the Capital was. We have had a chance to regroup.

The North is setting up blockades at all Southern ports to prevent European countries from bringing supplies to the Confederacy.

Barrett, this is going to be a long, costly war. New Haven Arms has had to add many jobs to keep up with the Union demands.

You and Brooke stay put. You are safe there.

Have not received any information from Brooke's family, but Titus and Annapurna are doing well. I will continue to keep you informed.

Your Friend, Cornelius

Everyone else had been watching Barrett from a short distance away, hoping for a smile, a glimmer of anything indicating good news, but he showed no emotion!

Hans strode over to Barrett. He knew the answer before he even asked, "What is it, cousin?"

Barrett lowered the paper and looked upward, almost as if he were praying.

Hans shifted his gaze to Brooke. "More bad news from America?"

Brooke nodded her head.

Turning her full focus to her husband, Brooke spoke straight from her heart. "We are returning to America, aren't we?" Her voice cracked with emotion.

"I need to serve my country; I can do no less."

"I don't want you to be wounded or killed. I already have to worry about my father and brothers. Now, you too?" Her eyes filled with tears.

He looked intently at her, noticing her confusion. "You don't understand."

"No, I don't. Tell me. What's more important than life... life with me?"

Barrett couldn't find the right words, but thoughts flooded his mind. *Will I have the strength to do what I feel I must do? How can I ever leave my beloved Brooke?*

He looked at his wife who was still covered in purple juice. He knew normally he would laugh at the sight, but feeling heavy hearted all he could do was muster a slight grin. "In the heart of every man lies the same desire—they long to be free from the bond of oppression and every evil. The soul yearns for freedom."

"Freedom?" she asked.

"Yes, you see, I need to help right a wrong."

"You're talking about freedom for the blacks?" A fresh batch of tears slid down her face.

"Yes. I'll try to explain. Remember the night we met Isaac Smith?"

Brooke nodded. "Of course, that is when I met the love of my life."

He paused. "I have been thinking a lot about Isaac Smith... John Brown. He put his life out there for his fellow human beings. He even watched two of his sons die for the same cause. I have asked myself repeatedly, did he really think it was worth it? Was it worth watching your children hanged in order to free the slaves? Then I remembered that God sent his son to die for us. Were we worth it? I love the scripture, *John 15:13: Greater love hath no man than this, that a man lay down his life for his friends.*

"Does this have to do with states' rights?"

"It does in a way, but the underlying problem is freedom for an enslaved people. Slavery is wrong."

She looked past him. "I can't argue that, but I love you and I don't want to lose you." As grief took a grip on her, she swung her arms around his neck. Struggling to contain the sob that threatened to choke her, she cried, "We have a life together, a future together, and besides, you have to compose your masterpiece."

Barrett couldn't speak, fighting his emotions.

In each other's arms, they prayed, asking God for wisdom, courage, and protection—not just for themselves, but also for their families, as well as their country.

Chapter Seventeen

March 1864
Union Training Camp, Pennsylvania

The young officer held his sword high, and then hastily lowered it signaling for the men to fire. The snap of the rifle hammers, the crack of the flint, and the pop of the powder caused the round pellets to hum as they raced towards the mark, thirty yards away.

The captain walked down the firing range to examine the targets closely. He discovered that the Minié balls that did hit the targets barely grazed them; most missed entirely. Not one hit the mark even close to the center.

Dissatisfied with the results, Captain Barrett von Weber shook his head, uttering under his breath, "Well men, back to the basics." He trudged back to the soldiers he was training. Not a word was spoken. Discipline was important to von Weber and the men knew when to talk. The stern look on his face told them that it was time for them to remain silent.

He peered at the men. Some of them were still boys in their teens and had never even seen a rifle up close, let alone fired one. Most of them came from the city and worked in manufacturing plants, banks, or stores. Many of the men standing before him had been drafted into the army. While others joined the military for the adventure, some felt a sense of duty... something males were expected to do.

Von Weber's expertise in weapons and hand-to-hand combat gave him an officer's rank when he signed on with the Union Army.

He knew his work was cut out for him, his responsibility great. He rubbed his forehead trying not to let his frustration be evident. After a long pause, he forced a look of calmness. "Men... gather around and let's start from the beginning."

Most of the men moved closer, every one of them had the highest admiration for the young officer who treated them with respect.

Von Weber began his prepared speech. "Gentlemen... your survival depends on how well you maneuver on the battlefield and how efficiently you handle your weapon."

Barrett waved a rifle in the air. "This is a Springfield rifle. When we are done here today, you will know how to handle it correctly."

"Sir?" a soldier near the back of the group spoke up.

Captain von Weber addressed the young man. "Yes, Private."

"Sir, meaning no disrespect, we have been over this before," he said stiffly.

Von Weber gave a nod of agreement. "I know it, soldier."

"Then why are you telling us again?"

Barrett sighed noticeably. He pointed in the direction of where they had been practicing. "Because out of the seventy-five men who just fired at those targets, only a handful of you actually hit them, and no one hit dead center."

Embarrassed, the soldier silenced himself.

Barrett began to pace back and forth holding the rifle even higher to get their full attention. "Men, this is your lifeline. How you use this weapon is the deciding factor on whether you return home to your family alive. Without proper use, you are a dead man. It is my job to see that you know how to load it quickly, aim it, and fire accurately. The quicker you learn how to prepare your rifle for the next round, the better your chance of survival. You will be taught how to clean and care for your weapon. You will also learn how to fight with a bayonet. What you do not want is a hand-to-hand fight, but if that happens, you have two possibilities—kill or be killed... and the second choice is not an option you want to consider. Gentlemen, you must keep your gunpowder clean and dry. Once it is wet, it is unusable and you will be forced into hand-to-hand combat."

Barrett hesitated as he stared at a boy on the front row who didn't look a day over fourteen. The captain put his rifle down and lowered his voice. "I want you to survive. I want you to live to see another day... to go home to your family. I only have a few days to teach you what I have learned in a lifetime. I feel responsible for each of you because if you fail on the battlefield and are killed, I did not do my job. That is why we are going over and over this until you get it. We will continue to review it until you hit that target, right square in the center, or the next group comes in and you are moved to the battlefield. So men, pay attention!"

Barrett noticed his good friend, Cornelius, standing under a nearby tent.

"Gentlemen, take a ten minute break and think about what I have said. Study your rifle. Get to know it because it will be your best friend on the battlefield! When I return, you will learn how to take it apart, clean it, and put it back together. Then you will concentrate on firing and hitting the targets."

Barrett walked over to Cornelius and greeted him with a hearty handshake. "What brings you here, my friend?"

"I have something to show you." Cornelius had placed a parcel, wrapped in a cream-colored muslin cloth, on a table. He picked it up, slowly removed the wrapping, and held the object out to Barrett.

Von Weber took the item from his friend and began examining it. "Oh my, a Henry repeating rifle. I don't see any of these around here. What an impressive rifle! Any changes?"

"It's improved, handles much better. The lever reacts quicker and the shells are brass now, not copper. Lincoln was impressed with the rifle you shot that day in Washington, as were some of the generals." He chuckled as he recalled the fond memories. "But getting them interested enough to buy them was another thing." He looked at the young troops waiting for Barrett to return. "Some of the Union soldiers have been purchasing these with their own money, and the Rebels now have a special name for them."

"Which is…?" Barrett asked, while checking out the mechanism of the rifle.

"That darn rifle that you load on Sunday and shoot all week," he laughed.

Barrett checked the chamber to make sure it was empty and then aimed it at a nearby tree. "Sure don't want these getting into the hands of the enemy. Handles nice… feels good in my hands… sixteen brass shells, you say?"

"Yes. The Union Army has agreed to buy five hundred of them to see how well they perform in battle."

"Interesting. I have run into many weapons that the Union soldiers purchased—Henry, Springfield, Colt, and even a few from Europe, which leads to a big problem."

"Ammunition!" Cornelius responded readily.

"Right… a rifle is no good without ammunition. The army cannot keep ammunition for all the different rifles. It costs too much, not practical. Logistics have been a major problem."

Cornelius agreed.

Barrett added, "I assume these weapons will be used for a specific purpose."

"Special teams, I understand." Cornelius continued, "As you know, it has become increasingly difficult during rainy season to keep the ammunition powder dry. And with the rainy season about here... well, what better time. In addition, we would like to gain the upper hand by firing more than one shot at a time. The new commanders believe this Henry can... well, putting in bluntly... kill more men quicker. This hopefully will result in less Union casualties."

Cornelius watched his friend inspect the rifle and shells. "Frankly, after three years of this awful war, the Union commanders are getting tired of the bloodshed! The Rebels are not going to give up without a fight, they have proven that."

Barrett let out a long, lengthy breath.

"I know you want to do your part in this war, Barrett."

"I am doing my part. The problem is many of the men think I am in this position because of who I am, or should I say, was?"

"I would not worry about what people think. You have a more important job instructing than you would on the battlefield. You are where you belong... teaching men how to use their weapons to survive. You have saved countless lives."

Barrett eyed Cornelius closely, and finally voiced his suspicion, "What really brings you here today? It's more than showing me your latest weapon."

"You know me too well," Cornelius chortled. "You are right. The new general wants you to teach a special group of men how to use these new weapons."

"New general?" Barrett's gaze stayed fixed on his friend.

"Yes. President Lincoln appointed Ulysses S. Grant the General of the Army. I believe you met him before."

"Oh yes, I remember him from Lincoln's celebration. I recall how he sat on that porch, smoking his cigar, and betting that I could hit the fence post." Barrett grinned, shaking his head.

"The man is rumored to be a drunkard, but he gets the job done."

Barrett nodded. "He wants me to go into the battlefield to test these weapons?"

Cornelius crossed his arms. "Yes, he does. Grant is now at Brandy Station, Virginia, preparing to go after Lee's army. Five hundred of these rifles are being sent there, as we speak. The plan is for you to be close behind. You will teach a special team of five hundred sharpshooters how to properly fire these rifles and keep them in top working condition. After that, those men will be sent to find Lee's army and destroy it... one man at a time."

"It's going to take more than five hundred men," Barrett quipped.

"True, but the goal is to get the top brass excited about this rifle. The old repeating rifle left this type of weapon with a stigma. Too many blew up in the soldiers' hands. And when the rifle did work—instead of making each bullet count—the men emptied the magazine. A soldier's ammunition was gone before he knew it. The thinking was to fire fast at an object, so it would take four or five shots to hit a target while the old musket would hit it with a single shot. It was costing the government too much for ammunition. That's where you come in—training the men to make every shot count."

Barrett remained silent, listening intently.

Cornelius went on, "What it also means is that if this rifle works in battle, the Union Army will purchase thousands more to equip each man with a new one. That would mean big money for New Haven Arms and make us as the leader in gun manufacturing."

"Seems ironic," Barrett muttered.

"What do you mean?"

"People making money by killing more people… faster."

Cornelius was slow to reply. "I agree."

Von Weber looked through the sight. "Is it precise?"

Cornelius reached inside his pocket and handed Barrett five rounds of ammunition.

Quietly, von Weber loaded them into the tubular magazine and paced to the shooting range where his men were waiting.

The men excitedly gathered around, fascinated by Barrett and the new weapon. They had heard the stories, and knew about the reputation he had as a sharpshooter.

"What's he holding?" one questioned another man in a soft voice.

"I don't know, but it sure would be easier to carry than these long, old guns we have now," another one responded.

Barrett signaled for the crowd to step back and be quiet. He took a stance and aimed the rifle at the furthest target. No one had come close to hitting the board, which was nothing more than a hastily painted face with a red nose. He slowly squeezed the trigger. The silence of the still morning air was shattered as the bullet hit the target right below the face.

The men cheered and continued whispering among themselves.

Barrett looked through a spyglass at the mark. Without a word, he made a few adjustments to the sight of the rifle and raised it to his shoulder.

The crowd hushed again.

When von Weber pulled the trigger, a blast echoed through the valley. The bullet flying through the air was precise, hitting the red nose on the face dead center.

With dropped jaws, some of the men stared at what was left of the target; others gawked at the captain who made the unbelievable shot.

One of the men mumbled, "That's impossible."

Barrett faced Cornelius. "Nice weapon. I like it. Easy on your shoulder and the sight is precise. If I were the General of the Army, I would order one for each of my men. The only problem is, this gun will take many lives."

"Rebel lives!" one of the soldiers who had been listening snickered.

Barrett glared at the soldier. "Yes, Rebels, but they are still human beings... maybe even your brother or father. Are you prepared for that?"

Ashamed, the man lowered his head.

Barrett turned his attention back to Cornelius. "What happens if the South gets their hands on rifles like these?"

The soldiers stared blankly at each other.

One of the privates in the crowd shouted, "They would slaughter us."

"That is correct," replied Cornelius.

Barrett handed the rifle back to his friend and crossed his arms over his chest.

"Fortunately, the ammunition is unique. The Confederates can't reproduce it. The rifle will only fire a .44 shell. Without the right ammo, the only use for this rifle is as a club," Cornelius added.

Barrett glanced at the weapon again. "I see the army's order as a challenge. When do I leave?"

"Thursday you will leave for Brandy Station by train."

Barrett questioned him further. "And the rifles?"

"They are on their way. The ammunition—five thousand rounds—is being transported separately. Both shipments will be closely guarded."

Barrett's eyes were clear and intense. He directed his words to Cornelius. "You put five hundred men on a ridge with these rifles and the battle is over. The enemy will be picked off like cans lined up on a fence." He took a deep breath. "Are you coming with me?"

"Me? No. This is your baby. The commanders are already convinced that you're the man for the job. Your job is to train the men, and at the same time convince the commanders that this is the rifle of the future. You, in essence, will be representing New Haven Arms."

Barrett cleared his dry throat. "Five thousand rounds will not go far."

"That's just for target practice. We have another fifty-thousand rounds coming soon after. The plan is for each soldier to go into the field with a hundred rounds."

"Even fifty thousand rounds will go quickly."

"The plans are to ship twenty-five thousand rounds every seven days, until the war is over."

"That will keep your company busy."

"Ah, yes… twenty four hours a day. We will have to hire more people… a lot more." Cornelius wrapped the gun back up.

"Where do you go from here?"

"I am going home to rest for a few days."

"Will you stop in and see how Brooke is doing?" Barrett's eyes lit up at the thought of his wife.

"Certainly. When was the last time you saw her?"

"Six weeks ago... briefly on her birthday. Maybe I can take some leave after this trip is over," Barrett mumbled, wondering if it would ever happen. The dismayed soldier looked heavenward. "I hate this war... so many men are dying needlessly. Will it ever end?"

Chapter Eighteen

March 28, 1864
Brandy Station, Virginia

The sky was still dark, but the darkness had that eerie quality it takes on when the sun begins to threaten it. The train whistle, sounding like a forlorn howl, added to the eeriness. The brakes hissed and screeched as the train finally halted long enough to allow a group of soldiers to cross the tracks.

The plethora of sounds didn't distract Captain von Weber. He was captivated by the hundreds of men marching in broken formation as he stared out the window of the train. It seemed as if they were being drawn like lambs to a slaughter. With pity, he watched them walk aimlessly to what could be their demise—their sunken empty eyes, their hollow faces, their weakened bodies. *How much time do they have before they become another nameless causality*? He tried to shrug the thought away, but it wouldn't leave.

Finally, the train continued to its destination.

Von Weber had visited many battlefields. One of his jobs was to evaluate a battle scene after the fighting was over. Had the soldiers been in the right formation? What should be done differently in the next skirmish to save lives?

He had seen hundreds of good men sprawled on the ground, dead or still suffering as they teetered on the brink of death. He often uttered prayers for those men and their families—their wives, sons and daughters, mothers and fathers, brothers and sisters. He looked at each gruesome scene, shook his head, and whispered repeatedly, "When will this senseless killing stop?"

When the train arrived at Brandy Station where Grant's winter quarters were located, a stern sergeant major paced out to meet von Weber.

The sergeant gave Barrett a lazy salute. "I'm Sergeant Major Perry. I take care of troop placement for General Grant. He sent me to pick you up."

"Thank you, Sergeant Major," von Weber replied, returning the salute.

"Come with me," he grunted. "Wagon is nearby."

Barrett's heart was heavy as they rode by thousands of dingy-white tents. He could see beaten down and exhausted men. The smoke from hundreds of fires was thick, causing many to cough, and the cold morning air did not help the soldiers' already weakened lungs. The camp was disease ridden. Food and clean water were scarce.

He noticed that each man carried an old Springfield rifle. *Pathetic... our men fighting a war with outdated equipment. They need modern weapons if they are to survive.*

The aloofness of the sergeant major took Barrett by surprise. Not one to be afraid of confrontation, he challenged, "Do you have a problem with me?"

The sergeant rudely replied, "I can't stand cowards who hide behind their rank or civilian influence."

Stunned, Barrett asked, "Is that what you think?"

"Not think... know!" he bluntly retorted. "I get tired of everyone saying... can't wait to see the Hymnist ... can't wait to hear him play. Well, to me you're just another Bible thumpin' preacher. And I had enough of those growing up."

Barrett was slow to reply. "I guess there is no use talking with you because your mind is already made up."

The sergeant major scowled at Barrett. "You got that right. Another thing I can't stand is a man who not only believes in a Higher Power, but quotes a book that is filled with tall tales."

Barrett looked dejected, but not for long. "I take it you are familiar with the Bible?"

"My mother took me to church every Sunday. She forced me to read it repeatedly. But, that God of hers could not save her from the typhoid that ran through our town. She prayed for a cure... I prayed for her to be cured... but it never happened. Even the priest died from it. Now, I know what you are going to say, it was all God's plan," he said scathingly. "God's plan? I suppose this war is also God's plan. No, sir." He accentuated the word 'sir' more as mockery than as a term of respect.

With that, the conversation was over. Neither man said anything more the rest of the trip.

The wagon stopped at a small, wooden building. Four men dressed in clean blue coats, each carrying a Springfield rifle, stood guard.

Barrett eyed them. *How sad! Even Grant's bodyguards do not have the new, updated weapons.*

Perry stepped out of the wagon and barked, "Wait here."

It had been four years since Barrett had seen Grant. Even that was not a real meeting, just a brief encounter.

The door squeaked open, and the sergeant major motioned for Barrett to follow him inside. The small building was dark and grimy. The smell of cigar smoke overpowered the faint aroma of coffee. The mixture of both smells made von Weber queasy for a second.

Barrett's attention was drawn to a man dressed in dark clothing, sitting alone in a dim corner. He assumed he was a high-ranking officer. He nodded a greeting, and von Weber responded the same way.

Lanterns illuminated a large table where a number of officers were conferring. A man leaning over a map on the table glanced up. In a gravelly voice, he spoke to the men around him, "Gentlemen, please leave so I can chat with the captain."

The men slowly exited the room, each glaring at Barrett on his way out.

After they had cleared the room, the man at the table stood up straight with a glass in one hand, and an unlit cigar in his mouth. "Captain Barrett von Weber, do you know who I am?"

Without hesitation, Barrett responded, "You are General Grant, sir. You were the man who believed I could hit the fence post at President Lincoln's celebration."

"Yes. I remember that day well!" he chuckled. He gestured to the man in the corner who remained seated. "This gentleman, although I use the term loosely, is General Sherman."

Sherman nodded.

Barrett responded, "Ah... I've heard stories about you, General Sherman."

"All good, I hope," Sherman snickered.

"I have heard you are a man who leaves no stones unturned."

"I like that better than some of the other things people have said. Although I do like to be called Uncle Billy... makes me feel part of the family."

Barrett gave a small grin, uncertain how to take the well-known general.

Grant ran a finger across his scruffy chin. "Captain von Weber, do you know why you are here?"

"I believe it is to train men how to use the new Henry rifle." Barrett's answer was swift.

"That is not exactly true... now." Grant hesitated as a frown creased his brow. "We have a new problem."

Barrett stepped closer.

Grant sighed. "I will get straight to the point. A few days ago, the Henry rifles and the ammunition shipments were stolen."

Barrett groaned, "No!" Trying to get a handle on the news, he paused before he spoke further. "Sir, if they get into the hands of the South, an entire battalion of Union soldiers could be wiped out. I thought precautions were being taken to ensure this wouldn't happen."

"All the men guarding the weapons were killed, and all the bodies were found except one. The uniforms were stripped off some of the soldiers. We later found out that the ammunition had also been stolen in the same way. So right now, we have a shipment of rifles and two shipments of ammunition heading somewhere—we just do not know where. We assume they must be headed to Lee's army."

Grant pointed to the map. "The Union successfully split the Confederate Army at Vicksburg. General Johnson is in control of one army, and Lee is in control of the other. We know where Johnson's army is and its size, but we have no idea about Lee's. That is why we need your help."

"Why me?"

"Because of who you are."

"And General Grant... just who am I?" Barrett kept direct eye contact with him.

"Why, you're the man that shot the top off that fence post over two hundred yards away. There are not many men who could do that, especially without a scope on the rifle." He shook his head, grinning. "I am in need of an excellent sharpshooter."

"For what purpose?" Barrett didn't blink, waiting for a response.

Grant glanced at Sherman, and then pointed to a rough map on the table in front of them. "Here we are. Here is Atlanta. General Sherman and I have devised a plan and Lincoln has agreed to it. Shortly, Sherman will march toward Atlanta. His job is to cut a path through the center of the Confederate states, causing utter havoc. As I said, the problem is Lee's army has apparently disappeared from the face of this earth. I have sent over a dozen scouting units out to find him and his army. Unfortunately, none of them have returned."

Barrett stared at the map, motionless.

Grant lit his cigar. "Many of my generals predict he is heading north. I personally think he's bedded down somewhere in Southern Virginia or Tennessee. The defeats at Gettysburg and Vicksburg have crushed his morale. He has not won many battles since. I think the old man is cooking up something special for us Bluebellies."

Von Weber swallowed hard. "Any possibility Lee has retreated, so he could send his troops to defend Richmond or Atlanta?"

"I wish that was the case, but I believe he has ordered Johnson to keep me busy fighting while his army regroups," Grant replied.

From the corner of the room, Sherman voiced, "No! I think Bobby Lee has hidden himself somewhere south of Virginia, and is waiting for a gift of five hundred rifles and fifty-five thousand rounds of ammunition."

A shudder ran through Barrett. "Sir, we have to move quickly before the weapons and ammunition reaches the battlefield. Where did the thefts take place?" His voice grew louder, more lively.

"Just inside the Virginia state line." Grant pointed to the location on the map. "It is unknown how many men were involved in each of the robberies. In all three cases, everyone guarding the shipments was killed, except one. We suspect those men were in on it and had help... a lot of it. The Union soldiers guarding the shipments were mowed down without having a chance to return fire."

Von Weber's eyes were clear, intense. "That's unbelievable. How could something like this happen?"

"It was definitely an inside job... pulled off with utmost secrecy. The Confederacy is losing the war. Our blockade is working, only a few ships from Europe make it through. The Southerners are starving. Their army is running out of ammo and guns. It is just a matter of time before they surrender."

Barrett cleared his throat. "General Grant, I think you underestimate the Confederates. They are hard to the core—many are backwoodsmen. They can last months in the harshest conditions by living off the land. They can bag a coon, or a squirrel for food, and eat mushrooms and tree bark. You are not up against Northern city dwellers like those that I have been training. The Rebels have a cause to fight for, no matter how feeble you think it is."

"Defending slavery is not a cause," Perry blurted out.

"You think they are only fighting for slavery?" Barrett asked, raising an eyebrow.

"Well, isn't that the cause of the war," the sergeant major snapped.

Barrett shook his head. "Many of the Southern politicians are fighting for slavery, but the average Southern citizen is fighting for something more."

"Like?" The sergeant major asked, waiting for a reply.

"Freedom—the right to exist without tyranny and the thumb of the government pressing down on them."

The smirk on Perry's face was evidence of his contempt. "Freedom... don't make me laugh. We are fighting for freedom for the slaves."

Anger rose quickly in his gut, but Barrett suppressed it. "You think that, but let me set you straight, Sergeant Major. The Northern politicians are trying to change the Southerners' way of thinking. Yes, the core issue is slavery, but Confederate soldiers are fighting for their individual rights to exist under their state constitution. They will follow their leaders like General Lee into battle, and if necessary, to their death."

Barrett stared at Grant. "Sir, you know General Lee and General Johnson. You know how they command, and how admired they are by their men. You also know how much they love this country—The United States of America—not just the Confederate States of America. They will never give up without a fight!"

The sergeant major was quick to reply. "That's why we have to cut off the head of the snake—Lee, and others like him. If we do that, it will end the war."

"The only way you will stop the South is to destroy it entirely." Barrett struggled to keep his voice even.

Grant glanced at Sherman and took a lengthy puff on his cigar. He shifted his gaze to Barrett. "You, sir, are astute. Lincoln should have put you on his staff from the beginning."

"General, what do you want from me?" Barrett exhaled through pursed lips.

"What I say here, stays here... understand?"

Von Weber nodded, but a sick feeling hit him like a freezing winter wind, taking his breath.

"General Sherman leaves in a couple days with seventy-five thousand men. Their orders are to march south to Atlanta, then to the sea, destroying everything in their path—railroads, cotton fields, manufacturing plants. Everything!"

Barrett stood straighter. "Sir, how can you supply seventy-five thousand men who are marching a thousand miles?"

His reply was swift and sure. "They will be living off the land. Taking what they need along the way."

"Taking what they need?" Barrett stiffened. "Sir, with all due respect, you are inviting rape and murder of innocent women and children."

Perry jumped in, cynically, "There are no innocent individuals in the time of...."

"Sergeant Major Perry, mind your tongue," Grant reprimanded.

Perry snapped to attention, silencing his words, anger covered his face.

Grant continued, "The men are bound by an oath. They are not to enter private homes, or hurt innocent civilians."

"You think that an oath will stop that?" Barrett clenched his jaw and waited.

"I pray that it will." Grant paced over to a small table against the wall and retrieved an item wrapped in burlap. He handed it to von Weber.

Barrett continued to speak, "General, with all due respect, if you allow a common soldier to take anything from a private citizen, North or South, you are asking for bigger problems. And if you think for a moment that these men will follow orders in a situation like that, then I am afraid, sir, you are sadly mistaken. I saw what these men look like. They have been away from their wives for months... years. They crave companionship and food, and will do whatever they want to get it. And you will have no control of them, sir."

Barrett looked down at the wrapped item he was holding. "What is this?"

Grant nodded his head "Go ahead, open it."

He removed the burlap. "It's a scoped Whitworth, a sharpshooter's rifle." Von Weber looked into Grant's eyes, moving closer to him. "It is better known as a sniper's rifle. I've fired one before, but never seen one with a scope like this."

Sergeant Major Perry added, "That's right. A good marksman can hit a deer at five hundred yards. An excellent marksman can hit a rabbit at five hundred yards. What can you do with it?"

Von Weber scanned the room, noticing all three men staring at him. "Ah... I'm beginning to understand the situation." He looked directly into Grant's eyes. "You want me to find General Lee and...." He paused, trying to frame his words wisely. "With all due respect, sir, I am a freedom fighter. I will fight and die, if necessary, for the freedom of this country, what it stands for, and for my fellow man. It's the last part that you may not understand—I will die for my fellow man... God would have me do no less. But sir, I have never been, nor will I ever be an assassin."

"You're disobeying a direct order from General Grant. That is considered treason and you can be sent in front of a firing squad," Perry shouted.

Barrett shot back. "Sergeant Major, General Grant has yet to order me to do it." He looked at Grant. "I obey one Supreme Commander and that is God Almighty. Again, I tell you, I will defend my country, my life, my family, and the lives of other innocent people from harm."

When Perry opened his mouth to make another comment, Grant quieted him. "Sergeant Major, back off." His face showed his seriousness.

"But, sir, this man...."

"This man is a righteous man, which is exactly why I chose him." He shifted his focus back to Barrett. "Captain von Weber, find those weapons, and ammunition... and make sure they are destroyed. And if you locate Lee and his army, let us know where they are as quickly as possible. Time is critical. Leave the rest to us."

Captain von Weber thought for a second. "I will find the rifles, and I will find Lee, but I will not assassinate the man." He took a deep breath. "However, I do have one condition."

"And that would be?" Grant inquired.

"I pick my own team."

Perry interrupted, "Why would you want to do that? I have some capable men ready to join you."

"I'm sure you do, but I need men I can trust."

"Done!" Grant agreed. "Pick your own men, but remember that if you are caught, you could be shot as spies."

Without hesitation, Barrett added, "I realize that, sir."

"Well then, Major von Weber, you better get a move on. Find Lee and his army before it's too late—for all of us."

"You said Major von Weber?" Perry questioned Grant.

"Yes, I thought seriously about promoting him to a colonel, but that would be too close to my rank. I do not intend to lose my job. Now, get a move on, Major."

Von Weber snapped his heels and saluted the general.

Grant returned the salute. "Sergeant Major, see to it that he gets everything he needs. Take him to General Custer to be briefed. And be civil to him... that's an order!"

"Yes, sir," Perry agreed.

Barrett headed to the door, but stopped abruptly. He turned back to General Grant. "Sir, if something happens and I fail to return, will you do me one favor?"

"What is that, Major?"

"Will you personally pay a visit to my wife, Brooke, and tell her... tell her I love her."

Stepping forward, the general extended his hand.

Barrett reciprocated with a heartfelt handshake.

"You have a beautiful wife. I could tell at that party how much she adores you. Major, you have my word on that. If this war is finished and you have not returned home, I will personally seek her out."

"Thank you, sir."

As the major turned to leave, General Sherman tipped his hat.

Barrett nodded back.

"Godspeed, Major. Godspeed," Sherman uttered.

Barrett stepped outside and took a breath of the smoky air. He looked heavenward, feeling like he had the weight of the world on his shoulders.

Inside the building, Sherman stood. "Interesting man."

"Indeed. I wish I had an army of soldiers like him," Grant stated with certainty.

"Yes, I hope Lee does not have men of Barrett von Weber's quality."

"True."

Sherman took a deep breath. "Ulysses, you have put a lot of trust in von Weber. Why are you so sure that he can do the job?"

Grant picked up his glass and examined it in the dim light. Seeing it was empty, he placed it back on the table. "Let me ask you a question. If you had a choice, would you pick a man like Davy Crockett, or God, to ride with you?"

Sherman laughed. "You know me... I'm not a religious man. I would have to pick Crockett—what a brave fighter he was."

"I would pick von Weber."

"You didn't put him in the mix!"

"Yes I did... I said Crockett or God. Von Weber walks with God. My goodness, how many men would disobey an order from the General of the Army for the cause of righteousness?"

"No man in his right mind." Sherman shook his head.

"Only a man who trusts God with his life."

Sherman stepped closer. "General, do you think he will do it? I mean kill Lee."

"No, but he will find him, so I'd better be ready to march when he does."

"I guess I'd better prepare for my march as well." Sherman picked up his hat.

"Indeed. History awaits you... it may not be good... but it awaits you."

Sherman shook Grant's hand and stepped out the door—into his uncertain future.

Chapter Nineteen

Von Weber followed Perry to an encampment of men that the sergeant major had personally selected to help find the missing shipments.

Barrett understood the importance on getting the right team together. He studied the hardened men as he traipsed through the camp. Not a smile appeared on any of them; the soldiers' eyes were cold, dark, empty. Almost three years of war had left confusion clouding the men's faces. Emotionless, they waited for the unknown events of the next day.

Von Weber noticed small pieces of paper nailed to trees and the sides of an outhouse. He walked closer to read a few of them.

Perry explained, "Men, women, and even some children come here and post notes looking for their family members. Not sure it does any good. It is a big country and these men have been all over the place. A soldier finding a note from his family ain't likely gonna happen."

A larger poster captured Barrett's interest. He moved closer to it.

"That there is a wanted poster. Lot of bad men out there going their own way, thinking war gives them the right to break the law. Many deserters from both sides are on a rampage of their own. The military has a price on their heads."

Barrett looked closer at the poster he was reading. "What about this one? Know anything about him?"

Perry looked at it and snickered. "He's a bad one. Don't know a lot about him. Raids the North and then disappears back into the South. People say he's one of The Gray Ghosts. All they know about him is the color of his horse. Not a lot to go on."

Barrett tore the paper off the wall, neatly folded it, and put it in his pocket. "I will need to keep a lookout for him and his gang."

Perry halted in front of a dozen men that he had chosen as potential recruits for the mission.

Even though Barrett was intent on picking his own team, he felt it would only be right to look objectively at Perry's selections.

Perry sounded confident as he spoke. "I've had a watchful eye on these men. They are cavalry trained from different units. Even though they do not know what the assignment is, they have volunteered. All have been through many a battle. Hard core to the bone. You will be impressed."

Von Weber shuffled from one foot to the other.

Perry barked at the soldiers perched next to the dusty road. "Fall in line men, so we can get your names."

Barrett eyed the men as they slowly made their way to their feet, mumbling words that he would never repeat. They stumbled into a short, crooked line. The men were rough; anyone could tell by their scars that they had been through battles. Some stood slumped. A couple others scratched their heads, in a daze. One yawned. A few dangled cigarettes from their mouths. Discipline was apparently not a major concern for these men.

Perry yanked the smokes from the men's mouths, "You know better than that," he muttered, throwing the cigarettes to the ground and grinding them into the dirt with his heel.

Barrett continued to size up the group.

He stopped in front of the one who had yawned. "You seem bored, soldier," Barrett charged.

"Hard night," the aging soldier replied. "I need to kill some more Johnny Rebs."

"Hard night you say?" Barrett leaned closer and sniffed the toothless soldier's breath. His body smelled unwashed, but his breath reeked of alcohol. "I bet it was." He stared at him for a moment, making the man uneasy. "What's your name, soldier?"

"Billy Moffit."

"Where are you from, Billy?"

"Nowhere in particular," the soldier grumbled.

"Do you know where you were born?"

"Pennsylvania."

"Pennsylvania. That's a big state... can you narrow that down for me? Where in Pennsylvania?" Barrett was becoming annoyed, but persisted.

"Does it really matter?" The soldier stood a little straighter.

"I suppose not. What did you do before the war?"

"Nothing really. Just traveled from town to town looking for odd jobs."

Barrett continued, "Where did you spend most of your time?"

"As close to a bar as I could, I suspect," the soldier chortled, amused with his remark.

The men beside him hooted.

Barrett was not entertained. He stared directly into Moffit's eyes without even a hint of a smile. "Married? Any children?"

"Tried gettin' hitched once. Didn't work for me. As for kids, I think I may have a few. The number of women I been with must have some extra mouths to feed somewhere. Not sure." He glanced at the other men, trying to coax them to laugh.

A few chuckled, nervously.

Barrett moved to the next man in line and stood nose-to-nose. "What about you? What's your story?"

"Me? I been in the army since I was a boy."

"How many years is that?"

"I 'spect 'bout ten."

Barrett noticed his rank. "And you're still a private?"

"Well...." The man smirked. "I fight a lot. That why I'm in army. Me good fighter. Never back down." He glared at Barrett, challenging the officer to select him.

"I see. Do you obey orders?" He waited for an answer, but never received one.

Barrett shook his head and continued down the line of men. "Anyone here ever killed a man?"

"In battle?" one asked.

"Humor me. In battle or out," Barrett shouted.

"I've killed dozens. We all have," a voice rang out.

Another yelled, "In battles and bars."

The men laughed.

Barrett looked hard at the soldier who made the comment.

The man moved his gaze to the ground and began scribbling in the dirt with his old, ratty boots.

"Thank you, gentlemen. You're dismissed." Realizing he was wasting his time, von Weber walked away.

Confused, Perry quizzed, "What's wrong, Major?"

"Not the right men!" Barrett responded, directly.

Perry let out a huff of breath, but decided it best not to comment.

Von Weber studied the dozens of men around him, many meandering aimlessly, staring into space. He could tell the men were beaten down, tired of fighting, wanting to go home.

Unexpectedly, Barrett shouted in a booming voice. "Gentlemen, listen up. I have been ordered to find Lee's army. I am in need of a half dozen soldiers who can live off the land, follow me, and obey my every command—men who are familiar with the lay of the land in the south. Are there any volunteers?"

As he spoke, some gave him a shooting glance or a quick, half-hearted salute; others ignored him as they milled around. Only the faint utterances of complaints could be heard.

"Told ya you weren't gonna get any volunteers. Those twelve men are your best bet," Perry sneered.

"Sergeant Major, those men will never obey any orders I give them. They will do what they want and listen to me only if it helps them." Barrett frowned.

He stepped closer to Perry and lowered his voice. "There is a good possibility that if we find the weapons, we may find gold, as well. If that happens, I know I would have no control over those men. None whatsoever! I want to do my job, find the stolen supplies, and locate Lee. I cannot do that if I spend all my time looking over my back."

A well-fit black man, dressed in a torn Union outfit, had been leaning on a nearby stump. Hearing Barrett's plea, he ambled over. "I go with ya, Massa."

"We need military persons, not slaves," Perry was swift to reply.

"Don't be hasty." Barrett raised his hand signaling for the sergeant major to stand down. "Soldier, do you know the area?"

"I cut lumber and delivered hogs over much of Virginia and Carolinas for Massa Roundtree. He dead now, so I sign up in blue army."

"I suppose you joined to fight for the cause," Perry scoffed.

"No, suh. I joined cuz I wanted to eat… and find my son."

"Your son?" Barrett angled his head.

"Yes, suh. He was born right before we got off the boat. Wife died birthin' him."

Barrett assumed he was talking about a slave ship, but didn't ask. "When was the last time you saw your boy?"

"That day my wife died. He be taken somewhere by the ship's captain."

"Are you a slave?"

"No, suh. Massa Roundtree won me in a card game, fair and square. Told me I was free. I not know what free means; I work for 'em 'til he dead. Tree fell on 'em. I try ta save 'em, but he dead just the same."

"Go sit down," Perry grumbled, frustrated. "You're wasting our time."

Barrett challenged Perry. "No! Come here, soldier. Sounds like Mr. Roundtree was a good man. What is your name?"

"He was good man... tried to help me find my boy. Massa Roundtree call me Jerry, so that what I call me. Jerry. Jerry Roundtree. He taught me everythin' I know."

"Well, that sure wasn't much. Now get back where you belong," Perry mumbled, shoving him away.

Major von Weber put his arm out, stopping the mean-spirited Perry.

Barrett turned to the onlookers. "Looks like I have one volunteer. His name is Jerry. Are there any other brave men here?"

"Mister, sounds like you're asking us to commit suicide. We be marching right into Rebel territory," someone charged.

Barrett eyed the challenger closer. "No! I'm asking for volunteers to help me find Lee's army. Let's put an end to this senseless killing, so we all can return to our families and farms. Soldier, you look like a farmer. I suspect you have a farm, don't you?"

"Had a real nice farm once. Raised hogs and sheep in Virginia—Highland County. Had a job in the local town, too. But, Rebels destroyed it in '62. Wrecked my town and my farm. Managed to get my family out before they ransacked my home and burnt it down."

Barrett stepped closer to him, his voice showing compassion. "I'm sorry to hear that, soldier. Where is your family now?"

"Wife and son died of 'monia that winter. Had no place to stay, thanks to the Rebs. So I joined the Union Army to pay them Southerners back for taking my home and family from me."

Barrett searched the soldier's rugged face. "You look like you can trap a rabbit, strip it, and cook it in twenty minutes."

"More like fifteen, sir."

"Then you're just the man I need. Join me and let's find Lee. Maybe we can persuade him to surrender."

The man forced a small smile.

A wrinkle-faced man who had been listening, stood up, brushed himself off, and strutted over to Barrett. He was dressed in an oversized Union coat and a Rebel officer's hat that covered his entire forehead. Three bloodstained holes in the front of his coat caught the major's attention. He assumed his clothing was taken from dead soldiers. A shiny, gold plated Confederate sword hung tight to his side.

A closer look revealed that he was an Indian. The man never said a word, just motioned with his hands. Barrett assumed he couldn't speak English. The Indian pointed to himself and then back to the major.

"You want to come with us?" von Weber asked slowly, enunciating clearly. He figured the man could understand a little English, even if he couldn't speak it.

The red-skinned man nodded.

"What can you do?"

The Indian moved his fingers as if they were walking, and then put his hand to his forehead looking around as if he was searching for something.

"You're a tracker?" Barrett inquired, understanding the motions.

The Indian nodded his head vigorously.

Another man stepped next to them and pointed to the Indian. "That there is Moccasin. That's what we call him anyway. We call him that because you can't hear him when he walks. He's a Cherokee Indian and he ain't got no tongue. Near as I can tell, he's from somewhere in Tennessee. Best tracker around... he could track a lizard in an acre of boulders if you asked him to."

Barrett shifted his gaze to the man who was talking. He was short, perhaps five feet tall. "What's your name, soldier?"

"Francis Wheaton, sir. Don't like the name Francis, so people call me 'Wheaty.' Anyhow, story goes that Moccasin was just a boy when Davy Crockett saved him from a mountain lion. Never left Crockett's side after that. Tracked with him all the way down to Texas. He got drunk a couple days before the Battle of the Alamo and got fresh with a senorita. A bunch of town folks thought they would teach him a lesson, so they cut out his tongue—left him in the alley to bleed to death. Problem was they also got drunk that night, so drunk they all passed out on the floor of the saloon. Moccasin here walked in with a knife that Jim Bowie had given him and scalped them all alive. I heard say that Moccasin was red that night, not because of his skin, if you get what I mean. He still has that same knife." The little man pointed to the sheath strapped to the Indian's side.

Barrett listened keenly.

Wheaty continued, "Story is, after he scalped them he took off running. He returned to the Alamo a few weeks later to join in the fight, but he was too late. The only thing he saw were the graves of his friends. He jus' wanted to die with them. I guess it is an Indian tradition that when you fail, you cut yourself. Moccasin has scars all over his arms, and has had a death wish ever since. Never got to fight and die bravely next to his friend, Davy Crockett. You should see him fight the Johnny Rebs. That officer's hat he's wearing is his souvenir from Gettysburg. Killed the Rebel officer in hand-to-hand combat. Killed another high-ranking Reb at the battle of Fredericksburg—I saw that one. That's where he got the sword. He always keeps a souvenir. He's not supposed to scalp anyone, so he takes something else."

"Does he understand us?" Barrett eyed the Indian.

"Oh, he understands us all right. Just can't talk. He can help lead us... that's for sure. He knows the South like the back of his hand."

"I noticed you said he can lead 'us.' Does that mean you are coming, too?"

The man nodded. "If he goes, I go. That Indian saved my life at Gettysburg."

A tall soldier leaning against a tree, laughed at von Weber. "Captain, you're crazier than a black bear being woke up in the middle of winter. I would like to join you in this adventure. If for no other reason than to watch what you do. It should be interesting—an old Indian without a tongue, a black man lookin' for his boy, a Southern farmer, and Tom Thumb. Looks like I will be the only normal one in the bunch."

"What's your story? You seem to be well versed. Few people have ever mentioned Tom Thumb from English folklore."

"Story? I have no story."

"We all have stories, Mr...."

"Alexander Budnikov. People call me Alex."

"That's Bulgarian, isn't it?"

"Yes, sir. Born, but not raised."

Barrett held his hand out. "Well, Alex, welcome to the team."

Another man quickly volunteered. "I come too. I go where my brother, Alex, go. Krasnov, sir. Boris Krasnov."

"Brothers, with different names?"

Alex replied, "Not blood brothers—brothers from the same country—Bulgaria."

"I actually have visited there, never saw so many trees in my life," von Weber declared with a smile.

The major turned to the farmer who had yet to commit. "Soldier, what about you?"

The farmer spit on the ground, and then fixed his gaze on the others who had moved to Barrett's side. "Is the darky really comin' with ya?"

Without hesitation, Barrett replied, "Yes, he is. Do you men have any objections to that?" he motioned to the other soldiers.

They shook their heads.

"No, sir. As I see, even though our skin is different, our blood is still red," Alex retorted.

"What about you?" Barrett turned back to the farmer. "Do you have a problem with Jerry, or Moccasin, for that matter?"

"I was raised with Indians. A problem with Jerry, suh? Nah! I just needed to know that there was someone as dumb as me going with you."

"What are you talking about, boy? We all fit in that category. Anyone volunteering for this job has got to be dumb," Alex shouted, halfway chuckling.

"Or brave," the major shot back.

Perry shook his head. "Major, you can't be serious. These men? I don't think you realize how important this mission is."

"Oh, I understand all right… that is why I have chosen these men. I believe I can trust them." He hesitated. "Besides, I have a special use for each one of them. They each have a contribution to make."

"I hope you know what you are doing, Major von Weber." Follow me, men… General Custer needs to fill you in. After that, I will take you to get your equipment."

"Custer?" Wheaty smiled. "The… General Custer?"

"The one and only," Perry answered bluntly.

"Do you know him?" Barrett asked Wheaty.

Wheaty chuckled. "Not personally, but I know of him. I was part of the 1st Michigan Cavalry at Gettysburg. He led an attack that busted right through the Rebel's line. I was hurt real bad only hours before. That is when Moccasin saved me. My horse was shot out from under me. I was about to be stabbed with a bayonet, and out of nowhere this Indian dressed in a Union outfit, jumped on top of the Reb and slashed his throat. He pulled me from underneath my horse and took me to safety. Messed up my leg bad. That's how Moccasin saved my life and how he got his hat."

"Cavalry? So you know about horses?"

"Do I know about horses? I used to race them in my hometown back in Michigan. My short size is good for something. Never lost a race… well, almost never."

"How about your leg?"

"Just like new."

Barrett turned back to the other men. "Okay, men, gather up your belongings, and let's go with the sergeant major."

The six men grabbed what little they had and followed close behind von Weber.

As they walked, Barrett reflected on the men behind him. *I am pleased with my selections. They certainly do not look like professional soldiers; we should easily blend in with the Southerners. This should be an interesting venture. We need to trust God to guide our way.*

Chapter Twenty

Barrett's mind raced with thoughts as he and the men followed Perry to Custer's tent. *We will be heading into enemy territory. How can I do my job, yet bring these men back alive? What is the best way to find those weapons, destroy them, and find Lee? Should we go back to the scene of the crime?*

A gust of wind jolted him back to reality.

When they reached the large tent, a lieutenant stepped out to greet them. "Lieutenant Roth, here."

Perry saluted the officer. "Sir, these are the men who will be headed out on the mission. This is Major von Weber."

Eyeing Barrett, the lieutenant saluted back. "Sergeant Major, you called him major, but I see captain bars on him."

"General Grant just promoted him to major, sir."

"I see. Thank you, I will take it from here."

Perry looked at Barrett grinning, and shook his head. "Good luck, Major—you are going to need it with this bunch."

Barrett turned his attention to Roth and the task ahead of him.

Without wasting time, the officer questioned, "Major, do you understand what your mission is?"

"Yes sir, I have been briefed, but they have not." He nodded in the direction of his men.

Speaking to the team of men, the lieutenant continued, "You will get the specifics in a moment. First, you are going to meet General Custer. Don't be shocked by his age; he is only twenty-four. Let me warn you, he is not in a good mood right now. It seems a deserter stole his horse last night and took off with it. That horse is as important to him as his new bride is. So be careful what you say to him, he can get rather perturbed."

They followed Roth into the tent where they noticed a thin man with long, blonde, curly hair leaning over a table. A single kerosene lantern hanging overhead illuminated his long nose, sunken eyes, and trimmed goatee.

"Well, I'll be hogtied," Wheaty excitedly spouted. "That is General Custer!"

Barrett turned to his men and ordered, "Attention!"

The men snapped to attention.

Barrett saluted the young general. "Sir, Major von Weber reporting."

Custer straightened and turned from the table, looking directly into von Weber's eyes. "At ease, Major."

The general stared down the line of men, eyeing them one-by-one. He scratched his chin. After a short time, he shifted his gaze to the lieutenant. "Land sakes, Lieutenant Roth, is this the best you can do?" He reached for a tin cup and brought it to his lips.

The lieutenant shrugged his shoulders, uncertain how to respond.

Custer handed his cup to the lieutenant and moved closer to examine Barrett. "Von Weber? German, I suppose."

"Yes, sir."

"I thought you were a major, but I see captain bars on you." The general pointed to Barrett's shoulder insignia.

"It is now, major. General Grant promoted me."

"Well, let's get the right rank on you."

Custer faced Roth. "See to it this man gets his gold leaf, Lieutenant."

"Yes, sir, right away."

Barrett added, "Also, Lieutenant Roth, I need civilian clothes for me and my men, including what an Indian would wear. I want us to blend with the southern population."

The young officer looked back at Custer who nodded his head in approval. He pulled the tent door back and exited.

Turning back to Barrett the general asked, "What did your family do in Germany?"

"They operated a winery, sir."

"A winery... I'm a whiskey man myself, but I have tasted some mighty fine wine. What did you do, Major, before all this insanity began?"

"I was a concert pianist. I wrote hymns."

"Von Weber?" The general's eyes grew wide "Ah, yes, the famous Hymnist."

"Yes, sir."

"Land sakes, you're a national treasure. You can't be leading this raid."

Barrett chuckled.

Custer walked closer to the men to scrutinize them. He stepped in front of each one, eyeing him from head to toe. He made his way down the line of misfits—a five-foot horse jockey, an Indian without a tongue, a black man, a farmer, and two men from Bulgaria. *They look like six ragamuffins.*

It took a couple minutes before Custer spoke. Finally, he laughed, "My word, where's the Irish-Arab?

"I'm part Irish," the farmer responded. "My mother was an O'Hara."

Custer stared at him. "Are you Arab?"

"No, sir. Ain't never seen no Arab. At least, I don't think so."

"Where are you from, soldier?"

"Virginia," Jackson replied.

"What did you do there?"

"I had a farm, sir, and made shoes, too," he answered proudly.

"Shoes. Good profession. I love boots… comfortable boots."

"We made those too, sir."

Custer stared at him for a moment and then cast his glance on the others. "Who on earth picked these men?"

"I did, sir," von Weber asserted.

Custer stepped in front of him, standing almost nose-to-nose.

"Major, may I ask why, out of thousands of soldiers, did you choose these… these six?" He rolled his eyes.

"Did not choose them, sir, they all volunteered."

"I see. But, you did accept them when they volunteered, correct?"

"Yes, sir. Jerry, the black one, along with Moccasin…."

"Don't tell me. He's an Indian, right?"

"Yes, sir. Jerry knows the country, and Moccasin, I understand is one of the best trackers in the world. Rumor has it he can track a lizard over an acre of boulders."

Custer shook his head. "No one can track anything over boulders."

"Moccasin can, sir. I seen him," the short man insisted.

Custer turned his focus to Wheaty. "And what did you do before the war?"

"I worked in a stable and was a horse jockey, sir. I rode with the 1st Michigan Cavalry at Gettysburg."

Curious, Custer probed further, "You don't say. Were you in the charge?"

"I was in an earlier one, sir. They killed Bobby, my horse. Moccasin here saved my life."

"So you were not in the one that I commanded?"

"No, sir."

Custer watched him. "Good thing. You would have been killed. One of the craziest things I ever did, but it worked."

"Yes, sir."

He turned to the tall, slim man. "And you, soldier, what did you do before the war?"

"Carpenter, sir, like Jesus."

Custer chuckled. "I see. What kind of carpentry?"

"I like building rockin' chairs, but because of my height I was hired to build buildings. Hardly ever needed a ladder." He grinned.

Turning to Barrett the general asked, "Major, why did you pick him? There must be some reason."

"He wanted to be part of it."

"I see. What about shorty here?" He pointed to the shortest soldier in the bunch.

"Thought his size might come in handy... besides, he's an excellent rider."

Custer looked at Barrett for a long moment. Finally, he shook his head and walked over to the large table. "Gentlemen, please surround the table. Can any of you read?"

Alex, Wheaty, and von Weber raised their hands.

Turning to the major, he pointed out, "You write music, so you'd better be able to read. Anyone else?"

"I can write my name," the farmer responded.

"Let me guess. Your name is X," Custer snorted.

"No, suh, its Jack, Jack Jackson."

Custer stared into space. "This can't be happening," he muttered to himself.

The well-known general let out a sigh of exasperation. "Okay, listen up, men. Major, how much have the men been told?"

"Very little, sir."

"All right, listen closely, men. Three shipments of supplies were stolen–one shipment of highly sophisticated rifles, and two shipments of the ammunition for those rifles. We presume by Southern sympathizers. If the South gets these weapons, they could wipe out an entire Union battalion in a matter of minutes. Now, this here is what we in the military call a map." There was no denying the sarcasm in his voice. He pointed to the display on the table. "It shows a bird's eye view of the land." Custer picked up a long stick and hit the map.

He peered at the Indian. "Can he understand me? Can any of you understand me?" His voice grew louder. He directed his words to no one in particular.

Moccasin nodded; others grumbled.

Custer tapped the locations on the map when he mentioned them. "We are here. This is Gettysburg. After the battle at Gettysburg, Lee's army divided and went different directions. We had a few battles in Chattanooga and Knoxville, and then we took up camp here." He continued pointing to the flat board. "Grant intends to take his army to the east to confront Lee. However, we must find Lee first. If we can't find him, Grant will put a large army between the Confederate Army and Washington and wait."

The men listened, absorbing the information the general shared.

"The rifles and ammunition left New Haven, Connecticut, up here." Custer tapped a spot on the map and then dragged the pointer downward. "The shipments started out on a military train and reached Cumberland, Maryland. For security, all three shipments left from there, by wagon, on different routes, with seasoned military escorts. Unfortunately, they never made it to their destination—Brandy Station."

Barrett looked around his men making sure they were attentive.

"Thirty Union Cavalrymen were ambushed while protecting the load of rifles near Warrington. The rifles were stolen and all of the soldiers killed... except one, Sergeant Everett Hornsby, who is still unaccounted for."

"Any idea who ambushed them?" Wheaty asked.

"No! All of the shipments were stolen the same day, but at different locations in Virginia. We know it was an inside job, and we know who some of the traitors are."

"Inside job... interesting," Barrett commented.

Custer continued, "The small shipment of ammo was ambushed and stolen at Auburn. All guards were brutally killed, except Sergeant Ashley Moses, who is missing."

As the general spoke, the men were getting a clear picture of the enormity of their mission.

Custer cleared his throat. "Now, the large shipment of ammo was hijacked the same day at Maymarket. Like the other locations, a massacre took place. Only one soldier was unaccounted for—Lieutenant Frank Abbott, who was in charge of that load. We assume the three missing men were all working together."

"How could such an elaborate scheme be carried out?" Barrett asked, never breaking eye contact with the general.

"Hornsby knew about the three shipments beforehand. Matter of fact, he was involved in the logistics of each wagon—where and when it would travel. But, a spy, a traitor? We never suspected that!" Custer exhaled hard, loud.

"Besides the three men, anyone else involved?" Barrett inquired.

"We don't know exactly who, but there had to have been!"

"I would think he would want to get rid of the merchandise quickly," Barrett speculated, stepping back. "I believe this was done for money. Hornsby and the others sold out because of greed."

Custer stared at Barrett. "Interesting theory. You know, that is entirely possible," he uttered softly, as if he was thinking aloud.

"Any idea where they went?"

Custer shrugged a shoulder. "That will be your job to find out. We believe that all three shipments will take this route and probably rendezvous here." The general moved his stick to Richmond, Virginia. "I would suggest that you, Captain, excuse me, Major, head straight down and cut the shipments off before they reach their final destination. When you find them, you are to destroy the contents, and then continue on to find Lee's army. We believe they are camped around this area here." Custer hit the tip of his stick on a spot west of Richmond.

"Beg ya pardon, General, but that be dumb." The black man tilted one side of his mouth.

"Excuse me, Private." Custer drew out the word Private.

"What do you mean, Jerry?" Barrett intervened.

"I been all over them thar hills and trails. Suh, ya can't move guns and ammo 'round. Too hard, they be spotted! There be soldiers everywhere along them hills, both blue and gray. Them rifles gotta be hidden somehow, and them movin' slow." Jerry drawled emphatically.

The Indian signed something to Wheaty.

"What did he say?" Custer asked, wiping his brow.

"He says he wants to start tracking where the rifles were stolen," Wheaty translated.

"That will put you three or four days behind them," the general surmised.

Wheaty's eyes grew large as he excitedly told Custer what his Indian friend had said. "Moccasin agrees with Jerry... he thinks the rifles are hidden, somehow disguised. Think about it... the thieves cannot take the chance on the military finding the weapons if they plan to sell them. As Jerry said, there are checkpoints everywhere, both Union and Confederate. Rifles are bulky and ammo weighs a lot, so special wagons would be needed to transport the loads."

"The Indian said all that?" the general asked, dumfounded.

"I may have added a few words," Wheaty smiled.

"I think Moccasin and Jerry are right," Barrett confirmed. "Someone out there has a ton of gold waiting to purchase those weapons. It may not even be the Confederate States. It could be a slave owner, military commander, or even a foreign country."

Custer stared at Barrett. "Major, I don't care how you do it—just find those weapons... or the ammo. One is no good without the other. Then find Lee... find him, and do whatever you can to get word back to General Grant on his whereabouts."

He paused for a moment. "Men, you will be on your own. You will only have the provisions you can carry on your back. You will be in enemy territory. If you are caught... you will be shot as spies."

Barrett knew how serious the mission was, but still, hearing Custer's words sent a shiver up his spine.

No one commented—each soldier was taking in the information and trying to submit it to his memory.

Light from the outside shown in as the tent door swung open and Lieutenant Roth entered. "Sir, I cannot find any gold leaf insignia anywhere. I did manage to gather clothing for the men, but some may not fit. Perry's getting the rest of the stuff. The Indian outfit is hard to find."

Confronting von Weber, Custer commented, "Your insignia does not really matter right now because you will be dressed in civilian clothes. Once you leave this post, you will no longer be working for the Union Army but for New Haven Arms. That way if you are caught... well you just may escape the gallows."

"Yes, sir," Barrett agreed.

"This war has brought out the worst in mankind—you may run into some of those scoundrels. Do not take prisoners and be sure to cover your tracks. Putting it bluntly, shoot first, and don't bother to ask questions... the other side will not. Finding these weapons is top priority. Understood?"

Custer looked at the interesting group of oddballs. Some nodded, others muttered, but all agreed on the importance of their assignment.

The general walked over to another table and pulled back a large covering. "Major, here is the equipment you need—weapons, and supplies. I am going to step back. You're in charge of your men now." He walked over to get a refill of coffee.

Barrett picked up one of the six Henry rifles on the table.

"What is that?" Alex gave a probing stare.

"It's a Henry .44 repeating rifle. Like the rifles that were stolen. These are a little older." Barrett handed one to the tall Bulgarian.

"What makes them be so special?" Jackson asked, wide-eyed.

Barrett was quick to reply. "It holds sixteen rounds of ammo. And you never have to worry about your powder getting wet because it is in a copper or brass case."

Wheaty jumped in, staring at the rifle. "You're joshin' me."

"No. I am quite serious." Barrett smiled.

Jack inspected the weapon, turning it from side to side. "Sixteen! That mean a good rifleman could take down sixteen men in...."

"As fast as he could aim and fire," Barrett finished his sentence.

"These were found on the battlefield. Their owners never made it home. Major... you only have three-hundred rounds so hopefully you will not get into a fight."

"Three-hundred rounds with the right men should be enough unless we run into the entire Confederate Army." Barrett smiled.

"My understanding is that you may have to do that," Custer said, raising his bushy eyebrows.

Barrett nodded, knowing that the general was right. He reached down, and picked up the burlap-wrapped item that Grant had given him. He put it on the table, untied the rope, and carefully removed the rifle.

"Whoa! A Whitworth! Never seen one with a scope!" Alex exclaimed.

"What is it?" Wheaty asked.

Barrett explained, "It is a Whitworth scoped rifle. I need to calibrate it before we leave. This rifle can hit a bull's eye at twelve hundred yards and may come in useful on our journey."

"Twelve hundred yards? Major, that's over a half a mile," Wheaty exclaimed.

"Impossible," replied Jackson.

Barrett patted the rifle as if it was an old friend. "No, not impossible. Alex, since you are familiar with this rifle, your job is to keep it safe. Once the sight on the scope is set, we must be very careful with it, or it could affect its accuracy."

"Yes, sir, you can count on me." Alex took the rifle from Barrett and clutched it like a newborn baby.

"Listen up, men! Wheaty, Jerry, and Moccasin will lead the way because they are familiar with the territory. We will start where the rifles were stolen and track them from there. If we find the rifles, we may eventually find the ammunition."

Barrett faced Custer. "General, can we hitch a train to where the ambush took place?"

"Done. Lieutenant, have a train ready to take these seven men to Warrington to meet their escorts. They will need horses and supplies...."

Barrett interrupted, "Nonmilitary... horses with no brands."

Custer looked at von Weber, "Right… very smart. Lieutenant Roth, you heard the man, get the horses!"

"Yes, sir."

Just then, Perry walked in carrying an armload of supplies. "Here are the rest of their clothes. I even managed to find some Indian garb."

"Thanks. Put everything here," Barrett pointed to the table.

"Sergeant Major, go with Lieutenant Roth and find some unmarked horses and put them on the train. The men and horses will need enough supplies for a couple weeks," Custer ordered.

"Yes, sir." Perry followed the lieutenant.

Barrett gave quick orders to his six soldiers. "When we leave this camp, we will be in civilian clothing, which could be good or bad."

"Give us bad, suh," retorted Jackson.

Barrett's voice grew louder. He spoke like a true leader, passionately. "We are Union soldiers, in civilian dress, in enemy territory. Even though we are representing New Haven Arms, if the Rebels catch us we could be tried as spies… or worse."

Wheaty interjected, "But, we are just trying to get something that was stolen from us."

"Still be considered a spy," von Weber uttered.

Sorting through the clothing, Barrett called Moccasin. "I hope you do not mind wearing this old Indian garb. Will it bother you?"

Moccasin grabbed it and raised his right fist, grinning.

"I take it that means it's all right."

Turning to the others, he continued, "We will be passing through some southern towns. You must remain civil and polite. No carousing with the women… or fighting with the men. There will be no drinking and no smoking. Am I understood?"

"Can we chew?" Jackson snickered.

"You could, but chewing would leave a trail that even a blind man could follow."

"Right, Major von Weber, no chewin'," Jackson responded swiftly.

The black man finally entered the conversation. "May I ask ya something, suh?"

"Go ahead, Jerry."

"What makes ya think that seven of us can take the stuff from 'em? There may be a hundred men guardin' that shipment."

Before he answered, Barrett told the men to pick out their clothing and get ready for the journey. He spoke while he put on an old pair of brown pants. "No, I don't think so. I would guess that only a few are traveling with the merchandise. If there were too many guards, they would draw too much attention."

Barrett faced Moccasin. "I've heard that you can find a lizard in an acre of rocks, I hope that is true because I need you to find a trail in a bloody battlefield."

"Good luck gentlemen," Custer boomed.

The small squad of soldiers saluted the general and quickly left, dressed in their new outfits.

They were four days behind the stolen shipments.

Barrett hoped Jerry was right and the people who stole the shipment were either lying low, or at least slowed down by changing and repacking the weapons. Either way, it could give them enough time to catch up.

Chapter Twenty-One

Drizzle continued throughout the day as the train made its way down the track. The vapor from the locomotive smokestack shot high into the air as it chugged along.

Barrett and his six men, along with the men operating the train, were the only ones aboard.

Only a handful of people knew what the seven men's orders were. However, it seemed that most everyone they came in contact with understood that anything Barrett requested, or any order he dished out, was to be fulfilled, no questions asked.

The three-hour private train ride gave the men the perfect opportunity to chat.

Barrett stretched his long legs out. "Men, since we will be together until we solve this war crime, I think it is important to get to know each other. I believe that it will take a bond... all of us working together, to make this mission successful and to help us be able to trust each other with our lives."

They all agreed readily.

Jack was the first to offer personal information. "This train is gonna stop close to my farm," he stated matter-of-factly.

"Really, Jack? Do your parents live close?" Barrett sat straighter on the hard seat.

"My family." A smile came to the soldier's face. "My family was a household of J's."

"J's?" Wheaty questioned.

"Yep. Folks were John and Janice Jackson. Had two brothers and a sister—Joe, Josiah, and Judith. Married the neighbor girl, Juliet. Guess that why she perfect for me—she was a J. We was young, I was fifteen; she jus' fourteen."

"That sure was young!" Alex shook his head.

"Farmin' is a hard life and you gotta start young!" He looked off in the distance as if he was in a different time and place. "Sho did love Juliet. She had the purdiest yella hair you ever seen. Didn't waste any time havin' a baby. She almost died giving birth to my son—named him Justin."

"Where does your family live now?" Wheaty asked.

"Dead—all of 'em! In '57 sickness came through our county... took Ma and Pa, my brothers, and my sissy. Don't know why me and Juliet and the baby got spared. Whole family went to church together every Sunday. Took two-hour, but we go every week, even durin' rainy time. Pa said, 'God took Sunday off, reckon we should too.'" A sad look came over his face. "I sho miss pa. Taught me how to live off the land. I got a job in the city to help s'port the family... I started workin' at a shoe store makin' mighty fine boots. Then the war broke out and everythin' changed. When the Rebels were beat in Sharpsburg, Maryland in' 62, they retreated right by my farm. Killed livestock and burnt my home. Barely got my wife and son out of thar. I shot three of them Graycoats before we got away."

"Did you kill them?" Alex asked.

"Don't know. Never returned ta see. I saw my house burnin', knew everythin' was gone. Sho strange."

"What was?"

Tears clouded his eyes. "I was a Southerner and attacked by them Rebels who should have protected me. After that, we headed north, weren't prepared for the harsh winter up thar—both Juliet and Justin died of 'monia. It was all because of them thar Rebels. That why I fight with Bluecoats. Hoped I meet up with them ones that burnt my farm. Fight every Rebel as if he be the one who robbed me of my family. What them Rebels sowed at my farm, I will one day reap when they're beat."

Wheaty put his arm around Jack.

Silence followed for a short time as the men pondered the horrors of war and how it personally affected them.

Finally, Barrett broke the tense quiet. "Thank you, Jack."

Barrett glanced at Moccasin, who was noticeably moved by Jacks' story.

The major was fascinated with the Indian. He noticed that his brown eyes were keenly watching, continuously alert. Sometimes Moccasin sat by the window of the train and would point out a bear, mountain lion, or even a small squirrel in a tree. Usually no one else saw it; however, he always knew something was there.

Barrett noticed that Jerry didn't say much. If he did talk, it was usually in the form of a question. Roundtree had taught him well, especially, how to live in a world that hated him because of his skin color.

Wheaty was a likable young man who never grew tired of talking. He was always kidding, telling jokes, and trying to get the others to laugh. He was also observant, probably due to the time he spent with Moccasin. They had taught each other a lot. His boisterous personality might be because of his size. At five feet, and that was pushing it, he literally looked up to everyone, and by talking made his presence known.

Boris rarely talked; he just followed orders. Barrett learned that the quiet man immigrated to the United States from Bulgaria to elude a war that was brewing in his country. Ironically, when he arrived in America, he ended up serving in a different war.

When Boris first arrived in America, he found himself on the streets of New York, knowing no English, and starving. One day he met a tall man from his home country who loved adventure and spoke his language. Before he knew it, he was following Alexander Budnikov to the battlefields of Pennsylvania and Virginia.

Alex came from a well-to-do family who moved to America when he was a young boy. He attended a private school in New York. When his parent's business failed and they lost everything, they decided to return to Bulgaria. He was old enough to stay in America, so he opted for that. He did some carpentry work, but soon grew tired of it because he wanted adventure. It was then he met Boris. They became friends and together joined the Union Army.

All the men had already known of Barrett von Weber, the Hymnist, even Jerry. In fact, he frequently hummed or sang one song in particular, *I Will Meet the Son at the End of My Journey*. To Roundtree, the song had a special meaning since he was trying to find his son, Caleb, stolen at birth fourteen long years ago.

It was late afternoon when the brakes screeched and the train carrying the little band of so-called civilians came to a grinding halt.

Barrett looked out the window and saw two riders in Northern blue uniforms waiting by the tracks.

The major and his comrades mounted their horses in the center freight car and waited. A limited amount of food and water were already packed in the saddlebags of the horses. When the door to the freight car flew open and a sturdy ramp fell to the ground, Barrett bounded off the train, leading on a brown stallion. The six others followed.

"Which one of you is von Weber?" One of the riders asked.

"Right here," Barrett spoke loudly.

The horsemen saluted the major, and he returned the gesture. "Follow us, sir. The site is not far from here."

The small posse followed the two Union soldiers for about fifteen minutes. They stopped at a small clearing where an obvious skirmish had taken place. Although there were no bodies, a struggle was evident from the hoof prints of the horses and the blood-stained grass. It appeared to be a one-sided struggle.

One of the Union riders faced Barrett, "Find the men who did this and make them pay for this heinous slaughter."

"Finding the shipments is first priority, but bringing these men to justice is also high on my agenda," von Weber voiced, looking over the terrain.

"Thank you, sir." The horsemen saluted and rode off.

Alex studied the area. "Major, how can we follow anything from here? With all the footprints, I don't believe even Moccasin can pick up the trail."

"It's our job to figure that out. Now let's get to work," Barrett ordered.

The Indian wasted no time jumping off his horse and squatting, searching for a clue, anything that would help.

"He'll find it. I know he will," Wheaty stated excitedly as he rode up next to Major von Weber.

Barrett nodded his head, dismounting from his horse. He studied a bloodstain and rubbed it into the soil with his shoe. Noticing a sizeable crop of trees on both sides of the clearing, he mentioned, "Seems like the perfect place for an ambush."

"They never saw it coming," Alex concurred, standing next to the major.

Barrett thought aloud. "Why should they have been concerned? The soldiers transporting the supplies believed they were safe in Northern territory. Nobody supposedly knew what they were hauling in the wagons, and the entire Union Army was only a few miles away. They were just delivering supplies... nothing more, nothing less–like a hundred times before. Why would they suspect there was a traitor among them, someone they trusted and respected?"

Von Weber stared at Alex, almost as if he was looking straight through him. "Good men died here, and I agree, they never saw it coming."

Barrett's mind reeled as he studied the horrendous scene—the hoof prints, the impressions of wagon wheels, the markings from where the bodies had been dragged away. *Where should we start? How can anyone find a trail in this mess? So much is riding on the success of this mission... God help us!*

The major observed Wheaty and Moccasin disappear into a grove of trees. Moments later, they reappeared, rushing past Barrett. Still looking at the ground, the Indian pointed from one spot to another.

The excitement on Wheaty's face was evident when he sprinted up to the Major. "Sir, Moccasin found the trail. I told you he could do it. I knew he would. Follow me!"

They walked a short distance and noticed the Indian crouched next to a number of hoof prints, examining them closely.

Wheaty spoke fast, animatedly, as he explained the discovery to Barrett. "Sir, we had to go back up the trail a ways to get some clean prints. The entire area had been messed up bad when the dead soldiers were dragged away, but we did find some good prints. Moccasin counted prints from twelve horses in the brush, which he thinks came from the attackers."

"So we are looking for twelve men with a wagon?" Alex blinked.

Wheaty shook his head decisively. "No, we are looking for thirteen men and two wagons. Moccasin figures the men fired at the Union soldiers from that grove of trees." He pointed to an area where the trees were thick with heavy underbrush. "That smart Indian found two distinctive hoof prints. One had a split shoe; the other had a nail sticking out one of his shoes. Evidently, the horse with the nail stopped, and allowed the other Union soldiers to go ahead."

"How does Moccasin know that?" Barrett asked.

"Sir, you can talk to him... he understands you." Wheaty grinned.

The Indian started signing something, and judging by his actions and facial expressions it was important. A few grunts and groans came from his mouth, but nothing understandable. Occasionally, he would glance at the others.

Wheaty watched his friend sign and relayed the message to the major and the other men. "When the horse with the nail stopped, he reared up. Moccasin thinks the rider was likely firing a pistol at that point."

Barrett shook his head sadly. "While they were being ambushed from the side, he shot his own comrades in the back. That would account for the rider staying behind the others."

Wheaty agreed, "Right, sir."

He continued conveying the Indian's message, adding his own words to make the story more exciting. "The other twelve men fired from the trees at the soldiers with the shipment. Sir, our troops never knew what hit them. I don't think they even fired a shot. As you saw, the ground at the ambush site was too muddled up, so Moccasin went on ahead to follow the prints. Both of the distinctive hoof prints are seen on down the road."

"So the rider on the horse with the nail in its shoe might just be Sergeant Everett Hornsby, the missing man," Barrett replied.

Wheaty cleared his throat. "That's the way I see it. Follow that track and you will eventually find Hornsby and the rifles."

The Indian hurried ahead, obviously with something on his mind. After kneeling and examining more clues, he stood and began waving his hands frantically.

"Look, he is waving at us. Moccasin is even quieter than most Indians, isn't he?" Wheaty laughed, tickled by his own humor.

Suddenly, the Indian jumped on his horse and sped off, still looking down, studying the ground.

Wheaty grabbed the reins of his horse. "Sir, he got the trail. A word to the wise—be prepared to follow... fast! It is sometimes hard to keep up with him."

"All right, men, looks like the hound has found the scent. Let's move!" Barrett quickly mounted his stallion and headed out at a full gallop, the others following close behind.

Hours later, Moccasin raised his hand to halt the other men. He dismounted and strode a short distance.

Wheaty got off his horse, grabbed his rife, and followed the Indian.

Barrett and the other men remained on their horses, watching Moccasin—weapons ready.

Moccasin began pulling away limbs and loose brush.

Wheaty put down his rifle and began to help the Indian.

"Alex, you and the others give them a hand, there must be something covered up," the major ordered.

Without saying a word, the men jumped off their horses and ran over to where the Indian was clearing brush.

Barrett grabbed his Henry rifle and stood guard.

When the last piece of foliage was pulled away, two wagons were exposed.

The major's jaw dropped. "Are they empty?"

Jerry climbed aboard a wagon and carefully pulled the canvas off. "Empty, suh," he shouted.

Alex climbed on the other wagon. "It's empty too, sir."

Barrett glanced around. "They moved the stuff to other wagons?"

Von Weber hadn't noticed that while they were inspecting the wagons, Moccasin and Wheaty had disappeared.

"Major, come here," Wheaty interrupted his thoughts, calling from the brush.

Barrett hurried over. "What is it?"

"Sir, we have found the rifle crates… they are empty." Wheaty pointed to a pile of wooden crates.

Barrett concluded, "The rifles must have been taken out, repacked, and put on other wagons, so they could make it through the checkpoints as they headed south."

Moccasin interrupted the discussion when he showed the major a set of Union clothing he had found stashed in the bushes.

"How can you possibly get through the lines with five hundred rifles?" Barrett asked, staring at the apparel. After a brief pause, he inquired, "Is there a sergeant patch on that coat?" he raised an eyebrow, waiting.

Wheaty held up the jacket showing a sergeant insignia.

"I bet that belongs to Everett Hornsby."

Sir, he apparently kept his boots."

"Major?" Jack spoke up. "I made boots 'fore. Military boots made up North are differ'nt than ones down South."

"Well, that could be their downfall. Find a Rebel wearing Union boots, and we just may find our culprit." Barrett forced a half-smile.

Jackson added, "That's if he be dressed in Rebel uniform. Could be dressed like us."

Barrett mounted his horse. "So, we do not know if we are looking for two wagons led by Rebels, or by civilians. That makes it difficult. Men, let's be on the lookout for a man wearing Union boots, dressed in civilian clothing, or in a Rebel uniform."

"With a horse that has a split shoe, or a nail sticking out of its shoe," Wheaty added.

"Not much to go on, but it's more than we started with." Barrett shifted in his saddle, trying to catch a better glimpse of the makeshift road nearby. "We need to know what way they went. How much time has passed? How far ahead of us are they?"

"We are about to find out. Give us details, Moccasin." Wheaty eyed his friend, waiting for him to sign.

As he signed, Wheaty interpreted, "They are headed due south at a slow speed, probably two days ahead of us."

"Why they be goin' that slow?" Jerry questioned.

"Apparently, they don't want to attract attention," Alex responded.

"I am sure it took a while to repack and hide those rifles," Barrett added.

"I wonder how they hid 'em rifles," Jerry stated.

Barrett shrugged. "Not sure, but let's hope we find them before they are sold."

"Sir, what about the ammunition?" Alex inquired.

"What about it?"

"Well, we have found the trail of the rifles, but how can we find the ammunition? Are we going to where the ammunition shipments were stolen? That could take days, maybe weeks." Alex crossed his arms.

Barrett smiled, his face relaxed. "I'm hoping we can convince those who have the rifles to let us know where they are taking them." He waved his Henry in front of Alex. "You know, a bit of friendly persuasion." He chuckled. "If that doesn't work, I don't know. We'll take it one day at a time. We started four days behind, now it looks like we are only a couple days back. I suspect that in the end, all three shipments will come together. Neither rifle nor ammo is any good without the other. If you have any better ideas, I would like to hear them."

Alex sighed. "I just hope we find one or the other… and soon. If we find them together, we may have a big problem."

Barrett nodded. "That is something that I do not want to even think about. Coming face-to-face with five hundred soldiers armed with Henry rifles is not my idea of a good day."

For a long moment, the seven men stared at each other contemplating the urgency of their mission.

Barrett studied the terrain and then started dishing out orders. "Okay, men, listen up. Moccasin will lead. Alex, you take the left flank. Wheaty you take the right. They are moving slow…very slow. They think they are safe, and in a way, they are—they have crossed into Confederate territory. Somehow, they have figured out a way to move the rifles south, without detection. I hope that we can do the same. Be on the lookout at all times! The hills will be swarming with Graycoats. Let's move!"

Chapter Twenty-Two

March 30, 1864
New Haven Connecticut

Birds happily chirped in the warm sunlight, undisturbed by the grief of war, or the suffering on all sides of them.

The dew was still on the ground when a stylish carriage pulled up to the von Weber home in New Haven, Connecticut.

Titus was taking Annapurna for his morning walk. When the young man saw the carriage, a big smile took over his face. He released the stallion's reins and ran as fast as he could toward the approaching visitors.

Titus arrived at the door of the carriage as it swung open. Out stepped Cornelius and a noticeably giddy Milly.

Titus greeted them in his typical friendly manner. "Good Morning, Massa Hall."

"Good morning, Titus. Looks like you have grown a foot since I last saw you. How is Annapurna doing?"

"He is doing fine, sir, but I think he is lonely for his Massa." Although Titus was talking to Cornelius, his gaze wandered to the young black girl next to the carriage.

Milly stood silent, blushing.

"I believe we all miss Master von Weber," Cornelius added truthfully.

"I won't be long." Cornelius winked at Milly. He turned and strode toward the house.

Cornelius enthusiastically knocked on the door.

William opened the door and greeted him, "Good morning, suh."

"Good morning, William. Is the lady of the house in?"

"Yes, suh. Please, come in."

Cornelius glanced back at Titus and Milly and smiled.

William rubbed his face. "I sure hope Titus behaves himself."

"Oh, fiddlesticks, William, it's young love." Cornelius handed William his hat and cane. "You should have seen me when I was his age. Every day I would find an excuse to walk by a pretty little redheaded gal that I was madly in love with."

A woman's voice sounded from the doorway. "But Margaret has blonde hair." Brooke walked to the visitor, smiling. Dressed in a pale-blue gown, she offered her hand.

Cornelius kissed it. "You keep getting more beautiful every day."

"Why, Cornelius, did you forget that my husband is the best shot in the state? You do not want to make him jealous. I do believe you are trying to change the subject. Who was this girl you were so in love with?"

"To be perfectly honest, it was my wife's sister. I was madly in love with her until I met Margaret. Good thing too, because her sister hated me. Still does, I think."

They laughed.

"Come into the parlor. I was just reading Charles Dickens' new novel—*A Tale of Two Cities*. William, will you bring us some tea, please?"

"Certainly, Miss Brooke," William responded.

"Ah, Charles Dickens. *It was the best of times, it was the worst of times, it was the age of wisdom, it was the age of foolishness....*"

Brooke smiled. "Why, Mr. Hall, you know Dickens."

"He is one of my favorite authors. I especially like that first paragraph, which was written in '59, I may add. It is truth for America today."

As the two sat across from each other visiting, Cornelius' face showed concern. He sensed something was different with Brooke. "I understand that you have been helping out as a nurse in prison camps."

"Yes. In fact, I received a letter yesterday from a good friend of Barrett's—Doctor Alexander. They are setting up a new prisoner of war camp in Elmira, New York, and he wanted to know if I would help in the hospital."

"Elmira? Barrett has relatives up there and a home, if I recall."

"Yes. I have already arranged for William, Prisse, and myself to stay there indefinitely. I want to keep busy. Of course, deep down inside, I know that I want to volunteer in case my brothers end up as prisoners. I need to do whatever I can."

"Why, Brooke, isn't that kind of looking at life in a dim light?"

"In a way, but it's better than the alternative." Brooke folded her hands in her lap.

"Which is?"

"Finding them in a cemetery."

"I see your point." His tone turned somber. "What news do you have of your family?"

"Charles and Samuel are serving together in the Georgia Cavalry. Rory is in charge of defending Savannah with the Cavalry Guard. Unbelievably, he was promoted to captain. Father is desperately trying to keep the company going. His textile business is booming, but he is not making money. He is busy making Confederate uniforms."

"I cannot imagine Rory as a captain, giving orders and the like. Bet he's enjoying that!" Cornelius groaned at the thought.

Brooke smiled in agreement. "Have you heard from my husband in recent days?"

"As a matter of fact I did, just a few days ago. That's what brings me here... he sends his love."

Her heart beat faster. "How is he? I get a letter from him almost every day, but he never really says what is going on there. I worry that it's more dangerous than he's letting me know. I think he does not want me to worry. Oh, how I miss him."

"He has an important job—teaching men how to use and care for their weapons properly."

"I'd rather have him teaching than fighting. Does he still wish he was in the thick of the battle?"

"I'm sure deep down he does, not because he wants to fight, but because he wants to do all he can do to end this senseless war. At the same time, I believe he knows his job is of extreme importance. As we speak, he is in Virginia teaching men how to use the new Henry rifle."

"Oh, I'm sure he is enthusiastic about that assignment." She shifted in her seat, trying to get more comfortable.

Cornelius noticed Brooke's hand softly rubbing her abdomen. He grinned and looked directly at her. "Anything you would like me to tell Barrett when I see him next?"

She crinkled her nose. "Now, Cornelius, what on earth are you talking about?"

"I have five children. My wife looked like you do all five times she was expecting. She had a certain glow about her, just as you have. I understand if you want to give the news to Barrett first?"

Before she had a chance to reply, William returned with their beverages. After he poured the tea, he held an exquisite silver tray loaded with goodies in front of Cornelius.

"Thank you, William," he said, removing a scone from the tray.

Cornelius took a sip. "Great tasting tea... just how I like it with zesty orange. Sylvia's recipe, I suspect."

"No, not exactly, but William tries his best. He watched her on several occasions, but even he admits his is missing something."

"Brooke, let's get back to the subject of importance. How far along are you? I could do the math, but you could save me the time." Cornelius grinned.

"All right... all right... you don't give up. About ten weeks... our baby is due in October."

"Congratulations. Any names picked out yet?"

"No, I will wait and see what Barrett wants to name the baby. I know he always talked about the patriot Nathan Hale. So, I would suspect if it's a boy, we would call him Nathan. I would love to give him the news in person. He said he would try to come home for a few days in May."

"I see no reason why he shouldn't be able to. The training should only take a couple weeks."

The chime of the large grandfather clock announced the hour. "Oh, my... I had better be going." Cornelius stood. "Margaret will have lunch ready for me. And, I think Titus and Milly have been by themselves long enough," he laughed.

"Need not worry about them, I been watching," William announced looking out the window, half-kidding.

Brooke joined in the laughter.

"When did you say you were heading to Elmira?"

"Late May. I hope to go up there with Barrett."

"Good. Please let me know when he returns." Cornelius reached over and gave her a kiss on the cheek. "Do not be concerned... your secret is safe with me."

Chapter Twenty-Three

April 1864
West Virginia

The full moon illuminated the thin, winding path, making it possible for the small band of soldiers to continue on their way long past dusk. They rode until the moon disappeared behind the clouds, making up a considerable amount of time.

Few words were spoken as the weary men ate their rations. Using their saddles as pillows, they hoped to catch a few hours of slumber. It had been a busy day and sleep was a much-welcomed necessity.

Barrett woke the travelers before dawn. Within minutes, they were on their way. He wanted to find the thieves before they escaped too deep into the South.

The dew was extremely heavy, which caused them to leave tracks. "If anyone is suspicious of us, they can follow us easy. Be vigilant at all times."

More than once the band of brothers hid off the trail while a small caravan of migrants slowly rode past in their covered wagons, most likely trying to escape the horrors of war. For the most part, soldiers from neither side bothered these travelers. The refugees were armed and would die defending their families if they were attacked.

Jerry seemed to be at the side of Barrett at all times. He felt it was his responsibility to protect the major. The two became close friends.

Von Weber continued to be amazed by Moccasin. The Indian's senses were keen, his awareness uncanny. He knew the way the sunlight would cast its shadows on a print making it stand out in the soil. Barrett would watch as the older man pushed his straight black hair from his face, crouch next to a fresh footprint, and read it like a road map. He had the utmost respect for the red-skinned man's ability to track something or someone. Hopefully, it would pay off in this vital search.

By the fourth day, Barrett believed they were closing in on Hornsby and his men.

It was mid-morning when they stopped at a fork in the road.

Moccasin abruptly jumped off his horse and studied the ground.

Watching him, Barrett told his men, "Stay here and be alert."

The major rode up to the Indian to see what he had discovered. "Moccasin, what is it? Did we lose the trail?"

The tracker pointed to the ground where dozens of horse and wagon prints muddled the path.

Barrett dismounted and examined the prints closer. "Looks like a lot of traffic came through here." He motioned for Wheaty to join them.

"What's going on, boss?" Wheaty asked.

"You tell me."

Wheaty knelt next to his Indian friend. "What do we have here?"

A lengthy exchange between the two of them began.

Finally, Wheaty stood, and explained to Barrett, "There were several wagons coming from different directions at various times."

"Which way did Hornsby go?"

Wheaty pointed to the right.

"Then let's follow him."

Wheaty explained further, "Sir, it seems we have a wagon that turned around heading east, following yet another wagon."

Barrett thought aloud. "Turned around? Why would they do that?"

Wheaty replied, "I don't know. Maybe the stolen shipments were supposed to meet here."

Puzzled, he looked at the Indian. "Moccasin, how fresh are these tracks headed east?"

"He says about an hour," Wheaty translated.

"I'm most curious about these tracks," Barrett voiced.

After a slight pause, Barrett decisively began dishing out orders to the men. "Jack, you and Boris stay here... hide and watch closely to see if anyone else comes by. Unless your life is in danger, do not confront anyone. The rest of you, come with me. Let's see who is making these tracks to the east. It appears that a wagon is following another wagon. Maybe this was the rendezvous point for all three shipments. Let's find out. Moccasin, lead the way." Von Weber pointed east.

The Indian tracker jumped on his horse and sped off.

As Barrett mounted his stallion, he reminded Jackson, "Remember to stay out of sight. Do not confront anyone if you can help it. We will return as soon as we can."

"Yes, suh," Jack shouted.

The four men followed Moccasin for twenty minutes when the tracks turned to the north.

Moving closer to Barrett, Alex asked, "Sir, if they had the stolen supplies, seems like they would not be heading back north."

"I thought the same thing, but we've come this far, we can't turn back now. We need to trust Moccasin." Barrett motioned for them to continue.

Minutes later, a number of shots rang out in the distance.

Barrett cast his eyes in that direction.

He noticed Moccasin seemed a bit unnerved by it, but continued forging ahead.

They proceeded cautiously, silently, for several minutes.

Suddenly, Moccasin jumped to the ground and motioned to Barrett that something unusual was ahead.

Barrett whispered to the others, "Dismount, ready your weapons!"

The major quietly got off his horse, tied it to a tree, and sprinted over to the Indian.

The others followed, vigilantly, watching for danger.

Crouching behind some bushes, they could see movement in the small clearing ahead, but could not make out what was happening.

Wheaty took out his spyglass and peered through it.

"What do you see?" Alex whispered.

"Looks like six Graycoats. There is something… or someone on the ground."

Wheaty kept looking through his glass and spotted a couple wagons with five men nearby. "Major, look to the left."

Barrett looked through the scope on his rifle and counted. "Looks like a total of eleven Confederate soldiers."

He turned his attention back to the half-dozen men standing in a group, laughing. Finally, one of the Rebels moved aside making it possible for the major to see two terrified women on the ground. "They have two women cornered," he whispered.

Barrett studied the scene. "The women must have been traveling in that covered wagon; perhaps they were trying to meet the caravan of migrants we saw yesterday. The Rebels must have followed them. But, I don't see any men."

"Surely the women were not traveling alone," Alex suggested.

"I would suspect the shots we heard a few minutes ago had something to do with that," Wheaty surmised.

Barrett peered through the scope, scanning the area closely. He could see some of the Rebels tossing things on the ground; one put something in his pocket. Still another held up a woman's undergarment, placed it near his body, and wiggled his hips. "They are pillaging the wagon."

The major turned to face his group of soldiers. "Listen closely, men. It looks like Rebels attacked that covered wagon. They may have already killed the men and they are about to do something horrible with those girls. Remember what General Custer told us to do—shoot first and don't bother asking questions," von Weber challenged. "If we don't intervene, those poor women will be raped and left for dead."

The major ordered, "Wheaty, you and Jerry get as close to the covered wagon as you can and take the three men out. Alex, you get the two men standing by the flat wagon."

Wheaty reeled around. "That leaves six, sir."

"Moccasin and I will get the rest. We have to move quickly! Signal to me when you are in place. Do not fire until I do... understand?"

"Yes, sir," the men chorused quietly.

Barrett added, "Men, this is the real thing... make your shells count. You have fifteen rounds in the magazine. Fire the weapon like I showed you."

He tapped Moccasin on the arm. "You stay with me."

The Indian nodded, aiming his old Springfield rifle at the gray-coated figures in the clearing.

Wheaty, Alex, and Jerry hurried to the left, drawing closer to the wagons.

Barrett continued watching through his scope. One of the men was trying to disrobe the younger woman forcefully, but she was attempting to fight back. The man hit her in the face, apparently knocking her out. "Hurry up, Wheaty," he whispered under his breath.

Von Weber turned his scope in the direction of his men and saw them wave, signaling they were ready.

Prepared for action, Barrett ordered, "Moccasin, wait until I fire, then shoot the man standing on the left."

Barrett aimed his rifle at the one who had struck the girl and slowly pulled the trigger, shattering the silence. Instantly, the bullet found its mark in the side of the man's head, downing the Rebel soldier. He fired again, killing a second Southerner.

When the Indian fired, the black smoke billowed from the Springfield's barrel, and the ball found its mark in the chest of the enemy.

The major shot again, hitting his target, intentionally wounding one of the attackers in the stomach.

One of the Rebel soldier's frightened horses reared up and took off galloping into the distance.

Meanwhile, Wheaty and the others opened fire, finding their assigned targets near the wagons.

Barrett fired two more times, hitting the last remaining Rebels.

Within seconds, the one-sided battle was over. The Graycoats never even managed to fire a shot.

The major stood and unexpectedly took aim at the escaping horse, and fired a shot, downing it.

He watched as his men rushed toward the wagons, prepared to fire if they saw any enemy movement. "Keep alert, men!" he shouted.

Wheaty quickly searched the covered wagon for any sign of life.

Alex and Jerry hurried over to the motionless men on the ground to make sure they were dead.

"Good... we are all accounted for," Barrett reported to Moccasin.

Alex noticed the wounded Rebel reach for his rifle and aim it at Wheaty. The Bulgarian wasted no time in shooting the attacker dead.

Barrett and Moccasin sprinted over to join the others.

"You missed one, sir, but I got him," Alex cited.

"No, I didn't miss. I wanted him alive, so we could gain some information." Barrett looked at the dead body.

"Sorry, sir, but he grabbed for his rifle," Alex added.

"You did what you had to do. The first response in a situation like this is survival. You did the right thing. Finish checking the rest of them and see if there is any life." He gestured toward the bodies.

"Why'd ya shoot the horse?" Jerry spoke up.

"I didn't want to, but we have no idea who else is out here. It is bad enough that we could have drawn attention by firing our rifles. I did not want to take a chance on a riderless horse creating more suspicion for us."

Barrett looked at the two wagons. "Jerry, help Wheaty inspect the wagons... see what they were carrying. Maybe they were some sort of scouting group. Hopefully, we can glean more information from the girls."

"Or, maybe they were deserters," Alex added.

"Or deserters," Barrett agreed.

Barrett walked over to the frightened girls and bent down. Paralyzed with fear, the older woman clung to the one who was still unconscious. *Her worn, hard face shows a difficult life. I bet she's a farmer's wife and that's her daughter. Poor girl looks to be only about sixteen.*

"Do what you want with me, but let my daughter go," the woman cried in a strong Spanish accent.

"Do not be frightened, we are not going to hurt you." Barrett's voice was tender, his eyes displayed compassion.

She glanced at the nearby brush. A fresh batch of tears rolled down her face.

Suspicious of her reaction, Barrett nodded his head in that direction.

Alex ran over to the dense shrubbery, backed up, and cast a shocked look toward Barrett. He surveyed the scene and then rushed back to the major and whispered in his ear, "Sir, they were shot! Three bodies—one adult male and two boys about eight and twelve."

The woman wailed, "It was my husband and sons. We were trying to get far away from this awful war."

"How long did they chase you?"

"Since early this morning. At first, my husband was not concerned because they were going in a different direction, but then they turned around and followed us. He knew we couldn't outrun them, so he decided to take a stand. We were no match for them."

Wheaty ran up carrying a heavy box. "Sir, you have got to see this. We found it in the flat wagon." He handed it to Barrett.

Von Weber removed an item from the box. "Interesting... looks like the missing ammo." Barrett glanced at the wagon. "Is this what the Rebels were hauling?"

"Yes."

"How many boxes are there?"

"I counted forty."

"Forty?" Barrett studied the ammo in his hand, and then quickly scanned the box, figuring in his head. "One hundred and twenty-five in a box... that's five thousand rounds of ammo. Any rifles?"

"No, sir," Wheaty swallowed hard.

A big smile came to Barrett's face as he placed the four shells in his coat pocket. "We have found the small shipment. Ashley Moses was in charge of that load. Is there any way we can verify that he is among the dead?"

"I can check their boots, sir," Wheaty offered.

Barrett stated, "I think this group turned and followed the covered wagon, obviously lusting for the women."

He eyed the older woman. "Anything you can tell me about the men who attacked your family?"

Still unsure if she should trust the group of men, she stayed silent.

Wheaty took his water pouch, dabbed some water on a rag, and wiped the forehead of the unconscious girl.

Slowly regaining consciousness, the girl looked around. When her eyes tracked to Moccasin, she screamed. Trembling with fear, she clung to her mother.

The Indian gave a half-smile taking a couple steps backward.

Barrett intervened, attempting to comfort her. "He is our Indian friend. He would never hurt you. He would defend you with his life... as would the rest of us." Continuing, he stated, "Now, tell me everything you know about the attackers. Did they say anything… names, places? Do you know anything that can help us find out who they were and where they were heading?"

"Why should we tell you?" the older woman questioned.

"We just saved your lives, for one," Alex replied smugly.

Barrett raised his hand motioning for him to remain silent.

"Massa Barrett, should we bury them bodies?" Jerry asked.

Kindly, the major asked the distraught woman, "What do you want us to do with your husband and sons?"

She could no longer hold back her tears. "Can you find a nice place where they can rest in peace?"

"Of course we can. Wheaty, Jerry, Alex, do what she asked."

"Yes, sir. What about the Rebels? What should we do with their bodies?" Wheaty waited for a response.

Barrett thought for a second. "They do not deserve to be buried, and time is important for us. Strip them for identification. One of them may even have a map to where they were headed. Hide their bodies in the brush, let the coyotes enjoy them."

"Yes, sir, the men responded in unison."

"What is your name?" the mother asked.

"Barrett. What is yours?"

"Margarita, and this is my daughter, Marisa."

"Are you Spanish?"

"Yes, we came from Spain eight years ago and settled in Charleston. We have relatives in Maryland. With food getting scarce, we decided to head there."

"My wife's family is from Spain," Barrett stated, trying to put the women at ease.

"What is her name?"

"My wife is Brooke. Her mother was Isadora Theresia Ambrosia Fortner."

A look of surprise took over her face, and then she touched her forehead, chest, and shoulders, symbolizing the cross, ending the gesture with kissing her thumb. At the same time, she recited the words, *En el nombre del Padre, del Hijo, y del Espíritu Santo. Amen.*

"What she say?" Wheaty questioned.

"In the name of the Father, the Son, and the Holy Spirit... Amen. She was praying," Barrett added.

Gazing deep into his eyes, the mother uttered, "I know that Isadora was a princess in the royal family. What is your full name, sir?"

"Von Weber... Barrett von Weber."

Her look of surprise continued. "The Hymnist?"

"Yes, the Hymnist." He smiled.

"We know your music from church. Why did the men call you, Major?"

"We are in civilian clothes, but honestly, I am a major in the Union Army."

"You fight for the North?"

"Yes, I fight for the North because that is where I am from, but my wife's family is from the South. That complicates family matters."

"I am sorry. This war has separated many families."

"And I'm sorry for your loss." Barrett caught a glimpse of his comrades carrying the bodies of her loved ones to the graves they were digging in a small patch of open ground, close to a grove of flowering trees. Jerry had taken the canvas from the wagon and was wrapping the corpses.

Barrett could only imagine how difficult this was for her. He tried to get more information, "It will help us if you can tell us where these men were from, where they were going, anything you overheard. We want to put an end to this bloody war and anything you know about them could help."

The girl, still clinging to her mother, spoke in a choked up voice, "I heard one of the men say, 'We don't have time for this. We have to get these supplies to Gilbert.'"

Her mother confirmed, "Oh, yes, they did say that."

"Gilbert? That could be a town or a person." Barrett called, "Jerry, come here."

"Yes, suh, Massa Barrett."

"Do you know of a town called Gilbert?"

"Gilbert? Ain't never heard of that one. Jackson, maybe he know."

Barrett turned his attention back to the girls. "You say you were heading north. Have you seen many Confederate soldiers since you left Charleston?"

"Yes. We saw thousands marching just a few days ago."

Von Weber continued, "Were they camping anywhere?"

"I don't know. They were just marching when we saw them."

"Which direction?"

"West."

He questioned Jerry, "What is west of here?"

"The rivers, suh, two rivers come together."

"Interesting." Barrett paused. "Maybe Gilbert is not a town, maybe it's a person, or even a boat."

Alex stated, "Sir, I guess this may have helped us."

"In what way?" Barrett asked.

"If the Rebels had not followed these women, they would still be ahead of us and maybe the exchange would have already taken place."

"What do we do with these women?" Wheaty inquired. "We can't just leave them here."

"Please, sir, don't leave us here alone," the mother pled.

Without hesitation, Barrett replied, "Miss, we will not abandon you. You are under our protection now. You are safe."

A look of relief shone on her face.

"Wheaty, get Moccasin over here. I have a job for him."

"Yes, sir."

Moccasin hurried over.

Barrett stood face-to-face with the Indian and placed his hands on his shoulders. "Remember that caravan we saw heading north?"

The Indian nodded.

"Find the caravan and leave these women with them, and then get back to us as quickly as you can. We are going to find out where these Rebels were headed. We are searching for a town, place, or person with the name Gilbert."

The women scowled at the Indian.

Barrett attempted to comfort them. "I can see you are frightened, but I trust this man with my life. I ask you to do the same. He will not hurt you. He would die protecting you. Trust him! Even though he cannot speak, he can understand anything you say."

The young girl managed a hesitant smile.

The Indian grinned broadly.

"Yes, sir, we will do that," the mother responded.

Barrett turned back to Moccasin. "My friend, hurry back. We need your tracking skills to continue our search."

Von Weber helped the victims to their feet. "Now go on your way with Moccasin."

Alex assisted the women into their covered wagon. "Do you know how to do this?" he asked, handing the mother the reins.

"Yes, thank you."

Moccasin mounted his horse and motioned for them to follow.

The mother shook the reins, yelling for the horses to go. Then, abruptly she stopped, staring straight ahead.

Barrett walked over to see if there was a problem.

She looked at the major, tears trickling down her grateful face. "God sent you to us! We thank you... and Him! I'll pray that God keeps you and your men safe as you complete your mission and then go home to your wife."

Barrett was visibly touched by her words. "And I will pray that you and your daughter get your life back together. Now go quickly. We have to get you to that caravan before it gets too far ahead. If things go well, Moccasin can have you there by tomorrow afternoon."

Major von Weber glanced at the profile of the rugged Indian astride his horse, confident he could depend on him.

The travelers waved before they disappeared down the trail.

Alex stepped closer to Barrett. "Sir, we are finished here."

"Did you find anything worth noting on the Rebels?"

"A few pictures. Three had Union boots on, but we cannot be sure one was Moses," Wheaty reported.

"Well, we are going to assume one was Moses. Let's hurry back to the crossroads to get Jack and Boris. Maybe Jack knows where or who Gilbert is."

"What do we do with the ammo?" Wheaty asked.

Barrett thought for a second before he spoke. "It will slow us down if we take it, and I certainly do not want to be caught with it. The only way to destroy it quickly is to burn it, but that will draw attention to us. If we bury it, we take a risk that someone may find it."

"Sir, what about tossing it in the river? The boxes will sink and the water will make it impossible to use," Wheaty suggested.

"Good idea. Let's get busy and dump the boxes in the deepest part of the river."

Chapter Twenty-Four

April 4, 1864
South Wales, Virginia

Silence filled the air, as the men retraced their steps on the trail.

Hours later, when they arrived at the crossroads, there was no sign of Jack and Boris.

"Where are they?" Barrett whispered to Wheaty.

Wheaty put his hands up to his mouth and gave a distinct birdcall.

There was rustling in the nearby brush as Jack and Boris rode their horses into the open.

"Here, suh. Heard lots of shots! Weren't sure what to do, so we do what you say and hide," Jack reported.

"Sorry it took a while, but we had a little problem we had to take care of," Barrett explained.

Jack looked past Barrett. "What is all the smoke?" He pointed to the southern sky.

"What smoke?" Barrett turned around, shifting his glance toward the billowing smoke in the distance. "How long has that been going on?"

"We was scared it was you. We been hearing shots thar a couple hours; smoke started 'bout an hour ago. It's been quiet since." Jack glanced around. "Where's Moccasin?"

"He is escorting a couple ladies to the caravan we saw yesterday."

"Ladies?" Jack's eyes widened.

"It's a long story. We found Moses and the small shipment of ammo and took care of that problem!" Barrett looked through his spyglass, viewing the smoky sky.

"Jack, is there a town down there?" Barrett asked.

"Don't know any town this close, but seems like new ones pop up every day 'round here. This here is gold minin' territory."

"Have you ever heard of a town called Gilbert?" Barrett asked.

"Gilbert?" Jack asked thinking aloud. "Not that I 'member. Jerry ever heard tell of it?"

"No, he hasn't."

"I wonder if that could be Gilbert." Wheaty stated, pointing to the drifting smoke.

"I've been wondering the same thing. Men, we have to change our plans. Instead of following the tracks of the wagon, we need to find out what is burning down there. Any guess how far away that is?" Barrett looked through the spyglass again.

Jack responded, "I reckon four or five miles as birds fly. Problem is, don't know what path gonna get us there."

Alex added, "I like the idea of flying like a bird, straight to it. I think it will be safer than taking any of these paths. But, what about Moccasin, sir?"

"He will be following our tracks... he will find us," Barrett responded with certainty.

"Major, what do you think we will see when we get down there?" Wheaty crossed his arms, waiting.

"Not sure, but I'm certain it will not be good. And, please stop calling me Major. Remember we are working undercover, so call me Barrett."

"How about Bear?" Wheaty grinned.

"Or Bear. After all, that's what some people call me."

"Not wanting to be disrespectful, sir, but why do they call you Bear?" Wheaty had been waiting for the right time to ask that question.

"That's what Barrett means in German," Alex cut in. "But I also heard that he's called that because he shot a bear from two thousand yards and saved his best friend's life."

"Two thousand yards... that not poss'ble." Jack's eyes opened huge. Then he added, "That true?"

Without missing a beat, Barrett responded, his expression serious. "The truth of the matter was it was more like fifteen hundred yards, and anyone can hit a bear from that distance... I mean they're as big as a barn."

All the men stared at him, but no one responded. None of the group knew if he was serious or kidding.

"Now, let's get back to the smoke. Moccasin could tell us exactly what kind of smoke that is," Barrett tipped up one side of his mouth.

"Suh?" Jerry spoke up. "That thar's wood burnin'. Seen it thousand times. Looks to be a buildin'... prob'ly several of them."

"What are you thinking, sir?" Wheaty searched the Major's eyes.

"I'm afraid we are about to see the brutality of war, the worst of mankind."

"Worse than we seen with them Rebs?" Jerry blinked.

"Oh, yes, for sure. Let's move out." Barrett motioned for them to follow.

Wheaty shifted his weight to the other stirrup. "Major... I mean Bear... I've been wondering something. When the war is over, will you continue to play the piano? You know you could probably become a famous bear hunter out west."

Everyone burst into laughter, helping to relieve the tenseness of the situation.

When the laughter subsided, Alex shot back, "You know, Wheaty, you could get a job carrying Tom Thumb's baggage."

Everyone laughed except Wheaty. "Who is this Tom Thumb everyone keeps calling me?" He tipped his face looking deeper into Alex's eyes.

Alex blurted out, "Tom Thumb is the smallest man in the world. He is in children's books and is no bigger than a man's thumb."

"Well, I certainly am bigger than a man's thumb. Aren't I?"

"You are. I am just glad to see you can take the men's kidding," Barrett added.

"Small as a man's thumb?" Wheaty muttered, glancing at his thumb. "Nah!"

Jerry rode closer to Barrett. "Suh, you sure Moccasin find us? After all, we leavin' the trail that followed them thar wagon tracks, ain't he 'specting us to be on the trail?"

"Don't have to worry about Moccasin finding us. With the trail we are leaving going through these woods, a blind man could follow us." Barrett rolled his eyes, grinning.

The team rode at a fast, but steady pace for the next couple of hours, most of the time in silence.

As they came up over a ridge, Barrett took out his spyglass and looked closer at the smoke, which was beginning to die down. "Too many trees to see clearly, but it does not appear to be a forest fire. Has to be some type of building, like Jerry said. I hope it stays burning until we get there. Besides the smell, it's the only way we will find the place."

"Suh, jus' thinkin'." Jack looked around, studying the terrain even further. "Been figurin' out where we be... we goin' straight south... so Fredericksburg must be a bit northeast. Jerry, what's that name of the town that them squatters started 'bout eight, ten years ago? You know them ones from Canada."

Jerry responded immediately. "South Wales. Massa Roundtree and I picked up a load of hogs thar once. Small town. Nice people. Friendly place."

"How many folks live there?" Barrett inquired.

"Near as I 'member, 'bout two hundred," Jerry responded.

"Friendly, you say?"

"Yes, suh, treated me good." Jerry replied, not taking his eyes off the smoke.

Barrett halted his horse; doubts clouded his face.

"Sir, you look upset," Wheaty commented.

"I'm concerned about what we will find. Something inside me says we are headed for big trouble." The wrinkles etched in his forehead were evidence of his apprehension.

"Major... I mean Bear... suh?"

"What is it, Jack?"

"You say somethin' 'bout Gilbert."

"Yes. That's what the woman heard the Rebels mention."

"Suh, I 'member place called Gilfred. A minin' town."

Barrett sat taller in his saddle. "Where is this mining town?"

Jack pointed due south. "Right on the river, 'bout two days away."

Barrett looked in the direction Jack was pointing. "After we see what the smoke is all about, we will go check that town out. Be on the alert at all times, men. There are good and bad soldiers in this area... probably from both sides."

The trek was slow. Snakes and other creatures hid in the thick vegetation. More than once, one of the men's horses was startled and nearly bitten by a hissing snake. Barrett knew they couldn't afford to lose their transportation.

Late afternoon, they neared the edge of the forest and spotted a clearing. The comrades tied their horses to some low branches and quietly crouched behind some shrubbery. Spreading some tree limbs apart, they had a clear view of the blackened town. The fire had died out, but the air reeked of smoke.

"Dear God, what happened here?" Wheaty exclaimed.

All eyes were on the charred ruins, some hot spots still smoldering.

"Sir, it looks like marauders have wiped out this town." Wheaty stated the obvious. "It looks like the charred remains of a ghost town."

"Only thing left standin' is the saloon," Jackson noted.

Their stomachs churned as they saw bodies of men, women, and children strewn throughout the town. Two old men left hanging from a tree in the middle of the town served as a sad reminder of the cruelty of war.

Barrett drew his pistol, issuing precise orders. "Proceed cautiously, men. Ready your weapons. Jerry, stay with the horses. Jack, stay hidden in the brush, and cover us. Alex and Boris, take the left side of the town. Wheaty, come with me—we will check that saloon. If you need help, make a lot of noise, and we'll come running."

"Yes, sir," Wheaty agreed, standing straighter.

"Move out, men!"

As they entered the town, they walked by a number of bodies that appeared to have been stabbed or shot, left in the street to be eaten by buzzards.

Wheaty chased the flesh-eating birds away. He noticed the naked body of a woman, probably in her twenties. He found a jacket on the ground nearby and covered her exposed body. *I shudder to think what happened to her before they killed her.*

The squeaking boards echoed through the valley, as Barrett walked up the steps of the saloon. Slowly, he inched the batwing door open.

Wheaty followed close behind the major as they entered the abandoned tavern.

A glut of broken and empty whiskey bottles and several tipped-over bar stools indicated that drunkenness and violence had taken over.

Barrett shook his head with disgust as he picked up an empty bottle.

"Wonder why they didn't burn this place down?" Wheaty grumbled.

The major remained silent.

With guns drawn, they wandered from room-to-room. There were no signs of life anywhere.

After their search was completed, the bewildered men joined Alex and Boris in the street.

"Sir, who do you think did this?" Wheaty inquired.

"Marauders... Southern or Northern, it's hard to tell." Barrett's response echoed the heaviness of his heart. "Alex, how many bodies did you find?"

"Just what we see in the street, and I saw a few in the burned out ruble," Alex answered.

"Alex, Boris, cut those bodies down from that tree." Barrett pointed to the hanging corpses.

"What happened to everyone else?" Wheaty asked, standing next to the major.

Barrett shrugged his shoulders, having no answer. He whistled, signaling Jerry and Jack to join them.

"Anyone thirsty?" Wheaty asked, walking over to the well. He pulled on the rope, but it seemed stuck, so he gave it a couple of hard tugs, finally loosening the pail.

Wheaty cupped his hands, ready to reach into the bucket to get a drink, when Jerry knocked the bucket off the side of the well.

"What you do that for?"

"Look! What's that?" Jerry pointed to crimson stains along the sides of the well.

Hearing the conversation, the major hurried over to get a closer look. He shouted, "Jerry, get a lantern from the saddlebag."

Roundtree hurriedly grabbed the lantern and returned to the well.

Barrett untied the bucket and secured the lantern to the rope.

The men surrounded the well and quietly watched the lantern lower in the hole.

"Not very deep," Wheaty confirmed as the lantern came to a sudden stop.

"Is that what I think it is?" Jack turned away.

The light from the lantern exposed a pile of bloodied bodies crammed in the small space.

Barrett shifted his gaze to the bottom of the well, hoping that what he had seen was not real, but knowing it was.

"The general was right," Wheaty's voice cracked.

"About what?" Alex questioned.

"General Custer warned us that we may not like what we see."

They pondered those words as Barrett tugged the lantern up. "Okay, men. Do not drink the water... it's contaminated."

Suddenly out of the corner of Jerry's eyes, he saw movement across the road. "Sir, we aren't alone."

"Shh... I see him... he went into the saloon. Alex and Boris, go around back—make sure no one comes out. Wheaty and Jack, come with me. Jerry, you stay here—let us know if you see anyone else. Be vigilant! Come on men... let's find out who is in the saloon."

Alex and Boris hurried down the smoldering street and crept around to the back of the saloon.

The others cautiously headed up the squeaky steps.

As the three men were ready to step into the saloon, a person with a knife suddenly lunged at the major. Barrett grabbed the stranger's arms, flipping him down the stairs and into the street. He jumped from the top step and in one quick action was on top of the attacker, pinning the person face down in the dust.

Wheaty rushed over to assist, but Barrett had everything under control. "Sir, one of these days you need to show me how you do that."

"Years of practice."

Wheaty gasped when they turned the captive over. "Sir... he's only a boy."

The boy struggled, trying his best to get out of Barrett's firm grip.

"Easy, young man. Why did you attack us?" Barrett asked the frightened youngster who was still flipping around.

Jack ran over and helped hold the boy's arms still. "We ain't gonna hurt ya," he shouted.

"The Bluecoats did! They killed my parents and everyone else."

"Bluecoats? Are you the only one left alive?" Barrett helped the struggling boy to his feet. He noticed that the lad's eyes shifted to a burned building down the street.

Hearing the commotion, the other men sprinted over.

Barrett pointed with his head to the spot where the boy kept looking. "Alex, Boris, check it out."

They rushed over to the charred ruins. Alex noticed a few loose branches and suspected they were covering something. He tossed them aside and waved Barrett over.

"Careful," Barrett said, handing the belligerent boy over to Jack and Wheaty. "Don't let him go... he's an active one!"

The major rushed over to see what they discovered.

"Sir, looks like a food cellar," Alex whispered, kneeling down to get a closer look.

Jack and Wheaty joined them, dragging the struggling youngster.

Barrett pointed his pistol toward the makeshift door. "Open it," he ordered.

Boris grabbed the side of the hidden door and pulled it open.

The men all stepped back, rifles aimed into the dark cellar.

Suddenly, the boy bit Wheaty's hand, and broke free. The lad picked up a loose board and swung it at Barrett.

"Major!" Jack warned.

Barrett flipped the child to the ground and then glared at Wheaty.

"Sorry, sir, he bit me," Wheaty confessed, rubbing his hand.

Barrett shifted his attention to the tall Bulgarian. "Alex, you're bigger than this boy. Contain him!"

"Yes, sir," Alex said, grabbing both of the boy's arms firmly.

Barrett peered into the dark cellar. "Come on out, or I will come in after you."

They heard a faint whimpering.

"Don't make me come in after you," Barrett's tone showed his seriousness.

"Please, sir. Don't hurt her. She's my sister," the boy begged.

Barrett eyed the now-subdued boy. Von Weber walked closer to him. "What's your name, young man?"

"Emmitt... Emmitt Shultz." The lad's voice cracked.

"Emmitt, Alex is going to let you go. I want you to go in that cellar and bring out whoever is there. We are not here to hurt you. If we were...."

The boy interrupted, "How do I know that?"

Barrett continued, "If we were going to hurt you, we would have done it by now."

"I don't believe you. You're going to hurt my sister like they did."

Barrett's voice took on a kinder tone. "Emmitt, by the loving grace of Jesus, I assure you, none of us here will hurt you, or anyone else, unless we feel our lives are threatened. We are here to help, now please bring out whoever is down there."

The boy stared at Barrett, wanting to believe, but still terrified.

Von Weber calmly stated, "Alex... let him go!"

The soldier released his grip on the boy.

Emmitt looked around, massaging his arm. He slowly began walking toward the hole.

Barrett grabbed the boy's arm as a reminder. "Don't make me come down and get you," he stated sternly.

The boy glared at him and then scrambled down the steep, dark steps.

"Sir, he may have a gun or a knife hidden down there," Wheaty whispered.

"I know, but it sounds like he is protecting his sister. Hopefully, now he understands we are here to help."

A few minutes passed.

"Sir... what should we do?" Wheaty asked.

"Patience... patience, Wheaty."

They could hear the faint sound of voices, but couldn't make out what was being said.

Finally, the boy's face appeared in the dark at the bottom of the steps.

Four of the men had rifles pointed directly at him. They noticed a frightened girl behind him, clutching his hand.

"Lower your rifles, men," the major ordered.

The sun was setting as the pair started up the stairs, the little remaining light illuminating the fear in their eyes.

As the youngsters reached the top step, von Weber slowly reached his hand out and moved the tangled, blonde hair out of the young girl's face.

Terrified, she pulled away, clinging tighter to her brother.

"Please, sir, don't hurt her!" the boy begged, his voice sounding desperate.

"We are not going to hurt her, or you. What is her name?" Barrett voiced, calmly.

A tear escaped from the corner of Emmitt's eye. "Her name is Chastity. She hasn't said a word since they… they had their way with her."

"Had their way?" Wheaty raised a questioning eyebrow.

Looking at the ground, the boy spoke, "The men in blue... they took her... they beat her and they… they did awful things to her."

Wheaty shook his head sadly. "Major, she can't be more than twelve or thirteen."

"She's thirteen, mister. She's my twin sister."

Barrett's heart ached for the girl. The smoke had blackened her face and clothing. He tried again to move her snarled, filthy hair from her face. Tears flooded her eyes leaving streaks through the soot on her cheeks. For a second, her eyes met his, and she noticed a compassionate look. At that moment, she realized Barrett was different from the men who had brutally attacked her, and she finally began to feel safe. She loosened the grip she had on her brother.

"Emmitt, please tell me what happened in this town. Who did this?"

The young boy dropped to the ground, exhausted. "Two nights ago we were attacked by a bunch of Bluecoats."

"Bluecoats, you mean Union soldiers?" Wheaty asked.

He nodded. "Yes, soldiers in blue coats… lots of them." Suddenly, Emmitt's eyes changed and terror took over. "They came in shooting!"

"You sure they were Union soldiers?" Wheaty found it hard to believe that his side was capable of such an atrocity.

"Oh, they were Bluecoats all right."

"How many were there?" Barrett asked.

"About thirty. I was out bow hunting when they got here. I came running back when I heard the first shots. I saw them Bluebelly Devils drag our women and children into the street."

"Where were the men of the town?" Wheaty asked.

"Gone… they took the guns in town and joined General Lee's army to fight the Northerners. My papa died in one of those battles. Only our mothers, sisters, a few boys younger than me, and a couple of old men were left." He paused. "We barely had enough food to stay alive. Little we had, we hid down here," he pointed to the cellar.

He closed his eyes for a moment. "Those Yankees rode in shooting and killing people with their swords."

"Swords... sounds like a cavalry unit," Barrett folded his arms. "Emmitt," he asked, almost afraid of the answer, "How many people did those Bluecoats kill?"

"Almost a hundred."

"Where are they? The bodies... what did they do with all of them?"

"Those men were here for two days... until they ran out of alcohol." His glazed eyes stared in the distance, and his mind drifted to a place he didn't want to revisit. "I can still hear the screams of the girls. I watched my best friend get killed by the leader of the group... he pushed that sword straight through Billy, laughing the whole time. I'll never forget that sword... gold with an ugly snake carved on the blade."

He hesitated as he tried to frame his words. "Many of the people ran into the church for safety... my mama did, too. Even the reverend and his family were in there. The leader told his men to set it on fire." He paused, searching for the strength to continue. "Most of the others were tossed in the well, some were still alive. I tried to get them out, but I couldn't. They took the girls into the saloon; they screamed and cried all night. I hid in the woods. I was so scared. By morning, most everyone was dead, or dying. Sir, the soldiers... they... they...."

His face changed; anger replaced fear. "I killed four of them soldiers. I will kill the rest of them when I find them. I will kill every Bluecoat I see."

"Not all Bluecoats are like that, Emmitt," Barrett said trying to ease the boy's hatred. "There are good and bad men on both sides." His thoughts flew to Brooke's family. *How can Alton and Rory be so different? Alton longs for peace; Rory lives to fight.*

Wheaty interrupted Barrett's thoughts. "How have we come to this?"

The young girl sat on the ground, quietly weeping.

Barrett watched her thoughtfully and then turned to her brother. "Emmitt, I am going to make you and your sister a promise. Tell me everything you can remember about those men—names you heard, what they looked like, what rank was on their uniforms. Did they have any scars, unusual boots... anything you can remember? And I promise you, I will do everything in my power to see that those men are brought to justice."

"Really?" A glint of hope shone in Emmitt's eyes.

"I give you my word, son. I'll do my best." He paused. "Another thing, how did you and your sister escape?"

"When night came, I ran to the root cellar. Most of the Bluebellies got real drunk, so later that night I snuck into the saloon and rescued Chastity."

"Don't know how you killed four of 'em," Jack stated.

"I found a bottle of whiskey in the cellar and put some stuff that they use for dead people in it." A mischievous grin came over his face. "I left it for them on the front porch."

"Dead people?" Alex had a puzzled look.

"Arsenic," Wheaty chimed in. "They use it to embalm people."

"Poisoned 'em?" Jack asked, eyebrows hunched together.

"Yep, didn't bother me at all watching them foam at the mouth. They were twitching on the ground like a chicken with its head cut off. Finally, one of their men shot them dead, to put them out of their misery, I guess. When that man stood there looking at them, I hit him over the head with that same bottle. I think I killed him! I grabbed my sister and ran to the cellar to hide. We heard gunfire the rest of the night. Next morning I heard a lot of commotion—sounded like horses galloping. I peeked out in time to see the last horse leaving, but the whole town was on fire." He lowered his head, and began sobbing, "I wanted to save them, but I couldn't. I was just too scared."

Wheaty put his arm around the young man. "You tried. You saved your sister's life."

"Yes, you are a courageous young man," Barrett added. "Is there any food or water down there?" He motioned with his head to the cellar.

"There's a little food, but no water."

Barrett took a long, deep breath. "We will have to go to the stream to get water. The well is certainly no good."

"Sir, what do we do with these two?" Alex asked.

"Get them some fresh water to start with." He forced a feeble smile.

"Yes, suh, I go," Jack volunteered.

"Take Boris with you... and be on the lookout. We don't know what way the attackers went or if they intend to come back. Don't think they will, but you never know. They may have left some incriminating evidence behind." He glanced at the youngsters.

"Yes, suh." Jack started to leave.

"Major, what will we do with them?" Wheaty asked. "We can't leave them here."

Barrett looked at the children. "No we can't. Jack," he yelled.

"Yes, suh." Jack spun around.

"Where is the closest town?"

"A day's ride from here—small town."

"Is that before or after Gilfred?"

"Before."

"How small is it?"

"Has a railroad... prob'ly six, seven hundred folks." Jack scratched his scruffy beard.

"That will work. We want it big enough that we don't bring any suspicion on us."

Barrett glanced around at what was left of the once-booming settlement. "Let's bury the dead now, so we can get an early start in the morning. Can't afford to lose any more time. We'll bed down here for the night."

"Where should we bury them?" Alex's eyes widened.

Barrett glanced at the girl who had crawled up on a nearby bench and fallen asleep. "We do not have the time or the manpower to bury them, or to bring them up from the well." He paused. "Put all the bodies in the well and fill it in—a mass grave! It's all we can do; it will have to be their burial grounds. Come on men, let's get started."

Barrett picked up the sleeping girl and carried her into the back room of the saloon. He gently laid her down in a bed, like a father holding his sleeping child.

Emmitt stayed next to her, protectively guarding his twin.

When they knew for certain she was asleep, Barrett and the boy returned to the main part of the saloon and strode over to a table. "Emmitt, sit down. I know it will be hard, but I need you to tell me everything you can about the men who did this to your sister and your friends. I want the attackers to pay for the crimes they committed here... every one of them. Was any rank ever mentioned? Any names?"

"I heard them mention the name, Rice... he was called lieutenant a couple times. And there was a Gibbon, or Gibbons... Captain Gibbons, I think. He seemed to be the leader. I hate him... he was the one that killed Billy."

"This Captain Gibbons gave the orders?"

"Yes. He told the men to have their fun."

The thought made Barrett's stomach queasy.

Alex and Boris burst into the saloon. "Sir, look what we found."

Barrett reached for the blue coat that Alex was holding and held it up to examine it.

"Sergeant stripes... interesting. The insignia looks like it's from the West Virginia Third Cavalry. Who's commanding the West Virginia Army?"

"Not sure, sir, but Wheaty will know. He knows everything," Alex chortled.

"Call him in."

"Yes, sir." He rushed to the door and called out, "Wheaty, Bear needs you."

Wheaty hurried in. "You call, sir?"

"Yes... who is in charge of the West Virginia Army?"

"Just West Virginia? Uh... that would be General David Hunter."

"General Hunter, you say?"

"Yes, sir, it's part of Sheridan's force."

"I know Sheridan, but I don't know Hunter." Barrett thought a moment and then turned to face Wheaty. "I don't think these men are with any unit. I think they are acting on their own. But I believe they had their orders."

"Orders to kill and rape innocent people?" Alex questioned.

"Probably to cause havoc in the South."

Alex shook his head in disgust. "What those soldiers did here was inexcusable."

"Yes, and I'm sure it's not the only town that it has happened to... there are many others."

"But, sir, this war will end one day... and when it does, the men who did crimes like this will have to pay." Wheaty emphasized the word "will."

"Unfortunately, not all soldiers are going to pay for their crimes," von Weber replied, sadly.

"But you said yourself that these men are going to pay," Emmitt voiced.

"I did say that and I meant it. The men who did this think there are no witnesses, but you are alive." Von Weber smiled, sending a message to the boy that he would keep his promise.

"But if them Bluecoats have orders for this, what we do 'bout it?" Jack asked, blinking rapidly.

"The military orders are precise. You obey the last command first, but you never obey a command that is contrary to the laws of God." Barrett stared straight ahead.

"Like killing an unarmed man, or raping women and children?" Wheaty shot back.

"Exactly." Barrett faced Emmitt. "Because there are witnesses, these men will be found and brought to justice. Now get some sleep. Wheaty, stay here and keep them safe."

"Yes, sir."

Von Weber walked through the batwing saloon doors and watched as Alex and Boris put the last body into the old well. They stood back for a moment with hats off and heads bowed. After a moment of silence, the two men took a couple picks they had found and began chipping away at the side of the well until it collapsed.

The citizens of this once-tranquil town now lay buried deep in the well.

When morning came, the men gathered the few supplies they could find for the youngsters—an old blanket and a ragged change of clothes.

Barrett took Chastity on his horse; Emmitt rode with Wheaty.

One final order came from the major. "Alex, burn the saloon... it doesn't seem right to burn down the church and leave the saloon standing. It's like this town never existed."

As they rode out of town, a spectacular sunrise brightening the sky served as a reminder that God was still in control.

Leaving the place Chastity always knew to be her home, she continued glancing back at the devastation, tears streaming down her sweet face.

After a little more than a day of traveling, they entered what appeared to be a peaceful town.

"Looks safe enough... almost like there is no war being fought," Wheaty acknowledged.

"Yes, but before the war ends, it will be touched," Barrett predicted.

The major gathered his men together and spoke calmly, "Listen up. Wheaty and I are going to take these children to the church for safekeeping. Stay out of sight. I do not want to arouse any suspicion. Be sure to keep a watchful eye for Moccasin, I hope he catches up to us soon."

As they rode into town, everything appeared peaceful. The sound of children's laughter as they played a game of tag in the street was refreshing. A couple elderly men sat in front of the hardware store playing a serious game of checkers; a lazy dog sprawled out at their feet.

A familiar melody from the piano in the church echoed through the town. Barrett smiled, recognizing the popular hymn as one he composed early in his career. He shook his head. *That seems like a lifetime ago!*

A man was sweeping the front steps of the church when they arrived. He looked up at them and smiled. "Good morning, may I help you?"

Barrett tipped his hat. "Are you the preacher?"

"Yes, sir. Name is Brother Jeffrey Voth."

"Preacher, I have a couple orphans here. Chastity and Emmitt are twins. A couple days ago, they witnessed some marauders kill their mother and everyone else in town. Their father was recently killed in the war. The girl... well... she has been severely traumatized, if you know what I mean."

Pastor Voth sighed. "What town was that?"

"South Wales."

"South Wales? I knew Brother Elbert, the preacher there. He was a good man. Lots of nice folks in South Wales." An expression of disbelief clouded his eyes.

"The town is no more." Barrett frowned.

The major started to help the girl off his horse, but she grabbed his neck and clung tight, whimpering.

"Chastity, I have to go. Trust me, you will be safe here." His heart was heavy.

Emmitt dismounted, ran to his sister, and protectively stretched his arms out for her. "I have her, come on, Chastity. They will be kind to us here."

She slowly released her grip on Barrett and slid off the horse into her brother's arms, still staring at von Weber's face, submitting it to memory.

Barrett reached into his pocket and jangled some coins. Pulling out a couple gold pieces, he stated, "I don't have much, but what I have is theirs." He handed the money to the preacher.

"Thank you, sir. God bless you!" Brother Voth examined the coins. "May I ask you, sir, why would you do this? These are hard times. Most men would leave children like these for dead."

"The Good Book says," *Inasmuch as ye have done it unto one of the least of these my brethren, ye have done it unto me.*

"You speak as a man who knows the Lord." The pastor shielded the sun with his hand as he looked at von Weber.

Wheaty snickered. *If he only knew the major is the Hymnist!*

"I was raised a Christian," Barrett beamed proudly.

"I see. Well, thank you, sir, for the offering. I really don't want to accept it, but these are hard times and…."

"No apology needed. I would give more if I could."

"Sir, I assure you, Chastity and Emmitt be well taken care of. You have my word!"

"Thank you, Reverend Voth. We must go, but Lord willing, I will stop by one day to see how they are doing."

"I pray the same. What is your name, sir?"

Barrett smiled. *I dare not tell him who I am.* "It is best that I remain anonymous, but I must say, I sure do like that piano tune."

"Thank you, sir. It's von Weber's, *God is Omnipotent.* I love the tune, but can't seem to find the lyrics for it."

"I don't think there are any words for it. How can there be? God is too beautiful and powerful to describe with human words."

The preacher stared at Barrett, speechless.

The major tipped his hat. "Good day, sir."

He and Wheaty turned their horses around and began to ride away.

The preacher watched them, scratching his head. Suddenly, a smile came to his face and he shouted, "My dream is to see him in concert one day—the Hymnist, I mean."

Barrett laughed heartily. "We will have to see what God has planned in your life... and his."

"Godspeed, sir."

Barrett waved and reined his horse into a comfortable trot.

The pastor continued to watch the strangers ride to the edge of town where four other horsemen greeted them. Within minutes, they disappeared out of sight.

Well, I'll be! Could that really be him? Nobody would believe me if I told them, so I guess I will just keep it to myself... for now.

He looked down at Emmitt and Chastity as his wife walked out to join him.

"Who were you talking to, dear?"

"You would not believe me if I told you." The preacher shook his head, still stunned.

The pastor's wife knelt down in front of the frightened girl. "Who do we have here? Why child... you look awful scared. Don't be. You are safe with us. Is this your brother?" She patted Emmitt's head.

The girl timidly nodded.

The loving woman put her arm around Chastity. With her other hand, she brushed the hair from her frightened eyes. "My, you are a beautiful young lady. You are safe now... both of you. Let's go in and get cleaned up." The woman stood and took the twins' hands, leading them into the church. "I was just about ready to make some cookies. Did you want to help?"

Chastity nodded, a slight smile turned up the corner of her mouth.

One more time, the preacher gazed off in the distance where the gentle rider and his companion had gone. He smiled, nodded his head, and then went inside and shut the door.

Chapter Twenty-Five

April 5, 1864
Gilfred, Virginia

Making sure the twins were safe had cost a significant amount of time, so the distance between the stolen rifles and Barrett's men had grown considerably. The major surmised that the detour had put them at least a full day and a half behind schedule. Still, Barrett had no doubt it had been the right thing for them to do.

They tried to retrace their steps back to where they had left the trail.

"Sir, I think we are lost," Alex admitted, shaking his head.

"I ain't lost, suh," Jack replied. "I know right where we at."

"I wish Moccasin were here to follow the tracks." Confusion reflected in Alex's eyes.

"Just give him some more time, hopefully he is nearing us. Anyway we are not following tracks right now because we are going to Gilfred," Barrett remarked.

"Jack, how much farther is it?" Von Weber tried not to let his exhaustion show.

"Be thar by mornin', suh."

They traveled on in silence, each man too weary to speak.

Just before sunset, a noise from the brush startled the team. A couple of them instinctively raised their rifles, aiming in that direction. Tension was high.

Barrett breathed a sigh of relief when their Indian friend bounded out of hiding. "Hold your fire, men. We don't want to hurt our tracker."

Moccasin rode closer to the major.

Barrett voiced, "Jack, continue leading, I need to talk to Moccasin. We will set up camp in about an hour."

Riding side-by-side, Barrett quizzed Moccasin. "Did you get the mother and daughter to safety?"

Moccasin nodded.

"Did someone take them in?"

He nodded again.

"You're sure they are safe?"

The Indian smiled broadly shaking his head. He pointed to Barrett, signing something.

"I'm sorry, I don't understand." Confused, Barrett called for Wheaty's help.

Watching from close behind them, Wheaty replied, "He said that the women are safe and they thank you for helping them."

"Well, thank you, Moccasin, for a job well done."

They continued their journey in silence until finally the dark, coupled with their exhaustion, overtook them.

"We will camp here," von Weber unenthusiastically announced. They reined the worn out horses to a stop and dismounted.

"Want me to start a fire, sir?" Alex asked. "This night air has brought a chill."

"We can't risk it at night. It could bring some unwanted visitors. Now, let's get a few hours of shuteye. We will take turns on watch. Wheaty and I will be first. Jerry and Boris take the second shift. Alex and Jack take the last. Moccasin, you rest... you earned it."

The Indian grabbed his blanket from his saddlebag and wandered off to find a place to sleep. He was out the moment his head hit the ground.

Before the sun rose, Alex woke Barrett up. "Sir, should we get some food?"

"Yes. Anyone else awake?" Barrett whispered.

"Jerry, Moccasin, and Boris are still sleeping... the rest of us are anxious to get started."

Yawning, Barrett made his way over to where the others were gathering firewood.

Barrett quietly ordered, "Let the others sleep a while. We'll spread out and catch a rabbit or something. Take your rifles with you, but do not fire. Use your knives. We don't want to attract attention." He grabbed his rifle and headed into the thick, dew-laden shrubbery, hoping to find some meat for breakfast.

Suddenly, gunshots shattered the tranquility of the morning—first one, and then another. "I told them not to shoot," the major muttered under his breath as he ran back towards camp.

As Barrett neared camp, he heard unfamiliar voices. He cautiously peered through some bushes. Jerry and Moccasin sat on the ground with their hands raised. Four rough-looking characters held them captive—two were dressed in civilian clothes, the others wore Rebel uniforms. As he scanned the scene, he noticed Boris sprawled face down in the dirt, close to where he slept.

A short, bearded, stocky man dressed in a dirty gray uniform questioned, "Should we hang these two, or cut their throats?"

"Hang the darky! Scalp the Indian! But don't shoot the gun again," a tall, lean man in civilian clothes, replied in a gravelly voice. "Then, grab their horses, and let's get out of here before 'em Bluecoats catch up to us."

One of the Rebels found a rope in the camp and tied it loosely around Jerry's neck.

Seething with anger, Barrett took his Henry from around his shoulder, keeping a watchful eye on the man who had tied the noose around Jerry's neck.

Another Rebel removed his knife from its sheath, and positioned himself behind Moccasin.

Barrett aimed carefully. When the Rebel moved the knife toward the Indian, the major fired, hitting the attacker between his cold, evil eyes.

Instantly, the major took aim again, and fired at the man who was tightening the noose around Jerry's neck. A shot through the head caused his body to immediately crumble to the ground, convulsing.

The tall man, who appeared to be the leader, immediately shifted his attention in the direction of the shots. He attempted to pull his pistol from the holster, just as Barrett's third shot rang out. The bullet found its mark in the man's mid-section, causing him to collapse.

Von Weber downed the last intruder before the Rebel had a chance to pull the trigger. He fell dead in a heap, pistol still in hand, next to the lifeless man who only seconds before was dishing out orders.

Wheaty and Jack rushed out from behind the trees as Barrett fired the last shot. They wasted no time hurrying to the aid of their comrades.

"Sorry, suh," Jerry said, his voice trembling. "Them Rebs s'prised us. Heard 'em yellin' and woke. They shot Boris goin' for his gun."

The major hurried to his fallen friend and rolled him over. There was no doubt, Boris was dead.

Alex dashed over to them. In silence, he towered over his friend's lifeless body, sadly lowering his head.

"Sorry, Alex," Jerry mumbled. "There was nuttin' we could do."

Alex bent over to pick up his long-time friend. Moccasin tried to help, but the Bulgarian motioned for him to leave. "He was my friend. I will bury him."

Wheaty walked over to Alex and placed his hand on his shoulder. "He was our friend, too. We would like to help."

Alex reluctantly agreed.

Barrett took over. "Moccasin, help Alex bury Boris. Jerry, make sure our horses are all accounted for. Jack, take a Henry and stand guard in the bushes. The shots may have aroused someone's curiosity. Wheaty, let's find out who these men are."

Wheaty and Barrett emptied the pockets of the dead men. There was no identification. A couple of them carried photographs, but nothing else.

"Sir, looks like they were after our horses, had none of their own. These men were obviously worn out! I think they had been in a battle and been running on foot for a long time," Wheaty surmised.

Jerry rushed over to Barrett. "Suh, horses are fine."

"Good. Jerry, what did those men say to you?" the major asked.

"One them said they better get goin' fore them Bluebellies showed up. What ya s'pose that meant?" Jerry's eyes widened.

"I suspect they were in a skirmish with the North the last couple days, but there are no active battles going on that I am aware of."

"Sir, look at this," Wheaty pointed to one of the dead men.

Barrett flipped the body over, studying him closer. "He is wearing civilian clothes, but has military boots on."

"Not just any military boots... Union boots." Wheaty added, "Sir, do you think this could be Abbott or Hornsby?"

"I think that is a good possibility. We are almost certain that Moses is dead, so that leaves the other two. That means we might be close to the stolen goods." Barrett scratched his head. "I wonder what happened."

Jerry cut in, "One of 'em said, Bluecoats attacked 'em."

Von Weber took a long deep breath. "Might have been the same marauders that destroyed South Wales. If so, who are they, and what are their orders, if they have any?"

"What should we do with the dead?" Wheaty asked.

"Hide them in the shrubbery. Let's hurry and get out of here before we have any more trouble."

The rest of the morning was quiet. Even Wheaty was at an unusual loss for words. Boris' death affected everyone. It was a reminder of how vulnerable they were. The Bulgarian was a quiet man, and for the most part, the rest of the men hardly knew he was there. Yet, he was still part of the group and would be missed, especially by Alex, his fellow countryman.

Barrett knew they had to get their minds focused. Massaging his temples, he pondered the situation. *It is possible that the Union has retrieved the rifles already. If that is the case, should we abandon our orders, or continue?* He was at a loss. He whispered a quick prayer for wisdom. *For now, we will continue.*

It was late afternoon when they trudged wearily into the Gilfred mining settlement. Three buildings and a stable made up the small town. Yet, what they saw was far different from what they hoped to see. Obviously, a battle had taken place. Bodies of soldiers in both gray and blue uniforms, as well as many civilians, littered the ground. There were even a few women and children.

Peering around, Wheaty cited, "It's deserted here, sir. It looks like there's not a living soul."

Barrett had a way of issuing orders that gave his men confidence in his authority. "Listen up, everyone. I want an exact count of how many Union, Confederate, and civilian bodies you find. And let me know if you see any wagons… especially if they have rifles or ammunition. Alex and Jack, inspect the two large buildings and the stable. Jerry and Wheaty, you check out the bodies—see if any can be identified."

Barrett faced Moccasin and spoke directly to him. "See if you can figure out what happened. If the stolen supplies were here… see if there are any tracks to follow."

The Indian hurried off.

Barrett walked over to three bodies in the street, all wearing Confederate uniforms. Two of them still had rifles in their hands; the other held a pistol. He took the pistol out of the lifeless man's hand and examined it. Speaking aloud, he said, "Colt .44, cavalry issued weapon." Searching the chamber, he muttered, "It's empty."

He wandered closer to a dead horse and noticed the initials, *US,* branded on a front shoulder. The markings on the left hip clearly read *1WV*. Barrett whispered, "1st West Virginia. What are they doing here? The group that attacked South Wales had the same insignia. This can't be a coincidence… it must be Gibbon's dirty work."

The major dropped the pistol to the ground. Staying alert, he walked up the steps into the smallest building. Much of the merchandise on the inside of the small workshop had been destroyed, but a few clocks still hung on the wall. A number of others cluttered a nearby table, parts scattered around them. He walked over, picked one up, and studied it. *I have not seen a clock like this since I left Germany—a Black Forest clock.* He examined the intricate details. *Nice workmanship.* A smile came to his face as memories surfaced. For a few minutes he was lost in the past, remembering the clocks in his home in Germany, and the sounds they made on the hour, like a symphony.

Barrett ambled outside and sat down on the steps of the old building. He stared at the scattered bodies. *Just what happened here?*

Alex, Jack, and Jerry ran up to him, slightly winded.

"Sir," Alex reported, "We counted twenty-three dead Union soldiers, twenty-four Confederate soldiers, and fifteen civilians—including two woman and three children who appear to be in their teens. Sir, a number of the Confederates and civilians were lined up and shot."

"You mean execution style?" Barrett's eyes grew wide.

"Yes, sir. And a couple of them had been tortured." Alex nodded, noticeably disturbed by the sight. "I noticed none of the civilians had a gun."

"Course not, 'ems Mennonites. Don't carry guns," Jack replied. "Peaceful people and hunt jus' for food."

"Did they run this gold operation?" Barrett asked, looking toward the river.

"Looks like it, if you can call it that. They probably panned for the residual gold from the mines up the river," Alex stated.

"Did you see any gold?" Barrett inquired, letting out a lengthy sigh.

They all shook their heads.

"That means there was either no gold here, or it was taken by whoever did this." Barrett added, "What did you find in the buildings?"

Alex struggled to keep his voice even. "Dead bodies! And, sir, behind the buildings were three large tents, each with six cots. I think there was a platoon of Confederates stationed here to protect the gold."

"That would make sense. The South is probably out of gold. Every ounce they find is worth a fortune. The government would want to protect it." Barrett peered in the direction of Moccasin and Wheaty who were kneeling beside some fresh tracks, examining them.

"We found some wagons down by the stable, but no rifles or ammunition," Alex continued.

Wheaty and Moccasin ran over to join them.

"Please give me something to go on. Did you figure anything out?" Barrett asked.

"Yes, sir," Wheaty said, wiping the sweat from his forehead. "Apparently, there was a lot of action here the last couple days. Near as we can tell about twenty Mennonites ran this mining town... probably three families—men, women and children."

"Then we can rule out the townspeople buying the guns," Barrett commented.

"I believe that is a correct assumption, sir."

"But everything points to the guns being here," the major pointed out.

Wheaty explained further, "Sir, the shipments were here. This was the meeting place. There's no doubt Hornsby also was here… we tracked his horse that has a nail through the shoe all around town. Eventually that horse left with two heavy wagons and five riders. We think both shipments combined here, which is why the loads were so heavy. The wagons came in from the same direction we did, but left the only other way out." He pointed to a partially eroded, rough road. "They went along the river. Near as Moccasin can tell, they must have left a couple days ago."

"I would have thought they would have had more than five soldiers guarding the shipment." Barrett rubbed his forehead.

Wheaty paused, "The tracks and footprints tell us a lot. The wagons apparently left before the battle began. We think the battle happened late yesterday, and by the looks of things, it was over quickly."

"Any idea how it played out?"

"Moccasin has a pretty good idea. He thinks the Rebels knew the Union troops were following them and set up an ambush for when they entered town. When they arrived, fighting erupted. The Union did not know a platoon of Confederates were already camped here." Wheaty crossed his arms.

"And the Confederates had no idea they were up against a seasoned Union cavalry unit." Barrett suggested. "Talk about a disaster waiting to happen!"

"Sir, Moccasin saw footprints from four men who escaped on foot heading east."

"That would probably be the men that killed Boris," Barrett surmised.

"Right," Wheaty agreed. "After the battle was over, the remaining Union soldiers ransacked this place. Most likely, they were looking for the gold. Looks like only seven or eight Union soldiers survived the battle, and they headed along the river chasing the wagons."

Barrett looked over at the corpses in the street. "They must have got their information from the soldiers they tortured."

"There are a number of 1st West Virginia horses by the river, as well as some others," Wheaty continued. "Sir, one of the horses belonged to General Custer… remember, it was stolen."

Barrett let out a lengthy sigh. "I guess that tells us these men must be acting on their own."

The look on Alex's face showed his concern. "Could the man who stole Custer's horse know about the stolen rifles?"

Barrett shrugged. "Let's just say, a tent isn't soundproof. Someone could have overheard the plans, stole Custer's horse, and took off." He paused, deep in thought. "I suspect that eight Union soldiers would not be heading south into enemy territory without a good reason—that would be suicide. They must believe the rifles or gold are on those wagons, maybe both."

"But how did the man that stole Custer's horse know to come here?" Alex asked.

"That is the unanswered question," the major confessed.

"Suh, goin' by river is slow. If we go back way we came, we can cut 'em off. Take maybe a day," Jack stated.

Barrett stood and brushed his pants off. "Let me summarize what we know. It is obvious they are not taking the shipment to Lee because there would be hundreds of men guarding them by now, so we can rule out going to Richmond, or Fredericksburg. We are far past those two cities and pretty darn close to North Carolina. I think the rifles are being sold to someone else. The Rebels did not anticipate Union soldiers bent on destruction in Gilfred and had to move fast. They may have spotted them ahead of time and that is why they left quickly with only a handful of guards. The rest of the men stayed behind to ambush Gibbons and his cavalry. Hornsby probably thought they could overtake them and catch up to the shipment. They did not expect such a large force, or a cavalry unit, which is why so many men were killed."

"It was unfortunate for the Mennonites who lived here—innocent, peace-loving people just trying to make an honest living," Alex added, sadly.

Barrett agreed, "You're right, Alex." He took a swig of water from his canteen. "So, Jack, you think we can catch them?"

"Yes, suh."

Barrett glanced down the old road. "Question is... who will have the stolen goods when we catch up to them? I am certainly not happy about fighting our own Union soldiers."

The men murmured in agreement.

"There's only one way to find out. Gentlemen, let's move! Let's get them!" Barrett's voice contained a fire, resolve.

"What about 'em dead?" Jerry asked.

"I am sorry, but we have to let them be."

"Even the women and children?"

"Yes, there are too many dead, and our mission is to get those rifles before the Confederate Army does." Barrett eyed his men one by one. "Or, whoever it is that is waiting for them."

"And to find Lee, right, sir?" Wheaty added.

"Yes, Wheaty."

Chapter Twenty-Six

April 8, 1864

The six riders pushed hard through the night, sleeping only a couple of hours.

Before dawn, they were on their journey again, still exhausted.

After a couple hours, they left the trail and began to climb a steep ridge.

It seemed that Moccasin's sense of smell was leading him. When they finally reached the top, he hurriedly dismounted and ran ahead, crouching close to the ground. Sensing the urgency of the situation, Barrett and the others watched the Indian, each man motionless, waiting breathlessly.

The tracker turned around and gestured for everyone to dismount and stay low to the ground.

Moccasin used his elbows to maneuver to the edge of a cliff. As he peered across the wide valley, his dark eyes widened, and fear took over his face.

Barrett fell on his stomach and edged his way next to the Indian guide.

The others followed, silently crawling over to join them.

Hearts racing, Barrett and his small group of men lay in stunned silence. As far as they could see was a sea of dingy, white and gray tents—thousands of them, all sizes.

Alex studied the scene through his spyglass. "Looks like the entire Confederate Army. What are they doing here?"

"I suspect waiting for orders," Barrett muttered, looking though the scope on his Henry rifle.

"What kind of orders?" Alex whispered.

"Isn't it obvious? We are in the Shenandoah Valley... he's planning to march to Washington, take it over, and end this miserable war."

"Really think he can do dat?" Jack asked.

Jerry's curiosity heightened. "Who is he?"

Wheaty scanned the valley. "He... is... there." Wheaty pointed to a large tent near the end of the encampment closest to them. "That's the old man himself... General Robert E. Lee. Never thought I would see him." Wheaty smiled, handing the spyglass to Jerry.

"Lee?" Alex whispered, focusing on the area. "Well, I'll be, he looks like my grandfather."

"He looks like everyone's grandfather," Wheaty commented.

"Don't look like mine," the black man, Jerry, said, causing everyone to chuckle.

"That is the funniest thing I have ever heard you say," Wheaty commented.

"Okay, men, quiet down," Barrett ordered.

Alex whispered, "Sir, if we killed him now, we would be heroes, and maybe even end this war. You know, what is that old saying? 'You cut the head off the serpent.'"

Barrett continued staring through his scope. "I don't think we would be heroes, and we definitely would not end the war."

"Surely it would help. I heard say that if it was not for him and Stonewall Jackson, this war would have been over a long time ago," Alex added.

Jerry handed the spyglass back to Wheaty. "Do you think you can hit him from here, Major?"

Barrett hesitated, looking over the scene in the valley. "It would be a stretch with my Henry, but not with the Whitworth."

Alex carefully unwrapped the rifle he had been protecting while they travelled the last few weeks. "Here, sir." He offered it to von Weber.

Barrett eyed the rifle and then Alex. Setting his Henry on the ground, he took the sharpshooter rifle and brought its scope to his eye. *Grant told me, if I get a shot to take it.* Peering through the scope, he focused on Lee just as the General turned and walked back into the tent.

"General Robert E. Lee," he whispered loud enough for his men to hear. "Any of you know what the 'E' stands for?" He lowered his rifle.

There was no reply.

"Neither do I." He chuckled. "Listen up, men. Our mission has changed."

"What?" Alex blinked.

"We need to get back to Brandy Station and tell General Grant that we found Lee and what looks to be the entire Confederate Army. Moccasin, how many men do you think are in this valley?"

The old Indian scanned the valley and then raised seven fingers.

"Seventy thousand?" Barrett gulped.

Moccasin nodded.

Barrett looked back through his scope and dished out new assignments. "Wheaty and Moccasin, head west, and then north to Brandy Station. Alex and Jack, head back the way we came. Whoever gets there first, tell Grant that seventy thousand Rebels are camped out west of Fredericksburg, close to Spotsylvania."

"Why teams of two? Why not all stay together?" Alex searched his face.

"Because right now the most important thing is to get word to Grant. We are in Confederate territory, splitting up will give us a better chance of reporting Lee's position to Grant. In addition, our mission is not complete... we are close to the rifles. We must destroy them before they get to the battlefield."

"Just you and Jerry are going after the shipment? Aren't you going to need Moccasin to track?" Wheaty sounded confused.

"We will be fine. Jerry knows the area."

Barrett put his hand out to shake their hands. "It has been great working with all of you. I could not have picked six better men. My heart is hurt that Boris did not live to see this."

Alex shook his hand. "I would like to see you take that shot before I go."

Barrett smiled. "Take that shot? You make it sound so... so formidable."

Alex peered over the cliff. "Wheaty, how far do you think that is?"

Wheaty looked over the terrain, measuring in his mind. "I'd say, twelve hundred yards."

"You do realize that once I pull the trigger, the entire Confederate Army will be after us."

"Yeah, but by the time they get up here, we will be long gone," Alex grinned.

Barrett loaded a single .45 hexagon bullet in the chamber. He would only have one chance to hit his target.

Alex and Jack watched the enemy through their spyglasses, pulses racing.

Through the Whitworth riflescope, Barrett observed General Lee step out of the tent and look around the camp. He could see his mouth moving. *He is probably saying good morning to his men, maybe even saying how peaceful the morning is.*

As the sun rose, the haze was beginning to lift. Amber and tangerine streaks painted the sky. Faint voices echoed across the valley. The aroma of burning firewood lazily drifted to the ridge where the men lay, waiting.

A man walked up to Lee and handed him a cup.

"Bad time to get a cup of coffee," Alex smirked.

Lee brought the cup closer, but first smelled the savory aroma. He took a sip, then turned and conversed with the same man, smiling. As he began to bring the mug to his lips, Barrett pulled the trigger.

The shot was deafening to the six men, but muffled to the soldiers in the valley below. Before anyone knew what was happening, the bullet found its mark. Lee's tin cup clanged as the shot rang out. Coffee splashed all over the astonished white-haired general's hand and sleeve. The bullet went through the cup and found its final resting place in one of the boards that held up the tent. The bullet's force tipped the tent slightly.

Immediately, guards surrounded Lee, scanning the horizon, searching for the source of the shot.

"You missed him," Alex charged, frowning at Barrett.

"No, he didn't. He hit exactly what he was aiming at," Wheaty was quick to reply.

"Major, you deliberately shot the cup... why?" Alex asked, confusion written all over his face.

Barrett looked through his scope as guards whisked Lee to safety. Other soldiers scurried around trying to find where the shot came from.

The major confessed, "I have met him before. He's a good man."

"Good? No, he's Rebel," Jack protested. "Killin' him coulda ended da war."

Wheaty smiled at the major. "You knew what you were doing all along."

Barrett chided his men, "Jack, he's an American, and I do not think it would have ended the war. I know how much his fellow soldiers love him. It would take the Confederates only a short time to figure out who fired that shot. I do not want to live the rest of my life looking over my shoulder. The six of us would have had to live out our lives in fear."

The major continued, "I have given you orders. Follow them! Hurry and get back to Grant! And if I do not see any of you again, it was an honor to have served with you. And Wheaty, return General Custer's horse to him... he may need it."

The four men stood and reluctantly backed away, careful to avoid being seen by the army below. They snapped to attention, and saluted their respected major.

Barrett returned the salute, still lying down.

The men quickly mounted their horses and sped off at full gallop.

"Jerry, let's move while we still can."

As the Confederate guards continued searching for the individual who fired the shot, Barrett stood and raised his rifle over his head.

"There he is," someone yelled, "Shoot him!"

Lee stepped out of the tent and stared at the man standing tall on the high ridge above.

The Confederate soldiers fired on the lone figure.

Lee smiled. "Hold your fire, men. He is out of range. You will never hit him, and you will never catch him. He knows exactly what he is doing."

"But, sir, he tried to kill you."

"No, he didn't. He hit exactly where he aimed. If he wanted to kill me, he would have, and he certainly would not have made his presence known." Lee stared at the silhouette of the man on the ridge. "If we had men like that, we would win this war!"

General Lee picked up the tin cup and examined it. "I would like to shake the hand of that man. He is some marksman!"

Lee looked at the man on the ridge, over a half mile away. Standing tall, the General saluted him.

Barrett returned the salute.

Jerry and von Weber mounted their horses and rode off.

Chapter Twenty-Seven

April 9, 1864

Thunder rumbled in the background, a reminder that it was rainy season in the South. A slight chill hung in the air.

Barrett and Jerry were determined to catch up to the stolen rifles and destroy them before it was too late. With seventy thousand Confederate troops breathing down their necks, they knew they had to move quickly. Not even rain would slow them down.

"Think anyone be followin' us?" Jerry felt his body tense.

"I pray not." Barrett spoke as his horse trotted along. The impact of the hooves on the soil sounded quiet in the eeriness of the morning. He had no idea if they were being followed, but he hoped that if the Confederates were chasing anyone, it would be them, and not Moccasin and Wheaty, or Alex and Jack. It was imperative that someone deliver the message to Grant. With Lee's army encamped in the Shenandoah Valley, he knew they must be waiting for the arrival of spring to launch an attack against Washington—and it was now spring. Grant needed to know Lee's position, so his army would be ready to defend the Union capitol.

Barrett was surprised that the road they were following did not have more Rebel troops stationed on it. There were security checkpoints located strategically along the road, usually on a bridge. He wondered how the rifles were getting through without being confiscated. Having to bypass the checkpoints slowed Barrett and Roundtree down considerably. They remained alert, always on the lookout for signs of trouble.

Finally, in the drizzle, they rode into a small town built on a gentle slope.

Barrett scanned the area, noting there was only one road through the town. "Gibbons and his Union soldiers would not go through this Rebel town. There must be a path up the hill somewhere that we missed." He pointed to the cliffs opposite the town. "But the heavy wagons had to come through here... no way they could have gone over those hills." He thought for a moment. "We will have to go into town because we need supplies. We know the wagons had to come this way, so let's keep our ears open and maybe we can learn something. We will act as if we are just passing through. Be careful what you say and do."

"I follow you, Massa. I be your slave," Jerry snickered.

Barrett gave Jerry a long look and smiled. "Yeah, I guess that will be the best way. Just walk behind me and stay close at all times."

"No need to tell me how to be slave. I got lots of practice, Massa."

Barrett eyed the black man. "I guess you have."

Cautiously, they rode to the old building marked, "General Store." They tied their horses to the hitching post, watching for the reaction of the townspeople. Most ignored them–a white man with a black slave was still commonplace in this area.

When they entered the store, Barrett walked up to the counter and ordered the needed supplies.

"Is that your slave?" the man at the counter questioned.

"To be perfectly honest, Jerry is a free man. He does work for me."

"Same as a slave," the storeowner grunted. "He doesn't steal, does he?"

"Jerry... steal? My word, no. He is the most honest person I know."

"No such thing as an honest darky," the man muttered under his breath, loud enough for Jerry to hear.

"Boss man, can we get some sugar candy?"

Barrett ignored Jerry, waiting for their supplies.

Roundtree noticed a few rough looking men in Confederate uniforms outside, inspecting their horses. He nudged Barrett's elbow.

Von Weber glanced out the window.

While the man behind the counter gathered their supplies, he caught a glimpse of what they were looking at. "They keep tabs on everyone and everything that goes through this town. Some people believe they are not even military... just some men hanging around causing trouble. Even been rumored that they check out people like you."

"Like me?" Barrett questioned.

"Yes, people who are just passing through town. Someone's always passing through, trying to flee the war."

"Why are they checking me out?"

"Some say that those bad eggs rob visitors a few miles outside of town. You are a prime target."

"Do they kill them?"

"Don't know. Never see or hear from them again. No bodies have ever been found, either. Had a small group of Confederates come through a few hours ago, but they left them alone."

"Confederates?" Barrett asked.

"Yeah. Five or six riders with two wagons. Looked like they been to battle and were heavily armed."

Barrett watched one of the men opening his saddlebag. Another showed keen interest in his rifle.

"Jerry, stay here."

"I go with you, Massa."

"No! You stay here and finish packing up the supplies." Barrett reached into his pocket, grabbed some Confederate money, and handed it to the shop owner. "Will this take care of my bill?"

The storekeeper eyed the money and smiled. "Sure will. I will take good care of you. Watch out for them, mister… they can be violent."

Barrett tipped his hat and walked toward the door. Before he exited, he noticed an ax handle, and picked it up, examining it. "Is this real hickory?"

"Yes, sir."

"Can I see how strong it is?"

The shopkeeper gave a crooked smile. "Help yourself."

Barrett strode out the door.

Jerry followed the storekeeper as he moved quickly from behind the counter and over to the window. A number of other people who had been shopping joined them, all anxious to catch a glimpse of the excitement in the street.

Barrett plopped the hickory stick over his shoulder and hurried down the crooked wooden steps. "May I help you, gentlemen?"

Startled, the three troublemakers looked up.

The man examining the rifle stopped what he was doing, glaring at von Weber.

"Who's asking?" one of them mocked.

"I am!" Barrett stepped closer, scowling at the man who was shuffling through his saddlebag.

The rough looking character grunted, throwing the bedroll and shaving supplies to the ground.

"Mister! You will stop what you are doing, pick up my belongings, and put them back exactly as you found them. Now!"

The man ignored Barrett, continuing to nose through his pack. "And just who do you think you are?" he quizzed.

"That's my saddlebag! And, what you are doing is illegal." Barrett's voice and manner indicated he was not to be trifled with.

"Sammy, do you hear anyone?" The thug turned to his cohort.

"Nope." The third man stepped from beside Jerry's horse and stormed toward Barrett. He unfastened his trigger strap and reached for his pistol.

In an instant, the major brought the hickory stick from his shoulder, crashing it across the man's gun hand. A piercing scream indicated that his bloody hand was broken, possibly shattered.

The soldier, who had been searching the saddlebags, pulled his knife. In one swift motion, Barrett brought the stick to the side of his head. The man crumpled to the ground in an unconscious heap.

The remaining man reached for his rifle, which was leaning against the hitching post. Wasting no time, Barrett brought the heavy stick down across the old Springfield rifle, cracking it in half. Calmly, he pointed the stick at the man. "Do you want to continue this?"

The man looked around and began to back away. "You don't know who you're dealing with, mister," he threatened.

"Yes, I do. You're the man who needs to take his friends and leave before you are permanently damaged, or worse. Grab your garbage and leave." The major scowled at the criminals.

"You could have killed us," the man with the bleeding hand screamed.

"Yes, I could have," calmly, Barrett agreed.

The men lifted their unconscious partner and dragged his body down the dirt road.

Barrett watched them limp down the street, never looking back.

He walked back into the store and examined the hickory stick. "Yup, it's real hickory." He leaned it against the wall. "Are my supplies ready?" he asked, as if nothing had happened.

"Almost." The shopkeeper gathered the remaining items and placed them on the counter.

Barrett grabbed an armful of supplies. "Thank you." He turned to walk away.

"Hey mister," the storekeeper shouted, "If you are headed south, there is a small clearing about a half mile out. It is rumored the robberies take place there."

"Thank you. I'll keep my eyes open." Barrett waved.

The man took a handful of peppermints and gave them to Jerry. "Take these."

"Ain't got no money."

"Consider it a gift. Thanks to your boss, those men should not be bothering me and my customers anymore."

"Thank you, suh." The excited black man walked out the door.

Barrett was already on his horse when Jerry came out of the store. "What are you smiling about?" he queried.

"The store man, he give me sugar candy."

"He did, did he?"

Jerry put one of the candies in his mouth and rolled his eyes with delight.

"Well...how is it?" Barrett asked.

"Ain't never tasted anything like it 'fore."

Barrett laughed as they headed out of town.

Twenty minutes later, Barrett had an uncanny feeling. *Something isn't right.* "Whoa," he halted his horse and instinctively removed his gun from his holster.

Roundtree stopped, grabbed his rifle, and looked around. "What is it, suh?" he whispered.

"Looks like something happened up ahead in that clearing. It must be where the ambushes were. Those troublemakers might be around here somewhere." Barrett glanced around, aware that the situation was tenuous.

Barrett spoke softly, "Jerry, they never saw you and may not know there are two of us. You go into the woods and come up from the side... and watch. Keep your Henry ready at all times. If they ambush me, take them out."

"What ya gonna do, suh?"

"I'm going straight through."

"Them could kill you, suh."

"Maybe. However, I think those men would rather see me squirm and beg for my life, than see me dead."

Not saying another word, the black man solemnly hurried into the woods, as ordered.

Barrett started down the trail, keeping an eye on the ground for any sign of fresh prints. Looking ahead, he noticed a clearing where a definite skirmish took place. Crushed down brush and muddled tracks from horses and wagons caught his attention. He dismounted and knelt on the ground to study the tracks. *Looks like two wagons have been here. Is that blood on the ground? They must have dragged something, or someone, off the path and into the woods.* Concern darkened his sweaty face.

In a split second, firing erupted from behind him. Men on horseback sped down the path toward him, shooting wildly. Barrett's horse took the first bullets and fell dead at his feet. He pulled his pistol out and fired in the direction of the oncoming riders. His first shots found their marks, hitting the lead rider and his horse. Both fell to the ground, tripping the next horse, which started a chain reaction. Another horse fell and the rider flew through the air hitting the ground headfirst. An additional rider was trampled in the chaos. Barrett emptied his shells into the remaining men, killing them.

Suddenly, three more riders charged out of the woods firing. With his pistol out of ammunition, Barrett jumped behind his lifeless horse. He desperately tried to get his Henry, but it was pinned underneath his horse. *Jerry, where are you?*

Realizing his situation was hopeless, he threw down his gun and raised his hands to surrender. *Anytime, Jerry.*

Abruptly, a blast of gunfire from the forest caused Barrett to jump behind his horse again. The three attackers shifted their attention from him, and began shooting blindly into the woods. Hit by shots fired from the woods, two of the men dropped over dead.

The gunfire ceased.

Aiming his pistol into the woods, the remaining rider shouted, "Come out with your hands up!"

Everything was quiet.

Seconds later, a black man stumbled from the forest—wounded and dazed.

The rider glanced at him and then at Barrett. He dismounted and aimed his pistol at Jerry.

Helpless, Barrett's heart pounded.

Two shots rang out!

Watching the unarmed black man crumble to the ground, the attacker laughed aloud—an evil sound that resonated through the forest.

Barrett screamed, "No!" and charged toward the killer.

The man turned his pistol on the major.

God help me!

The attacker pulled the trigger. The hammer clicked, he pulled the trigger again, and another click. Angrily, he threw the empty pistol at Barrett and searched for another weapon.

It was too late!

In one blow, von Weber thrust his hand into the man's neck, breaking it. The man fell to the ground in a lifeless heap.

Barrett ran to Jerry who lay face down in a pool of blood. As he turned him over, the injured man groaned. He noticed several bullet holes in his chest. The dark blood indicated his comrade would not survive.

The major held the head of his dying friend in his lap. "You did good, Jerry."

"Suh, sorry I was late. There dead people in the woods. I tripped over 'em." His voice grew weaker with each word.

Barrett sat silent.

Jerry whimpered, "Not gonna make it, am I, suh?"

A tear rolled down Barrett's cheek. "No, my friend, you're not."

The black man took a deep, labored breath. "Suh, I have a confession 'bout my boy."

"If you want me to find him, I will try. I will tell him what a brave man his father was," Barrett's voice cracked.

"You don't have to, suh. Know what happen to him, just couldn't admit it. Searchin' for him gave me somethin' to live for." Each breath was getting shallower.

"Where is your boy?"

"Truth is... he born dead. I heard the splash when they throwed him in the ocean. Never got to hold him. Lost my wife and baby that day." Jerry's eyes glistened with tears.

"I'm sorry. I have never had a child, so I cannot possibly know how you feel. Although, as a child, I knew how it felt to be held, safe in my father's arms. Soon you'll be safe in your Father's arms."

Blood seeped from Jerry's mouth.

"My father?" It took every ounce of remaining strength for Jerry to get the words out.

"Yes, your Heavenly Father."

"Oh, yes, I know Jesus." Jerry turned his head as if he was looking for something. "Massa Barrett, suh?"

"Barrett to you, Sergeant Roundtree."

"Sergeant?"

Barrett fought back the tears. "Since I am the ranking officer in battle, I have the authority to give you a field rank... that makes you, Sergeant Jerry Roundtree."

The black man smiled weakly. "Barrett?"

"Yes, Sergeant Roundtree."

"I like dat."

Barrett was unable to respond.

"I got words for grave marker."

Another tear tumbled from Barrett's face and hit the hard ground. "And what may that be?"

"*I Will Meet the Son at the End of My Journey.*"

Barrett closed his eyes, knowing they were the lyrics to a hymn that he had written—the song Jerry frequently sang.

"Oh my... there my boy, get to hold my son.... get to hold my son," Jerry groaned, staring heavenward.

Barrett finally forced his eyes open. He wiped his eyes with the sleeve of his jacket. When his vision cleared, he looked at his trusted friend, whose eyes were now closed.

Jerry was gone.

The peaceful countenance on the black man's face caused von Weber to smile. Standing, he stared at the body of Sergeant Jerry Roundtree and uttered, "You are finally free... free in the arms of Jesus."

He buried his friend close to a tall oak tree, next to a brook. When he was finished, he stepped back and prayed silently.

Taking time to survey the area, Barrett tried to capture the landmarks in his memory, hoping that one day he would return.

Looking at the fresh grave one last time, he made a promise, "I'll be back, my friend. I'll be back."

Chapter Twenty-Eight

April 11, 1864

Barrett was on his own now and the responsibility on his shoulders mounted steadily.

He tramped back into the woods searching for Jerry's horse. He quickly found the animal, untethered him, and mounted the impressive steed.

Within seconds, he was on his way. Pushing the horse to his limit, he would do everything in his power to catch up to the Union soldiers.

Late at night, after riding hard all day, he rested his horse and his own aching body. Exhausted, he slept fitfully for a couple hours.

The next morning he was on his way before sunrise. Fearing that staying on the road was too dangerous, he made his way guardedly through the woods.

At one point, gunfire echoed eerily through the valley.

He continued vigilantly, watching and listening for signs of trouble.

Mid-morning, he heard two gunshots nearby, followed by another.

Not seeing anything unusual, Barrett soon stopped by a brook for a needed drink. Reaching into the water with cupped hands, he jumped back, startled! To his horror, the face of a man stared back at him from below the surface.

Once he calmed, he dragged the corpse out of the water and checked him for identification. The man was dressed in a Confederate captain's uniform. When he opened the jacket, von Weber noticed he wore civilian clothes underneath the uniform.

That is strange. I bet that when he left the South, he was going to take off the uniform to blend in with the population. Judging by the Union boots he is wearing, this has to be Hornsby. He flipped the body over and discovered the man had been shot twice in his back. *This probably was from the shots I just heard... the killer is nearby!*

Barrett stepped into the stirrup and swung into his saddle. He closed his eyes and drew a long breath through his nose. With a slight bit of leg pressure, he requested a canter, but instantly reined his horse to a stop when he spied something in the tall grass. Uncertain what it was, he took his gun out of his holster and strode over to get a closer look. "Well, what happened to you?" He stared at a dead man in a Union lieutenant's uniform. "I wonder who you are." A closer look revealed the soldier had been shot in the back of the head with a single bullet. "Looks like you may have been running with the wrong company."

After checking the area for any other suspicious activity, the exhausted, lone soldier pushed on.

Late morning, Barrett heard more gunfire, this time coming from ahead of him.

He continued further into the brush cautiously. Hearing voices, but unable to discern what was being said, he dismounted and continued on foot, until the voices were directly in front of him.

Barrett peeked through the thick trees and noticed a single wagon. He snuck over to it. Tarps that had covered the load had been removed. Several large, pine boxes caught his attention. Looking inside the few that were open, an awful realization hit him! *Coffins...dead Rebels! So, that is how they have been getting through the lines. No one would ever attempt to stop wagons carrying dead soldiers.* The stink almost made him vomit.

Cold metal touched his neck and a booming voice from behind startled him. "Anyone ya know?"

Barrett froze.

"Now drop the pistol and turn 'round."

Barrett turned around and stared into the eyes of a toothless man, dressed in a dirty blue uniform, who was aiming a gun directly at him. He groaned. "Oh, yes, I remember... Moffit... Billy Moffit. I should have recognized you by your lack of teeth!" he scoffed.

Moffit scowled with a toothless smirk. "Hey, Quinn, look who I found."

A couple men rushed over.

The taller of the men immediately recognized Barrett. "Well, well, if it's not the captain, or should I say, major?" his eyes narrowed, and then brightened with a dangerous glint.

Barrett exhaled hard. "You are one of the men Sergeant Perry tried to hook me up with for my mission." Things were beginning to add up in Barrett's mind. *I need to play along until I can get the upper hand. I know what these men are capable of—they have left a bloody trail of death and destruction.*

The soldier sliced him with a glare. "What should we do with him?" Moffit spit on Barrett's boots.

"Not sure. For now… tie him up with the other prisoner."

Moffit jammed his gun into the major's back and shoved him over to a tree where a frightened man sat tied.

"What we gonna do with 'em?" one of the men hissed.

Barrett scanned the scene. He counted five men, a few of them aiming rifles directly at him.

"You already asked that question, Billy. Man, you sure are dumb," a rough-looking, full-bearded man replied.

"Ain't no reason to hurt my feelin's, Sonny," the toothless man cried out.

"Sorry, Billy. I jus' teasin'."

"Will you two dummies shut up and let me think," Quinn shouted.

"Wonder what the captain would do?" Sonny asked, thinking aloud.

"He and the lieutenant ain't here… means I'm in charge," Quinn was growing impatient.

"Killing Rebels is one thing, but a Union officer… not sure 'bout that." Sonny retorted.

"I suspect the major knows a lot about us," Quinn jeered.

"I say take care of these two now… they are dead weight." Moffit's eyes flashed evil.

"Yes, but not yet. We might get information out of them," Quinn shot back.

"What you mean?" Moffit's bloodshot eyes widened.

"Stop the questions, you're driving me crazy," Quinn barked.

"Major, forgive them… they are not the sharpest knives in the drawer, if you know what I mean," Quinn chuckled.

"Is Sergeant Perry part of this?" Barrett kept his tone calm.

"Are you serious? That man is all military."

"How did you manage to beat me down here?" Barrett questioned Quinn.

"That be because of Lieutenant Rice," Sonny foolishly jumped in.

"Idiot, shut up," Quinn snorted.

"It ain't gonna matter, he dead man," Moffit barked, shoving Barrett to the ground.

"Rice? I don't know him." Von Weber sat with his back against the tree as Moffit roughly tied him to it. He noted a man sitting on the other side of the tree… head down.

Quinn arrogantly grinned. "Yeah, guess you are curious about how this all came about. Well, I'll tell you." He knelt down in front of the major. "All we was told was that we were chasing a number of wagons into the South. But, I overheard a lot of things... something to do with special rifles. Near as I can tell, Rice planned this entire thing. I guess the theft was supposed to be at Brandy Station, late at night. Rice had worked out all the details. The plan was to take the rifles out of the crates, replace them with rocks, and leave. By the time the military figured out what really happened, everyone would have been long gone. Good scheme, huh?"

"Rice planned all that?" Barrett asked.

"Yep, but it seems that a couple of his cohorts, Abbott and Hornsby, had other ideas. Rice was mad when he found out, so he stole a horse and...."

"Talk about dumb, Rice stole General Custer's horse," Sonny butted in.

Quinn cackled. "Right after Sergeant Major Perry and you met with us, the general ordered a bunch of us to find the man who stole his horse. Custer was steamin' mad."

Barrett quizzed further, "Let me guess, the platoon was led by Captain Gibbons, right?"

"You catch on quick."

"Are you all from the 1st West Virginia?"

"Not likely. We from Pennsylvania. Only horses we could find were from that unit." Quinn spit some chewing tobacco on the ground between Barrett's feet. "We caught Rice about thirty miles from Brandy Station."

"Like I said, him real dumb. Went the wrong direction the night he stole General's horse," Sonny snorted.

"That's a fact. Captain Gibbons was going to hang him on the spot until they had a conversation that changed things. Don't know what was said, but next thing I knew, we were marching full speed south chasin' these here wagons."

"Murdering innocent people along the way," Barrett growled through gritted teeth.

Quinn stood; his face red with rage. "They were all Confederates! When I find those rifles, I am going to enjoy letting Billy kill you."

Moffit's toothless smile grew large.

All of a sudden, Quinn seemed to snap, "Empty the entire wagon. Bust open the pine boxes! Dump the bodies out. Must be something we ain't seen."

"But, Quinn, they stink. Heat's rottin' 'em real bad. Keep tellin' you, wagon is empty. Everything must have been put in the other wagon," Moffit whined.

"Let's see what he knows?" Sonny griped, pointing to the man next to Barrett.

"Believe me, he don't know nothing. Met men like him before—they just read the Bible and farm. Besides he don't speak much English." Quinn shook his head, disgusted.

"Maybe they really were takin' dead Rebels back to be buried," Sonny stroked his bearded chin.

"Yeah, maybe the rifles were on the other wagon. Why did the lieutenant and the captain leave in such a hurry?" a stout, red-haired man joined the conversation.

"Captain said he had to go and check something out, but he gave us orders, and left me in charge." Quinn glared at the red-haired man. "I told you to stop asking questions, Red. Go check out the wagon!"

As Red stomped toward the wagon, he muttered, "Sure seems strange that he left right after torturin' that Rebel." He gestured toward the dead man tied to a nearby tree.

"Captain gave us orders–dump the wagon into the river and get rid of the Mennonite. First, let's tear this wagon apart." Noticeably irritated, Quinn stormed toward the wagon with his men.

Barrett and the stranger were left alone, tied together.

Von Weber looked around. Four dead men were sprawled on the ground. A fifth man was tied to another tree, slumped over, dead.

Keeping an eye on the action at the wagon, the major whispered to the man by him, "Who are you? And what is your role in this?"

"I not know. I speak little English. I told take dead men to Atlanta."

The frightened man was hard to understand, but by his accent, von Weber could tell he was German.

Responding in German, Barrett continued, "Please listen carefully. I am a major in the Union Army. I was sent here to find stolen rifles and ammunition. Do you have any idea where they might be?"

"No. I know nothing. I am only a clockmaker."

The conversation continued in German.

"What's your name?"

"Oscar Schwartz."

"Did you make the clocks back in that gold mining town?"

The German laughed, cynically. "Gold mining town... is that what you call it? We never found any gold there."

Barrett listened intently, hoping for answers to help him.

"Yes, those are my clocks. My wife and I came from Germany three years ago with our two sons. We settled in Charleston, but moved to Gilfred to strike it rich... find gold. There was no gold there, so I started making clocks."

"Judging by your workmanship, I suspect you come from the Black Forest in Germany."

The Mennonite's face perked up. "Why, yes, how did you know?"

"My family has purchased many clocks from that area."

"Your family? What is your family name?"

"Von Weber!"

"Von Weber? From the winery?"

"Yes." Barrett kept a watchful eye on the men who were tearing the wagon apart desperately searching for something.

"I have met some of the von Webers, but I do not know you. I delivered a large clock to them years ago."

"I am their son, Barrett."

"Barrett von Weber... the well-known Hymnist?" The Mennonite grinned, feeling like he found a long-lost friend.

"Yes, that's me. Was your family still in Gilfred?" Barrett asked.

"No! My wife went to Charleston a couple weeks ago with our boys. There is a large Mennonite settlement there. I was going to finish my clocks and join her in a few weeks."

Barrett was relieved that the man's family was not in the town when the bloodshed occurred. He made a decision not to tell him about the horrible scene he witnessed in Gilfred. At least, not yet.

"You must tell me what you know, Oscar."

The German took a deep breath and continued whispering in his native language. "The men here jumped us an hour ago and killed those three men who are lying on the ground. They tortured two others trying to get information from them, before killing them. So far, they have left me alone. I told them I don't know anything."

"What do they want? What do you think they are looking for?"

"They keep asking about guns and gold."

"Were you hauling guns?"

"No! I was hauling soldiers killed in battle. Ezra and I were hired to take the dead soldiers home to Savannah and Atlanta. One of the dead was some general."

Barrett shifted his position, trying to get more comfortable.

"Some soldiers came earlier this morning and picked up one of the wagons and left for Savannah."

This stirred von Weber's interest. "So, one of the wagons has already left! Do these men here know that?"

"Yes, I believe so."

Barrett continued to probe the Mennonite for information. "How many men left Gilfred with you?"

"Ezra and I left in wagons with five soldiers on horseback. We left in a hurry."

"Any idea why the rush?"

He stared into the distance, reliving the scene. "Things were crazy. All the soldiers were running around like something big was about to happen. I saw them setting up barricades in the street. I think Union soldiers were coming. Ezra and I were glad to leave."

"You took the wagons?"

"Yes, Ezra and I were hired to build two heavy wagons with special compartments under them."

"Compartments? For what?"

"I don't know. We were paid ahead of time, quite well."

"When was that?"

"Sometime in March. We finished about a week ago."

"I need to know everything that happened this past week," von Weber delved deeper.

"It began a few days ago when the wagons came into town carrying these coffins. The coffins were all transferred into the wagons we made. A couple more wagons came by later that evening. The Confederates worked all night unloading the goods from them and putting them in the secret compartments we made. We took off before sunrise."

"Who was in charge?"

"A man named Hornsby. He wore civilian clothes until we left... then he put on a Confederate uniform... made himself a captain at that."

Must have been the dead man in the river. Knew it was Hornsby. "What happened next?"

"We hurried along. I noticed the soldiers with us were always looking back to see if anyone was following us. It made Ezra and me nervous. As I said, earlier this morning, a company of Confederate soldiers met us here and took Ezra's wagon. We were then told to deliver the bodies in my wagon to Atlanta. While we were resting, we were ambushed by these men." He motioned his head toward the men at the wagon. "They killed Ezra immediately, even though he was unarmed. He was a good man—had a wife and six children."

"I'm sorry about your friend."

Oscar hesitated, "These men here... do you plan on killing them?"

"If I have to, I will. I cannot let these rifles kill more innocent people like Ezra. I have to stop it here. Tell me more."

Schwartz looked up into the sky, taking a deep breath. "You see that soldier tied to that tree?"

"Yes."

"The captain threatened to cut his fingers off if he refused to talk."

"So did he talk?"

"Yes, and I heard everything he said."

"Continue."

Oscar lowered his voice even more. "The men here do not know it, but Gibbons and Rice chased after Hornsby."

"Why would they go after Hornsby?"

"Because of the sacks."

"The sacks... what sacks?"

"The sacks the soldiers from Savannah gave them early this morning. By the way they were carrying them, I suspect gold was in them."

"Gold... are you sure?"

"They were heavy. That man who picked up the other wagon had two sacks strung across his horse when he came. He handed the bags to Hornsby and left with the wagon. Never said a word."

Confused, Barrett quizzed, "Oscar, tell me about the man with the bags."

"I never heard his name, but he was the same man who paid us to build the wagons. He had a small, well-armed army with him."

"How many men?"

"I would say about twenty, with well-trained horses and swords."

"Sounds like a cavalry unit. Did you hear any names?"

"They just called him Captain. He was pretty proud of it, too."

"What did he look like?"

"He was dressed in a gray uniform. Young man, rather short, with black hair. Oh yes, he rode a spectacular black horse with a red mane."

Barrett grimaced as a thought ran through his mind.

Oscar continued, "Hornsby left almost immediately with the bags, heading north. The captain took the wagon and his men, heading east to Savannah. We were ordered to continue on to Atlanta with this wagon."

Barrett observed a couple of the Rebels as they took a wrapped body out of one of the coffins and tossed him to the ground. "Ain't nothing in here," one shouted, holding his nose.

Von Weber could smell the decay even from where he was. *They can't find any rifles. Have we all been fooled? Maybe this wagon was a decoy and all the rifles were on the wagon that left.*

He shifted his focus back to Oscar. "Who is this Gibbons?"

"He seemed to be the leader of these men. Tortured the dead man by that tree, and then slit his throat. His last order was to push the wagon into the deepest part of the river, take care of me, and then head west to join Sherman. I am sure Gibbons and Rice went after Hornsby. Then you showed up."

"Gibbons just left?"

"About an hour ago."

"That means if I would have been using the road, I would have run into him." Barrett sighed. *The other dead man must have been Rice. Looks like Gibbons got greedy.*

Von Weber kept twisting his hands, desperately trying to slip them from the knot. "Why haven't they killed you and dumped the wagon like Gibbons ordered?"

"Busy. That man, Quinn, thinks there is gold, or some kind of special rifles worth a fortune on the wagon."

"I suspect when they are done tearing the wagon apart they will kill both of us," Barrett whispered.

The clockmaker was silent.

Von Weber spoke again, this time with new resolve. "We are going to have to fight back."

"I am a Mennonite. I cannot hurt another person."

"Not even in self-defense?"

"Not even in self-defense."

"That puts me in a bad position."

"What do you mean?"

"There are five of them and one of me. It could be two. I know you know how to fire a gun... you hunt to feed your family."

"But, I cannot hurt another person." Oscar stayed determined.

"You know, Oscar, I consider myself a Godly man. I pray, attend church when I can, and read the Bible, but I will still defend myself and those who cannot defend themselves. I feel that is a responsibility that God has given me."

"We have been taught that to take another man's life is sinful. I cannot go against my teaching." Oscar rested his head back on the tree.

"Then, I will honor your belief."

Their conversation was interrupted when Sonny bellowed, "Man, this thing is heavy."

Barrett watched two men push one of the coffins out of the wagon. When it hit the ground, the force split the pine box open. A decayed body tumbled to the ground, the stench overtaking the thieves. They turned their heads in disgust. When they turned back, their eyes grew twice their normal size—rifles were scattered on the ground.

"What the...?" Red jumped off the wagon to investigate, the whole time fanning his face to get rid of the awful odor. He picked up one of the rifles and studied it. "What is this?"

"I seen one of them before. They never run out of balls," Sonny added.

"You crazy!"

"No, I mean it. You can fire that thing all day and it continues to shoot."

The men rushed over to the other side of the wagon. "Quinn, look what fell out of a coffin! There's a whole bunch of 'em." Sonny held up a rifle, smiling from ear-to-ear.

Quinn grabbed the rife, eyes gleaming. "This is what we have been looking for! Break open the rest of the coffins, men," he ordered, excitedly.

Examining the new rifle, Quinn pulled the trigger repeatedly. Nothing happened! Finally, he took a Minié ball out of his pocket, and tried to shove it in the barrel, but it didn't fit.

Barrett watched the frustrated man's antics and found him comical. He chuckled aloud.

Quinn rushed over. "What are you laughin' about?"

Von Weber's frown darkened.

"Do you know about these things?" He held up one of the new rifles.

"Yes... they are Henry rimfire rifles. They take special bullets," Barrett replied, hesitantly.

"Where are the bullets?"

"How would I know?" The major's displeasure of the question was evident.

"I was not talking to you, I was talking to him." He pointed to the Mennonite. "Where are the bullets?"

Oscar sounded nervous. "I told you I not know about these rifles... or bullets. I hired to take dead soldiers home to Atlanta. That all I know."

A loud crash interrupted them. Another coffin burst open, spilling a corpse and more rifles to the ground.

Quinn shoved the rifle close to Barrett's face, and shouted, "Is it true these things never run out of balls?"

"Like I said, they don't fire balls, they fire bullets. Each rifle holds sixteen rounds, and then you have to reload it."

"Where do you put the powder?" Quinn was getting angrier by the minute.

"The powder is in the shell."

"The rifles are no good without the ammunition, so both of them must be in the coffins," Quinn yelled, glancing at the wagon. He threw the empty rifle to the ground and stormed back to the wagon.

Barrett's mouth tipped as he remembered the shells in his pocket that he had taken out of the box when they rescued the women–four shells for a Henry rifle. *Thank you, Lord.*

There was fire in Quinn's eyes as he dished out orders to his men. "Open every coffin. Find that ammo! It's got to be here! If we can get the bullets to these guns, we can command an army, or sell them together and make a fortune."

Two men began shoving the coffins off the wagons. If one didn't break open, a couple men on the ground used their rifles as crowbars to pry the lid off. The smell was horrendous as the coffins split open. Some of the men tied a bandana around their face, which really didn't help; others just took a deep breath and held their nose.

Barrett continued watching, sizing up the situation, and waiting for his opportunity. He knew exactly who was holding the weapons and which man was the biggest threat.

Oscar breathed a sigh of relief when he felt the rope holding his hands loosen. Barrett had worked the knots loose, freeing both of them.

With his foot, von Weber slowly dragged the empty Henry rifle that Quinn dropped, closer to him. He reached into his pocket and clutched the four shells. Keeping the rifle on the ground, he inconspicuously began loading the ammo. At the same time, the major whispered, "Oscar, listen closely. I only have four shells... there are five of them. When I make my move, you need to get the rifle Quinn leaned against that tree over there and get it to me. We will need to act fast. Can you do that?"

"Yes."

After Barrett loaded the fourth shell, he inched the weapon into his hands, and whispered, "Go!"

Oscar wasted no time running toward the tree.

At the same time, Barrett sprang up.

Sonny caught a glimpse of him and reached for his pistol.

Von Weber fired, killing the man instantly. In a quick motion, he fired at the other man in the wagon, who grabbed his chest and fell to the ground in a heap.

Red, who minutes ago, had used his rifle as a crowbar had unknowingly bent the barrel. When he pulled the trigger, the gun blew up in his face, blinding him. Dropping the weapon, he held his eyes, screaming, "My eyes... my eyes!" He fell off the side of the wagon, hit his head on a coffin, and broke his neck. Ironically, he fell on top of a decaying corpse.

Von Weber turned his attention to the last two men—Quinn and Moffit—who had been busy gathering rifles. Barrett's third shot hit Moffit between the eyes. The ruthless soldier fell to the ground, toothless mouth wide open.

Quinn drew his pistol and jumped to the ground as Barrett fired. The bullet hit his rib cage, dizziness and pain overtook him.

Von Weber moved a step closer.

When Quinn heard the click of the rifle, he realized Barrett was out of ammunition. He struggled to his feet, clutching his bloody side with his hand. With his other hand, he aimed his pistol at Barrett.

A deafening shot rang out from behind the major. He could tell by its sound, and the smell of the smoke, that it was from a Springfield rifle.

Quinn fell to the ground, dead.

Barrett glanced behind him and saw Oscar holding the rifle, trembling. In shock, the Mennonite dropped the weapon.

For a short time, no words were spoken as Oscar stared at Barrett with glazed eyes.

Eventually, the clockmaker spoke, "Now what?"

They rushed to the wagon. "How do you get into the secret compartments?"

Oscar reached under the wagon and pulled a lever. The side dropped down exposing dozens of boxes. Barrett removed one of them and peered inside. "Did the wagon that left this morning have the same amount of boxes?"

"It can hold the same amount. I was never told anything," Oscar straightened.

"How many coffins did he take?"

"I believe six."

"We must destroy these rifles and ammunition, and then I have to stop him," Barrett sounded determined.

"I'll go with you."

"No, it is too dangerous. I will have to ride fast to catch up to the Rebels."

Oscar's face and voice held certain tenacity. "They will travel slower than us because they are loaded down with the rifles. Let's load up these coffins and continue on to Atlanta. We can do this!"

"No! I can't let you do that… you have a wife and family. You should return home."

"Don't you?"

Thoughts of Brooke flashed through Barrett's mind. "Yes, I do."

"Then, let me help. Together, we can do this." Oscar paused. "Is it true?"

"Is what true?"

"Can you really fire that rifle all day?"

"It takes shells... sixteen of them." Barrett grinned.

"I saw you take down four men in seconds. If this weapon gets into the wrong hands, many men will be killed. I do not want that," Oscar rubbed his wrists where they had been tied.

"Nor do I."

"Then let's get going. We might be able to catch up to him."

"No need to... I know where he is going." A chill ran down Barrett's arm.

A look of confusion took over the clockmaker's face. "How do you know that?"

"Did the captain's horse have two red socks on the hind legs?"

"Why yes, how did you know that?" Oscar shot a questioning look.

"Let's just say, I know this man."

Chapter Twenty-Nine

May 1864

The road to Savannah was long and tedious.

Many Confederate troops stood at attention along the roadside, removing their hats, and saluting the wagon as it passed. Barrett noticed that the soldiers were exhausted and gaunt from what seemed to be a never-ending, futile war. Three years of bloodshed had taken a toll on what was left of the Southern troops, their families, and their country.

Barrett and Oscar pressed on, hauling the soldiers who had died on the battlefield. To pass the time, the men chatted like old friends—discussing their families, the war, and their hopes for the future.

Finally, the duo arrived in the bustling seaport of Savannah.

Barrett faced his companion. "This is as far as we travel together, Brother Oscar."

The Mennonite looked at von Weber confused.

"How do you know where to go from here? Do you know who bought the rifles?"

"I have a pretty good idea."

Von Weber climbed off the wagon and walked over to the horse tied to the back. "What happens after this, I must face on my own. And you... you have some brave men to take home to their families."

"Sir, it's been an honor traveling with you." Sadness crept into the Mennonite's eyes.

"The honor was mine. I suspect you will go back to making those beautiful clocks."

"Yes, I will." He nodded confidently.

"Good. You create something people can treasure. Your clocks bring smiles into a world that's gone mad."

"Sir?" The clockmaker hesitated.

Barrett glanced up at him as he checked the saddle cinch on his horse.

"Thanks for saving my life. They would have tortured me for information as they did the others… and then killed me."

Von Weber scratched his head. "As I remember, you saved my life. Are you all right with what we did?"

"I do not regret it, if that's what you mean. It was justified. I know that now. If I had not done it… a great man would have been killed."

"Maybe we will see each other again." Barrett's voice was earnest.

"I hope so."

Barrett mounted his horse, ready to face an uncertain future.

"Mr. von Weber?" Oscar blinked.

"Yes."

"Look me up after the war. I will have a special clock waiting for you."

Barrett rode his horse over to the wagon and extended his hand to his comrade. "I will look forward to that." He tipped his hat and rode off.

The Mennonite watched as the major disappeared down the road. *Lord, be with this man of God. Keep him safe, so he can return to his beloved bride.*

As von Weber neared Annalise, worried thoughts bombarded his mind. *Should I wait for the cover of darkness? If I were Rory, where would I hide the rifles? And, what would I use them for?*

Barrett tethered his horse to a tree in the forest, not far from the house. Suddenly an idea hit him. Rory would probably hide the wagon in the old barn, north of the house. Brooke said no one uses it anymore.

Creeping cautiously through the forest, Barrett soon was overlooking the old hay barn. He lay prone, viewing the area through his spyglass.

A trio of horses nearby munched contentedly on a patch of grass.

He observed two men with bandannas tied over their faces as they exited the barn. When they opened the large doors to go back in, Barrett caught a clear glimpse of the wagon inside. Standing next to the wagon was Rory—his lips were moving and he was pointing at something. The major could hear muffled voices, but could not discern what was being said. He assumed his brother-in-law was dishing out orders.

Through the large, open doors, Barrett noted empty coffins on the ground. The hidden compartments on the wagon had been opened and the boxes of ammunition removed.

Rory disappeared into the blackness of the barn's interior.

Barrett waited and planned his next move. He watched as the men returned the corpses to the coffins, replaced the lids, and loaded them back on the wagon.

Barrett whispered, "Well, Brother Rory, I see you have been busy. Looks like you have enough weapons and ammunition to run a small, but powerful army. Did you think you could get away with this? No, you can't! I will stop you from going any further."

Within a short time, the wagon pulled out, two horses tied to the back of it.

Rory strutted out of the barn, peered around, shoved the large creaking door shut, and locked it. He mounted his horse and sped off.

The major stood to his feet and tucked his spyglass into his pocket. It's time to find out the truth. I have to see this for myself—up close.

When he was certain Rory was out of the area, Barrett ran to the front of the rustic barn. It was locked! He peaked through a knothole. It was dark inside, except for rays of light creeping through the cracks in the walls. The nauseating smell from decaying bodies lingered in the air, a sad reminder of the ugliness of war.

He ran to the side door and discovered that a board secured it from the inside. Barrett scanned the area to make sure he was alone and then removed his knife. Forcing the blade through a crack in the oak wood, he lifted the board, and pushed the door open enough to wiggle through.

A shaft of light through the opening revealed Rory's prize. The rifles were lined up along a wall; the boxes of ammunition evenly spaced in front of them.

Von Weber stood motionless, staring. *I wonder how many lives were lost... for this!*

Barrett heard the sound of horses' hooves pounding the ground. Someone was coming. He knew it was too late to escape into the woods, so he quickly ran over and shut the door. Barely able to see, he scurried up the ladder to the loft and hid behind some stacked hay. With pulse racing, he watched, and listened... and waited!

When the barn door squeaked open, five men entered. One was Rory, the others Barrett didn't recognize. Two wore Confederate officer uniforms; the others were dressed in a suit and tie. Looked like they might be some of Rory's political friends.

The eager officers rushed over to examine the modern rifles that were illuminated by sunlight from the open door.

Picking a rifle up, one man boasted, "Look at this! Impressive! There is something good about the Northerners... they certainly know how to make a splendid rifle." He laughed heartily.

The men dressed in business suits held their noses. "What is that stench?"

Rory ignored the comment.

Barrett wiped sweat from his brow and prayed for God's protection.

"How many rifles are here?" an officer asked.

"Here, there are two hundred and fifty... with thirty thousand rounds of ammunition," Rory replied smugly. "But we have a total of five hundred at our disposal."

Unable to take his eyes off the gun he was stroking, one officer pressed further,

"How many shells will each rifle hold?"

"Sixteen," Rory's reply came quickly.

"You mean a man does not have to reload this every time he fires?" One of the other men shook his head in disbelief.

"That is correct, Senator. We could mow down an entire division of Bluebellies in a matter of minutes," Rory bragged, almost feeling the victory.

"Can we get more ammo?"

"No, this is it. But with this, we can cause enough damage to the Billy Yanks front line to crush their morale and win the war—easily!" Rory folded his arms.

"What is your plan, Captain?" One of the politicians searched Fortner's eyes.

"We are going to arm two hundred and fifty of our best marksmen, and I am going to lead them into battle," Rory replied.

The officer challenged the cocky, young captain. "You do know that the latest military information states that General Sherman is marching south with a huge army. He's only a couple weeks away from Atlanta. If he reaches that city and overtakes it, the South is doomed."

Rory's dark eyes lit up. "By the time, they reach Atlanta... we will be ready for them."

The same officer questioned, "How? What are we going to do?"

"Besides what's here, there are two hundred fifty additional rifles headed to Atlanta. Hopefully, they are there by now. I have enlisted two hundred and fifty more of the finest sharpshooters in Georgia, who are going to set up an ambush outside Atlanta. We will send them Bluebellies running north faster than a jackrabbit."

Rory picked up a rifle, aimed it at the roof, and mumbled, "The problem for them Bluebellies is... I will be waiting there with General Johnson and his army. Sherman will never know what hit him. We will crush them." Rory raised his clenched fist. "And I will take great pleasure in killing Sherman personally."

"What if the North has these same weapons?" a senator asked.

"They don't. These rifles were headed to the battlefield to be used against us, when we hijacked the shipment. Funny how fate works," Rory cackled. "But, they are now in our hands and will be used against them."

Barrett's heart thudded hard in his chest, fingering his gun, still in the holster.

Rory puffed out his chest. "I understand General Lee is marching towards Washington, as we speak. Brilliant plan, isn't it, men?"

One of the officers patted Rory vigorously on the back. "You, sir, will make a fine general one day... very soon."

"That's what I am counting on. However, more importantly, I'm really looking toward the Presidency of these Confederate States... all thirty-eight states. The Union will be one again... with a new flag, a new future, and a new president... me!"

Listening from his hiding spot, Rory's arrogance was almost more than Barrett could bear. Bile rose in his throat.

"Now if you would excuse me, gentlemen. I do not want Father to get suspicious, so I need to make it to supper on time. He is already questioning me about why I was gone so long to Atlanta. He had no idea I was picking up these weapons, or that I have been leading raids into Virginia. I will contact you in the next couple days."

The men slapped each other on the back and left, leaving Rory standing by himself. Barrett watched as his brother-in-law picked up one of the rifles and pretended to fire it, like a child with a play gun. The conceited man hooted, "Now, if I could just have the privilege of using one of these rifles against my sister's husband, my life would be complete!"

A chill ran through Barrett. He toyed with the idea of stopping Rory right then and there—with one bullet, but decided against it.

Brooke's rebellious brother put the rifle down and protectively covered the stolen weapons with a tarp. He turned to leave, but just before he closed the door, he glanced back, muttering, "President Rory Fortner... the name fits."

His evil laugh sent shivers up Barrett's spine.

The out-of-control Fortner son closed the door and locked it from the outside.

Barrett climbed down from the loft. If I burn this barn down, the rifles and everything else will be destroyed. Whatever happens, I cannot let these weapons leave here.

Von Weber made sure he left nothing out of place and then returned to the safety of the secluded wooded area on the hillside to await his next move.

Hours later, under the cover of darkness, he left his horse in the woods, and ran to the rear of the Fortner's house. He climbed up the back terrace, scrambled through an open window, and hid in Alton's bedroom. He could hear voices downstairs, but they were so faint he could not make out who was talking.

Pulling his pistol out of its holster, he sat in a dark corner, waiting, praying.

Finally, he heard the sound of footsteps coming down the hall. "Suh, do you want me to turn the bed down for you?" a voice sounded from outside the door.

"No, thank you, Brennan... I think I will read a while before I turn in."

"Would you like some tea?"

"No, thank you... my belly is still full from supper. I will see you in the morning."

"Yes, suh. Good night."

Alton stepped into his bedroom, closing the door behind him.

Barrett watched his father-in-law stride over to his bed, set a lantern on the nightstand, and grab his Bible. When Alton reached over to increase the flame on his wall lantern, the light revealed the silhouette of a person sitting in the corner.

Startled, Alton gasped, "What...?"

The major spoke quietly. "Shh... Sir, it's me, Barrett."

"Barrett, what on earth are you doing here?" He moved closer and saw the pistol aimed in his direction. "Is Brooke with you? What is the meaning of this? Where is my daughter? Is she all right?"

"Please calm down, sir. I have not seen Brooke since January. Alton, I am sorry, but I have to make sure you are not part of this... this...." His voice trailed off as he gazed at his pistol.

"Part of what?" Alton's eyes widened.

"Sit on your bed... and do not talk too loud. I'm sorry, but I will be forced to shoot anyone who comes through that door." An ache settled in Barrett's heart.

"Why on earth? Son, what is going on? Help me understand... please." Alton's lower lip trembled.

"Do you have any idea what your youngest son has been doing?"

"What are you talking about? Rory? What has he done now?"

Barrett sighed heavily. "Are you missing any money... gold, precisely? I do not think he could have gotten the gold from the banks. The South does not have any gold left, so I suspect he must have gotten it from here... from you."

"I have gold here, yes, but I am sure it's not missing?"

"When was the last time you checked it?"

"I'm not in the habit of counting my money every day."

"Maybe you should count it right now. Can we get to your safe without anyone seeing us?" Barrett swallowed hard.

"We can do that easily."

"Let's go." Barrett pointed in the direction of the door with his gun.

Alton cracked his knuckles. "If I didn't know you, I would suspect you were trying to rob me."

"That may have already been done."

Alton walked over to a picture of his late wife, which was hanging on the wall.

"What are you doing?" Barrett questioned impatiently.

"Do you think I'm crazy enough to put the safe in my study?"

"Well, there is one there. I saw it."

"Yes, but it's a dummy—just a little cash and a few papers in it." Alton removed the picture of his wife that hung above the large stone fireplace. Then he pulled on an odd shaped stone that opened a hidden compartment. A combination safe was inside.

"This is where I keep all of my valuables. This safe is fire and tamper proof."

"Does anyone else know its location, or the combination?"

"Only my three sons... and Brooke. Now you. I installed it myself, years ago."

Barrett groaned.

Alton pulled the door of the safe open and pulled out several stacks of Federal currency.

"Why, Mr. Fortner, these bills are the latest notes issued by the government. You are hoarding United States currency." Barrett forced a smile.

Alton grinned. "I'm a realist. I know that one day soon Confederate money will be worthless, and the legal tender will be United States currency—the greenback. I still have to trade around here with Confederate money, which I keep downstairs. When I can, I buy gold and silver with it. I know that when the country falls the banks will follow, and so will its currency. The price for everything will rise a hundredfold. I intend to be ready."

"I understand."

"See. All of my gold is in these two bags. Safe and sound." Alton pointed into his safe.

"Take the bags out and see what's in them," Barrett demanded.

Fortner shook his head. "All right, but this is crazy." Alton grabbed two large bags and pulled them out of the safe. His body tensed up when he lifted them and dumped the contents of one on the floor. He gazed in horror when rocks scattered everywhere! "My gold! My gold! It's gone! The future of Annalise!" He fingered the worthless stones. The heartsick man poured the contents of the other bag on the floor—more rocks!

Feeling nauseated, Barrett put his gun away. "When was the last time you saw the gold?"

"I told you, I don't count it very often. I have not been in this safe for over a month. No reason to."

Despondent, Alton shook his fist. In a loud voice, the angry father growled, "Rory!"

He spun around to leave, but Barrett stepped in front of him.

"Get out of my way," Alton said loudly, anger consuming him.

"Calm down," Barrett whispered. "I have something I must show you first."

"Now?"

"Not now because no one knows I'm here. Do you still visit your wife's grave every morning?"

"Yes, I rarely miss a day."

"Meet me there in the morning."

"I have to confront Rory," Alton scowled, determined.

"Sir, I cannot let you do that. I have to show you something first."

Barrett turned to leave. "I pray I can trust you. If not, your daughter will not have a husband."

"You can trust me. I want to know where my gold is." An ache settled in Alton's heart.

"Do not mention this to anyone, and do not approach Rory. Understand?"

"As you say. I will clean up this mess now, and meet you at my wife's grave just before sunrise."

Barrett climbed down the balcony and dropped to the ground. Running, he disappeared into the darkness.

Chapter Thirty

May 7, 1864

In the early morning dew, Alton rode up the hill to the burial site, as he did every day. Nearing the summit, he could see his son-in-law already waiting for him. The sun still had not risen, but the light silhouetted Barrett on his horse—a silent reminder of what he had to face. The hurting father uttered a silent prayer asking for strength for the day, one he knew would be difficult.

Alton placed the flowers on his wife's grave, said a quick prayer, and mounted his horse.

As he followed Barrett to the barn, neither man spoke.

When they arrived at the front door of the barn, Alton grumbled, "Why is this barn locked up like this?"

Barrett led him around to the side door. Using his knife, he entered the same way he did the day before. Alton followed cautiously.

Since darkness engulfed the barn, Alton lit one of the lanterns and handed it to Barrett. "Okay. What is it that is so important?"

Barrett walked over to a tarp and pulled it down, exposing the rifles and ammunition.

A look of disbelief spread across Alton's face. He picked one up. "This looks like the rifle you gave me when I first met you."

"Yes. It's the newest model!"

"Why are they here?" Afraid of what was to come, Alton's voice tightened.

"Rory bought them and stored them here."

"Bought them? With my gold?"

"Yes. With your gold—blood money!" Barrett lowered his head.

"What do you mean?" A frown creased the older man's brow.

"I hate to tell you this, Alton, but many men were slaughtered because of these weapons. In fact, men, women, and children were murdered for these rifles."

Alton couldn't respond. Feeling dizzy, he leaned against a nearby post for support.

"Sir, I have been following these rifles for over a month. There are thirty thousand rounds of ammunition here. Rory intends to use them to attack Sherman and his forces, while Lee marches on Washington. He has aspirations of becoming a general and ultimately, President Rory Fortner... leader of the thirty-eight Confederate States."

The elder Fortner hesitated, in an effort to get a grip on his emotions. He finally spoke, his voice filled with determination. "Well, his job is a lot harder now. I heard from reliable sources that Lee's march on Washington was stopped in Spotsylvania, Virginia. Grant was waiting for him."

Barrett closed his eyes in relief. *That means Wheaty, Moccasin, Alex, or Jack must have successfully informed Grant where Lee was encamped.* "Thank you, Lord," he uttered aloud.

Alton, still in shock, shook his head. "That boy is delusional." Still holding the rifle, he faced Barrett. "What should we do, son?"

"I would like to see where the trail leads and who else is involved. However, I cannot allow these weapons and ammunition to leave here. The uncontrolled madness needs to stop... now! There's only one way," his voice trailed off.

Alton thought for a second and then glanced at his lantern. "You will need some place to hide until the war is over. You will never make it back North alive."

"I know, but I cannot stay here. That will put your life in danger."

"Listen to me. You must hide here until we can figure out how to get you to safety. If Sherman is marching toward Atlanta, you can catch up to him and there you will be safe."

"Alton, I want you to know that I do not agree with what General Sherman is doing, but I do understand his reasoning."

"I heard say that his army is leaving a path of destruction a hundred miles wide straight into the South. Thousands of acres of good farmland are being turned into wasteland. They are destroying railroads, manufacturing plants, everything. When they are finished, there will be no South. God help us when they get to Atlanta."

Alton stared at the ground, shaking his head. Finally, he fixed his gaze on his son-in-law. "You can stay in Titus' old room above the stable. I will see to it you get food every day. You'll be safe there, for a while, anyway."

Barrett shook his head. "I can't do that. It will put your life at risk."

"Rory is in charge of the Savannah Guard. He is gone most days. Everyone else here will obey me and protect you."

"Have you heard from Charles and Samuel?"

"No, I have not. I fear for my sons. This war..." he could not finish the sentence.

Barrett nodded and then peered around at the weapons. "Now, what do we do with these?"

"Will the shells burn?"

"They will explode when the fire gets hot. Problem is they will be projectiles. All bullets have to land somewhere. We have to make sure no one is near here when they explode."

"It's a chance we have to take, son." Alton's voice was certain. "It has to be done!"

"After we do this... then what?" Barrett blinked.

"My gold is gone and I have to confront Rory about that. He must know it is coming. After all, he is the only one here who knows the combination of my safe. He has to realize that one of these days, I am going to open those bags of gold... and find rocks."

"That may be a brutal meeting."

"It's past due. He may have destroyed Annalise. I don't think I can ever forgive him for that." Anger and pain clouded his face.

Barrett's heart broke for the older man. "There is one more thing." He reached into his coat pocket and pulled out a wrinkled piece of paper. "I saw this in Virginia. I wanted to believe it wasn't true, but I'm afraid it is." He handed the paper to his father-in-law.

With shaking hands, Alton carefully unfolded it.

Barrett held up the hissing lantern, so Alton could read it.

Wanted dead or alive: $1,000 reward.
Male... Height 5'6"... 140 pounds... black hair.
Last seen riding a black horse with red mane, tail, and socks on his rear legs. Wanted for the cold-blooded murder of twenty-two men, women, and children.

Alton moaned. "That's Dark Shadow. He is the only horse I have ever seen that fits that description." Alton raised his fist high. "Rory, what have you done? You have brought the wrath of God upon this family."

After giving his father-in-law a few minutes to grieve, Barrett broke the quiet tension. "Alton, I see that Annalise seems to have been unscathed by the war."

"Yes, but I fear it's coming our way. If Sherman hits Atlanta, he may head to the sea continuing his destruction… and Annalise will be directly in his path."

Barrett watched Alton for a moment and felt sorrowful. He had worked this land for many years and tried to raise his children in the fear of the Lord. Now, both his land and family were in the path of destruction.

"Let's finish this job! I want to get home to Brooke."

Alton's face perked up at the mention of Brooke's name. "I haven't had a chance to ask, how my daughter is?"

"I have not seen her for nearly eight months."

An expression of sadness fell upon Alton's face. "And I have not heard from her either. I am sure she writes me, but since this nation is split, letters rarely make it this far. I pray she is safe."

"She is safe where she is… and she has William, Prisse, and Titus to look after her."

Barrett took a step closer to the door. "Sir, I am not sure how long I can stay here—Rory is bound to find out. When that happens, all of our lives will be in danger."

"I will let my staff know you will be staying in the loft above the stable, and under no circumstances are they to tell anyone. They will cooperate."

"Not sure how long that will work out." The major's voice cracked.

Alton eyed Barrett. "You're sure you don't want to continue following the trail and see who else is behind this?" He motioned toward the weapons.

"Yes. I am certain of that. The killing must stop. We must end it here, now, at Annalise." Barrett's voice was definitive.

"Okay, I will do this, so it will be me who is responsible, if anyone asks," Alton stated sternly.

"I'm not leaving the barn without you, in case anything goes wrong. We will light it and run… together." Barrett walked over to the door and pushed it open.

Without any more thought, Alton tossed the lantern on the rifles, causing it to break. Lamp oil quickly spread over the dry hay, flames instantly shot up!

The father sprinted toward the door to join Barrett.

Moments later, the duo reached the stable and they heard the explosions begin.

Alton said, "Quickly! Hide upstairs! Do not show your face until I send word that it is safe. If you hear anyone come up there, get into the closet, where there is a little hiding place. I need to act as if I know nothing about the fire."

"What about my horse? Rory may ask where he came from."

"I will have one of my stable boys mix him with the herd. Now go upstairs! I'll take care of the rest."

"My prayers are with you." Barrett waved, bounding up the stairs of the stable.

"We are going to need them, son!"

In order to look inconspicuous, Alton rushed back to the house.

Rory, dressed in his nightclothes, stormed out of the house to see what the commotion was.

Alton acted shocked, confused. "Rory, what in tarnation is that? Are we being attacked?"

Rory ignored the question. He just yelled. "No, No, No." Running past his father to the stable, he jumped on the first horse he could find. He sped off toward the blazing barn.

Alton noticed his house staff watching the distant flames. With his son out of hearing range, he thought it was the perfect opportunity to brief them.

"Brennan, Sylvia... come here quickly!"

Confused, they hurried over.

"Now listen to me... this is just between the three of us."

"Yes, suh, Massa Alton," Brennan agreed.

"Barrett is hiding in the loft above the stable. If Rory finds out, he will kill him."

"Why Massa Rory want to kill Massa Barrett?" Brennan blinked.

"Don't worry about that. Just do what I say. He will need to stay there until we can find a way to get him to a safe place."

Neither said a word, listening.

"He will need food and water. See to it that he gets it secretly. Under no circumstances is Rory ever to know about his brother-in-law being here. Understood?"

"Yes, Massa you can count on us," Brennan responded.

"Yes, suh... we sure do love Massa Barrett," Sylvia added.

"Now you stay here and don't worry about what is happening at the barn."

Several workers had sleepily staggered out of their nearby homes, watching the flames in the distance.

One of the grounds staff sprinted up to him, out of breath. "What shall we do, Massa?"

"Simon, get the water wagon and as many people as you can to the fire at the old barn. I am heading there now."

Men grabbed shovels, picks, and rakes and followed the large wagon with water barrels as it raced toward the fire.

By the time Rory reached the fire, the barn was completely engulfed in flames. Ammo was still exploding sporadically.

"No! No! How? What happened?" Rory fell to the ground slamming his fists into the dirt.

Minutes later, Alton showed up with the water wagon and the additional help.

"What we do, Massa Alton?" Simon asked, running up to Alton.

"Nothing, we can do... just let it burn. But we have to make sure it does not spread to the woods." He lowered his head sadly.

"Let it burn? You cannot let it burn. My whole life is in that barn." Rory sprinted up to one of the workers holding a bucket of water and shoved him. "What are you waiting for? Get fire lines going! Put that fire out! That's an order!"

Rory shouted at his father, "You let this happen! You went on your ride this morning and should have seen the fire from the cemetery. You could have stopped it!" He eyed his father with contempt.

"Rory, what is going on? This old barn is empty!" he shouted. "What are all those explosions? They sound like guns firing," Alton questioned his son.

The despondent son grabbed his father's jacket and began to shake him wildly. "My life is ruined. All ruined," he wailed.

He pushed his father down, jumped on his horse, and sped off.

Chapter Thirty-One

May 1864
Elmira Prison

The woman held her breath and watched as the fly buzzed around her face and landed on her sleeve. She eyed it for a second and then it flew off, finally landing on a wall. Bang! A folded newspaper came smashing down and crushed it. "I hate flies and mosquitoes," she complained.

Brooke smiled at her. "We seem to have an abundance of both around here, Helen."

The woman looked around for another fly. Finding one, she smacked her newspaper down again. "Got it! Six out of seven. One of my better days."

Brooke giggled.

Helen sat down on the old, wobbly chair at the table in front of Brooke. She lifted her head a bit and eyeballed the young woman's mid-section. "How's the baby?"

Brooke rubbed her abdomen. "Kicking up a storm. He must be a boy. He already knows Kung Fu, like his father."

They both laughed, a sound not heard often these days.

A single gunfire shot from outside caused both of them to jump, interrupting their conversation. Their smiles disappeared as fast as they came. They both sat in stunned silence for a moment, not knowing if the gunfire hit a fleeing prisoner, or was meant to scare one away from the wall.

Their minds were put at ease when they heard one of the guards yell, "You got that rabbit, Ben. We gonna have a nice meal tonight."

Helen took a deep, calming breath. "I cannot believe how fast this camp has deteriorated. They used to call it Camp Rathbun, then Elmira. I can see why they call it Hellmira now. The filth these men live in is horrible."

She peered around the small room, which was part of a large wooden structure used for a hospital. The patients' beds were in a number of tents attached to the side of the building.

Brooke dropped her chin and gave her friend a sad, crooked smile. "When I first signed on to work here, I thought it would be a way to help people. You know, to show the Southerners that Northerners care about them. But after only two months, it seems the Northerners are more bent on teaching these prisoners a lesson than rehabilitating them."

Helen sighed. "You seem down today."

"I'm concerned for Barrett. Why have I not heard from him? Not even a letter. He used to write me every day."

Helen cupped her hands over Brooke's. "I doubt his mail can even get through."

"Not even a message?"

"A message... that is just as hard. Does he know to reach you here?"

Brooke shrugged her shoulders. "Titus is at home in Connecticut. Cornelius has been trying to locate Barrett. He even contacted President Lincoln. The last thing we heard was that he was headed to Virginia to train soldiers." She wiped away a single tear. "I look at the conditions of this place, and I shudder to think what the Union soldiers are going through in the prisons down there. Helen, I am afraid that Barrett may be in one of them."

Helen blew out a sad breath that lumped in the deepest part of her soul.

Prisse opened the door a crack and peeked in. "Miss Brooke, it's time to make rounds and check our patients."

Helen stared at Brooke, still holding her hand. "Honey, let's make the rounds and then we can go into town and visit the church. We can pray for Barrett, Gordon, and Walker, too."

Brooke's expression changed to pity for her coworker. "Oh, Helen, I am thinking of myself and not taking into consideration that your husband is a prisoner on one of those horrible ships. I'm sorry." She jumped from her chair, walked around the table, and gave her friend a heartfelt embrace.

Helen's eyes grew misty.

Brooke added, "Your son, Walker, have you heard from him? Will he return home soon?"

"I think so. They managed to save his leg, but he will walk with a limp the rest of his life. He is one of the fortunate ones." She bit her lip.

The friends linked arms and followed Prisse into the next room—a large tent with dozens of cots—all holding sick and wounded soldiers.

"Miss Brooke, are you feeling all right?" her handmaid, Prisse, asked.

"You asked me that question only ten minutes prior," Brooke lovingly chided as she repositioned a prisoner's head on a limp pillow.

"I know, Miss Brooke, but William gave me strict orders to keep an eye on you." Prisse shifted the man's legs to a different position.

"You are doing a splendid job, my dear," Helen encouraged.

Prisse fell silent. Stepping back, she gazed at the long line of beds filled with soldiers. Many patients groaned in pain, others lay motionless, on the brink of death.

"Miss Brooke, do you really think we are doing any good here? The soldiers... they die no matter what we do."

Brooke looked forlornly at the unconscious prisoner she was caring for. "I know it seems hopeless, but we must continue to help, hope, and pray that they make it until the end of this awful war, when they can return to their families."

"There you are," a loud voice interrupted.

"Good Morning, Dr. Wey," Brooke drawled.

"Hello, Doctor," Prisse said, pulling a sheet down and tucking it under the thin, straw mattress."

"Good morning, Prisse. Young lady, you never cease to amaze me."

"What you mean, Dr. Wey?" she angled her head.

"You are always keeping busy. You never leave any stone unturned."

"I am not turning any stones, Dr. Wey, just patients."

He chuckled. "It is a figure of speech. I mean, you always make sure everything is the best it can be."

Prisse blushed.

The doctor turned his attention to Brooke and Helen. "Ladies, we have nearly a hundred prisoners coming in shortly. They have had a long trip and will be worn out. Get the equipment ready and check them for disease, or wounds, then separate them accordingly. We can only give beds to the men whose lives are in danger. There is not enough room for anyone else."

"Doctor, we have been losing men at a rapid rate. They have been dying by the dozens every day." A sigh escaped from Brooke.

"I know, but I am doing the best I can. We just do not have the supplies, facilities, or the manpower to save them. What's more, I'm afraid it will only get worse."

"What do you mean, Doctor Wey?" Brooke felt her heart quicken.

"When winter hits... these weak men are apt to freeze to death."

"We need to get more blankets and be prepared," Brooke's frustration was noticeable.

The doctor shrugged his shoulders. "That is not going to happen. These prisoners are low priority."

"How would we like it if our Northern soldiers were treated like that?"

The doctor stopped what he was doing and stared at Brooke for a long moment. He finally broke the quiet, "I have heard horror stories about what has been happening at the prisoner of war camps down South where our Northern troops are being held. I was told, their newest camp crams twenty-five thousand of our men on fifteen acres."

"Fifteen acres? Twenty-five thousand men? That is twice what we have here. Doctor, that is inhumane. What we are doing here is cruel... I can't even imagine those horrible conditions," Brooke's voice cracked with emotion.

"I can't either, but there is absolutely nothing we can do about it." The doctor stared off into space. "I have asked for help here, but doubt that it will ever come. How do you think I feel? I am just one doctor from a local town trying to help out."

A loud voice boomed from the doorway, "The prisoners are here."

"Okay, girls, check each man as he comes in. Separate them according to their needs and we will see if we can help them," the doctor's voice faded as he walked away.

"Come on ladies, let's do our job," Brooke challenged.

They stepped out of the tent and watched as almost a hundred men marched slowly toward them, guarded by only a dozen Union soldiers.

A hefty, gray-haired army sergeant, carrying a horsewhip, ordered the men to halt. He boomed, "Listen up, men. This is going to be your home until we tell you otherwise. I want you to form a single line by that door. You are going to be checked over by these nurses. If I even catch you looking at them, you will get a swift hit in the head with my quirt. So, don't you dare look at them, or touch them... understand?"

The prisoners murmured, some moaned.

"Now form a single line and give your name and rank to Private Nelson. Move!" the old sergeant barked.

A young soldier sitting at the table logged the name of each Confederate prisoner coming through the line. After that, the captive stepped to the next area where Brooke and the other nurses would check him over for apparent wounds or sickness.

Most of the prisoners were weak and gaunt. Many limped from wounds suffered on the battlefield. Some were seriously ill.

The sergeant sat nearby keeping a watchful eye on each man. "Get to movin'," he bellowed, trying to hurry the line along. "Ain't got all day!"

Brooke and the other nurses gave each man a small smile, but most of them did not notice it, fearing the sergeant would follow through with his threat. One soldier after another kept his eyes glued to the ground.

As one man neared Brooke, his knees buckled and he collapsed. Alertly, she and another nurse caught him before he hit the ground.

Seeing the prisoner stagger, the sergeant clutched his whip.

Brooke raised her hand protectively, "Don't you dare hit this man." She scowled at the hard-hearted sergeant.

He gave her a cross look, but backed away.

"Doctor, this man collapsed."

Dr. Wey rushed over to him and looked in his eyes. From the bones in his face and the color of his skin, he could tell he was suffering from malnutrition.

"Prisse, get this man some soup."

"Yes, Dr. Wey." She scurried off.

"Brooke, we can't give another cot to a malnutrition man. We need it for the wounded. Sit him over there and have Prisse feed him." The doctor pointed to a rickety chair.

"Yes, sir." Brooke helped the weak man sit in a chair in the corner of the crowded room.

From time to time, the sergeant hit his whip against the palm of his hand, reminding the prisoners he was boss.

Private Nelsen continued checking the men in. "Name and rank, city and state," he shouted to the next man in line.

The prisoner responded weakly, "Lieutenant Charles Fortner from…."

"Speak up, soldier, speak up!" Nelson yelled.

The prisoner took a deep breath and replied a little louder, "Lieutenant Charles M. Fortner, from Savannah, Georgia."

Brooke dropped what she was doing and spun around, almost afraid to hope. Barely recognizing the thin, frail man, she ran to him. Tears burned her eyes. "Charles? Is that really you?"

Everyone nearby watched as the prisoner slowly looked up and saw a nurse running toward him—a woman he immediately recognized as his sister. He took a step closer to her, but stopped abruptly when the sergeant raised his whip.

Brooke screamed, "Sergeant, let him go… he's my brother." She swung her arms around Charles' neck and held him in a long, tearful reunion.

Broken by what he had gone through in the war, and finally seeing and feeling someone he loved, the soldier could not contain his emotions. Tears streamed down his cheeks.

The sergeant stared blankly, uncertain what to do. He finally turned back to the line of men. "Keep the line movin'! We ain't got all day." For a brief time, he chose to ignore the sibling reunion.

Charles held tight to his sister, trembling. Brooke helped him to a quieter area. "Get some water," she sobbed.

Helen quickly retrieved a tin cup from a nearby table and filled it with water.

Brooke brought the cup to Charles mouth so he could take a sip. Then he placed his hand over hers and tipped the cup to his lips, gulping the water down.

She handed the cup to her friend to fill again.

Charles stared at Brooke. Finally, in a muffled voice, he cried out, "Samuel is dead. Our brother is dead."

Not saying a word, she closed her eyes and pulled Charles' head closer to her. Undeterred by anything or anyone around them, they wept.

The sergeant stomped over to them. "Nurse, get that prisoner back in line. We got work to do," he ordered.

Seeing the emotional scene playing out before them, Helen snapped back, "Let them be. Let them at least have a few moments."

The sergeant persisted, "We need to get these other men checked in. We do not have time for this nonsense."

Doctor Wey heard the shouting and walked over to them. "What is going on? What is all this noise?"

"This nurse here left her post," the sergeant scowled.

"It's her brother," Helen reported. "She just found out that her other brother is dead. Give them a little peace for heaven's sake."

Just then, Prisse rushed in with a cup of soup. "My, this smells good... we fix you up good...." She glanced up and saw Brooke embracing a man. His dirty face was thin, his eyes sunken, his beard rough, but she knew it was Charles. She put the soup on the table and walked slowly toward them.

Charles opened his tear-filled eyes when he heard Prisse.

"Massa Charles... is that really you?"

He could not speak, nodding his head.

She joined the embrace.

Doctor Wey glanced around the room. "Everyone else get back to work! Let them have a little privacy."

"Sir, I cannot leave this prisoner in here by himself," the sergeant snarled.

"Sergeant, what is he going to do? Look at him! Is he going to beat his sister up and try to escape? Now do what I tell you. Give them some space, and let's get these other men taken care of."

"All right, sir, but I will have to bring this before Colonel Colt."

"Colt may be in charge of this camp, but I am in charge of this... this so-called hospital, so do as I instruct!"

The irate sergeant stormed away.

Brooke responded, "Thank you, Doctor Wey."

Facing Helen, she said, "Continue checking the prisoners in, I will be with you in a moment."

The doctor glanced back at Brooke and Charles and shook his head sadly. "I loathe war."

Holding her brother's hand, Brooke asked, "Are you certain Samuel is dead?"

He responded softly, "Yes. He died at Gettysburg. I saw it happen. We were with General Pickett, attacking the Union line. As we charged up the hill, I saw Samuel go down after being hit. I could not get to him because of all the fighting. We were being slaughtered, so the remaining few of us retreated. I rushed back to our brother and held him in my arms." Charles seemed to be in a daze, trying to collect his thoughts. Finally, he found the strength to continue, "Blood poured from his mouth, but he just looked at me and then... then he went limp."

Tears streamed down Brooke's face. "What happened to his body?"

"I knew I had to take him home... back to Annalise. I was carrying him back to camp when I felt a terrible pain in my leg and collapsed. Next thing I knew, I was a prisoner. I had been shot in the leg."

"And Samuel?"

"I never knew what happened to his body." Charles took another sip of water; some dribbled down his scruffy beard.

Brooke brushed his long stringy hair away from his face with her hand. "That battle was a year ago, where have you been?"

"I have been in several prison camps. I have lost count."

"Does Father know about Samuel?"

"I am not sure. Don't know how he could."

"What about Rory?" she asked, handing him another cup of water.

Charles grabbed it with both hands and gulped it down. "Last I heard Rory was promoted to captain."

"Captain? Of what?"

"Most people don't know it but..." he moved closer to Brooke's ear and whispered, "he is one of the Gray Ghosts."

"What? I have heard of them, but I thought the Gray Ghosts were a story people made up, a myth."

"No! They are real. They are a cavalry unit led by Colonel John Mosby. Rory is one of their leaders. I've heard that he has been leading raids into Virginia and bringing back guns and supplies." He looked directly into his sister's teary eyes and took a deep breath. "Brooke, I hate to tell you this, but he has a price on his head for killing women and children."

She gasped, "Oh, no! How could that be?"

"Word has it that he led a raid on a Virginia town and something terrible went wrong. His men went wild and began firing on everyone. When it was over, twenty some people were killed… some women and children."

"How do you know Rory was involved in this?"

"I heard men talking about it. Other prisoners. Then I read a poster at a train station a while back, when we were being moved."

"I don't understand." Brooke felt sick to her stomach.

"It's Dark Shadow."

"What?" She raised an eyebrow.

"The flyer gave the description of a black horse with a red mane and red socks on the rear legs."

Brooke groaned. "That describes Dark Shadow perfectly."

"Right."

"You must be mistaken. Rory would never endanger Dark Shadow in the war."

"Rory hated Dark Shadow after the race—he blamed him for losing to Barrett. He actually has gone into many battles with that horse."

Brooke shook her head in disbelief.

Doctor Wey approached them, concern written on his face. "How is your brother doing?"

"He is dehydrated." Brooke put her arm around her brother's shoulder.

"Understandable. How long have you been a prisoner, son?" He studied Charles.

"Going on a year."

Brooke pled, "Doctor, what can we do? I can't let him live like the rest of the prisoners here. I just can't."

The doctor drew a loud breath and crossed his arms. "Unfortunately, you do not have anything to say about it. Your job is to be nurse, not a judge. You can't free this man, nor can I." Wey stared at the prisoner. "Did you say you were an officer?"

Charles responded with a nod. "Lieutenant… cavalry."

"Well, rank does have its privileges, sometimes good… sometimes bad. In this case, it may be to your advantage. We would have to separate you from the rest of the men because you're an officer. Not sure why they haven't already done so." Dr. Wey spoke as if he was thinking aloud.

Brooke breathed a sigh of relief.

Suddenly, Charles mouth turned up at one corner. "My sister, I have been so busy feeling sorry for myself, I did not notice you are pregnant." A hint of a sparkle appeared in his eyes. "When is my niece or nephew due?"

"In about a month."

"How is Barrett? I mean, where is he?"

She gave a sad shrug and turned to get him another drink. "He is a captain in the Union Army… somewhere. I haven't heard from him since January."

"January? That's seven, eight months ago."

She could not respond; sadness gripped her.

The doctor noticed the sergeant getting more infuriated by the minute, so he spoke up, "Brooke, if the other prisoners here find out this man's brother-in-law is a Union officer… well, his life would be in jeopardy. Of course, the higher ups running this prison would see that as a problem solving itself... one less mouth to feed, one less prisoner to care for. I cannot free this man, but because he is an officer, I can see that he is separated from the enlisted men. I might be able to allow him to work in the hospital for the time being. I will have to okay it with the prison commander."

Brooke's eyes showed a hint of hope. "Mr. Colt seems to be a fair man. And since Barrett was a friend to his brother, perhaps that might make a difference."

"What do you mean a friend?" Charles asked.

"Major Henry Colt is in charge of this prison."

"Colt?" Charles questioned.

Brooke explained, "Barrett has a gold plated Colt revolver on his trophy shelf. It was given to him by Samuel Colt himself—Henry Colt's brother, after he won the pistol competition years ago. He used one of Colt's pistols in the finals."

She shifted her gaze back to Wey. "Doctor, do you really think he may be permitted to work in the hospital?"

"I believe so. Your brother will at least get clean water and a small meal. But, you must remember, he is still a prisoner of war and will have to be treated as such."

"I understand." Her eyes narrowed with his tone.

Wey tried to sound hopeful. "I will talk to the commander… but I am not promising anything."

"That is all I can ask."

"In the meantime, he can stay here as a patient."

"Thank you, Dr. Wey." She looked at her brother—thin, frail, but alive, and felt great joy. On the other hand, she mourned for Samuel. "Father is going to be heartbroken when he hears of Samuel's death."

"And when he hears about Rory," Charles muttered.

Brooke grabbed her brother around his neck. "At least you are safe, for now. I pray my husband is, also."

She briefly looked heavenward. *Lord, protect my husband, the father of my baby. Watch over him every minute of every day. And Father, please end this senseless war!*

Chapter Thirty-Two

May 20, 1864

A couple weeks after the fire, a sullen Rory still had not said a word to Alton or anyone on the estate staff. He would awake before dawn and be gone the rest of the day. When he came home, often late at night, he went straight to his room. An uncomfortable atmosphere filled the air at Annalise.

One morning at breakfast, Rory finally broke the tense silence. "I'm going to be gone for a couple weeks," he grunted.

Alton looked up from his plate of eggs and sausage. "Where do you go for weeks at a time?"

"I do military maneuvers with my men," Rory replied curtly, helping himself to another portion of grits.

Almost immediately, the expression on Alton's face changed when he realized it was time to confront Rory. His eyes were clear, intense. "Son, I have to ask you a question." He bit his lower lip and decided it would be best to get straight to the point. "Where is it?"

"Where is what?" Making no eye contact, Rory continued to shovel food into his mouth.

"My gold! It is all gone… and you are the only one living in this house who knows the combination to my safe," Alton spoke through gritted teeth.

"Don't know what you're talking about. One of the slaves must have taken it," he said with a sarcastic overtone.

"You know we have no slaves here. Never have. I pay them a fair wage. And they did not take it… you did!"

Anxiously, Rory peered out the window, ignoring his father. He noticed a servant headed to the stable with a tray full of food—he sat up straighter and squinted.

"Rory, where is my gold? All of it is gone, replaced by worthless stones. Without that gold, we can lose everything when the war is over. It will be the end of Annalise!" Alton's voice grew louder with each word.

"Think I care?" Rory stood up from the table, walked over to the window, and watched the servant enter the horse stable. He could almost feel his father's piercing gaze burn straight through him, but he refused to look back at him. He sipped his orange tea.

"You should care, Rory. It has given you a comfortable life." Alton declined a fresh hot biscuit when Seymour held the plate in front of him.

Rory folded his arms across his midsection in a hostile stance and glared at his father. "I don't know about that. You can always use your greenbacks you have hidden away. Save the farm with that Federal money."

Alton stared at his son. *He seems so cold, callous. Who is this man? I don't know him anymore.* He noticed the captain bars on Rory's uniform glisten when the sunrays hit them. Sadness overwhelmed Alton when he thought about his youngest son's role in the war.

The father took a deep breath and let it out slowly. "How would you know about that money? Are you admitting that you stole my gold?"

"No! I did nothing of the sort. I did not steal... bought some needed supplies for the South... to defend it. It is better than hoarding the gold, like you were doing."

Alton leaned forward cupping his hands together. "When you say supplies, you mean rifles, don't you? Is that what you mean?"

For a few seconds, Rory looked too stunned to move or speak. His face turned red with anger. "I can't believe it! You set the fire!" The realization was almost more than the son could bear. He sounded beyond angry, frantic.

"Yes, I did. When I found those rifles, I knew they were meant for no good."

Rory threw his half-filled glass of tea, narrowly missing his father, and began screaming, "Those guns were meant to save the Confederate States of America! Father, I can have you hanged for what have you done!"

He looked out the window and seemed to calm down. His tone was no longer a shout, but sharp, cold. "Who are you hiding in the stable?"

"What?" Alton nervously sipped his now-cold coffee.

"Abby walked into the stable with a tray of food a few minutes ago. I do not think she is going on a picnic, and I don't think we feed the pigs that good. Who is hiding there?"

Alton did not respond; his pulse started to race.

Eyeing the stable, Rory pulled his gun from the holster and started toward the door. "We will soon see!"

"No! Son, sit down!" Alton was panic-stricken. He reached out to stop his out-of-control son.

"I am sick of you ordering me around." Furious, Rory took the butt of the gun and hit his father in the back of the head.

Alton fell to the floor and grabbed his head as blood oozed from the wound.

Two servants ran to his aid and helped him to his feet.

Alton glared at his son. "What happened to the little boy I raised... the little boy that I used to take fishing every day... the little boy I bounced on my knee?" Alton's hands were bloody from holding his wounded head.

"The little boy grew up, sir. He grew up," Rory stressed the word "sir," scorning his father.

Alton pulled the paper that Barrett had given him from his side pocket and tossed it at his son. "What is this? Is this true?"

Rory cast a questioning look at his father.

"Is this really you? Have you done these evil things?"

Rory bent over with his gun in hand and picked up the paper, now red from the blood on his father's hand. He read the wanted poster silently; an emotionless stare covered his face. "Where did you get this?" he shouted, trembling with anger.

"Is it true? Is this really you?"

Rory looked past his father, a trance-like expression covering his face.

"The description fits you." Alton clenched his shaking, bloody hands.

"There are hundreds of men who fit that description." The younger man remained defiant.

"Not riding Dark Shadow. The description of the horse can only be Dark Shadow. Is it true?" Alton's voice cracked with emotion—sadness taking over.

There was silence for a moment while Rory stared at the paper. "Things just went wrong." He shifted his gaze toward his father, his face filled with hatred. "But they were Yankees... Bluebellies... the scum of the earth... they deserved to die."

"They were unarmed men, innocent women, and children." Alton's heavy heart left lines around his eyes and mouth.

"They were Northern scum, sir. Not fit to live," Rory hissed.

Alton shook his head; unable to speak, he fought back tears.

"I asked you, who is in the stable, Father?" Suddenly it hit him and a sly grin came to his face. "I should have known... Barrett... von... Weber!" He stormed out of the dining room.

In desperation, Alton grabbed his arm, shouting, "No, son! I beg of you, don't! Don't have more regrets... stop this madness, now!"

Rory glared at his father's hand on his arm. Filled with disgust, he ordered, "Take your hand off me, or I will hit you again. My Confederate cavalry will be here any moment. Then, I will have to make the decision of what to do with you. Destroying government property and harboring a Union officer are extremely serious charges. I may have to watch you hang, Father." Laughing scornfully, he jerked his arm from his father's grasp. He checked his gun to make sure it was loaded and stomped out the door.

The servant girl, who had taken the tray into the stable, walked past him and offered a slight smile.

Without warning, Rory took his free hand, grabbed her by the neck, and pinned her against the side of the stable. "Where is he?"

Terrified, she cried, "The room upstairs."

He released his grip on her, slapped her hard with his open hand. She fell to the ground, sobbing.

Not saying another word, he entered the stable. Out of control, he stomped up the narrow stairway. When he reached the top, he saw the tray of food on a small table. Heart pounding, he gazed around the small room. Trying to sound calm, he demanded, "Come out, Mr. von Weber. Meet me like a man, not like the coward I know you are."

There was silence.

"Twenty Confederate cavalry troops are on the way here, as we speak. You cannot get away. Come out and die like a man, or be hanged. Either way, you are dead! Problem is... what do I do with my father?"

Continued silence.

"Think about it. If you are found here, you and Father will be hanged together. Harboring Union loyalists, especially men like you, is a hanging offense. I cannot stop that. If you come out now, I can guarantee my father's safety. I will say he turned you in. Better yet, maybe I'll not say anything. I will just kill you and bury you somewhere... certainly not in Father's precious cemetery."

Barrett burst out of the closet, aiming a pistol at Rory's head, while Rory pointed his gun at Barrett.

"Ah, yes, I knew it was you. Now what am I going to do with you?"

Barrett challenged him, "Why did you kill those innocent people?"

"Why, Barrett, what makes you think I did that? Even if I did... we all know there are no innocent people in time of war. There are just casualties of war."

With guns still aimed at each other, Barrett appealed, "It looks like we have a standoff. Let me go, and I will face your troops."

"Oh, that would be fun to watch. You being shot a hundred times. My men would love that! And, I would love to see your body painfully twitch as each steel ball hits you. The problem is that I want to have the pleasure of shooting you. I want to do it." His voice sounded like a spoiled child having a tantrum.

"I have never understood why you hate me so much?"

"It's because you're easy to hate. That's why."

"That's not an honest answer."

"No, but it's the only answer you are going to get. Now, this can end one of two ways. You put your gun down and surrender, at which time I will decide if I will kill you, and Father will get a reprimand. On the other hand, maybe I will turn you over to the guards and they will hang you. Maybe today, right here at Annalise. They are upset with what Sherman is doing to the South right now. I am sure they would love to make an example of you. There's no way I could stop them."

"There is a third way." Barrett's palms were sweating, but he sounded calm, sure of himself.

"And what is that?"

"Let me go! Let me take my chances out there," Barrett gestured with his head to the outside.

"You know if I do that, you might just get away and kill some of my friends. No, I like it my way."

There was no denying the fire in Barrett's eyes or the sincerity in his tone as he spoke. "I only have five rounds of ammo here. I will kill you first—you know I never miss my target. And right now, this gun is pointing directly at your head. I could fire before you even had a chance to return fire. And after that, I could kill four of your friends. Do you want to take that chance?"

Rory's obnoxious grin disappeared as he pondered Barrett's words. He knew his brother-in-law was right, so decided to play along. "Perhaps you are right. I think I will let you go... on foot. No horse!"

"How fair is that?"

After a minute Rory spoke up, "All right. Since we are related, I will let you keep your horse, and I will even give you a five-minute head start. I really do not want my father to hang, so nothing will be said about you living in this loft. You just stopped by the estate hoping to find sanctuary and Father turned you away. Oh, my... he is going to owe me... owe me his life."

Rory pointed his gun in the direction of the stairs. "Go! Get on your horse. I would suggest you don't ride north just yet, because my cavalry unit is coming from that direction. As I said, I want to be there when they cut you down. I want to watch you suffer."

Barrett slowly walked to the stairs and started to back down, his pistol still aimed at Rory.

Fortner followed him down the narrow stairway.

Barrett untied a saddled horse and slowly mounted him.

"I guess I can get you for stealing a horse, also. That is certainly a hanging offense," Rory cackled.

Alton watched from the porch, blood still oozing down his head as Barrett backed his horse out of the stables.

"My, I get the feeling you do not trust me. See, this is my word." Rory emptied his pistol and threw the gun on the ground. "Go! Go! Get out of here. I will come after you in five minutes... and I will be riding Dark Shadow. It is a race you will not win this time."

Barrett glanced at Alton sitting on the porch, but didn't speak. He swiftly kicked his horse to get him to take off in a gallop down the road.

Immediately, Rory ran to his horse and reached across the saddle, pulling his rifle out of its sleeve. He stepped into the open for an easy shot. "Five minutes are up!" he said, laughing. He aimed the rifle at Barrett's back. "Die, you Bluebelly Devil!"

As a shot rang out, Barrett's horse reared up. Von Weber pulled his gun, to return fire, but stopped when he noticed Rory standing with his rifle in hand, holding his abdomen. A crimson stain appeared on the front of his clean, gray uniform.

Barrett shifted his gaze to the house and saw Alton standing at the railing, holding the rifle Barrett had given him as a gift—The Henry.

Rory slowly turned, struggling to stand up. He saw his father holding the rifle, still aimed at him. "Father, how could you?" he gasped.

Alton dropped the rifle and ran to his bleeding son.

Rory collapsed into his father's arms. When Alton stared into the eyes of his youngest son, he remembered those brown eyes as a baby, as a child. A dam of tears broke. "I'm sorry, my son. I could not let you do it! It was wrong, just like the things you have been doing the past couple of years... taking innocent lives!"

"I could have been president."

"No, Son. We just don't want to admit it, but the war has been lost for some time. Our Southern pride has destroyed this land we love."

Rory's eyes were rolling into his head and dizziness overtook him.

"Why, Son? Why have you been so consumed with hatred for Barrett?"

Rory coughed a couple times, blood trickling from his mouth. Staring straight into the morning sky, he spoke, "From the moment I met him, I realized he was everything I always wanted to be. I knew he would be someone you would love."

"But Son, I have always loved you. I never expected, or demanded anything special from you. You are my son and I loved and respected you for who you were. But you began doing evil things, sinful things."

"I always wanted to make you proud." Rory sputtered, finally looking into his father's eyes.

"I was proud to be your father. I loved you!"

"Do you still love me, Father? After all I have done, do you still love me?"

Large tears built up in Alton's eyes as he thought about his son's words. Before he had time to respond, Rory's eyes grew wide, and an expression of fear took hold of him. Then his eyes rolled back and he was perfectly still. Death had come.

The father's tears fell, landing on his son's lifeless face. "Yes, son. Despite what you have done... I still love you. How could I not? You're my son... my boy."

Alton screamed in anger, and then began wailing, mourning what could have been. After a time, he looked heavenward and then stared at Rory's lifeless body. Wiping away the tears that had fallen on his son's face, he cried, "My tears can never wash away your sins, but the blood of Jesus can." Then, laying his head on his son, he sobbed.

Barrett watched from nearby—helpless, sorrowful.

After a short time, Seymour, Brennan, and Sylvia ran over to help Alton.

"Brennan, I'll take care of Massa Alton," Sylvia ordered, taking charge. "Get rid of the guns and clean up the blood. Seymour, take Rory's body to the barn and hide it. We will take care of it later."

Despondent, Alton clung to his dead son, rocking him.

Barrett dismounted and stood close by, wanting to help, but uncertain what to do.

"You must go, Massa Barrett. We'll take care of this," Sylvia strongly voiced.

Just then, a couple children came running. "Sylvia, them Graycoats are comin'! Them Graycoats are comin'!"

Sylvia dished out orders. "Quickly, get Massa Alton up the stairs and sit him on the porch where he can see what's happenin'. Massa Barrett, you go before they find you. Hurry! We'll take care of things here. Massa Alton, he be all right."

With tearful eyes, the distraught father faced Barrett. "Go, my son. Go! This was not your fault. Run! Make it safely through this awful war. My family has been through enough. I don't want my daughter to be a widow."

Brennan tried to reassure von Weber. "Massa Alton be all right. We take care of everythin'. No need to worry, Massa Barrett."

Barrett's horse reared up, then took off at a full gallop.

"You bring back Miss Brooke when this war over. You hear me?" Sylvia yelled. Barrett waved as he sped off.

Brennan assisted Alton up the steps. "Sorry, Massa Alton."

Alton peered at his servant. "Brennan, you did the right thing getting me the rifle. You did the right thing."

Brennan helped Alton change his bloody shirt and positioned him in his rocking chair on the porch. His loyal dog sat beside him.

Alton watched Seymour and another servant carry the guns and Rory's body into the stable.

Another worker hurried over with a rake and spread fresh dirt over Rory's pool of blood.

Minutes later, a small platoon of Confederate soldiers rode down the lane and stopped in front of the house.

Sylvia greeted them cheerfully, smiling as though nothing had happened.

"Good morning, gentlemen," Alton's voice sounded subdued.

"Good morning, sir. Is Captain Fortner here?"

"Rory... uh, Rory...?" Just hearing his name was almost more than he could bear.

Sylvia took over. "Captain Rory had an early breakfast and left. Said he be gone 'bout three weeks."

"He was supposed to wait for us." The soldier sounded bewildered.

"Massa Rory said somethin' 'bout meetin' with a man name Mosby," Sylvia continued calmly, relieved that she had overheard Rory mention him before.

The man who was talking stood in the stirrups and looked around to the others. "I understand... when Colonel Mosby calls, you run."

The sergeant looked at Alton with sharp eyes. "Mr. Fortner, you do not look well. Have you already heard the news?"

Confused, Alton cocked his head.

Sylvia noticed him struggling, so intervened. "Massa Alton very sick. Might be catchin' 'monia. He got terrible wet fightin' our fire couple weeks back."

"Sorry to be the one to inform you, but we have news from the battlefield."

Alton swallowed hard, fearful of what was coming

The sergeant dismounted and walked up the steps. He solemnly took his hat off and snapped to attention.

The other men on the horses removed their hats and held them in front of their chests, showing their respect.

The soldier handed Alton a cream-colored paper. "I am sorry this is late, sir. With the battlefields so far away and the thousands of casualties in the war, it is impossible to get updates to the next of kin in a timely manner."

Alton stared at the letter, holding it away from him. His heart pounded. With trembling hands, he handed it back to the sergeant. "If you will, Sergeant."

"Yes, sir." The soldier opened the envelope and read the letter aloud.

Dear Mr. Alton Fortner,

I regret to inform you that your son, Lieutenant Samuel Fortner, died a hero's death at Gettysburg. He led his company in a charge taking the hill and saved the lives of many men.

I also regret to inform you that your other son, Lieutenant Charles Fortner, is reported as missing. We are uncertain if he is a Prisoner of War, or a casualty. I sincerely regret the sacrifices you and your family have had to make for the defense of the South. May God look down on you and your family and give you comfort at this time of loss.

President Jefferson Davis

Alton stared at the sergeant and weakly replied, "Samuel is dead. How am I going to be able to tell his wife and children?" He paused. "And, what happened to Charles?"

"He is missing, sir. We are not sure if he was captured or what." The sergeant looked around nervously. "Sir, on behalf of the great State of Georgia, you have our condolences."

Alton gazed off in the distance, speechless.

"Sir, I must get my men back to Savannah. I do not know what Rory's new orders are, but I am certain he will do what needs to be done to preserve this great country. We are preparing for General Sherman. If you have not heard, his forces are getting ready to attack Atlanta and some believe he will be heading this way soon. We will be ready for him. If he heads to Savannah, he will hit a brick wall and will be defeated. That's a guarantee."

He saluted Alton.

"Sergeant?" Alton quietly spoke.

"Yes, sir."

"Is there any chance of getting Samuel's body returned to us?"

"Uh, sir." The man was uncertain how to answer that question. "Not at this time, Mr. Fortner. I would suspect the bodies were buried where they fell. Maybe after the war, sir, we can sort things out."

Alton's eyes clouded.

"Sir, you can be proud of all three of your sons."

Alton looked at the man with a blank stare.

The sergeant snapped to attention, put his hat on, and turned to leave. He mounted his horse and rode off with the rest of his men.

Rory was buried in the family cemetery. On his gravestone was his name, nothing else. Next to him was a tombstone for Samuel.

As Alton stood in front of the two new markers, he poured out his heart to God. *Lord, I beseech You that if it be Your will, my son, Charles, will be found alive and unharmed. And God, I pray that Barrett will make it through this war and return home safely to his bride. God, please protect what is left of my family.*

Chapter Thirty-Three

July 18, 1864
Cool Spring, Virginia

The old warhorse had grown weary with the pace that Barrett was forcing him to gallop, but somehow kept going.

Still deep in the South and with Rebel troops scattered in every direction, the exhausted major's biggest fear was that someone would recognize him. Although he was thinner and his beard had grown considerably, if someone studied his facial features, he might still be recognizable. And, most folks would instantly know the Hymnist was a Northerner.

Three days had passed with Barrett traveling mostly off the road in wooded areas. With each mile, he grew more anxious to get home to his wife, and catch up on some needed rest.

After a few hours of restless sleep, Barrett examined his horse. Lifting one of its legs, he said, "You seem to be holding up all right, old man. Soon you will be able to rest and eat all you want. Just hold on for a couple more days. With any luck, we may run into a Union patrol and get some help." He patted his faithful steed on the neck.

After he loaded up the few items he had, Barrett continued on his way. It was dawn and the sun was just beginning to peek through the deep mist in the beautiful Shenandoah Valley.

Barrett arrived at a large clearing at the edge of a forest. The fog was thick. He looked over the terrain. *Impossible to know what lies ahead.* In the distance, he could barely make out the treetops around the perimeter. Directly in front of him stretched a lovely field of grass, dotted with wildflowers. He quietly muttered, "Well... I can go around... or I can go across." He patted his horse's nose. "What ya think, boy?" The horse nudged forward. "Yeah, I'm thinking the same thing. I want to get home." Without further delay, the homesick man and his horse started across the large, open field, first at a trot, and then at a slower, more cautious gait.

Halfway across the vast field, he sensed something amiss. *This is not right. It's too quiet!* He brought his horse to a sudden stop and looked through the now-golden haze. Silently, he watched and listened with every ounce of his being.

A loud pop echoed across the valley, shattering the ominous quiet. He heard muffled voices in the distance. To his right, he saw hundreds of flashes speeding across the meadow in a straight line. Then he heard the dull thuds of something hitting the ground around him.

Barrett knew he was in imminent danger! He leaned back in his saddle and hit the rear of his horse, urging him forward. Within seconds, the noise around him became deafening. Dazzling flashes surrounded him. The smoke from the gunpowder of military cannons and Springfield rifles quickly replaced the haze. He was in the middle of a battlefield!

He crouched down in the saddle as low as he could to avoid being hit by either enemy, or friendly fire. He feared that he was as close to being rescued, as he was to being captured. He did not know which way to turn. Making a split-second decision, he kept his horse moving at full speed in the same direction.

His worst fear became reality when Minié balls found their target, hitting Barrett's horse. His trusted companion fell lifeless to the ground. The momentum of the horse going down sent Barrett flying through the air, tumbling onto a man who had been killed in the battle.

Through the lifting fog, he could see men in blue rushing past him. The scene was chaotic. His only thoughts were on survival. He quickly took the dead Union soldier's blue hat and Springfield rifle. Barrett ran toward what he believed to be the safety of the Union lines.

Suddenly, there was a flash of light directly in front of him. An intense pain penetrated his side. He was hit! He struggled to his feet, and saw the soldier who had shot him reloading. Barrett somehow found strength to use the empty rifle to hit the Confederate, who crumpled to the ground. Von Weber raised the bayonet to end the man's life, but to his surprise, he looked into the face of a young boy, perhaps fourteen-years-old. He thrust the bayonet into the ground, next to the terrified young lad's chest.

When the boy's eyes opened, tears flowed down his cheeks.

Barrett stood over him. "Go home, son! Go home," he whispered.

At that moment, von Weber felt a piercing pain in his head. Everything went black.

The sounds around him were loud. However, it was not the noise that roused him, it was the horrible stench.

For a time, the light blinded him. Slowly his eyes began to focus on his surroundings. He noticed fir planks in front of him. His right hand was tied to the side of a wagon; his other hand painfully secured behind him. Trying to gather his bearings, he lay still for a moment. *Where am I? What happened to me?*

Finally, his ears caught the sounds of a deep, gruff voice singing an old, familiar spiritual. *Nobody know the trials I seen. Nobody knows for sure. Nobody knows but Jesus.*

Barrett moaned. He felt like his head had been hit with a hammer.

"Dr. Benton, Dr. Benton... him awake," an unknown voice nearby announced.

A man wearing a white coat, driving the wagon, looked back. "Well, well, I thought we lost you. Can't have that!" He spoke with an unusual accent.

"Where... where am I?" Barrett asked weakly.

"Southern Georgia."

"Georgia? I thought I was in Virginia." He blinked a few times, still trying to adjust to the light.

"You were... three weeks ago."

"What? How did I get here?" Barrett licked his parched lips.

"Isaac moved you."

A black man looking down at him smiled, proudly displaying his big, white teeth and wide eyes.

The white man in the front continued, "He has been taking care of you the last three weeks. Everyone else wanted to leave you for dead, but for some reason Isaac took a likin' to you."

Barrett forced a small grin. "He has a good voice, nice baritone, but he needs to learn the right words."

"What you mean?" the black man looked like his feelings were hurt.

Von Weber managed to weakly sing, *Nobody knows the trouble I've seen. Nobody knows but Jesus.*

The black man's voice grew louder. "That's what I sung... right, boss? That's what I sung."

"No, Isaac, I believe the man is right."

The black man shook his head forlornly.

The driver added, "Like I said, Isaac has taken a real likin' to you. Now me… I really can't get my emotions wrapped up in a piano player."

"You…" Barrett's throat was so dry he coughed, "you know who I am?"

"I sure do… I saw you play in Paris back in '60. I recall you had a ravishing young Spanish senorita by your side." He laughed, amused by his own humor.

"My wife, Brooke." Sadness overcame Barrett at the mention of her name.

"Yes, I remember." The doctor's voice trailed off as his mind strayed to his own wife.

Silence hung in the air for a short time as the old wagon bumped along the rough trail, jarring the injured man.

Finally, Barrett broke the quiet. "Doctor, will I be able to play the piano again?"

"That depends."

"On what?"

"If you make it through this godforsaken war. Countless men have died… thousands more will die." He shook his head sorrowfully. "Too many, way too many."

Barrett felt like flies were eating him alive and desperately wanted to shoo them away. He groaned, partially due to the pain, partially from frustration.

The doctor eyed the flies swarming around Barrett. "Not much you can do about them. There are too many of them and the conditions are ripe for mating."

"If you untie me, I can at least swat them away. Why am I tied up anyway? I can't go anywhere."

"Isaac, tell the man what happened last time he was loose."

"You were like a snake in a rat's nest. You tore into the Rebels like a crazy man. Took three of 'em out. They was gonna shoot you, but I calmed ya down."

"May I ask how?"

"You have two pretty good size bumps on your head—one is from a bullet creasin' your skull, and the second is from me hitting ya with a board."

"A board? Why a board?"

"Only thing I could find that wasn't lead."

"Well, I guess I can appreciate that. And it explains my horrible headache." Barrett's nose crinkled. "Did I kill them?"

"The Rebels? No, just beat 'em up bad." Isaac chuckled.

"What is that stink?" Barrett inquired, making an awful face.

The driver grinned. "Stink? Isaac, you smell anything?"

"No, suh, reckon I don't."

"It smells dreadful."

"Oh, that smell... that's death... plain and simple," the doctor responded.

Barrett was all too familiar with the smell of death. He hated it as much today as he did at the onset of the war. He tried to reposition himself. "You didn't answer my question... will I be able to play the piano again?"

The driver slowed the wagon a bit. "Oh, I understand what you are asking... you are wondering if you are missing any limbs. No, you took a pellet to the head and one to your side. The boy whose life you spared saved yours. He brought you to me when I happened by. You will have a scar, but your hair should cover it. Your side got infected, like most wounds in this war. I'll tell you a dirty secret... some of the Confederate soldiers pack their ammo in sheep dung. They know it will infect the wound and eventually kill a person. Then, you got pneumonia. Just not your month."

"So, you're a doctor?"

"Of sorts."

"So, that's what happened to me?"

"Yes, you had a real bad infection, besides pneumonia."

"Dr. Benton used a gallon of whiskey to clean the wounds," Isaac reported.

"I don't remember any of that," Barrett confessed.

The black man added, "Everybody else does. You scream like a banshee."

"I sure am thirsty." Von Weber struggled to move his head and look around. He noticed dozens of beaten-down men walking nearby, some in old, filthy blue trousers and grimy shirts. Others wore only under garments. He could see only a few armed Confederate soldiers guarding them.

He was in an open wagon with no cover, no shade. Near him lay two men, not moving.

The doctor noticed Barrett glancing around. "It's too late to worry about them... they didn't make it. Just haven't had time to stop and bury them."

Isaac held a tin cup of water to Barrett's lips and he gulped it down. "Where are we going?"

"We are going to Camp Sumter," Benton responded.

"South Carolina?"

"You wish. You are thinking of Fort Sumter, where the war began. No, the place we're going is better known as Andersonville, where the war has ended for many men. It is a Union prison camp that most refer to as hell."

"Where is it located?"

"You ask too many questions," the white man shot back.

"South of Atlanta," the black man mumbled while checking Barrett's bandages.

"I've never heard of Andersonville," Barrett commented.

"It's one of the biggest cities in Georgia... built in 1864," the driver answered, snickering.

"I don't understand."

"You will when you get there. But, you may be a lucky one."

"Why is that?"

The doctor added, "It all depends on if you, Mr. von Weber, are an officer, enlisted man, or a spy. You were found wearing an enlisted man's hat and civilian clothes. But, I would find it surprising if a man with your ability and wealth was not an officer. Like I said, it depends."

"I'm not a spy. Grant commissioned me a major a few months ago."

"Major? What are you doing down here?"

"Is this an interrogation or what?"

"Sir, let me explain something to you." The doctor's demeanor changed from lighthearted to serious. "I have never been to Andersonville, but I have heard horror stories. If what I have heard is true, Isaac and I will have our hands full. We have been ordered to take care of the prison hospital. It seems the conditions are so bad that the doctors that were in charge of it have turned into patients. So, if you think you have seen inhumanities in this bloody war, let me tell you, you have not seen anything yet." He began laughing.

"Why are you laughing?" Barrett asked.

"Oh, if you only knew, if you only knew." The doctor shook his head.

Barrett cleared his throat. "I detect an English accent."

"Not English... Australian."

"Australian, like in kangaroos?"

"Precisely, chap," the doctor smiled.

"What are you doing here fighting our war?"

"I guess you can say we were drafted—Isaac and me."

"Drafted? I'm confused." Barrett's eyes widened.

"Our ship was sailing to Canada when it was attacked and sunk by a Confederate ship. We were captured! When they found out I was a doctor, and Isaac here was my associate, they freed us on the condition that we serve with them. The South is in desperate need of doctors—good doctors.

We figured being alive and trying to save men was better than being dead. Even made me a major." He pointed to the insignia on his white coat.

"So, you're not in this war by choice."

"Oh, mercy no. We are survivors, like you, I suspect."

"Does anyone else here know who I am?"

"No. We will try to keep it concealed for now. Isaac thinks you will be safe with us. When you get well, you can work with us in the hospital. I have no idea what you were doing down here when they caught you, but they will probably think you were a spy. A spy has only one outcome... the firing squad."

Barrett exhaled loudly. "I might as well tell you. I was going home, riding across a field, when my horse was shot out from under me. I saw a group of Union soldiers rush past me, but because it was foggy, I could not see the battle lines. I assumed the soldiers were attacking, I never realized they were actually retreating. I grabbed a hat from one of the fallen Union soldiers and headed to the Northern side. At least, I thought it was! That ended up being a big mistake on my part because I ran right into an attacking Rebel line."

Barrett's arms and fingers were numb from the tight rope. "Any possibility I can get my hands free?"

"Depends on if you are going to do some of that fancy fighting you're so good at. What is it called, Ku Fu, or something?"

"Kung Fu... Chinese fighting technique."

"Doctor, 'member, when we saw some them little Chinamen fighting in that cage in Australia." Isaac's big eyes grew.

"Yes, I do remember that. The things those men did were unbelievable."

"Whacha think, Boss? Untie him?"

The doctor eyed Barrett. "Anyone looking for you?"

"I'm sure my wife is."

"Ha, ha. I am sure my wife is looking for me, too. I left her ten months ago in England. Isaac and I were attending a royal medical conference there. Nothing royal about it. Seems like the king needed medical personnel in Canada—a cholera outbreak, I heard. Anyhow, Isaac and I jumped the next ship to the king's royal country. Not that we wanted to, but when the king says go... a loyal subject goes. Not like the riff raff hooligans in America." The man winked in a kidding manner. "As luck would have it, our ship was sunk... and here we are."

Benton finally answered Isaac, "Go ahead and untie him. I think he is harmless enough."

He turned to Barrett and asked, "What should we call you?"

"How about Dr. Barrett," von Weber shot back.

"Ah... Dr. Barrett. Has a nice sound. What do you think, Isaac?"

"Sounds good to me, Boss. Question is... what happens when Dr. Barrett here goes into the operating room to cut an arm or leg off?"

"I'm not squeamish, if that's what you think. However, I would prefer to hold the man down rather than to cut." Barrett watched Isaac untie the rope.

"Understandable. All right, Dr. Barrett. My name is Noel Benton, and this here is Isaac Noble."

Isaac helped Barrett sit up.

Barrett massaged his wrists. "Now, what is the plan? How long before we reach this... this Camp Sumter?"

"Well, that depends," Benton stated.

"Depends on what?"

"Look around you. There are over three hundred prisoners with us."

Barrett looked at the soldiers trudging beside the wagon. "I noticed that they look pretty worn down, but what is stopping them from escaping? I see only a handful of guards."

Doctor Benton replied, "Well, for one... where would they go? They are too sick, hurt, and exhausted to run. When we first started this march, there were only forty of them. The further we marched, the more prisoners we added." He pointed in front of them. "See that wagon up ahead?"

Barrett looked at a wagon rolling along about two hundred feet in front of them. Three men seated inside were keenly watching the prisoners, each holding a long barrel rifle.

"There is one behind us, also. Each man in that wagon is a... what do the Rebels call it, Isaac?"

"Tree frog."

"Right, tree frog... an expert sharpshooter. They love to target practice with two-legged game... if you know what I mean."

Barrett studied the men in the wagon, observing that their eyes never left their potential targets.

"Yes, they had a lot of fun the first few days. These two dead men were some of the unlucky ones. They dragged themselves back here, wanting Isaac and me to save their lives. Trouble was they were already dead—just didn't know it, and so we loaded them up to give them a little hope."

Barrett glanced at the Union soldiers, most of them staring into space, never talking, simply plodding along.

"What are you thinking?" Benton asked.

"I should be with them... I am one of them. I feel guilty riding here."

"Don't. You are an officer, or a civilian, we do not know which they'll decide. However, rank does have its privileges."

"But how... I mean...." Barrett couldn't frame his words right.

"This is a loose band of Confederates. They were ordered to march these men to Andersonville and collect more on the way, if they found them. Honestly, there is no one in charge."

"What about you?"

"Me?" He laughed. "Isaac, the Hymnist wants to know if I'm in charge."

Isaac laughed robustly. "If he only knew Boss Man, if he only knew."

Both continued the bout of laughter.

"You need to only know this... we have marched over a hundred miles out of our way to avoid Atlanta. Want to know why?" Before Barrett could reply, the doctor continued, "It is because Atlanta is under siege by General Sherman. This war will be over soon. When Atlanta falls, the South will soon follow."

"Then what?" Barrett asked.

"Then... Isaac and I can return home." Taking a deep breath, he peered at the haphazard line of Union soldiers, some with no shoes, others limping. "Hopefully, we can all go home." He hesitated, and then looked at Barrett. "After all, we are prisoners, even the Rebels who are guarding us. We are all prisoners in some way."

Barrett stared at the doctor and his assistant, trying to understand what they had gone through.

Looking heavenward, he uttered a silent prayer for them, for himself, and for his sweet Brooke.

Chapter Thirty-Four

August 14, 1864
Andersonville

Lightning zigzagged across the darkening sky, and then came a loud clap of thunder, but the weather didn't faze the soldiers.

The trip to Andersonville had been long and difficult, and to make matters worse, it had been pouring for weeks. Even though the rain that fell on them was the only shower the prisoners would get, the constant downpour frustrated everyone. The soldiers trudged along trying to pick their feet up, but the mud stuck to their old worn shoes, and made their tired feet so heavy it was almost impossible to walk. Some of them marched in their bare feet, which made it easier until they came upon a sharp rock lying beneath the surface. Even the horses stumbled in the mire.

The wagons carrying the guards were covered, but still the blowing precipitation drenched the men inside. When a wagon became stuck, the guards stayed seated and forced the weak, sick prisoners to push it out of the mud.

The only positive thing was that the overcast skies brought cooler than normal August temperatures.

Every day that the rain continued, the conditions deteriorated more.

When a prisoner fell, due to the slick mud, or perhaps because of exhaustion, a couple other men would pick him up and drag him along.

Occasionally, one of the Rebels would fire a shot over the heads of the prisoners as a reminder that there was no escape—no end in sight.

Doctor Benton and Isaac had their hands full trying to keep the men moving. The weakened soldiers' morale, along with their wretched physical condition, was at an all-time low. It eventually got to the point that when a prisoner couldn't continue on his own, he was tossed into the "dead wagon," even if he were still alive.

The Rebels were afraid that General Sherman and his forces were camped nearby. Therefore, the soggy march continued. Days blended into weeks.

After weeks of sustained rain, it finally stopped.

Late afternoon on a steamy summer day, the small band of walking dead arrived at Andersonville. They would likely spend their final days of the war at this prison, leaving only by death, or surrender of the South.

"Can we pull this off? What if someone recognizes me?" Barrett asked the doctor as they neared the gate to the prison camp.

"Leave it to me. If anyone does know you, he will have a hard time recognizing you with that beard and long hair. Besides, you did study to become a doctor, so it's not really as if we are hiding who you are. You're my associate, Dr. Barrett."

"I can do this," Barrett said, trying to convince himself as they got off the wagon.

A thin, lanky man, with a scraggly beard met them at the giant wooden gate. Dressed neatly in a Rebel uniform, his right arm was strapped tightly to his side.

Barrett immediately noticed the soldier's piercing eyes, which seemed to look right through him. He shuddered.

The man saluted Dr. Benton with a sharp salute. "Good afternoon, Doctor. I am Captain Henry Wirz. Am I glad to see you!"

The doctor returned a lazy salute. "I hope I can say the same."

"I notice a strong English accent," Wirz replied.

"And I notice a strong European accent," Benton's mouth turned up one corner.

"That is correct. I am from Zurich, Switzerland."

Doctor Benton held his hand out to shake the captain's outstretched hand. "Zurich is a beautiful city."

"You have been there?" Wirz took a step closer.

"I studied medicine in Paris and took a short leave to Zurich."

"Paris, France?"

"Ah, yes. During the peaceful times."

"Those times were few and far between," Wirz chuckled. "It seems we have a bit in common... I studied there, also. I was in the medical field before this war broke out. I hope to continue down that path when the war is over."

"I hope to go home." Benton forced a small grin.

"And where might that be?"

"Australia."

"Australia? What are you doing here?"

"Trying to save lives… and you?"

"Trying to stay alive." The captain shifted his focus to Isaac. "Is this your slave?"

"In a way… he does the dirty work."

"Like?"

"He removes limbs surgically, so hopefully men can live another day," the doctor responded.

"Really?" He glared at Isaac. "A black man helping in the infirmary, doctoring… not sure how the men will like that. Guess we'll see."

Wirz turned his head to the sky and noticed a large, dark cloud, pushing its way through the white clouds that had previously covered the sky. It moved, as if on a mission.

Fixing his attention on Barrett, Wirz stared at him with penetrating eyes.

Von Weber stood at attention, unnerved.

The captain squinted as he tried to get a closer look at the bandage on von Weber's head. "You look like you've been in battle, sir."

Doctor Benton hurriedly took over. "This is Dr. Barrett. Just joined my staff. He was wounded in a battle last month at Cool Spring, Virginia."

"Oh, really… heard we whipped them Bluecoats bad there."

Barrett responded readily, "I wouldn't know. When the battle began, I felt something hit my side and then my head. Everything went black! Next thing I knew, I was in the hands of my fellow physicians."

Wirz eyed him closer. "You look familiar. I forget names, but never forget a face. Have you ever been to Kentucky, or Louisiana?"

"No, sir, I don't believe I have," Barrett snickered nervously.

"You sure look familiar. What do you do?" Wirz persisted.

"I assist Dr. Benton." Von Weber replied matter-of-factly, hoping it was enough information for the inquisitive captain.

"He is going to need all the help he can get." Wirz glanced up at the threatening sky. "Looks like another toad strangler comin'. We got so much rain the last few weeks that it washed away some of the makeshift housing of our prisoners. On the bright side, it washed away some of the filth, too. Maybe it will take away the dysentery and cholera in this overcrowded hell-hole," he snorted.

"Maybe, but if it does, they will probably be replaced by pneumonia—and as a doctor, I have no defense against that." Benton's eyes turned to study the unusual sky formation.

"Point well taken, Doctor."

Just then, a few large raindrops plopped on the captain's hat. He stared upward. "Looks like the devil is beating his wife." Wirz laughed, again amused with his humor. "Now, I have to excuse myself. I need to give my famous speech to these new prisoners. You know, let them know the reality of the situation. Not that anything I say could ever prepare them for what is to come."

Wirz walked away with a limp that seemed to be caused more by his dead arm than anything else. He slowly climbed the steps toward a Confederate flag waving in the now-gusting wind.

Peering at the large group of new prisoners, Wirz took his gun out of its holster and waved it in the air. Without warning, he fired it. Now that he had everyone's attention, he spoke loud and precise. "Welcome to Camp Sumter. My name is Captain Wirz... you will call me, 'sir.' This will be your home from now on. You will leave here one of two ways—either flat on your back with your feet sticking up, or as free men when this war is over. You will notice that these conditions are not like home. Your first instinct will be to run. Let me warn you right now... escape is not possible. You are in the middle of nowhere. A fifteen-foot high fence surrounds the entire perimeter of this place. Notice the cannons that are aimed at the prison." He pointed with his pistol to a nearby hill. "They are ready for any sign of trouble. When you enter these gates, you will notice a small fence between you and the main fence. It marks what we call the 'dead line.' If you so much as tap your foot in that area, the guards in the pigeon roost will shoot you. No questions asked! If you are found digging a tunnel under the fence, you will be shot on sight. If you succeed in building a tunnel and try to escape, I will personally shoot you when you pop your head through the hole."

He pointed to the nearby wooden towers. "Those guards sitting up there in those pigeon roosts have only one job and that is to kill anyone who tries to escape. The guards will coax you into stepping over that line—they dream of shooting Yanks." He scowled at the prisoners. "Do I make myself clear?"

There was a slight murmuring among the battered bunch of newcomers.

"I repeat... do I make myself clear?"

Their response was a little louder.

"If there is work to do, they'll be no mollygrubbing. No slackers allowed 'round here."

Wirz eyed the sky again and decided to wrap things up so that he could seek shelter from the looming storm. "Sergeant, get these men inside," Wirz ordered a man who was standing near.

"Yes, sir. Open the gate!" the sergeant shouted.

The large gate began to swing open.

Wirz walked down the steps and over to the doctors. "I know I sound mean, but I must have total obedience. With so many prisoners, and so few guards, that's the way it's got to be."

Barrett's jaw dropped when he saw what was inside the gate. For a second, he imagined what it must have looked like when the meadow was green and the small brook running through it was the drinking hole for deer and other wildlife.

The unbearable stench jolted him back to reality. He blinked. What was left of the creek was nothing but raw sewage. Thousands of men meandering around were skeletons, skin covering their emaciated bones. Some were naked.

Wirz noticed the horrified look on Barrett's face. "You will get used to the smell. This is a good day. As I said, the rains have washed much of the smut away. We got over thirty thousand men in a prison made for ten thousand. I barely got enough vittles to feed my own guards." He stopped talking, staring in the distance. For a short time, his mind seemed to drift to another time, another place.

Rumbling thunder jarred him back to the situation at hand. "Corporal Shea," he shouted.

A short, thin man rushed up to them and stood at attention. His hat was so low on his brow, it was hard to discern his age. "Yes, sir," he replied in a nasally voice.

"Show these new doctors to the hospital. They will be taking over Ward Seven."

"Yes, sir. Follow me." The four men walked the perimeter, outside the prison fence, at times catching a glimpse of the horror inside.

At one place, Barrett stopped for a second and peered through one of the slits in the tall wooden fence. Hundreds of crude tents were everywhere. With the rain beginning again, the Union prisoners did not even try to seek shelter. Thousands of muddy, malnourished men aimlessly moved around.

Barrett stared at the ominous cloud that had settled directly over the prison camp.

The threat of rain did not deter the corporal. "That there is the dead house." He pointed to a fenced area. "Ain't really a building. We get rid of dozens of them Yanks every day. I've shot at a few trying to escape. Less mouths to feed." The young man stated, coldly.

"Does that bother you?" Dr. Benton boldly asked.

"No. What's it matter to you?"

"I'm a doctor. My job is to save lives."

"I'm a soldier. My job is to kill Bluecoats. They rape and murder our Southern gals. They don't deserve to live. Them's vermin."

Doctor Benton knew anything he said would be futile, so he remained silent.

As they approached a small gate, it opened. A wagon, surrounded by guards, pulled out in front of them. Barrett's stomach churned when he noticed it was carrying dead men heaped up like garbage, their leathery skin blackened by the sun. The corpses were so thin that there was no way to know how many were in the wagon.

"Don't know why the captain even takes the time to bury them yanks. Must have a heart in him somewhere!" Shea smiled a devilish grin.

Light rain began.

Von Weber peered inside the gate. He noticed a man dressed in a brown cloak, surrounded by a handful of prisoners. A pile of bodies was nearby.

Barrett overheard one of the prisoners say, "Father, we have enough dead for another load."

The prisoners began to load another wagon with the bodies.

The man in the cloak turned and noticed Barrett.

"You have a priest here?" Barrett asked Shea, uncomfortable with the way the man was staring at him.

"Oh, don't mind him. The crazy priest thinks he can help the Yanks. Once he went into town and came back with a wagon full of bread for the prisoners. Father Whelan is a crazy, old coot."

"That cloud looks mean, we better get under cover," Dr. Benton warned.

"You get used to it. Gonna get wet one way or another... sweat or rain. Don't matter which," Shea replied.

Barrett watched as thousands of emaciated men gazed at the sky with a growing sense of awe. The mysterious cloud hovered directly above the dead house.

Even the nervous guards stared in wonder at the cloud suspended over the prison, looking still and powerful.

The endless drone of misery from the sick and dying became muted for a short time.

A soft rain fell gently upon the earth.

Barrett heard the same prisoner continue speaking to the priest, "Father, you pray and pray, but it's as though God does not hear you. Why doesn't God care about us?"

Suddenly, from the heavens came a thunderous, deafening roar. Then, from the heart of the deep, dark cloud, a great bolt of blinding lightning struck the earth at the dead line. It hit with such force that the men staffing the cannons quickly prepared for battle.

"We're under attack," a guard yelled.

With weapons in hand, the guards prepared to meet an attack from the Northerners.

Then, there was another tremendous explosion, so powerful that many of the weaker men were hurled to the ground.

The deafening noise caused Isaac and Dr. Benton to run for cover.

An eruption of earth and steam filled the air. Instantly, water gushed from the broken ground, spraying into the air, and coursing into the prison—fresh, clean water!

Barrett watched, awestruck by the power of the Creator.

The lightning struck a few feet from where Father Whelan stood, amazed.

"I didn't mean it in a bad way," the terrified soldier who had been talking to the priest shouted, falling to his knees. He crawled over to the water bursting up from the ground. Tasting it, he cried, "Oh, thank you, God. It tastes so sweet."

Father Whelan watched as the prisoners hurried toward the new source of fresh water. He then looked over at Barrett. Slowly, he raised his hand and waved.

Barrett hesitated, and then waved back.

The priest smiled. "I believe God is watching over us." Recognizing the Hymnist, he added, "Maybe in more ways than one."

Barrett caught up to Isaac and the doctor, and followed them to their new jobs in Ward Seven.

"This here be your hospital tent," Shea announced in a strong Southern accent. "The hospital been made bigger, so when everyone here died off, they just kept it empty 'til you came." The corporal opened the flap of the tent and entered.

Wide eyed, the doctors looked around. Bloodstained sheets scattered on the ground caught their immediate attention.

Barrett wondered if the swarming flies were finding refuge from the rain inside the infirmary, until he remembered how many were outside the tent. The horrific smell was unlike anything he had ever smelled before. His stomach was queasy, his heart sick.

"This is clean?" Dr. Benton glared at the muddy floor.

The soldier laughed. "Only cleaning it gets is when the rains come. As you can see, a river runs right through here. You think the flies are bad now, wait 'till you see them skeeters—they're bigger than flies. There's a swamp nearby... I heard say there's a 'gator in it."

"Where are the beds?" Dr. Benton asked, scratching his head.

"Beds? You jokin', mister? The beds are the ground."

"Boss, we can't help the men in this filth," Isaac shook his head.

Infuriated by his comment, the corporal gave the black man a hateful look. "You speak when asked, boy." Impulsively, he raised his rifle butt to hit Isaac.

In one swift motion, Barrett grabbed the soldier's arm, immediately disarming and throwing him to the ground.

"What ya think ya doin'?" the corporal grumbled, lying in the mud. "How you do that? Who are you anyhow, mister?"

"That is Dr. Barrett, and I am Dr. Benton. The man you were about to hit is our associate, Isaac." Benton pointed his finger at Shea's chest, his stern face showing his seriousness. "If you ever raise a hand against him again, I will have you court-martialed."

"He just a darky. What difference it make?" Shea struggled to his feet.

"It makes a difference to me," the doctor retorted.

"They have to learn to obey—darkies and worthless Yanks."

"Not in front of me."

"But I heard tell these Yanks raped and killed our women, ravaged our towns. Everybody knows that."

Barrett stepped in. "Just because you heard something does not make it true. I have not only heard about, but I have seen for myself many atrocities that Southern soldiers have done."

"What do atros... atrocities mean?"

"It means horrible things. From now on, all prisoners here are treated with dignity. When did we turn into animals?" Barrett's face was red with anger.

"They need to know who is boss." The obnoxious corporal was not about to give up.

Benton stepped in, "Well, we all know who is boss of Ward Seven. I am... Dr. Barrett is... and even Isaac."

"Ain't gonna take no orders from a darky." Shea's eyes spit fire, hatred.

The doctor snorted in disgust. "You may not want to, but when you get sick, and I mean when, because you will, Isaac will be the first person you come to. He will point you to the right place. You really do not want him to be your enemy. Isaac has saved many lives, both Southern and Northern, so let's just leave it at that."

The soldier glared at Isaac. "This is where you sleep and work. I'm finished here." He stormed out of the tent, fuming.

Doctor Benton traipsed over to the so-called surgical room and picked up a few of the grimy instruments. "Gentlemen, I see why this place is called hell."

The overwhelmed men stared at their surroundings, unsure where to begin.

Just then, a tall, cleanly dressed man, carrying papers under his arm, burst into the tent. He rushed past the men, as if he did not notice them. Walking into the next room, he sat in an old chair in front of a small table and began writing.

"Excuse me." Dr. Benton shot him a look of confusion.

The man raised his hand and continued to write.

"I don't think he wants to talk with you right now," Barrett whispered. "He seems to be a man on a mission."

They watched as the busy man jotted some notes on a list and then wrote something on a paper next to it.

Finally, he glanced up. "Are you the new doctors?"

"Yes, we are." Benton introduced his medical team to the stranger.

"My name is Atwater... Private Dorence Atwater."

"Pardon me, but you have a Union outfit on, are you a prisoner?" Benton inquired.

"Yes, my job is to keep track of the prisoners and submit a detailed report to Captain Wirz."

"How long have you been a prisoner, Private Atwater?"

He put his pen down and began to explain, "I was one of the first to come here. When Captain Wirz found out I was good with the pen, he put me in charge of making this list of the prisoners who die here. It was not bad the first couple of months, but the prisoners just kept coming... and dying. This was the ideal location to set up a prison. The South began closing all their other prisons a few months ago and started sending prisoners down here. It is too far south for the Union to rescue us, and the nearby town and train station make it convenient."

"The prisoners who came with us had to walk for weeks," Dr. Benton stated.

"That is because of Sherman. He has destroyed half the railroads in the South. I heard that his men wrapped the rails around trees so they can never be used again."

"Wrapped around trees? How they do that?" Isaac asked.

"I don't know details. Just what I heard. They call them Sherman's neckties," Atwater seemed pleased to disclose the information.

"So you were one of the first to arrive here?" Barrett inquired.

"Yes. This prison was built to house ten thousand men, but within a few months, there were over twenty thousand. It has been enlarged, but it is still much too small."

"How many prisoners are here right now?" Barrett gestured with his hand toward the outside.

"My guess is thirty-two thousand."

"Thirty-two thousand men on how many acres?"

"Roughly twenty six."

"Did you say twenty six?" Barrett's eyes opened wider.

"Yes. I figured it's about six square feet per person. And with the miserable conditions—lack of food, clothing, and shelter—come disease and crime. Men began robbing and killing their fellow comrades. There was no law in the prison, and very little the guards could do about it, or wanted to do about it. Finally, some of the prisoners approached Captain Wirz, and he gave the okay to capture those who were robbing and killing. About a hundred and fifty men were captured. Imagine—prisoners capturing prisoners!" He snickered. "Six ringleaders were given a trial by their fellow prisoners, and then hanged for all to see. Since then, the robbing and murdering has decreased."

Barrett probed further. "Any women here?"

Atwater had a quiet voice, but talked fast, "Only a couple nuns coming in once in a while and a few nurses. There have been reports that a few women have dressed up like men to be near their husbands. One of them died a couple months ago, that's how they found out she was a women. You see, the prisoners are stripped when they die, so their clothes can be used for others. Imagine the shock! Unbelievably, we even had a baby born in the prison last spring. When Captain Wirz found out, he had them removed from the compound. Now the mother and child live in the town close by."

"How many guards are here?" Barrett asked.

"About twelve hundred. They are not exempt from getting sick and dying either. Some days it seems we have as many guards coming to the medical facilities as prisoners." Atwater shuffled his papers. "In reality, no one wants to come to the hospital because they are afraid they will never leave alive."

Benton spoke up, "You mean to tell me some will refuse medical treatment because they are afraid they will die here?"

"Sad, isn't it? But remember, the death rate for doctors isn't very good either."

"Well, we will have to change that." Benton forged a small smile.

"Good luck. We have had days when more than a hundred men have died. Every morning the wagons drive through the prison and pick up the dead." He shook his head, sadly.

Barrett took a step closer to Atwater and spoke quietly, "Okay, tell us who we can count on if we need help? Who is our enemy and should be avoided—both Union and Confederate?"

"The priest—Father Whelan, will help in any way he can. Captain Wirz allows him to mingle with the prisoners. Be cautious of the guards, most of them cannot be trusted, especially Corporal Shea, who you had the pleasure of already meeting. He spends a lot of time here in the hospital and is extremely cruel to the prisoners."

"What about Captain Wirz?"

"Captain Wirz is difficult to figure out. On one hand, he is a tyrant. On the other, he will try to help, but his hands are tied. He was given an impossible task because this prison has tripled its capacity. He believes he has to run it with an iron fist, or he will lose control."

Barrett folded his arms. "Why do they have a captain in charge of a place like this? I would think it would be more suitable for a colonel, or even a general."

"I have wondered the same thing."

"What is the biggest obstacle we will face?" Benton asked, still seeking information.

"We have no medicine," Atwater reported, without hesitation.

"Does that mean the guards are the ones getting the medicine and food?"

"To be perfectly honest, there is little food or medicine for them, or the prisoners. I have seen the prisoners go without, but I have also seen the guards have very little. The hard fact is that the North has banned all medicine as contraband. I know a couple countries in Europe have been sending medical supplies, but it has been confiscated by the Union."

"Are you sure about that?" Barrett asked.

"Yes. I also know that there will be no exchange of prisoners."

Von Weber looked surprised. "But, I heard from good sources that the South has been trying to exchange prisoners."

"That may be true, but the fact is the North has suspended it. Grant said if we trade prisoners, we would just be fighting them down the road, so no more exchanges. If you will excuse me, I have to leave. There is another dead wagon getting ready to be loaded. I need to be there." Atwater left as fast as he appeared.

Doctor Benton cleared his throat and addressed his team. "Men, we have a big job ahead of us. Let's start by cleaning up this place. We need to dry out the inside and keep it dry. Might be able to get a few of the healthier prisoners to help."

He stepped closer to Isaac. "Since we can't get medical supplies, we may have to resort to natural remedies."

"Natural remedies?" Barrett blinked, wondering how the doctor would respond.

"Yes, like maggots to clean wounds and leaches to suck bruises. Some roots and leaves from plants can be used for medicines and food. Many of the old remedies from Australia can help. Men, let's go about saving lives, so that these men can return home to their families." Benton rubbed his hands together. "Let's get to work!"

Chapter Thirty-Five

September 1864

When the rain finally stopped, the September heat and humidity, coupled with the filthy environment, made perfect breeding grounds for all types of diseases.

Within days, Ward Seven was full to capacity with sick and injured prisoners.

Isaac, knowledgeable about medicine, became involved in all aspects of patient care. The black man tried to stay away from the guards, especially Shea. The corporal seemed to watch everything he did, eyeing him with suspicion.

The prisoners had less and less food to eat as time passed. What few supplies they received had to make it past the guards first. Sometimes the prisoners went days without a morsel of food, growing weaker all the time. Everyone knew that with winter approaching, there would be even less provisions available. Every day the conditions of the camp, and the men, worsened.

The doctors from Ward Seven took on the responsibility of going into the prison to look for those who were sick or hurt, but refused to go to the hospital. The three of them would often follow the dead wagon through the camp. While dead prisoners were loaded on one wagon, Benton and his staff loaded the sick and dying on another. Many still refused to go to the hospital with them. If they were going to die, they wanted to die with their comrades.

Corporal Shea stayed nearby when the doctors made their rounds. If any of the prisoners got out of line, he would restore order in a hurry.

Atrocities were commonplace, not just by the guards, but also among the prisoners. With no officers in charge, there was no chain of command, so chaos reigned. Everyone quickly learned to be cautious, scared for his life.

The prisoners formed groups to watch over each other. Someone would always stay alert, watching. Even though they had little, there was always a person who wanted it, whether it was a blanket, a morsel of food, or even a walking stick.

While making rounds in the prison one morning, the doctors watched a number of fellow prisoners trying in vain to subdue a man.

"I want to be free," the desperate man cried, "I want to be free!" Escaping their grasp, the distressed man ran to the dead line. When he stepped over it, a bullet from one of the towers instantly hit him in the stomach. Helpless, he crumbled to the ground.

Doctor Benton instinctively ran toward him.

"Stop! I wouldn't do that if I was you, Doctor," Shea warned.

Ignoring his warning, Benton was about to step over the dead line when a bullet hit the dirt directly in front of him.

"Told ya," Shea chuckled.

"Are you crazy? I'm Doctor Benton, and I need to help this man," the doctor yelled to the two men in the tower.

"No one is allowed in that area," a young boy from the pigeon roost shouted. "The first bullet was a warning, but the next one will get you."

Barrett called out to the lad who fired the shot, "What rank are you, soldier?"

"Private, but it don't matter. Captain Wirz told me to shoot anyone who crosses the dead line. Just doin' my job!"

Barrett glared at the fellow in the tower who was still aiming his weapon at the doctor. "He certainly didn't mean doctors. Private, that man is Major Benton. He is a Confederate officer and outranks Captain Wirz, thus overturning his order. He could have you court-martialed right now. If you shoot him, you will be charged with murder. The penalty for assaulting an officer is death. Do you understand what I am saying, Private."

"Our orders are to shoot anyone who steps over the line," the other lad insisted, voice quivering.

Barrett's facial expression was harsh, his voice commanding. "Then let me explain it in a way you will understand. You see, we are going to retrieve the wounded prisoner. If you so much as fire a shot in this direction, you will regret it. If you ever need medical assistance… and you will… do not bother coming to the hospital. You will not get any help. But really, that will not matter because if you shoot one of us, both of you boys will be brought up on murder charges and hanged by morning. You did your job, now back off!"

There was no response from the tower.

Barrett gestured toward the men around him. "There are hundreds of witnesses against you—both Union and Confederate."

"We have orders to shoot. We follow orders!" one of the boys repeated, nervously.

"How old are you, soldier?" Barrett inquired.

"Sixteen."

"Sixteen? You really want to die so young?" Barrett didn't even blink.

Shea watched the exchange with interest. *I wonder who's going to win.*

Barrett continued, "You boys have your whole life ahead of you. That farm you want to start, that young woman you want to court and marry. And children… well, that legacy will be gone if you shoot the good doctor here. I guarantee it."

Confused, the two boys looked at each other blankly.

After a pause, one of them said, "I plan to marry Sue Martin. I sure ain't gonna die for the likes of them. Let them get the Bluebelly and be gone." He spit.

Turning to the doctors, the shooter shouted, "All right, get him, but hurry up."

Barrett and Benton ran to the wounded man.

The soldier's breathing was labored. Benton touched his chest and felt nothing but bones. "He's still alive. Let's get him to the hospital!"

Barrett picked up the wounded man who weighed less than a hundred pounds. The prisoner stared into von Weber's eyes and spoke loudly, "I see freedom… I am finally free." With that, he went limp.

Doctor Benton checked his pulse to see if there was any life. "He's gone."

Barrett closed the man's eyes, then sadly carried him to the dead wagon and carefully placed his body in it. "He's free, Doc… he's free."

Benton nodded his head, understanding what he meant.

Corporal Shea had been watching Barrett the entire time. He muttered under his breath, "Why does he care so much about these people? They are nobody to him, yet he defends and protects them with his life?" He shook his head, confused.

Every time the doctors entered the prison, they saw more inhumanity.

On one of their morning rounds, they stopped to check a patient who refused to come to the hospital. The frail man sat under a makeshift tent made from an old sheet with small tree limbs supporting it. He walked with the aid of a crude crutch. "Morning, Doc! Morning, Dr. Barrett!"

"Morning, Everett," Barrett responded cheerfully.

"See you brought the devil with you again." Everett said, gesturing his head toward Shea.

"He is not a bad man once you get to know him." Barrett smiled.

"Oh, he bad alright."

"How are you feeling this morning?" Benton asked, kneeling next to the man who always brought a smile to his face.

"About the same... still kickin', Doc."

"I have not seen Frank in a couple days." Von Weber looked around.

"He is over there, down by the sewer."

They spotted a lone figure sitting on the bank of the filthy creek.

"What is he doing?" Barrett asked. "Most men do everything they can to stay away from there."

"Not sure. Been there for a couple days. Comes to the tent at night, but goes to the same spot and sits all day long. Guess he goes there to get away from everyone. Prob'ly this prison has messed up his brain, like it has the rest of us." He shrugged his shoulders.

Doctor Benton turned his attention to Everett. "You sure we can't talk you into coming with us to the hospital. It's a lot cleaner than it used to be."

"No! Everyone goes in, but no one comes out alive." The patient was emphatic.

Barrett noticed three suspicious looking prisoners weaving their way through the crowd, approaching Frank.

A big man, carrying a long stick, yelled to the prisoner sitting on the bank of the creek. "What ya got there, Turner?"

"Nothin'," Frank replied.

Barrett walked closer to listen.

"You sure look like your hidin' somethin' there."

One of the trio kicked Frank Turner, pushing him over, exposing his hidden treasure.

There it was—a beautiful, wild strawberry plant with three berries—two red and one still green.

"Strawberries!" The third man yelled, grabbing for the tantalizing fruit. His reach was cut short when the big man crashed the stick across his arm. "Ouch! Sal, that hurt."

Frank struggled to his knees in an effort to protect the berries with his body.

Instantly, Sal's stick came across the back of Turner's head, and then he stomped his face in the sludge.

Barrett and Dr. Benton rushed over to help Frank.

"I'm gonna have those strawberries!" Sal announced.

The trio began arguing among themselves, each determined to win the battle for the berries.

Not backing down, another yelled, "No! They are mine."

A fight erupted with Frank in the middle of it.

Barrett stepped in, trying to separate the scrapping men.

Sal raised his hickory stick to strike Frank one more time, but von Weber grabbed it out of his hand. He kicked the big man's legs out from under him causing him to collapse in the raw sewage.

From a short distance away, Corporal Shea shook his head, laughing heartily.

One of Sal's sidekicks, almost in tears, stood up, crying, "We crushed them strawberries while we fought. Don't that beat all?"

Sal scowled as he stood to his feet, stunned. "Who do you think you are?" he challenged Barrett.

When von Weber and the big man met eye-to-eye, a surprised look appeared on the man's face, and then an unusual smile. "Well, well, well, if it isn't Captain von Weber, or should I say, Major?"

Barrett took a step closer to the man that he took down. Glaring at him, he barked, "And if it isn't Sergeant Major Perry... how did you get here?"

"More importantly, how did you get here? This is an enlisted man's prison." Perry tried to yank his stick from Barrett's grasp, but von Weber quickly pulled it back out of his reach.

Perry looked down at the crushed strawberries." Looks like no one gets the berries." His malicious laugh echoed through the prison camp.

Barrett shuddered, perhaps from fear, perhaps because of the evil Perry represented.

"Boys, let's get out of here. See you around, Major." Perry turned to leave.

"Sal, what did you hit me on the head for? That hurt," one of his men complained, rubbing his head.

"Shut up. Let's go."

Barrett questioned Perry, "Why do they call you Sal?"

"That's what they call me here. What do they call you?" he gave Barrett a sly grin.

Von Weber didn't answer. He just watched them walk away.

Using a single crutch, Everett slowly made his way over to where Barrett stood. "That was Sal. He's a mean one. Takes what he wants when he wants it."

Barrett nodded in agreement. *Perry could cause me a lot of trouble; he knows who I am.* He groaned.

Doctor Benton was examining the beaten man, trying to determine the extent of his injuries.

"Is Frank all right?" Everett asked, concern written on his face.

Barrett bent down and picked up something from the ground. He walked back to the wagon, poured some clean water from his canteen on it, and then put the item in his pocket. He walked over to where the doctor was caring for the battered man.

The doctor spoke softly, "They beat him senseless. Look what they did to his face. He's not going to make it. Do you know that man with the stick?"

"Unfortunately... we have met." Barrett knelt next to the injured man.

Frank's eyes were sunken and his bloody face showed every bone. Von Weber gently propped the dying man's head on his knee, retrieved the item from his pocket, and showed it to him. The man's eyes grew wide as he stared at a red, ripe strawberry. Von Weber moved the fruit around the man's lips, gently squeezing the juice from it, so Frank could enjoy the taste. His eyes closed as he savored the perfect strawberry. When Barrett placed the berry into the man's mouth, a smile came to his face... and then a look of peace. He could not say anything, he could not move—but his eyes showed his gratitude. He took his last breath. Barrett closed Frank's eyes.

Everett, who had been watching nearby, asked quietly, "Is he dead?"

"Yes. I'm sorry... he's gone," Dr. Benton sadly stated.

Corporal Shea was touched by what he had witnessed, but tried not to show it. The last thing he wanted was for anyone to see him expressing pity or tenderness—it might be mistaken as a sign of weakness.

Barrett stood, staring at the dead man. He shook his head. "Why, Lord? Why?"

Everett interrupted the conversation Barrett was having with God. "May I?"

"What?" the major asked, confused.

"That stick you are holding used to be my other crutch, but Sal stole it from me a couple weeks ago."

Von Weber handed him the crutch and smiled.

Chapter Thirty-Six

October 1864

On an especially cool fall morning, the doctors were bandaging a patient when the makeshift door to the hospital flew open. Corporal Shea and four guards stepped in.

Shea walked up to Benton. "Doctor, I have orders to take Barrett to see Captain Wirz."

Barrett's heart began racing, but he kept his eyes on the patient he was tending.

"May I ask why?" Benton asked.

Shea sighed. "I didn't ask. I only do what I am told."

"I will go with him," Benton said, protectively.

Barrett responded readily, "Doctor, you better stay here with the patients, they need you."

"You sure?"

"Yes." Barrett nodded.

"Is he under arrest or something?" the doctor pressed Shea for more information.

"I was just told to bring some guards with me and fetch Dr. Barrett."

"Let us not keep the captain waiting," Barrett said, gathering his hat.

Isaac shot Benton a look of concern.

Without another word, Shea and the other guards marched Barrett to the captain's quarters. Two armed men stood guard out front.

They entered the small building Wirz used for his office. It was not fancy—simply a large desk, a couple of chairs, and a few framed pictures on the wall.

Finally, after what seemed like an eternity, a door behind the desk opened, and Captain Wirz strode in.

"You may go, Corporal Shea," Wirz said in broken English.

"You may need me. This man could be dangerous. I saw him in action the other day."

"I don't think so. Go, now!" Wirz insisted sternly from behind his desk.

Shea left reluctantly, glancing back.

"Have a seat Mister Barrett von Weber."

Barrett stared at the captain, not surprised. "How did you figure it out?"

"An old friend of yours told me."

"Let me guess... Sergeant Perry." Barrett snorted in disgust.

"Correct."

"Trust me... he is not an old friend."

"I didn't think so. He said some interesting things about you. He said you were a major, called you a spy."

Barrett cleared his throat. "The major thing is correct, but the spy thing is not. I was sent south on a mission to retrieve some rifles that were stolen by some Union soldiers. They wanted to make a quick dollar at the price of innocent lives—both North and South, if that makes me a spy, then so be it"

"Were you sent by the United States Government?"

"Yes, but I also represented New Haven Arms." Von Weber's throat sounded dry.

"Ah, the rifle company. I heard about the new rifle they have. They say you can load it on Monday and fire it all week, or something like that."

Barrett did not respond.

Wirz stared at von Weber; his piercing eyes seemed to go right through him. "I saw you perform in Atlanta before the war. I believe it was right before you were wed."

"Hope you enjoyed it." Barrett forced a feeble smile that he feared wasn't convincing.

"I did, very much so."

There was an awkward silence for a moment as Barrett waited.

"What should I do with you?"

Von Weber said nothing.

Wirz continued, "I have heard from some of the prisoners and guards that you are a fair man and do your job well. Do you have training as a physician?"

"I studied to become a doctor for a year in Paris. That is what my parents wanted me to be. They felt that medical experience would be helpful for a missionary."

"Ah... what changed your mind?"

"I felt the Lord was leading me to music, not missions. I had already performed in the great concert halls in Europe and the United States."

Wirz stood. "Come." He walked over and opened the door to an adjoining room.

Confused, Barrett followed the captain.

The room was empty except an old piano and a rocking chair. He pointed to the piano. "Would you honor me with a song?"

"It has been a long time." Barrett's heart raced. He paced over to the piano, pulled out a rickety bench, and sat down. He took a deep, relaxing breath. "Any song in particular?"

"Ah… could you play my favorite, "How Magnificent Your Love for Me?"

Wirz walked over and opened the door leading to the outside, and then sat in the rocking chair.

A smile forged on Barrett's face as he repositioned himself. Stretching out his long fingers, he cracked his knuckles, and began to play.

The captain closed his eyes, taking in every note.

The beautiful sound resonated out the door and over the prison walls. It was as if the Hymnist had never stopped playing the piano. His fingers glided effortlessly over the old ivory keys in such a way that anyone within earshot was in awe.

Calm engulfed the entire prison as thousands of men stood motionless, tears flowing from their eyes. Even the guards were immobile, solemn. All fixed on the marvelous sound that transported them back to a different time and place.

When the Hymnist played the last chord, he just sat still, caught up in the emotion of the moment.

Wirz's eyes remained closed.

For a few minutes, nothing was said.

Finally, Wirz opened his eyes and gave a long, heavy sigh. "Now what do I do with you?" He raised his good hand and scratched his neatly trimmed beard. "I cannot put you with the other men—too dangerous. Besides, you are an officer. I would have to send you to Camp Oglethorpe, in Macon. But, with Sherman so close, I dare not release any of my guards to take you. The only other alternative is to let you continue helping at the hospital."

Barrett stared directly into the captain's eyes. "You're telling me that I can continue what I have been doing?"

"That is correct. Maybe you can come back and bless me with another song soon."

"What about Perry?"

"Perry abuses his own men, preys on the helpless. As far as I am concerned, he is a traitor. I despise traitors from either side. I suspect after this war is over, he will be treated as such."

"And you? After the war, how will you be treated?" Barrett asked.

"Me?" He took a deep breath. "You and I both know that it is just a matter of time before the South loses this war. As for me, I did what I had to do with what I had. I would like to think that people would consider the position I was in. I suspect, at worst, I will get a little jail time."

"And then?"

"And then I will take my wife and family and begin to live again. Maybe return to Europe. I talk about becoming a doctor after this war is over, but you and I know that will never happen. This dead arm will prevent me from doing that." He hit his lame arm. "But like you, I am sure God has a plan for my life."

"I am sure He does." Barrett stood.

Captain Wirz saluted him.

The grateful major returned the salute.

"Corporal Shea," shouted Wirz.

The soldier ran in. "Yes, sir."

"Take Dr. Barrett back to the hospital. There are too many men sick and dying. He is needed there."

"But sir, I thought...."

"Corporal, you are to obey, not think. We have doctors dying from sickness and we cannot afford to lose another one for any reason."

"Yes, sir."

"Another thing, Corporal... you finally got your wish."

"What is that, sir?" Shea's eyes widened.

"As much as I hate to lose a good man, I know how much you have wanted to get in on the action... on the battlefield."

Shea waited in silent anticipation.

"You and eight other guards leave next week to join General Johnson. He needs men like you to defend Atlanta. Good luck, Corporal."

A big grin took over Shea's face. He snapped to attention and saluted Wirz. "Thank you, sir."

"No thank you needed. Just do not let Sherman come down here. I don't want to be responsible for what I would have to do with the prisoners. I certainly couldn't let thirty-three thousand soldiers go free." Wirz looked past Shea to one of the cannons aimed directly toward the inside of the prison compound and sighed heavily.

On the way back to the hospital, Shea gloated, "Now I can kill all the Bluebellies I want."

"Have you ever been in battle?" Barrett asked.

"That there is none of your business."

"Just wondering if you were a man of conscience, or what."

"Have never killed a man if that's what you mean, but I have beaten 'em close to it."

"You mean you beat a prisoner?" Barrett said remembering what Private Atwater had said about Shea.

"What's it to you?"

"Just thinking… it is a lot different beating an unarmed man who is dying of starvation than to meet a six-foot tall, well-trained military man on the battlefield."

"That is not your worry. I'll do fine. Don't know why the captain let you go anyhow. To me, your nothin' but Yankee trash," Shea's tone was cold, his voice callous.

Barrett did not say anything more. It was a useless argument. He knew the corporal's trip into battle would not be as glorious as the man would like to think. It never was.

With fall in the air, the nights became cooler, the days shorter.

Corporal Shea was gone, but others eagerly stepped into his place, harassing, beating, and intimidating the prisoners.

"How many men are we going to lose because of the cold?" Dr. Benton asked while making his rounds one morning, not expecting an answer.

Barrett and Isaac listened with concern. Their own bodies were feeling the pain from deprivation of nourishment and clean water. Von Weber had lost fifteen pounds since arriving at the camp; everyday it became more noticeable. They knew as winter took over, things would only get worse.

Chapter Thirty-Seven

November 1864

It was a cool fall day in Washington. Most of the leaves had already lost their battle for life—at least for the year. However, the brown oak leaves refused to submit to Mother Nature and continued clinging to their birthplace.

The black carriage rode up the long, circular driveway of the North Lawn of the White House. The two horses pulling the carriage halted in front of the stately mansion.

"I will wait for you here," the black man announced, stepping out.

"No, William, please come with me." Brooke received his hand as he helped her down the high step.

"But Missy, this is the president's house. I can't go in there."

"I have heard it said that it is the people's house, which is all the more reason that you should come with me." Brooke faced him, unwilling to back down.

"But, they think I am your slave."

"Then I will set them straight. Barrett von Weber employs you. Do you not get paid each month?"

"Yes, Miss Brooke, I certainly do," William answered sheepishly.

She looked at him curiously. "William, what do you do with the money you earn?"

"Nothing, Miss Brooke... I just put it in a box beside my bed. Never know when I might need it."

"You should go out and buy some nice things." Brooke giggled quietly at the suggestion.

"Like what, Missy? I reckon I have all I need... food... shelter. You take good care of me. What more do I need?"

She smiled, and then took his hand and tugged on it. "Come with me and meet the president. After that, William, we are going shopping."

"Ah, Miss Brooke, I don't want to be a bother." His voice trailed off.

"No bother. It will be fun. You'll see." She winked at him.

"Just the same, Missy... I need to brush the horses down. Don't want them to get sick."

"All right, William. Have your way. I am not sure how long I will be."

"No problem. I be here."

She turned and walked up the steps, passing two guards who were standing in front of the giant residence. Stopping, she glanced back at William. "We are still going shopping when I am done here!"

The black man responded with a big smile.

Brooke walked confidently up to the large mahogany doors and knocked loudly.

The door opened quickly.

A small man stood inside; an armed guard close by. "What may I do for you, ma'am?" he said, in a somewhat harsh tone.

"I have come to speak to the president." Brooke sounded businesslike.

"You have to follow the correct procedure and be approved. You cannot come and knock on the door of the White House and expect to get in. Good day, madam." He began to shut the door.

"I have written a dozen letters and have yet to receive a reply. Do you know who I am?" Brooke's voice elevated, indicating her frustration.

The man opened the door all the way. "I am well aware of who you are, Miss von Weber. The fact remains that an invitation is required to visit the president at his home. I am in charge of that." He again began to close the door.

Two guards stood nearby observing Brooke, sternly.

From a distance, William watched, uncertain what to do.

Persistent, Brooke put her foot in the door. "I did not come all this way for nothing... and it is Mrs. von Weber."

"Mr. Lincoln does not have time to listen to sad stories about how Southern prisoners are not being treated properly or fed right. He has greater concerns than that right now. So, if you will excuse me, ma'am, I must go. I am a busy man. When you get an invitation, you can return. Or, maybe you can catch the president at one of the fundraisers. Good day." The stubborn man was about to close the door all the way when a woman's voice sounded from inside the hallway.

"Brooke von Weber, is that you?" The familiar face of Mrs. Lincoln appeared next to the man. The president's wife reached past him, pulling open the door.

The First Lady turned to him, "You may go, Mr. Reese. I will take care of our guest."

"Mrs. Lincoln, with all due respect, President Lincoln does not have time for this kind of disruption today."

"Let him be the judge of that." She reached her hand out to Brooke and pulled her close for a hug. "How have you been, my dear?" Without waiting for an answer, she pulled back and stared at Brooke. "I heard a rumor that you were going to have a baby. Now one of two things has happened. It was just that... a rumor... or you already had the baby. Now, which is it?" she asked with a warm smile.

"I gave birth to a baby boy last month."

"Healthy?"

"Yes, and I may add, he is the most handsome lad in the world."

"Judging by the looks of your husband and you, I predicted that to be true." She smiled and then a sad look came to her face. "Have you heard anything from Barrett?"

"No, ma'am, not since January."

"I pray he is all right. Cornelius has been here a number of times petitioning the president to find your husband. I think that is the reason Albert acted the way he did at the door." She scowled at the president's assistant.

"Mrs. Lincoln, like I said, the president has more pressing things on his mind right now. It is my job to make sure his time is used wisely... protect him from unnecessary interruptions."

"Mr. Reese, if we ever get to the point where we as leaders cannot listen to the people of this land, it is time for us to close shop." The president's wife took Brooke's hand and led her to a nearby room, Reese followed. She opened the door slowly and peeked inside.

President Lincoln sat behind a large desk, reading. He removed his spectacles and greeted his guests with a huge grin.

Reese immediately spoke up, "Sir, I apologize for the intrusion, but this woman demands to speak to you. I tried to explain how busy you are and that you did not have time for this nonsense."

"Albert, when I woke up this morning, I was given a local newspaper, the one I hold in my hand right now. It had some negative remarks about a President Abraham Lincoln. Next to the article was the photo of a rather homely looking man and under that picture was the caption, *President Abraham Lincoln*. Now, if I am not mistaken, that ugly cuss looks a lot like me, and absolutely nothing like you. I make the decisions, not you."

"I'm sorry, Mr. President. I thought...."

Lincoln stood and walked around the desk. "Please don't do that. Let me do the thinking and you follow my orders. That way, if and when I make a mistake, the blame will be solely on my shoulders... not yours. Now, please let me spend some uninterrupted time with this young lady. You may go!"

"Yes, sir." Albert's look was not one of approval as he rushed out of the room.

The president extended his hand to Brooke, who readily grabbed it with her white-gloved hands.

"My, you look as ravishing as ever. How long has it been... four... five years?"

"I believe four years, Mr. President." He released his grasp on Brooke and took his wife's hand. "Please call me, Abe. Mrs. von Weber, we were about to have a little lunch on the back porch, would you join us?"

"Why, thank you Mr. Presi... Abe. I would be honored."

Reese sat at a small desk in the hallway, glaring at Brooke as they walked out of the study.

"Albert, would you see to it that we set an extra plate for lunch?"

"Yes, sir, Mr. President."

Lincoln spoke softly to the two women. "You have to excuse Albert. Word came last week that his son had been wounded at Boydton Plank Road. The battle happened almost a month ago. We learn the outcome of many of these battles weeks later."

"I hope his injury is not serious." Brooke's face reflected her concern.

"He may lose an arm. It saddens me that many have lost so much during this war."

The three walked onto a large veranda and sat down at a small, round table. A small vase of pink roses rested in the center of a delicate, white, embroidered tablecloth.

Reese stationed himself nearby.

"A bit cooler, but still a nice day to eat outside," the president stated.

He held a chair for Brooke, and then one for his wife.

Brooke watched him. *He is walking slower now. He has aged considerably in the four years he has been in office. I guess war does that to a leader.*

When the food was served, she stared at the plate in front of her. On the fine china was a helping of brown beans, a small piece of salt pork, and a piece of cornbread. Water was the beverage.

"I see by your expression you are surprised by the food," the president grinned.

Unsure how to answer, Brooke commented shyly, "It is quite fine, but it is not what I would expect the leader of the country to eat. I have dined with kings and leaders all over the world and the meals were quite lavish."

He chuckled. "Yes, this is anything but lavish. Brooke, let me tell you something that only a few people know. When I sent our young men to war, I told my staff that twice a week we would eat the kind of food the troops eat. Why should we eat better than they do? By the way, my staff wasn't happy with the idea, but agreed! I also begin and end my day in prayer for those serving the country. Why do I do that? Because of a little advice that your husband gave me before he left four years ago. 'If you are going to lead... do so from your knees.' I did not heed that wisdom until after the war began. That's when I realized I needed guidance from a sovereign God."

The small talk continued while they ate their simple, but tasty meal.

"Now, what brings you here, young lady... and I know it's not the food."

"I need help. I am a nurse at Elmira prison. Are you aware of that place?"

"As a matter of fact, I am. Fort Rathbun. I have heard the scuttlebutt of the goings on there. And yes, I even know that the prisoners call it 'Hellmira.'"

Brooke looked directly into the eyes of the president, hoping she could share her heart honestly, openly. "Mr. President, it is neither scuttlebutt, nor simply rumors. We desperately need supplies. Men are dying from the lack of food, unsanitary conditions, inadequate shelter, and the scarcity of medical supplies. Prisoners are dying from the cold. Sir, they need blankets badly."

"Brooke, I understand you are concerned for the safety and well-being of these men. I am certain you mean well. I know how difficult it must be having your brothers serving on behalf of the South. I am confused. I received a briefing from my staff just two weeks ago, assuring me that the four thousand prisoners at Fort Rathbun are being adequately cared for."

Brooke looked stunned. *I have to make him understand what is really going on.* "Sir, not to be disrespectful, but you are not being told the facts. There are not four thousand men at Elmira! There are over ten thousand! I work in the hospital and see hundreds of patients each day suffering from scurvy, diarrhea, and dysentery. And, Mr. President, dozens are needlessly dying every day. Every day! Many could be saved with just a warm blanket and a good meal." Her eyes showed her passion.

Her voice cracked as she talked about her own family. "Yes, I am concerned because one of my brothers is a prisoner of war, and another has been killed in battle. God only knows what has happened to my youngest brother and my father. I am also anxious about my husband, whom I have not heard from in ten months. He could be a prisoner in one of the Confederate prisons, and I have heard horror stories of how they are treated. Now, I know there are many here in Washington who would like nothing better than to see these Rebels done away with. Putting everything else aside, they are men, whether they are North or South, blue or gray, they are human beings. Still someone's father, brother, or son. The soldiers did not start this war… this war was started in congress."

Lincoln looked at her with sadness. "Albert," he spoke loud enough for Reese to hear him.

"Yes, sir, Mr. President."

"On my desk is a letter I have written. Please bring it to me."

"Yes, sir."

President Lincoln turned to face Brooke. "I never wanted this war. I wanted to lead our free nation to prosperity. My desire was to continue the freedoms that our forefathers had envisioned. It has grieved me to see so many men on both sides, the strength of our nation, give their lives for what they believe is right."

Reese returned and handed the president an envelope.

"Thank you, Albert." Lincoln held it in his hands as if he were protecting it.

"Recently, I received a memo, which announced the death of five young men—brothers. Actually, they were mere boys from Boston. I felt the need to write to their grieving mother. It was something as the president, as a leader, I had to do. I would like to read my response to you."

Brooke looked on with curiosity. She wiped her mouth with her linen napkin.

President Lincoln began reading:

Executive Mansion, Washington, Nov 21, 1864

To Mrs. Bixby, Boston, Mass.

Dear Madam,

I have been shown in the files of the War Department a statement of the Adjutant General of Massachusetts that you are the mother of five sons who have died gloriously on the field of battle.

I feel how weak and fruitless must be any word of mine which should attempt to beguile you from the grief of a loss so overwhelming. But I cannot refrain from tendering you the consolation that may be found in the thanks of the republic they died to save. I pray that our Heavenly Father may assuage the anguish of your bereavement, and leave you only the cherished memory of the loved and lost, and the solemn pride that must be yours to have laid so costly a sacrifice upon the altar of freedom.

Yours, very sincerely and respectfully,

A. Lincoln

Brooke could see tears forming in President Lincoln's eyes. He put the letter back in the envelope and gently laid it on the table. His eyes met hers. She realized they were the eyes of a president who had sacrificed much in this war.

For a short time, no one spoke, all pondering the words in the powerful letter.

Upon finishing the meal, Reese approached the president. "Sir, we must leave shortly for the Capital."

"Going into the lion's den again. Okay, Albert. Thank You." Lincoln finished the last few sips of his water and put his cup back on the table. He looked up as a flock of geese flew overhead. "I love to watch sights like that. Notice how the leader drifts back out of line behind the others. When my presidency is over, I hope to do the same. I think Mary and I will head back to Springfield and die old, never to be remembered." He perked up. "But before that, I want to visit Jerusalem. Ever been to The Holy Land, young lady?"

"No, I have not. I believe my husband has been there a few times. There are very few places he has never visited."

"I have heard that he is an adventurous man."

Brooke smiled.

"Mrs. von Weber, I don't know why I was misinformed, but I believe every word you told me. And, I will get to the bottom of this. In the meantime, I will give you the supplies you request. Regardless of what many of my fellow politicians on both sides think, the people of the South are still part of this Union. One of these days, we will be a united nation again. I want history to show that my presidency was not part of tearing the country down, but building it up, and bringing it together. I pray I live to see that day. I want to thank you for your support, and I trust that your husband returns to you and your son safe and sound. I wish to hear the Hymnist play his inspirational music once again." Lincoln stood, took Brooke's hand, and kissed it.

Brooke wiped away the tears of joy in her eyes; she was encouraged by the president's words.

"I will instruct Albert to make sure you get everything that you requested." Lincoln eyed his aide who was listening to the conversation and repeated, "Everything!"

Albert nodded his head obediently.

"Thank you, Mr. President. I will be forever grateful."

"Please enjoy some girl talk with my wife." Lincoln bent over and gave his wife, Mary, a kiss on her forehead. "If you will excuse me, I must bid you farewell."

Albert handed Lincoln his stovepipe top hat. He placed it on his head, which made his six-foot, four-inch frame, look even taller.

Brooke smiled. *He is certainly a giant in my eyes.* She watched him as he disappeared into the house. An uneasy feeling washed over her, one that she could not shake. She had a strange feeling that she would never see that great man again.

Chapter Thirty-Eight

December 1864

There was a good amount of snow on the ground when the old locomotive pulled into the bustling train station at Elmira, New York. The train next to it was carrying supplies that President Lincoln had ordered for the prison. Thanks to the persuasion of a Southern belle named Brooke von Weber, the nation's leader had ordered a generous amount of medicine, food, blankets, and other necessities to be sent to the prison.

The old locomotive that just rolled in had a different type of cargo— over a hundred new prisoners. Most captured only weeks before when General Sherman's forces began the siege of Atlanta.

Brooke, Helen, Prisse, and a number of railroad employees were unloading the supplies from the train and loading them into nearby wagons.

"You met the president. What was he like? Is he as tall as they say?" Helen probed, wanting to know all the details of Brooke's recent visit to Washington.

"President Lincoln seemed pleased to help in this way. Although some people around him were not. He was kind, and yes, he is tall... very tall." Brooke peered over her shoulder at the nearby train.

The prisoners were slowly stepping off.

A sad look took over Brooke's face. *That's pitiful... they are crammed in a livestock car and herded like cattle.*

Noticing her friend's gloomy look, Helen asked, "How can men treat each other this way?" She stretched her aching back.

"I don't know, but it is awful."

The women watched while the Confederate prisoners left the train. They marched in a broken line down the street toward the prison—some in chains, others on crutches. Stronger soldiers helped those who were missing limbs.

Many townspeople stood on the side of the road yelling obscenities to the unwelcomed prisoners.

A group of children ran up and threw rocks at a couple of them. The guards chased them away, but not until after they had done their damage.

The men were all filthy; many were wearing blood stained clothing. It was obvious they had not had a bath for weeks, maybe months.

Most held their heads low. They were beaten down—both physically and mentally. Nothing much mattered anymore—even the two attractive young women they walked past didn't catch their attention.

Finally, the wagons were loaded with the much-needed provisions.

"I sure don't look forward to unloading all these supplies," Helen murmured, climbing aboard one of the wagons. "It's going to take hours. We sure could use some help."

Brooke agreed. "Maybe a new prisoner could help." She shouted to the soldier in charge of the prisoners, "Sergeant Hatfield."

"Yes, ma'am?" He strutted over to the wagon.

"Can we get a prisoner to help unload these wagons?"

"Ma'am with all due respect, they are prisoners, some are murderers. Besides, they are not healthy enough to do any kind of labor. Look at them." He gave an exhausted snicker.

"That one looks healthy and harmless enough," Helen said, pointing to one of the prisoners walking close to them. "Unless you want to help?" She was sure the sergeant was not interested in assisting them.

The sergeant glanced back at the Rebel. "Hey, you there!" He pointed to him.

A Confederate prisoner pointed to himself, his eyes questioning the guard.

"Yes, you! See to it that all these supplies are put away when we arrive. And don't even think about stealing anything, or touching the women."

"Climb aboard, soldier." Brooke grinned at the prisoner.

Confused, he climbed in the seat next to her on the wagon.

One whiff and Brooke commented, "You need a bath, soldier."

"Been a long time, ma'am."

She noticed the man kept his eyes on Sergeant Hatfield. "Relax. His bark is worse than his bite. What's your name?"

"Shea, ma'am... Corporal Bartley Shea."

"You know how to handle these?" she gladly handed him the reins.

"Yes, ma'am."

He eyed Prisse who was driving the wagon in front of them. "She a slave, ma'am?"

"There are no slaves here, soldier. Where are you from?"

"Atlanta, ma'am. Well, really a small town outside Atlanta."

"I'm from Savannah," Brooke shot back.

"Savannah? Thought you sounded like a Southern belle. You a prisoner here?"

"No, I'm a nurse. My husband is from Connecticut."

"You're married to a Northerner?" He shook the reins to signal for the team of horses to proceed.

"He's a good man. I love him with my whole heart," she drawled, a sparkle in her eye.

Shea did not speak. Matter of fact, the rest of the way to the prison hospital, he was quiet, reflective.

When the wagon arrived at its destination, she handed him an armload of blankets and picked up a pile for herself. "Follow me, I'll show you where these go."

They worked into late afternoon. Prisse passed the supplies off the wagon, and the helpers delivered them to the hospital storage area.

Shea scowled at the black woman, but the sergeant kept an eye on him and was never far off, realizing the prisoner's disapproval of Prisse.

As Helen grabbed some towels off the wagon, Brooke advised, "Please see to it that these are put in the storage room out back."

"Sure," Helen said with a grin.

"She seems happy," Shea noticed.

"Oh, she is. Her son has returned home from the war. She also recently found out that her soldier husband is alive and coming home. He had been held captive on a Confederate prison ship. She has much to be thankful for."

"I heard them ships are nasty," Shea frowned.

"That is what I heard, too."

"How was he freed?"

"Jumped overboard with three other men. Water temperature was near freezing. He was the only one that made it safely to shore. The good Lord was watching out for him. He was rescued by a fishing vessel and taken to a Union garrison where he is getting the best of care. He should come home in a couple weeks." Brooke couldn't help but smile; she was thrilled for her friend. Many families were not having the same happy ending that Helen had. Quickly, Brooke's smile turned to a look of concern as she thought of her own husband, her own family.

Doctor Wey rushed in, interrupting her thoughts. "Look at all these supplies, aren't they wonderful?"

Brooke agreed, "Yes, President Lincoln really cares about the soldiers. He believes them to be Americans even though they are from the South. He does not consider them our enemy."

The doctor hunched a shoulder. "I'm sure the fact that he knows your husband had a lot to do with your success. Hopefully, we may be able to save a few lives with these supplies."

Brooke's eyes brightened. "Did you hear about Helen's husband?"

"Yes, so happy that he managed to escape. Now we need to pray that you hear from Barrett," Wey added.

"Oh, Dr. Wey, I know he is alive... I can feel it in my heart. I only wish I would hear from him."

"Brooke, the war will be over soon. I heard that Sherman took over Atlanta."

Shea, walking past them with an armful of goods, overheard their conversation. He came to a stop and stared straight ahead, shocked by the news. *Could it be true?*

"Sherman's headed to the sea," Wey continued.

"The sea?" Brooke repeated, her brown eyes filling with tears.

"Yes. They believe he is headed to Savannah." Dr. Wey looked concerned. "I am sorry to tell you that, Brooke. I know you are worried about your family."

"Charles needs to know about this."

"It will be hard for us to get word to him now that he is at the officer's prison at Johnson's Island," Wey added.

"I need to go and visit him soon... maybe this weekend."

"This war will all be over within a few months," Dr. Wey predicted.

"I wonder if there will be any South left."

They were both wondering what the future held.

The doctor shook his head and walked off.

Brooke continued unloading the wagons, her thoughts racing. *Both sides are guilty of the atrocities of war—the inhumane treatment of their fellow man. It's pitiful the way men have been used as pawns to fulfill politician's dreams. Then again, it is war. So sad!*

"Sherman took Atlanta?" Shea asked Brooke as they continued to work.

"Yes, he did."

Shea went on, "Heard he was killin' everyone and destroyin' everything in his path. That he was leavin' a trail a hundred miles wide."

"Well, I hope that is a little exaggerated."

"I overheard your conversation with the doctor. Who is Charles?"

"My brother... he was captured at Gettysburg. He was in General Pickett's brigade."

"Your brother fought for the South?"

"Yes, all three of my brothers did. The youngest, Samuel, was killed at Gettysburg in the same battle."

Just then, Prisse walked over holding a tray with a bowl of warm soup and a cup of tea. "Miss Brooke, here is your lunch."

"Thank you, Prisse. Just put it on the table, please."

"Yes, Miss Brooke."

Shea watched the black woman walk over and place the tray on the table.

He continued making conversation with Brooke, "Ma'am, sorry to hear about your brother. And you say you have no idea where you husband is?"

"No. I haven't seen him since January. He went to Virginia, and I have not heard from him since. I pray he is safe. Sure hope he is not a prisoner at Andersonville."

"Andersonville?" Shea swallowed hard.

"Yes, it's a prison camp in Georgia. I hear it is awful." She straightened her back. "Well, that's the last of the supplies. Thanks for your help, soldier. Before you leave, I want you to sit down and have a little soup and tea."

"Ma'am, I can't eat your lunch."

"Oh, nonsense. You were a big help. Please, sit down, and enjoy it. Once you walk through those doors, you will find out how bad a prison can be."

"Can't be worse than Andersonville," he muttered under his breath.

"Pardon me?" Brooke questioned.

"I said that I was glad to help a fellow Southerner." He pulled out the rickety chair and sat down at the table. He took a few sips of the soup and closed his eyes, savoring the taste. Raising the spoon to his lips, he asked, "What is your husband's name?"

"Barrett von Weber."

Shea began coughing, struggling to catch his breath.

"Are you all right?" Brooke asked, leaning over the table, concerned that he was choking on the soup.

He cleared his throat. "Yes, ma'am, I'm fine."

For a short time, her big brown eyes captivated him. When he realized he was staring, he quickly turned his head. "Sorry, ma'am. Didn't mean to stare."

Just then, Sergeant Hatfield walked in. "There you are, Corporal. What are you doing?" He rushed over to take away his food.

Brooke stepped in front of the sergeant. "Let him finish eating. He was a big help, and he is being rewarded for his hard work."

"With all due respect, ma'am, just because you are a nurse here, does not give you the right to overstep my authority."

"Why Sergeant, what on earth do you mean? That is my lunch, and if I want to give it away, I will, and to whomever I want. Besides, this is a hospital... patients must have nourishment to keep up their strength."

The sergeant bit his lip and backed to the door. "Corporal, finish up and fast! The fun is over, time for you to join your friends."

"Sergeant, I better not hear of you treating this man badly," Brooke brazenly added.

Hatfield sighed. "I am just looking after you, ma'am."

"I know you mean well."

When Shea finished his small meal, he walked toward the sergeant. "I'm ready."

Hatfield did not say any more. He just opened the door and motioned for Shea to enter the prison.

"You know how funny this is?" Shea commented on his way past the sergeant.

"Do not talk to me unless I ask you to," Hatfield barked.

"I just wanna tell you, I been where you are." He glanced back at Brooke who was cleaning up the dishes. "I won't cause you any problems."

"See to it you don't."

As Shea marched into the prison, a recurring thought hounded him. *I was so cruel to her husband, yet she has been so kind to me.*

A couple weeks passed. Being one of the healthier prisoners, Shea had been assigned more responsibilities. Many chores were in the hospital, thanks to Brooke. She liked the young man and asked for his help whenever she had the opportunity.

He would watch with curiosity as the dark haired woman cared for the prisoners. He remembered her husband doing the same, not only for the Union prisoners, but also for the Confederate guards, always showing compassion.

It was a cold December morning, nearing Christmas. The temperature had been dropping every day and the winter snows had begun.

Corporal Shea checked into the medical facility complaining about a hurting ankle.

Doctor Wey examined him. "Ankle seems to be okay. You must have twisted it helping the other day. Speaking of that, I want to thank you for all the help you have been around here."

Brooke walked in. "Morning Dr. Wey… morning Corporal Shea."

Good morning, Brooke. "Seems like Corporal Shea sprained his ankle. Let's just wrap it. I think he'll be all right." He faced Shea, "If I didn't know you better, I would say you were faking it."

The corporal smiled at the doctor.

"Well, looks like you have been working too hard," Brooke acknowledged, bandaging the man's ankle.

"May I ask you a question, Nurse Brooke?"

"Yes."

"Why do you do what you do?"

"What do you mean? Enlighten me."

"This!" Shea motioned around. "Why do you help us? We are the enemy."

"No! You are not the enemy. I have had this discussion with my husband many times. As he and I both see it, we are all Americans. Sure, we have our differences, but we are still Americans. My family came here from Germany and Spain for a better life. What about your relatives?"

"I'm Irish. My family came to America, too. Grandfather said he got tired of the English tellin' him what to do." He forged a small smile.

"We all came here for a better life, so we should be able to get along."

"Do you think that will ever happen?"

"Yes, but at such a terrible cost."

"You went to the President of the United States and asked for supplies for Southern prisoners. Why? And, why on earth, did he agree?"

"President Lincoln is a good man. He knew it was the right thing to do." She paused. "I have not heard from my husband for eleven months. He's also a good man. He will go out of his way to defend the helpless. That is how we met. He came to my rescue in a small town far away from my home. That seems so long ago." Her mind drifted back to better times with Barrett, and her eyes lit up.

Shea listened, his heart heavy.

As Brooke continued to care for the patient, she added proudly, "My husband is a great musician. He writes hymns and is known as the Hymnist. If you are a churchgoing man, you probably would have heard of him."

Still, he said nothing.

"If he is a prisoner, I pray that he's being treated right. I can do no less for the prisoners here." She looked directly into Shea's eyes. "Your ankle looks fine."

"I have a confession, Nurse Brooke."

"There's nothing wrong with your ankle, is there?" Smiling, she angled her head, waiting for his answer.

"No, ma'am. Please don't tell the sergeant, but I had to see you."

"Don't tell me you have a hankering for your nurse. If so, I have to say, I'm very much in love with my husband, and I have a baby at home."

"No, ma'am. I needed to talk to you about... about your husband." He hung his head.

"My husband? What about him?" Her eyes grew wide.

Sheepishly, he confessed, "I know where he is."

She jumped up! "What?" Brooke's heart began pounding. She took a deep breath in an effort to calm herself.

"I was afraid ta tell you 'fore now." He paused, trying to cushion the blow he knew his words would cause. "I was a prison guard at Andersonville."

Covering her mouth with her hands, she gasped, "Andersonville?"

Shea reluctantly continued, "I was there when he was brought in. He came in with about three hundred other prisoners, along with a doctor, and his slave. Your husband had been wounded."

Tears stung her eyes. "Is he... is he?"

"Alive... yes... very much so. They call him Dr. Barrett. He helps in the hospital."

"Is he all right? How bad was he hurt? Please tell me everything you know." Her eyes showed concern.

"Yes, ma'am. He was wounded on the battlefield—shot in the side, and another bullet grazed his head. Suffered from pneumonia, but the prison doctors saved him."

Shea took a deep breath. "I have to admit..." he put his head down, ashamed, "I was not nice to him. I was not kind to any of the prisoners. I feel bad about that now."

Brooke's voice cracked with emotion. "When did you last see Barrett?"

"September. Left to fight with General Johnson." His eyes focused on the ceiling. "We was gonna stop Sherman. Ha. What a joke that was. Captured me the third day. His force was too large, too well-trained."

Brooke took her handkerchief and wiped her eyes.

Shea paused to give the nurse time to calm her emotions. "Don't know if he's still there. Heard say the Confederates was gonna close Andersonville and send 'em prisoners other places. Sherman was close and they was scared he'd free 'em prisoners. Thirty-two thousand prisoners on the loose in Georgia—no tellin' what damage they'd do to farms and the folks who run 'em."

Brooke was afraid to ask the question that haunted her. "Is it true what I have heard about Andersonville?"

Shea thought, trying to form the right words. "Yes, ma'am. Hard to say which place is worse, here or Andersonville. We suffer from the cold here... they suffer from the heat. Not sure what's worse." There was a lengthy pause. "Nurse, may I ask you somethin'?"

"Yes." She wiped a stray tear.

"I have noticed your faith."

"My faith?"

"Yes. I see you prayin' over these men." He motioned to the dozens of men lying in the hospital. "Men, who are your enemy, but you still pray for 'em. I don't understand."

"They are not my enemy. They may be the enemy of the United States government, but not mine."

"I realize that now. I treated all 'em Union solders like enemies. I now know 'em just doing their job, like me. I've been a guard and prisoner, so I've seen both sides of hate, and both sides of good. I'm a changed man."

"In what way?"

"For the better."

She let him continue talking.

"I'd like to have faith like you. I want to be able to love my enemy?" he pled.

She saw his brokenness.

"Nurse, I was a guard at Andersonville for a year. I helped build that place—hell on earth for thousands of men. I am guilty of heinous crimes." Tears of remorse trickled down his cheeks. "Don't wanna go to hell when I die."

"Do you have a family?"

"I have a wife and two children. At least, I did. Haven't seen or heard from 'em for almost four years. When the call came to battle, I was one of the first to go. My only thought was to kill 'em Yanks. Don't know why, just knew I had to."

"You're still so young. How old were you when you left home?"

"Nineteen."

"Just a boy. Bartley, give me your hand."

"My hand, why?"

"So we can pray. Let's pray for your wife and children. Let's pray for the men at Andersonville... and the ones here at Elmira. Let's pray for an end to this awful war, so we can all get back to living our lives. Pray that this hate will stop and that this nation will once again be united."

He couldn't speak.

Brooke bowed her head with the soldier and prayed. Her prayer ended with thanksgiving to God because she now knew her husband was alive. Maybe an end to the horror was in sight.

Chapter Thirty-Nine

April 10, 1865

It was an unusually quiet Monday morning at Elmira Prison. Everyone capable of helping was doing his or her daily chores.

Brooke showed up with her son, anxious to show him off. She knew the happy baby always brightened the day for the patients and the staff in the hospital.

Corporal Shea enjoyed listening to Nathan's babble—a pleasant sound he had not heard for many years. *Oh, how I miss my boys. I hope that they are well.*

A sharp noise echoed through the prison! A soldier in a Union uniform rode his horse full speed around the compound, yelling.

Church bells throughout the town were ringing.

"What is that racket?" Brooke rushed out of the hospital.

"What in tarnation is he saying," Helen asked, joining her.

"Something about the war." Brooke waved the horseman over.

The rider halted his horse in front of them; a huge smile encompassed his face.

"What is all the commotion? What's going on?" Brooke asked.

Over the noise of the bells, the man voiced loudly, "Morning, ma'am," he said, tipping his hat. "The war is over! General Lee surrendered to General Grant at Appomattox, Virginia, on Sunday Morning."

"The war... the war is over! Lee surrendered! Lee surrendered!" Helen shrieked at the top of her lungs, hugging Brooke.

Brooke held tight to Helen and her son, numb by the news she had waited so long to hear.

Unsure how Shea would react, she immediately turned to watch his expression. He seemed wobbly as he stood, and then fell to his knees, bursting into tears. "The war is over. Thank you, Lord. I can finally go home to my family."

The two nurses knelt beside him.

Brooke began to pray, her voice filled with emotion. *Dear Lord, thank you for ending this horrible war. God help us as we return to our lives. Please give comfort and protection to our loved ones scattered around this world. Give them safety and courage as they return home. To You, Lord, we give praise!*

Nearly a thousand miles away at Andersonville Prison, a similar event was taking place.

"Everett, you still won't come to the hospital for treatment?" Barrett asked, once again challenging his prisoner friend to accept medical help.

"Told you a thousand times, if I go in there, I'll never come out alive."

Barrett shook his head. "Well, as you always say, you're still kicking."

They laughed.

"Things are a lot better since Sal left," Everett admitted.

"Yes. I'm sure he has found some other poor soul to terrorize, or maybe someone bigger has put him in his place." Barrett grinned.

Von Weber glanced around the prison. "I am sure glad that so many men were transferred to other prisons. It's hard to believe that only a few months ago this place was home to over thirty-two thousand Union soldiers. The harsh winter sure has taken its toll. Glad spring is here, except now come the rains."

"How many men you 'spect are still here?" Everett shifted his position trying to get comfortable.

"I say about eight thousand."

"You and Dr. Benton have always looked after us, but you have not been immune to the dreadful conditions at the prison either."

"Yes, neither have the guards. We all have suffered from scurvy, diarrhea, dysentery, lice, and all the other diseases."

The loud beating of drums echoed through the prison, disrupting their conversation. The large wooden gates opened slowly.

Wirz, recently promoted to major, proudly rode in on his horse. He spoke to the prisoners, loud and precise. "Gentlemen, the war is over! You are now free to go home." It was short and to the point. He turned his horse around and it cantered back out.

However, this time the gates did not close—they remained wide open.

Barrett noticed that there were no longer any watchmen in the towers.

All was quiet as the prisoners blankly stared at each other, uncertain what to do. The time in captivity had made them fearful of everyone and everything. They were afraid to step forward, afraid they would be shot trying to escape.

"Think it's a trap, Dr. Barrett?" Everett cast a questioning look.

"No, I don't think so. Until we know for sure, don't do anything foolish. I'll go back to the hospital and see if Dr. Benton knows anything."

Barrett rushed back to Ward Seven. The hospital still housed sick and wounded men, many teetering on the brink of death.

"Well, Mister von Weber. When will I be able to see you in concert again?"

Barrett recognized the voice behind him, but it sounded different. He spun around. "Isaac?" He gave the black man a strange look. "Something's different. That did not sound like you."

Isaac laughed, "You were not the only one who was trying to deceive the Confederacy."

"I don't understand." Barrett's face showed his confusion.

Just then, Dr. Benton joined them, no longer dressed in his Confederate uniform or usual white coat. "Doctor, we need to get going. I found a ride to New Orleans. From there, we can catch a ship to England. I talked with the other doctors. They told us to get out while we can and they would take over our responsibilities."

Barrett stared at the two men. "Doctor?" he questioned.

The black man who saved his life, laughed. "Let me introduce myself. I am actually Dr. Benjamin Noble."

"Benjamin Noble? The well-known doctor and philanthropist from England?"

Barrett was baffled.

"The one and only," the black man gave his usual broad smile, big white teeth sparkling.

Barrett studied the black man he had known as Isaac for the last nine months. "I don't understand? I thought you were Dr. Benton's assistant."

Benton chuckled. "Oh, mercy no. Why do you think Isaac... Dr. Noble... was in the operating room with me all the time? I was really his assistant."

"But... why?"

Noble explained, "After our ship was sunk, we were rescued by a small Confederate boat. They had no idea who I was, only that I was black... a slave. I would have ended up on the sale block, but Dr. Benton devised a plan... this plan. We reversed roles, so to speak."

"You both played the role very well." Barrett shook his head, smiling.

"It was I who saw you in a concert in Paris." Noble confessed. "I never forget a face. The moment that young boy brought your wounded body to us, I recognized you. I knew that if for any reason I was where I was, it was to save your life."

Benton put his hand on Barrett's shoulder. "And save your life he did. As I said that day in the wagon, Dr. Noble stayed with you day and night nursing your wounds and pneumonia. Without him, there is no doubt you would have died. Do you know that he is a world authority on pneumonia? You would have died with any other doctor... especially me." Benton laughed. "I'm still in training."

"Nonsense. What you have done the past year makes you a doctor. I will make sure that happens when we get back to England." Noble's mouth tipped as he assured his partner.

"Thank you, Dr. Noble," Benton replied.

Barrett looked at the big man he had come to respect and reached his hand out.

"Thank you for saving my life, my friend, Dr. Noble."

"I would like to say it was my job." He took Barrett's hand and shook it firmly. "But truthfully, I was so moved at your concert that night in Paris, I wanted to see you in concert again."

"I'm sure that can be arranged," Barrett sincerely agreed.

Benton looked around anxiously. "Doctor, we must leave now. The Yanks will be here any time, and when that happens, who knows if they will consider us friend or foe. We are not going to stay around and find out... we're going home!"

"England or Australia?" Barrett asked.

"England first, to pick up our wives, and then we are off to Australia. I will never leave that country again. Let the rest of the world fight among themselves," Benton insisted. "I want no part of any war!"

Noble grinned from ear-to-ear, excited about his future. "I am going to Australia with Dr. Benton. They have some remarkable remedies that the natives have used for centuries."

"If I ever get to Australia, I will definitely do a concert." Barrett grinned.

"I'll hold you to it," Noble acknowledged warmly.

Barrett watched his friends walk away. He would miss them.

He glanced around the prison camp, which was emptying out fast. His pulse started racing with the hope that soon he would be holding Brooke in his arms.

Gathering his few personal belongings, the weakened Major von Weber walked through the prison and out the front gate.

The only guards remaining were the ones stationed in front of Major Wirz's office. One of them recognized the Hymnist and, not saying a word, stepped aside.

Barrett knocked on the office door.

A voice with a strong Swiss accent answered, "Enter."

Sitting at a table, staring at a picture, was the man who commanded the prison camp. Major Heinrich Hartmann Wirz smiled when he saw von Weber. "To what do I owe this visit?"

"Just thought I would stop in and say goodbye."

"Good bye, Barrett von Weber," Wirz said matter-of-factly.

Barrett turned to leave.

"Sir," Wirz cried out.

Barrett eyed the man whose future was uncertain, the man so many loathed.

"Will you play one more hymn for me?"

"Anything in particular?"

"Yes. *I Paid the Price for Your Sins.*"

Having played many hymns for Wirz in the last nine months, Barrett knew the routine. He opened the door so any remaining prisoners could hear, and then sat at the piano and began to play. The music echoed throughout the now almost empty prison, and was heard for a long distance by the men walking to freedom. When he finished the song, he stood, walked over to the door, and started to leave.

"Sir," Major Wirz called out.

Barrett turned around.

Wirz's red face was streaked from tears that had left trails down his cheeks and settled into his straggly beard. He stood, straightened his uniform, snapped to attention, and saluted von Weber.

Barrett slowly returned the salute.

Wirz sat back down and continued staring at the picture of his wife and child.

Leaving the old wooden structure, Barrett traipsed out the gate, not looking back.

He walked briskly and before long noticed a man lying in a small field of wildflowers. "Everett, is that you?" He cautiously approached the newly freed soldier.

"Yes, sir."

"Are you all right?"

"Never been better."

"Why are you lying there?"

"I'm smelling freedom, sir. Green grass and wildflowers—what could be better?"

Barrett smiled. "Having your wife lay next to you."

Everett laughed. "You got me on that one."

Barrett sat next to him. "What is your plan?"

"I'm going home. They said to go to the Mississippi and catch a paddleboat to St. Louis."

"St. Louis? My home is in Connecticut, but I have family in Savannah. Maybe I should go to Savannah... it would be closer." Barrett rubbed his long, tangled beard.

A nearby Rebel soldier in a tattered uniform overheard Barrett's comment. "I would not advise heading to Savannah. The war is over for Lee and Johnson, but there are many factions still fighting against Sherman. Besides, there is nothing left of Atlanta, or Savannah... Sherman saw to that."

"Where are you headed?" Barrett asked.

"Going home to Jackson, Mississippi. Been away from my family for four long years. I fought with Jackson, Pickett, and Lee. Heard there was a train leaving here that would take prisoners to Vicksburg, and will be stopping at my hometown." He paused. "I heard the rails in the North are still running. They were hardly touched. About the only one left in the South is this one here—heading west." He pulled out a small piece of paper and began rolling it around some tobacco. "You say you're from Connecticut?"

"Yes. New Haven," Barrett replied.

The soldier put the smoke in his mouth and lit it. "Don't believe Connecticut was even touched by the war."

Barrett was relieved. "How can I get in touch with my family?"

"In Connecticut?" He blew smoke into the air.

"Yes."

"There may still be a telegraph station in Vicksburg... probably be your best bet. Once you take the riverboat to St. Louis, you can catch a train to Connecticut and be home in no time."

"Thank you for the information, soldier."

The helpful stranger waved and began to walk away. Then he stopped and turned around. "You know for the last four years, I been killing you Bluecoats... only because I was told to. Now that the war is over... well, I know my way around here pretty good. Come with me, and I will help get you to the Mississippi."

"Well, thank you, sir."

"The war is over and it's time the North and South start getting along. Name's Spencer McGee. Got a farm outside Jackson with seven kids and a wife. Like I said, have not seen them in nearly four years."

Barrett helped Everett to his feet.

The two walked closer to the soldier who had befriended them. "Name is Barrett von Weber, and this is Everett."

"The Hymnist? I wondered if that was you. Could tell by your height. You're a legend. Everyone talks about Barrett von Weber. Next to Stonewall Jackson, and Robert E. Lee, your name is mentioned around the campfire—the bear, the horse race. I even heard a couple officers talk about the time you shot the top of the fencepost from two thousand yards. There were rumors that you were a prisoner at Andersonville." He stopped talking when he realized he was rambling.

Barrett shrugged his shoulders. "Well, it was not two thousand yards, and I would rather be known by my music."

"Oh, that, too. We sang your hymns around the campfire, also." He turned to Everett, "Will you be able to walk with us?"

"Don't worry about me, boy. I survived eleven months in this hole, and I would walk across hot coals to get home."

The two Union soldiers looked back one last time at the tall, wooden fence surrounding the prison where they had been confined.

Without speaking, they began their march to freedom.

They had only walked a short distance when they noticed a few black men digging in a nearby field. As far as the eye could see, were mounds of dirt. Barrett realized that they were looking at the final resting place of over thirteen thousand men who died at Andersonville.

One of the gravediggers looked up, wiped his brow of sweat, and stared at the three men.

Barrett stopped walking, stood at attention, and saluted the fallen heroes.

Everett dropped his crutch and stood at attention, joined by the Rebel. Together, with wet eyes, they united with von Weber in an emotional salute.

Silently, they began their long journey to the Mississippi River.

Chapter Forty

April 16, 1865

The rumble of thunder didn't muffle the loud knock that echoed through the lower floor of the von Weber mansion in New Haven.

William opened the door, and greeted a pale Cornelius Hall who stood under the awning, sheltered from the rain. "Massa Hall, good to see you. We just arrived home from Elmira."

Cornelius's tone seemed flat as he spoke. "William, please get everybody? I have some news that they all need to hear." The visitor appeared greatly distressed.

William invited the guest inside, placed his wet umbrella in the stand near the door, and hung his hat on a hook near several others. He wondered what could be the reason for the urgent request.

"Please follow me, sir. Miss Brooke is in the study with Little von Weber." He used the name he had fondly called the baby even before he was born. "Miss Brooke, Massa Hall is here. He needs to talk with you."

Brooke had just finished nursing the baby and was burping him. "Why Cornelius, what a pleasant surprise! How are you on this fine Easter Sunday? Did you enjoy church services today?" She started to stand to greet the long-time family friend.

"Brooke, I have some bad news to give you, please stay seated."

Ignoring his request, she stood, and handed the baby to Prisse. Taking a deep breath, she closed her eyes, and mouthed a silent prayer. She could see their family friend was shaken and tried to brace herself for the worst. In an effort to calm herself, she took another deep breath.

Seeing her concern, Cornelius tried to put her mind at ease. "Brooke, you can relax, it has nothing to do with Barrett. In fact, I received information this morning that all of the prisoners at Andersonville have been released. They are being transported to the Mississippi where they will go up the river to St. Louis. From there, they will be going home. Brooke, if Barrett is among them, he should be heading home soon."

Relief overwhelmed her.

Cornelius added, "I have taken the liberty to order a coach for you, Prisse, William, your son, and myself to meet Barrett in St. Louis. We will be able to take a train much of the way, so the trip should not be too difficult."

"Oh, thank you, Cornelius, you have made my day. You have always been there to help when I needed it. How can I ever repay you? I thought you were bringing bad news because you looked so serious."

"My dear, you never have to worry about repaying me for anything. Your husband is my best friend. In the past two years, I have lost much sleep, but my prayer time has deepened." He hesitated, and she could see tension lingering in his eyes.

There must be more bad news. She hugged her shoulders, her mind racing. *Maybe Barrett had lost a limb, or his sight. Perhaps he will never be able to play the piano again.* She took a deep, steadying breath.

"Brooke, there is bad news. I regret to inform you that President Lincoln was shot Friday night. He passed away Saturday morning."

Her eyes welled up instantly. She felt like she couldn't move, couldn't breathe. With her head lowered, she somehow found the strength to ask, "How is Mrs. Lincoln?"

"She is in the state of shock. She was sitting next to him at the theater when the assassin shot him. There is a nationwide manhunt for the killer and the others in his party."

For a moment no one spoke, each absorbed in thought.

Brooke finally added, "Tell me Cornelius, did a Southerner do this horrible act? If so, the healing for this nation will be that much more difficult."

"I have not heard. Everything is still sketchy. An actor named Booth shot him. Such a tragedy!" He shook his head sorrowfully.

A fresh batch of tears slid down her face. "April 14th? He was shot on Good Friday! How sad! He died the day Christians were remembering Christ's death."

The friends stared at each other, not knowing what to say, what to do. Memories crowded their troubled minds.

Barrett and his traveling companions huddled close in the cattle car of the slow moving train. So many men were squeezed together that there was no room for any of them to sit down.

"I think we would get there faster if we walked," Everett joked.

Some of the men nearby responded with weak laughter.

Barrett watched through the slats of the railroad car as hundreds of soldiers in both blue and gray uniforms plodded along on the side of the tracks. The line seemed endless. The smiles that most wore were so broad, and their bodies so thin, their grins literally went from ear-to-ear. I *guess that is where the expression, "Smiling from ear to ear" came from.* Barrett chuckled.

"How some of those men can walk is beyond me. But walk to freedom they will, they must." Barrett shook his head with wonder.

"Sounds like that could be words to one of your hymns," Everett responded.

"One day, maybe they will be."

The train stopped at Jackson, Mississippi, where McGee said his goodbyes to his new friends.

"I pray that your wife and children are well," Barrett said to the Rebel soldier before he jumped off the railroad car.

With a quick wave, McGee took off fast toward the crowd at the railroad station.

Everett watched as the man dropped everything that he was carrying, mobbed by a group of excited people. "Hey, Barrett, take a gander." He gestured with his head to the activity outside.

Barrett gazed with interest at the sight and smiled at the cause of the commotion—McGee's wife and children were enthusiastically welcoming him home.

Everett commented, "I wonder how long they have been waiting."

Barrett replied, "Four long years."

"I count eight kids," Everett replied.

Von Weber quickly counted heads and continued smiling. "He must have left without knowing she was with child again. What a pleasant surprise for him."

Both men laughed as the train continued on its slow journey.

Finally, at Vicksburg, the train came to the end of the line. The former prisoners stepped out and joined the thousands of other men, searching, and waiting for information about what they were to do next. Used to taking orders, they had a difficult time thinking for themselves and making decisions.

Studying the crowd, Barrett asked Everett, "Is it me, or do you think something is not right?" He sensed an uneasy, peculiar feeling in the air.

Everett nodded. "I feel it, also. What do you think is going on?"

Barrett simply shrugged his shoulders. Making his way to the telegraph station, he walked up to a window where a white-haired man was busy sending a message. Von Weber noticed a long list of names in front of the telegraph operator. "Name?" The man asked nonchalantly as he worked the keys, not looking up.

"I would like to send a telegraph to Cornelius Hall at New Haven Arms in Connecticut."

"Not sure it will reach there. The war has destroyed many of the lines, besides the wire's been busy since the report on Lincoln. What do you want the message to say?"

"What report on Lincoln?" Barrett shot back, without blinking.

"Didn't you hear? Lincoln was shot and killed."

Barrett stepped back for a second, disbelief covering his face.

"What do you want the telegraph to say?" the man asked again. Finally, he stopped typing, grabbed a feather pen, and looked up at the stunned von Weber.

Barrett could hardly speak. "Uh... alive... well... coming home... Barrett."

Writing it down, the busy man commented, 'I will send this out immediately, but like I said, not sure they will get it. You from one of the prisons?"

"Yes."

"Pardon me, but you seem a little lost, mister."

"I think I am more shocked about President Lincoln than lost. But I guess I am a little lost, too."

"Trying to get home to Connecticut?"

"Yes."

"The Union Army is paying the paddleboats pretty good to take you prisoners up the Mississippi. Even more for officers. Most of the men are getting off in Cairo, but you can get as far as St Louis. Be easier to catch a train there."

"Is there a certain paddleboat I should catch?"

"Your best bet is to take the *Sultana* from here to St. Louis. From there, you can catch a train all the way to Connecticut. *Sultana* will be docking at the pier in the morning. I understand she has had some mechanical problems, so will be under repair for the day. If you can wait that long, that is your best bet. Otherwise, stand in line with the other thousands of men and go on one of the other paddleboats that will be leaving sooner. The *Sultana* is one of the newest and biggest paddleboats on the Mississippi."

"The *Sultana*?"

"Yes, sir."

"Thank you for the information. Can you add that to the message?" Barrett turned and left without waiting for a response, his mind whirling.

He brought the news of Lincoln's death to Everett who was resting on a small grassy knoll. His friend's face displayed no expression with the news. Three years of war, and one year in a prison camp, had made him calloused to news of death.

"I understand there is a paddleboat called *Sultana* leaving in the morning. We can get on it. The man at the telegraph station said that is our best bet."

"Barrett, I think that it is time you headed home, and let me find my own way." Everett rubbed his crusty, tired eyes.

"I can't do that. We have been through too much together... I won't leave you."

"Barrett, not only am I am slowing you down, and keeping you from getting into the arms of your sweet Brooke, but I'm pushing myself too hard. I'm afraid if I am not careful and continue at this pace, I could fall and break one of these fragile bones. And if that happens, I may never walk again. My friend, I really need to take a few days to rest. It is clean here. Connecticut is a lot farther than Illinois. You have a long ways to go. Me? I'm almost home, just up the river a bit. Furthermore, once I am on that paddleboat, I will have to stand for hours with all the pushing and shoving. No, not yet."

Barrett could see his comrade's determination. "All right. I understand." He shook his hand. "Stop by one of my concerts sometime. I'll have a front row seat reserved for you."

"I'll do that."

Barrett slowly backed away. Finally nodding his head, he turned and meandered toward the Mississippi River.

Chapter Forty-One

April 24, 1865
Vicksburg

The large steamboat limped its way into port, yet most people waiting for her on the riverbank could not hear or tell anything was wrong. After all, her slow speed could be contributed to the swollen Mississippi and the record spring rainfall. Ships found it easy to travel down the river, but going upstream against the heavy flow was a different story.

The closer she got, the louder the water thrashing the paddle wheel sounded as it strained against the powerful current.

Finally, Barrett could make out the name of the struggling steamboat. On the side was the name... *Sultana*. He breathed a sigh of relief knowing he was at the right place. *I am finally going home to Brooke!*

"Sounds like a boiler problem to me," a man next to Barrett stated, trying to make conversation.

"How can you tell?"

"Been around the river all my life. Worked on the St. Louis docks, even was on a steamboat for a while."

Barrett eyed the returning prisoner who looked like he had fared better than most of the returnees. "Can it be repaired quickly?"

"Can be. May not be done right, but they can fix it, if they really want to. It's best to replace the entire boiler, but most the time they just patch it. I reckon it's all about money."

"You from St. Louis?" Barrett wondered.

"No... Ohio. The jobs were in St. Louis. Work on the docks was hard. When the war broke out, I became an infantryman. Room and board... easy work... or so I thought. Was I ever wrong! I Joined the 65th Ohio Infantry.

Spent three years fighting for the North. The last twelve months I have been stuck in Cahaba Prison in Alabama."

"Cahaba... never heard of that one." Barrett continued the friendly banter.

"After a time, I s'pose they were all the same. Which one were you in?"

"Andersonville!"

The man eyed Barrett for a moment, sizing him up. "Well, maybe they weren't all the same. Is it true that over ten thousand Union soldiers died there?" Word of the atrocities at Andersonville had circulated among the men confined in other prisons.

"Last count I heard was over thirteen thousand." Barrett stared at the murky, overflowing Mississippi River. "Thirteen thousand innocent souls died a slow, agonizing death in that snake pit they called a prison."

The men stood quietly for a long moment each caught up in his own thoughts.

Finally breaking the silence, the man asked Barrett, "Why would God do that?"

Anger flashed in Barrett's eyes. He pointed a finger at the man and spoke, each word growing louder. "Why would God do that? Blame it on the people who ran the prison! Blame it on the Confederacy! Blame it on the war itself! But, hear me... don't blame God! He is a God of peace and love. Do you realize that if all men obeyed what the scriptures say, there would be none of this?" Barrett motioned at the hundreds of returnees lined up, waiting for their turn to board the *Sultana*. All wore scars of battle and imprisonment—some visible, other internal ones would linger in their minds for a lifetime. He took a deep breath, and his voice calmed. "Just that one simple commandment that Jesus gave us—*Love thy neighbor as thy self.* If we would just obey that one, what we have endured, and the senseless slaughter of the past four years would never have happened."

He continued, "God's love is unconditional. His peace is eternal. He is merciful. It is men who did this. Call it greed, hate, prejudice... call it whatever you want, but I assure you, sir, God did not cause this. We did it to ourselves. All of it! And the sad truth of the matter, this is not the first time, nor will it be the last." He bowed his head in prayer.

The man remained quiet, reflecting von Weber's words.

Barrett stood on the deck, gazing at the giant Mississippi River. Softly he began singing one of his hymns.

As I look out on the water,

As I gaze upon the sea,
I see Your love's unending,
Because I know, You died for me.

A few men around him joined in. Before long, many on the pier were singing. Those who did not know the song quickly learned the tune and did their best to join the others.

The beauty of the mountains,
The fragrance of a rose,
I know that You love me,
Because I'm the one You chose.

Even the passengers already on the *Sultana* stepped closer to the rail and listened to the chorus of men singing.

The repairs to the *Sultana* were almost complete when the anxious soldiers finally began boarding the riverboat.

Barrett was one of the first to walk up the gangplank, glancing at the men around him as he trudged aboard the vessel.

A Union officer sat in a chair with a pen in hand, keeping track of how many men were boarding. "Give me your name, rank, and state or unit."

"Major Barrett von Weber, Connecticut."

"Welcome home, sir." He stared at him with a slight smile.

"Thank you, but I'm not home quite yet."

A deckhand announced to anyone who would listen, "No pushing, or shoving. Captain Mason is the captain of this ship, and I have orders to send everyone to the front or the top deck."

Barrett made his way to the bow where there would be cover in case of rain—the skies looked gloomy.

Standing close to him was a young woman holding a baby in her arms.

Barrett smiled when he saw the sleeping infant. "A boy or girl?" he asked, as other Union soldiers crowded around the young mother. Concerned for her safety, von Weber protectively moved closer to her.

The jittery woman's eyes reflected anxiety as soldiers crowded closer. "A girl. She is two months old."

"What is her name?" Barrett continued the chatter, hoping to put the frightened mother at ease.

"Josie."

"That's a pretty name. My name is Barrett. Are you just traveling up the river, or are you waiting for someone?"

"I am looking for my father. I received a wire last week saying that he had been released. Told me to meet him on the *Sultana*. I came from Canton, Ohio. I sure hope he comes. He has been a prisoner for a long time at Blackshear Prison Camp. I have missed him and my husband greatly."

"Blackshear? That's another prison I have never heard of. Where is your husband?"

"He is still fighting with Sherman. I haven't heard from him for five months. I pray he is still alive." She shook her head sadly.

Barrett watched as hundreds of men trudged up the gangplank, most of them slowly making their way to the top deck.

More returnees shoved close to the young woman.

"Gentlemen," Barrett shouted. "We have a young lady with a baby here. Give her some space and treat her with respect. Remember we are Northern gentlemen, not ruffians."

Another man joined von Weber. "Move! Let's give the young lady some room."

The nearby men took a step back.

Barrett couldn't help but chuckle at some of the men boarding the ship. Many were so thin and frail, yet they had enough energy to do the jig. Most of the men were celebrating with broad smiles and an extra bounce in their step. They were finally free!

The crewmen continued shouting, "Move all the way to the front. There is space on the upper deck and below. Everyone wants to go home, so make room."

Barrett couldn't shake his growing concern—*I wonder how many can fit on this steamboat. They keep coming aboard.* "Anyone know what the capacity of this steamboat is?" he asked anyone who would answer.

"I think between three hundred seventy-five and four hundred," a spry, gray-haired man behind him responded.

"Well, I think we passed that long ago."

"I heard the captain of the ship is getting five dollars a head," a voice cried out.

"What can happen even if it sinks? How bad could it be? We are only sailing on a river." Another man in the crowd laughed.

Barrett let a loud sigh escape. "No! It is not just a river... it's the Mighty Mississippi."

Another added, "Old Man River is like a woman, there's no controlling her." He roared with laughter at his own joke.

Some of the men enjoyed his humor, while others were serious. A definite nervous tension filled the air.

One voice in the crowd spoke up, "It sure is nice to see a woman again."

"And a baby," another voice cracked.

The uncomfortable woman continued to watch below as an endless line of men stepped from land to the gangplank of the *Sultana*. Suddenly, a smile of recognition swept across her face. She waved to a man boarding. "Josie, there's your grandpa."

Barrett smiled as he watched the young mother's look of apprehension turn to one of joy.

As the man neared his daughter, the smile on Barrett's face disappeared. *Oh no! It can't be!*

The man hugged his daughter and beamed when she proudly introduced him to his granddaughter. "Daddy, this is Josie." The grandfather snuggled the baby close, still smiling—a smile that vanished when he looked up and noticed Barrett.

"Well, well, well, if it is not Sergeant Major Perry... or should I say Sal?" Barrett sneered, remembering the way the man had said something similar to him at Andersonville.

The blood drained from Perry's face. He scanned the crowd around them, searching for others who could also recognize him.

"What are you doing here?" Perry asked with raised eyebrows.

"Same thing you are... going home," Barrett responded curtly. His anger was evident by the expression on his face.

Perry smiled nervously at his daughter.

"Do you two know each other?" she asked with wide eyes.

"We have met on a number of occasions," Barrett replied.

"An old friend?" she persisted.

"I will let Sal answer that." Barrett's shoulders stiffened.

"Sal... who is Sal?" Her confusion showed.

Perry handed the baby back to his daughter. "Honey, I need to talk to this man for a moment." He stepped between his daughter and Barrett.

Crossing his arms, he addressed Barrett forcefully, "Move over... I want to have words with you."

Barrett stepped back a few feet.

Perry moved within inches of his face. "Listen, the war is over. What happened at Andersonville is in the past. It is time to start our lives over."

"Forget the past? What happened at Andersonville is not over... it never will be!"

"Keep your voice quiet. I don't want to upset my daughter. Listen to me... it was about survival in the camp, nothing more," Perry whispered.

"That's where you are wrong. It was more than that. It was about our comrades. We had the responsibility to help one another survive, to protect each other. What you did... the men you beat up... men like Frank... over a strawberry! Let's just say... God will judge your actions. Those men also wanted to hold their grandchildren like you are doing today, but they will never have that chance... because of you!"

"Keep your voice down," Perry shot back, glancing at his daughter.

"You want me to forget what happened there? I can't do that."

"The war is over! We need to forget what happened during our imprisonment. Let's forget and move on," Perry insisted.

"You were a leader. You were in the position to help men, but instead, you took advantage of the weak, the helpless." Barrett's face was red with rage; anger consumed him. "I suppose you want to be friends! Should we forgive and forget?" His voice was loud, his words cynical.

Perry lowered his head, his voice now quivering. "I admit I was wrong... I have to live with what I have done the rest of my life. I know that some of what I did cost the lives of men... good men. Was it worth it? Yes, I survived. Was it right? No, it was horribly wrong."

"How can something be wrong, but worth it?"

"I guess it depends on where you are standing."

"That's right... problem is you are standing... and they are six-feet under."

Perry jabbed his finger into Barrett's chest. "You stay out of my life! Leave me alone!" He moved away from von Weber, and stepped to the other side of his daughter who stood between them. Putting his arm around her shoulders, he stared sadly into the cold Mississippi River.

The conversation was over. Nothing more needed to be said.

Perry knew that this was a battle he could never win, nor did he deserve to.

Barrett pitied him on one hand; on the other hand, he detested him.

The returnees continued to board the vessel for hours.

Finally, the ship's crew halted the boarding process.

To keep things under control during the trip, a company of armed Union soldiers boarded.

The gangplank creaked as it lifted.

Cheering erupted from the war-weary men.

With the boilers now repaired, they could begin their journey up the swollen river, heading home.

The *Sultana's* whistle sounded a loud, long blast. The ropes were released from their cleats, and the paddle began its motion churning the water and forcing the boat to move forward.

The clanging boilers and hissing smokestacks caused some passengers to cover their ears. The boat shuddered as it plodded along, slowly at first, but then with increasing speed and thrust.

Barrett wasn't sure who started the tune, but on the top deck, someone began singing. It was a song von Weber knew well—one of his first hymns. The lyrics seemed fitting—*I'm Going Home.*

> *I'm going home. I'm going home.*
> *Been traveling in this distant land.*
> *No more pain, I no longer roam.*
> *I'm going home, I'm going home.*

The *Sultana* struggled up the Mississippi at a slow pace, traveling on through the dark of night.

The next day the ship docked for a short time at Helena. Much-needed coal and supplies were quickly loaded.

While they waited, Barrett listened to the men conversing, occasionally chiming in.

"Cannot wait to hug my children," one worn-out returnee said.

"I can't wait to hug my wife," a toothless man grinned.

"I can't wait to get a full plate of taters and beef," still another stated.

"Turkey for me... I sure miss turkey." The man closed his eyes, picturing the moment.

Suddenly, a shout interrupted the chatter. "Look! Someone on the dock is taking a photograph of us."

Barrett peered at the dock where a man had set up his camera, preparing to shoot a picture of the modern steamship.

The men who were physically able, rushed to the side of the boat, forcing their way towards the railing to get a better view.

Barrett feared the railing would collapse. That was when his concern that there were far too many men on board became reality—the boat began to tilt. He grabbed hold of the railing. *Lord, please help!*

"Get back to the other side! Get back to the other side!" a voice ordered. "This is the Captain of the *Sultana*. Get back to your position, or you will capsize this boat."

The passengers obeyed and gradually the ship was righted.

The picture had been taken.

Barrett watched the photographer fold his tripod and traipse away.

Finally, the *Sultana* was again on its way to Memphis.

They arrived at their destination late afternoon.

Quickly the crew began taking on more supplies and coal.

Barrett elected to stay on board—comfortable, he was afraid he would lose his spot if he left. His thoughts centered on Brooke and home.

Finally, at midnight, the steamer continued its slow voyage up the Mississippi.

Chapter Forty-Two

2 AM April 27, 1865
On the Mississippi River

The *Sultana* journeyed slowly up the murky Mississippi River in the early hours of the morning.

The night seemed endless to the anxious returnees.

The passengers bundled up the best they could, but still those on the decks were shivering. Some of them huddled close to the two large smokestacks that provided much-needed heat. Others crowded together to share their body heat.

Although the boat was overcrowded, it was cleaner and much more comfortable than the wretched places they had been. No one complained about the cold. Even though most of the returnees had no idea what they would face when they returned home, at least they were finally free.

Most of the men welcomed sleep and did not fight to stay awake as the hours dragged on. In their weakened condition, they needed rest.

Barrett was sitting on the deck, his back propped against the wall, the railing only a few feet in front of him. There was barely enough room for men to step over him. Sleep had not yet overtaken the pianist. His mind flooded with thoughts of home. *What about Brooke? Her father? Is there any chance that Annalise survived?*

He glanced around. Perry's daughter lay sleeping on the deck, not too far from Barrett, her snoozing child clutched in her arms. Von Weber and a couple of the other men nearby had sacrificed their coats to cover the mother and baby.

Her father, Sergeant Major Perry, stood a few feet from her, leaning on the railing, staring out into the darkness.

Von Weber wondered what Perry was thinking. Were his thoughts on his family, or would the evil deeds that he had done while he was a prisoner consume him? *No wonder he can't sleep.*

Barrett couldn't help but notice an eerie silence on the foggy night; he shuddered.

Suddenly, a faint hissing sound caught his attention.

Then, a loud noise that sounded like metal rubbing against metal shattered the quiet night.

An old soldier lying near the warm smokestack commented, "Sounds like the boilers are working extra hard tonight. Hard to sleep with that clatter."

A man close to him replied, "Let 'em work... that heat feels good." Exhausted, the man closed his eyes and returned to slumber. He didn't even hear the hissing sound growing longer and louder until it was a shrill whistle.

Without further warning, a powerful, loud explosion rocked the boat.

In an instant, the blast hurled the unsuspecting men sleeping near the boilers through the air and into the water. Countless others were blown off the deck into the frigid Mississippi River.

The explosion slammed Barrett forward. Trying to gain his bearings, he clung to the railing, which was all that separated him from the cold water. He shook his head in an effort to make sense of what was happening; the events around him seemed to be occurring in slow motion. Still groggy, he used the broken railing to pull himself up.

He noticed the air that had been cold instantly became steaming. Red-hot coals showered from above and hissed when they hit the water. He felt intense pain in his neck from the sparks raining down.

The sky was on fire!

Barrett blinked, trying to focus. A bright light caused by the blast suddenly turned shadowy as men from the deck above were catapulted over the side, many on fire, their screams horrific.

Out of the corner of his eyes, he saw Perry helplessly flip over the railing.

The young woman screamed when she saw her father plummet into the cold river. "Father, Father!" Sobbing, she rushed to the railing.

The scene was chaotic. Those around the woman scrambled, desperately trying to escape the imminent disaster. All the pushing and shoving made the rail collapse, and the terrified mother plunged into the cold river, still clinging to her baby.

Her blood curdling screams were more than Barrett could bear. Instinctively, he jumped into the water to rescue her.

Lifeless bodies floated around von Weber. The smell of burnt flesh was overpowering.

He glanced at what was left of the burning *Sultana*. The once-proud vessel heading upstream was now disabled and at the mercy of the strong current of the Mississippi forcing it downstream. Orange flames rose high into the night sky; the fire was so bright it illuminated the horrific scene like the noonday sun.

Barrett heard the young woman screaming, "My baby... my baby! Help me!" He could see her being swept downstream, desperately trying to hold her baby out of the water, but seemingly losing the battle.

Von Weber swam as hard as he could to get to her. Grabbing the terrified mother's long hair, he pulled her closer. "Don't struggle... don't struggle. Lie on your back and hand me Josie." Trying to keep his voice calm, he told the frantic woman, "Do exactly what I tell you and you will be all right. Now give the baby to me!"

Frantically, she handed her crying daughter to him.

Lying on his back, he placed the baby on his chest. "Float on your back and lock arms with me. Do not panic, we'll let the river guide us. If you struggle, you'll pull us all under. Eventually we'll grab onto something, or reach shore. You have to trust me!"

Stretching her arm out, she locked elbows with him.

Together, they were dragged down the raging river.

Barrett noticed some men clinging to large chunks of wood, and tried to take hold of a plank, but couldn't grab it with only one hand.

He saw the flaming hulk of the *Sultana* being pulled downstream by the current. Bodies and debris littered the water. Survivors struggled to keep afloat.

He shouted out to the only One who could help him. *Lord, help us get to shore before the river claims us!*

Chapter Forty-Three

2 AM April 27, 1865

On the Banks of the Mississippi

The warm campfire added comfort on the brisk night.

The four men camped by the river were involved in a spirited poker game. "Ha-ha... three jacks," a boisterous, hefty man gloated, thumping his cards down on the flat tree stump they were using as their table.

Annoyed by his good luck, the other three men tossed their cards down. "You have been lucky all night... you must be cheating."

"It's all in how the cards are dealt." He scooted a bunch of coins his direction. "That's why they call me Chance," he boasted.

Before he could pocket the money, an explosion knocked one of the card players out of his chair, onto the ground, rocking the quiet of the night.

Flashes of light instantly lit up the dark sky.

The startled men jumped up, staring at the river, fear invading their hearts.

"What the... what happened?" the man who fell off his chair yelped.

"Give you odds the boiler exploded on that steamship that passed us an hour ago," another man said, looking toward the flames spewing into the sky.

"Taylor, I told you the boilers were working too hard when it floated by," another grumbled.

"Looks like a bad one. Bet they felt it in Memphis." Taylor grabbed his jacket. "Reckon they can see the flames, too. Boys, the fishing starts early. What did Jesus say about fishers of men? In this case, we really will be fishing for men. Leonard, Posey, grab the lanterns! Chance, let's get our boats in the water! Posey, go with Chance. Leonard, come with me. We need to look for survivors… fast!"

"Yup, more important things to do." Chance replied, quickly pocketing his winnings.

"Taylor, you think them's Bluecoats?" Leonard asked, grabbing a couple nearby lanterns.

"What difference does that make? Whoever they are, they need our help," Taylor replied.

The men hurriedly uncovered their two small fishing boats. Having made rescues before, they knew what to expect, so they tossed their fishing equipment out of the boats, knowing it would be in their way. Pushing the boats into the water, they jumped into them.

Posey and Leonard attached the lanterns to poles hanging over the water in the front and back of the vessels.

"These lanterns will only last a couple hours," Chance shouted loud enough that the men in both boats heard him. The cold night air caused their voices to easily be heard over a great distance. "So I brung some extra oil. May be a long night."

"Good thinkin' Chance. With the river swollen the way it is, it has covered a lot of trees. Some survivors may have found refuge in them. There's no way of knowing what's hidden under the water. Be careful… don't wanna sink our boats," Taylor warned.

As the men rowed upstream against the strong current, the light of the lantern illuminated the concern on Taylor's face. "I have seen enough shipwrecks on this river to know that bodies of both living and dead will soon be passing by. We will only have a split second to pull them in."

Barely were the words out of his mouth, when they felt a hard thud against one of the boats, followed by another, and another. The men stopped rowing and peered over the side.

Chance stretched the lantern as far over the water as he could.

Paralyzed by fear and uncertainty, the men stared at the gruesome scene and tried to comprehend the enormity of the situation as a number of bodies floated by.

"Let's get the gaffs and start bringing the bodies into the boat," Posey hollered.

"No!" Taylor ordered, "There are too many of them. We should grab only the living."

"Oh, dear Lord," Leonard yelled, "I have never seen anything like this—there are hundreds of dead out there."

"What is that smell?" Chance asked, hanging up the lantern and grabbing the gaff.

"That's burning flesh," Posey replied.

"Be careful! If we take on too many, they will capsize us. Just look for the living," Taylor reminded them.

Posey rowed over to a body, and Chance pulled it closer to check for any sign of life. Seeing the victim's badly burned face, he moaned, "I think I am going to get sick."

A continuous stream of bodies and debris jostled the fishing boats.

"There are so many bodies... maybe two ships collided." Taylor shook his head.

Using gaffs and oars, they continued the gruesome task of weeding out the living from the dead.

"There... look over on that plank," Posey yelled, pointing to a man clinging to a small, unrecognizable part of the steamship.

"We will get him. You keep looking for survivors," Taylor told the rescuers in the other boat.

"I see some men clinging to the trees along the shore." Chance said, pointing in the general direction.

"Forget them—they are safe for now! Get the ones in the river first. The temperature and the strong current will soon drag them under," Taylor stated, noticeably distressed.

The men continued to pick up survivors. Within minutes, the small boats were filled.

"Chance, we have to head to shore. We can't take on any more," Taylor urgently reported.

"Let's put over on the east side. I see lights there. Might be able to get more help," Chance shouted from the other boat.

"Quiet! I heard something!" Posey stopped rowing, "Do you hear that?"

The men listened carefully.

"Do you hear a baby?" Chance asked.

Posey gasped. "Yes... Lord have mercy... it's somewhere in front of us!"

Chance extended the lantern as far as he could reach. "Over there." He motioned straight ahead. "God help us... there's a baby on that man. Grab them before they pass by!"

They rowed closer. Much to their relief, the man was still conscious, but they knew time was not on their side.

Chance shouted urgently, "Mister, hand me the baby. Hand me that baby!"

With his left hand and long, strong fingers, Barrett removed the crying baby from his chest and handed her to the rescuer.

Chance passed the infant to one of the survivors in the boat. Taking his coat off, he handed it to the same man. "Wrap the baby in my coat. Keep it warm."

"Yes, sir," the frail solider replied, through chattering teeth.

Just then, Taylor's rescue boat pulled alongside to help. "Give me your hand," Leonard shouted to Barrett.

"Take the girl first," von Weber replied weakly.

The rescuer tried to pull the unconscious woman aboard, but was unable to get a firm grip.

"Grab her by the hair," Barrett muttered.

Leonard grabbed her hair, pulling her closer.

One of the recently rescued men reached over the side, placed his arms around the woman's waist, and helped pull her into the overcrowded boat.

Taylor shouted, "Now, give me your hand!" He reached out to Barrett just as a large chunk of debris collided with his boat. The force knocked them into Chance's boat, crushing von Weber between the two boats.

Barrett disappeared under the water.

"Where did he go? Where is he?" Chance shouted frantically as he grabbed his lantern and held it over the edge of the boat. He jumped to the other side, looking desperately for the victim. "Sir... where are you? You saved these two people, help us save you, mister. Please say something!"

The only reply was haunting silence.

"He's gone. So close," the soldier holding the baby muttered.

"Is the woman all right?" Taylor asked.

Leonard's voice quivered, "Think so. Passed out from the cold. We need to get these people to the fire. Then we can come back and look for more survivors."

Taylor pointed to some lighted torches on the riverbank where several other boats were being launched. "It looks like help is on the way!"

Some people on the bank were grabbing bodies that were floating by.

Unfortunately, most of the victims were already dead.

As the fishing boats rowed to shore, Taylor talked about Barrett's heroism. "I wish we could have saved that man. He sacrificed his life for this woman and her baby. Think he was the father?"

"No tellin'. Never saw him before," Leonard said, rowing faster.

"Where you from?" Chance asked, holding the lantern closer to illuminate the rescued men's faces.

"Just released from Andersonville," the man holding the baby replied.

"Explains it! No wonder you are so boney," Posey commented.

"It's ironic," Chance said, watching another lifeless body float past them.

"What's that?" Taylor hollered from the other boat.

"To go through this awful war, spend time in that hellhole of a prison, and then die on your way home to freedom. To drown at that... they deserve better." Chance stood, removed his hat, and held it over his heart.

Everyone in both boats quieted and offered a moment of silence to honor the victims.

Chance looked out over the flooded river. "Maybe someone downstream will rescue that brave man."

"Not likely. Water is too fast, too cold, and it gets darker down river. Not much, if any, chance of his survival," Taylor added, sadly.

"You say the woman is fine?" Chance asked.

"Think so," Leonard said, shivering. "Need to get her and the others to shelter and some dry clothes."

Shaking his head, Chance lamented, "I have never seen anything like this... so many bodies... why so many?"

"The ship was overloaded. Heard someone say there were over two thousand men aboard," one of the survivors muttered.

"What steamship was it?" Chance asked.

"The *Sultana*," he replied.

"*Sultana*! Can't put two thousand men on a boat that only holds four hundred," Taylor shot back.

"Well, apparently they did."

"Fools," Taylor coughed.

While the boats rowed toward shore, they continued bumping into more bodies. Some men in the river were still conscious and held to the side of the boats. "Hold on men. There is no more room in here. Don't struggle, or you'll tip us and we'll all die... just hold on and we'll get you to shore."

Exhausted, drenched, and cold, they finally managed to reach dry land.

The rescue continued throughout the night.

By late morning, bodies were strewn along the banks of the Mississippi, toward Memphis. Some were in neatly laid rows, others scattered. Some had blankets or sheets covering them. Many were burned beyond recognition. Most had drowned, not because they didn't know how to swim, but because they were too weak.

Chapter Forty-Four

8 AM April 27, 1865
St Louis, Missouri

The city of St. Louis was bustling. Citizens were preparing for thousands of Union troops who were expected to reunite with their family members.

Brooke and Cornelius rode in a spacious, upscale carriage from the train station toward a new hotel overlooking the river. They chatted as they neared their destination.

"Cornelius, there is something I have always wanted to ask you," Brooke announced, peering out the window at the busy streets.

"Okay," he replied, putting down the book that he had been reading.

"Barrett and you have a close relationship, one that I have not been able to fully understand. At first, I thought it was a father-son type, but I believe it's more than that."

"Ah, yes, I understand what you mean." He sat back in his seat.

William listened intently, also wondering.

Prisse rocked the baby, anxious to hear the older man's reply.

"Is it a secret the two of you share, or what?" Brooke drawled.

"A secret? No, not really. It all goes back to that bear story that people talk about."

"Is it really true?" Brooke's smile of anticipation lit up her face.

"Most certainly! However, there's more to the story than what you heard. You see, I had a son Barrett's age."

"Yes... Jonathan. Barrett mentioned him many times." Brooke blinked.

"They were the best of friends. Those boys did everything together. Every year at Thanksgiving, Jonathan and I, along with Barrett and his father, would go turkey hunting. We never shot any, but Barrett... well, he could hit a knothole in a barn at five hundred yards with his eyes closed."

Cornelius chuckled. "I have seen the best men in the world shoot, but I have never seen anyone quite like Barrett. Gifted with a sharp eye and a steady hand, he would hit that target precisely every time." His face beamed with astonishment.

He continued, "One particular day, we walked about four miles from home and set up camp. Time for the four of us to rough it."

Brooke giggled. "I just can't see you roughing it."

"Oh, I loved taking my son fishing and hunting. Barrett and Jonathan had just turned sixteen. My boy sprained his ankle stepping in a rabbit hole, so he stayed back at camp. We walked about twenty minutes and hit the top of a ridge. We could see the camp very clearly from where we were. I can still picture the vivid colors of the trees that fall."

After a thoughtful pause, Cornelius went on, "We continued hiking a bit. It was a quiet day and we could hear everything echo throughout the valley. However, we were not prepared to hear the deathly screams coming from camp. Barrett scurried up a tree to find out what was happening, and shouted, 'Bear in the camp.'" Cornelius took a deep breath. "I can only estimate, but it was over a half a mile as the crow flies... at least fourteen hundred yards away... an impossible shot. Especially sitting in a tree. I will never forget the sound of Barrett's rifle—his shot sounded like a cannon going off. The growling stopped, and then I heard Jonathan yell, 'You got 'em!' Sure enough, Barrett had shot the animal in the chest."

"So the story is true," Brooke commented, grinning with pride.

"Yes, it is."

"My husband saved your son's life."

"He did. Actually twice."

"Twice?"

"What I am going to tell you now, very few people know. It's something that we all have tried to forget. I was running frantically back to camp when I heard a young girl scream."

"A girl?"

"Yes. You see there was a little girl named Lanie... I believe she was about twelve. She had a hankering on both the boys and was out looking for them. When she walked into camp, she screamed, rousing the wounded bear. Normally the animal would have been dead, but in this case... well, the shot came from too far away. The animal was too big."

Cornelius stared into space. "When I arrived at camp, Jonathan lay on the ground, bleeding from where the bear had slashed his arm with his powerful claws. The girl was screaming and throwing rocks at the beast, trying to veer it away from my son. She saved my boy, but...." He swallowed hard and a tear came to his eye. "I felt helpless, paralyzed by fear, and I watched as the giant animal came at the girl. Finally, I raised my rifle and pulled the trigger... nothing... all I heard was a click. Suddenly, a shot rang out, hitting the beast in the head... killing it. I looked up and saw Barrett on the ridge, holding his rifle, some eight hundred yards away. His second shot did the animal in. However, Lanie was already dead... mauled by that ferocious beast. You know, Jonathan always felt guilty for not being able to defend her. So did I. And Barrett, well, he blamed himself for not killing the animal with the first shot."

Cornelius' face showed how moved he was as he recalled that fateful day. "Because of that experience, Barrett always taught his soldiers, if you are shooting to kill, aim for the head."

"Whatever happened to Jonathan?"

"He died of pneumonia two years later." Cornelius' eyes were wet.

The story touched Brooke's heart. In silence, she thought about the heartache her husband endured. She finally understood the strong bond between Barrett and Cornelius.

The horses whinnied as they pulled the coach up to the front of the upscale hotel.

A friendly bellhop assisted Brooke and the others out of the buggy.

"I will check us in and see if we have any telegrams," Cornelius stated.

"I have never been this far west before," Brooke said to the bellhop as he unloaded their bags.

Watching a paddleboat floating down the river, she commented, "So this is the famous Mississippi. Is it true it runs backwards?"

The man snickered, "It happened in 1812. We had an earthquake south of here and the ground shifted. The river ran backwards and caused large waterfalls. I heard it was a remarkable sight. The Mighty Miss has a mind of her own, goes wherever she wants."

Cornelius came out of the hotel, and eagerly strode over to Brooke waving a paper.

"What's it say?" she asked excitedly.

"It's a wire from my office, from Barrett. They received it four days ago from Vicksburg, Mississippi and forwarded it here."

"Hurry and read it!"

Alive. Well. Coming home. S.S. Sultana.

Brooke could not speak; tears welled in her eyes.

She took her baby from Prisse and kissed him on the cheek. "Son, you're finally going to meet Daddy. He's coming home!"

"Talkin' 'bout your husband, Ma'am?" the bellhop asked.

"Oh, yes. He's just been released from a Southern prison camp." She shifted her gaze back to the river.

"Heard they're comin' here on steamboats. The men that do not get off in Cairo, will be arrivin' here in two or three days."

"Oh, I can't wait to see him," Brooke squealed.

The joyful moment was interrupted when a messenger boy bumped into Cornelius. "Whoa! Where are you going in such a hurry, young man?" he chided him.

"I have to deliver these telegraphs."

"Must be very important," Hall stated, half-smiling.

"Yes, sir, it is. A steamboat sunk in Memphis."

The boy rushed into the lobby of the hotel where he handed a wire to the attendant at the desk. Then he ran out quickly, heading to his next destination.

Cornelius hurried to the front desk, Brooke followed close behind. "What does that wire say?" he asked.

The attendant read the paper aloud, *Overloaded Sultana sinks north of Memphis. Heavy casualties.*

Brooke could barely speak, but managed to whisper, "Oh no... Barrett."

Cornelius' voice took on urgency as he spoke to the attendant, "We need to get to Memphis fast. How do we do that, sir?"

"Peterson... Ansell Peterson can take you. When do you want to leave?"

"Immediately."

The clerk spoke directly to the bellhop. "Troy, go and fetch Ansell. Tell him he has a job... quickly!"

As word of the horrible maritime disaster spread, many other worried families rushed to Memphis to discover the fate of their loved ones.

Chapter Forty-Five

April 29, 1865
Banks of the Mississippi

The bodies of the soldiers from the *Sultana* lined the banks of the Mississippi, near Memphis.

A solemn Brooke carefully stepped over one body after another, tears staining her face. She looked stunning in a flowing white dress. Jet-black hair tastefully tucked under her lace-trimmed white bonnet accented her angelic appearance.

Time-after-time William and Cornelius pulled back a sheet to see if the corpse was recognizable to them. The Spanish beauty breathed a sigh of relief when they shook their heads signifying it wasn't her husband. Yet, sadness overwhelmed Brooke knowing someone, somewhere, would be waiting for a husband, father, son, or brother to come home... and he wouldn't be returning.

Their search had begun on a barge that housed hundreds of dead from the recent maritime disaster. Even though she worked at Elmira and saw much death and suffering, it never became any easier. Yet, nothing could compare to the heart-wrenching search for her own husband.

Each victim was a unique individual, yet the faces had certain similar characteristics—rough beard, boney cheeks, and bulging eyes. She was beginning to wonder if she would recognize her love at all.

A young man nearby became physically ill while searching for his father. The sight of the *Sultana* fatalities, some burned beyond recognition, was too much for him. Finally, he had to give up, and walk away without recovering his beloved father's body.

Brooke needed to be certain. She whispered a prayer: *Lord, if my husband is here, please help us find him.*

The gruesome search dragged on hour after hour, body after body.

Dozens of other people were on a similar mission.

One time in particular, William pulled the sheet down to look at the remains of a soldier. A nearby scream startled them. Brooke turned to see a woman staring at the body. William stepped aside, and the woman ran over and fell next to the corpse. A handsome young man knelt beside her and put his arm around her. Then he looked at the dead man and nodded his head. They had found their missing loved one.

Brooke's stunned eyes caught the man's pained look. He walked over to her and explained, "That is her husband... my stepfather."

"He looks much too old to be fighting in a war," Brooke stated.

He was. I was supposed to be in the Union Army, but he insisted on taking my place. That should be me lying there," his voice cracked. "He wanted me to finish my schooling, make something of myself."

"Did you?" her eyebrows raised.

"Yes. I am going to medical school. I plan on being a doctor."

"Then, you will honor his death with your life."

"I will," he said, grateful for the words of wisdom she had conveyed to him. "What is your name?" he asked.

"Brooke... Brooke von Weber."

A strange look spread across his face. "You're not related to the Hymnist, are you?"

"Yes, he is my husband. I have not heard from him, so I fear the worst. I believe he was aboard the *Sultana*." Her voice broke, "I hope we can at least find his body."

"My father... stepfather, wrote me a letter from Andersonville. Father Whelan, a priest at the prison, sent it to me. My stepfather told me how bad it was there. His only treasured times were when he would hear piano music coming from outside the prison wall. It was not like saloon music, it sounded like a concert pianist... playing hymns of praise. He kept trying to find out who it was and finally the priest told him that it was the Hymnist."

"You must understand my father was not a religious man, at least, not when I was a boy. He had no idea who the Hymnist was. I did, of course, and so did my mother. I pray that my stepfather made peace with God because of your husband's music."

Brooke wiped a tear. "Thank you for the kind words."

She eyed William and Cornelius, who were still looking for Barrett. Then, her eyes turned to the distraught wife. "I am sorry for your loss."

"Yes, but at least now that we know he is dead, we can take him home and give him a proper burial. His grandchildren and their children will always know that their Grandpa fought bravely in the war and died coming home to them. That is better than never knowing what happened to him."

The young man glanced back at the hundreds of bodies. "I pray you can find your husband. His music has touched the hearts of so many people, like my stepfather." He paused, thinking about the letter. "Funny thing."

"What is funny?" she asked with wide eyes, wondering about humor in the midst of so much despair.

"I wonder if your husband realized when he was playing that piano at Andersonville that he was probably playing to the largest audience anyone has ever played to. I heard there were over thirty thousand men there. An audience of thirty thousand, that is amazing!"

She smiled, "That is amazing."

Brooke noticed a tall figure dressed in dark clothes walking their direction. She gave an inquisitive look. *That looks like death walking toward us.*

The young man took her hand and kissed it. "God be with you and may He answer your prayer the way you desire." He glanced at his mother. "I best be comforting her."

Brooke watched him kneel next to his mother and put his arm around her tenderly. Together they wept, memories crowding their minds.

Brooke's heart ached for them. *Father, grant them Your peace.*

The wind suddenly changed direction and the smell of decaying bodies became overwhelming. Looking around, she noticed that Cornelius and William were now some distance away. *I had better catch up to them. New thoughts bombarded her. Is this effort futile? Maybe we should stop looking, perhaps it is better to let his memory live. Seeing his decaying corpse may end up to be a nightmare.*

With the wind blowing in her face, and her mind occupied by what the young man's stepfather did for him, she did not hear the stranger dressed in dark clothes coming up behind her. His voice startled her, "Woman, why do you seek the living among the dead?"

She turned slowly to see where the familiar voice came from. Her heart beat faster. The tall dark figure she had seen wandering only minutes before stood directly in the path of the setting sun. She could not see who it was, but she hoped. Oh, how she hoped! The mysterious person stepped out of the sun's rays and revealed himself to her. A dam of tears broke, coursing down her cheeks. Standing before her, only a few feet away, was the love of her life—her precious Barrett.

Unable to speak, she slowly removed her bonnet, her black hair falling down around her shoulders. Brooke rushed to him, threw her arms around him, and sobbed uncontrollably.

Barrett held her head tight to his chest and kissed her long hair, tears flooding his eyes, also.

For a span of several moments, it was only them.

Cornelius looked up, disbelief clouding his face. He pointed to the reunited couple. "William, look!"

The black man was about to uncover another body when he saw Brooke hugging a tall, thin man. "Well, I be. Massa Barrett is that you?" He whispered, "Oh, Lord, can it be?"

Holding his wife close, Barrett took a long, deep breath. "Oh, how I have missed your soft touch!"

Still unable to speak, she clung to her long-lost husband, never wanting to let go.

He barely noticed the pain from his injured ribs or his head wound.

Finally, freeing his right arm, Barrett pulled Cornelius into a welcoming hug.

"Good to see you, son," Cornelius stated with misty eyes.

"You don't know how relieved I am seeing all of you."

When Barrett shifted his attention to William, his faithful employee extended his hand. The Hymnist readily grabbed it, smiling, "Nice handshake."

William returned a wide smile. "Massa Barrett, we were afraid you were dead!"

"I didn't think I was going to make it." He paused, trying to frame his thoughts. "I remember what sounded like an explosion on the boat, and being forced into the railing in front of me. I vaguely recall being in the water holding a baby."

"A baby?" Brooke repeated, shocked.

"Yes. Next thing I knew, I woke up in a small fishing shack. One of the locals had pulled me from the river, unconscious."

Brooke looked heavenward, smiling.

She took her husband's hand and led him back to the carriage that would take them to the hotel where Prisse and Little von Weber were waiting. On the way, Brooke thought of ways to tell her husband that he was a father, but decided to wait and introduce him to his son in person.

Barrett looked at Cornelius, "So you received my telegraph?"

"Not until we arrived in St. Louis."

"St. Louis?"

Cornelius added, "Yes, we heard that the Andersonville prisoners had been released and were headed to St. Louis."

"How did you know I was in Andersonville?"

"Met an old friend of yours... Corporal Shea," Brooke squeezed her husband's hand.

"Corporal Shea?"

"Yes, he became a prisoner at the place I was working."

"He was a prisoner? Where were you working?" Barrett questioned, confused.

"I was a nurse at the Confederate Prison camp in Elmira, New York."

"Elmira... the old military compound. I trained some soldiers up there. What are the odds that Shea would be a prisoner at the same camp where you worked? I trust he is well."

"Very much so. He told us all about you and what you were doing in Andersonville."

"It's a small world," Barrett grinned.

Brooke's face saddened. "You heard about President Lincoln?"

"Yes, I did. Tragic day for America." He looked out the window.

After a moment, Barrett sighed. "Brooke, I need to tell you about Rory."

"You mean what a scoundrel he turned out to be?"

"That and also, well, I managed to get to Annalise last summer." He took both of Brooke's hands and stared into her eyes.

"You did? How is Father?" she asked, excitedly.

"He was tired and worn out, but thankful to be alive. Brooke, Rory... Rory is dead."

She did not respond, never asked how it happened.

Brooke hesitated and then looked directly into Barrett's deep blue eyes. Her voice cracked with emotion, "So is Samuel... he was killed at Gettysburg. Charles was captured... he spent two years as a prisoner."

"Is he still alive? Has Charles been released?"

"Yes, he is alive, and I heard he was supposed to be released." Brooke continued, "My love, what about Annalise? Has it been spared?"

Barrett's creases in his forehead showed his distress. "It was untouched in July. However, Sherman's forces were marching that direction, and he was destroying everything. I heard that Atlanta and Savannah are in ruins. Darling, Annalise was right in his path! I am afraid your home is rubble by now. I pray that your father survived." He lowered his head.

Tears flowed as she leaned her head on his shoulder. "What now?" Brooke asked, knowing their future was uncertain.

"I'm not sure. I want to get as far away from this horror as possible."

"Germany?"

"That is what I was thinking."

"Before we leave, could we find out how my father is?"

"Yes, we can certainly do that. We might be able to catch a ship going to Germany from Charleston or Savannah, depending how bad the ports were destroyed."

When the coach pulled up in front of the hotel, Prisse noticed Barrett with them. She hurried to them, smiling, and handed the baby to Brooke.

Looking into her husband's eyes, Brooke announced, "My love, I proudly introduce you to your son, our son, Nathan. I hope you do not mind, but I had to give him a name, so I named him after one of your heroes... Nathan Hale."

Stunned, Barrett stared at his son who was wrapped in white linen. He carefully took him from his wife's arms and gently kissed his cheek. As he pulled the baby close, tears began to flow. "God has been good to me. He has blessed me... protected me." He looked heavenward. *Thank you, Lord. You have made me the happiest man in the world!*

Chapter Forty-Six

September 1865
Annalise

The cooler than average temperatures brought an early fall to the Northeast. In late September, the von Weber family left their home in New Haven, Connecticut. William, Prisse, Titus, and even Annapurna accompanied them on their trek to Annalise.

A cloud of unrest hung over the land. There were lingering armies in the South that had not surrendered. Many soldiers headed west to start a new life.

The rebuilding of the railroad had begun, so they took the train as far south as they could. Then, the journey continued in a less comfortable mode of transportation—a carriage.

The devastation saddened them as they passed through the once-beautiful Shenandoah Valley, known as the breadbasket of the South. Now, it was nothing but a wasteland.

Brooke fought back tears as she witnessed the desolation in Georgia. The beautiful homes, estates, even the forests, had been laid to rubble. Many people sought shelter in tents, or simple sheds made out of burnt wood. It was worse than she ever imagined. Her heart ached.

The couple was silent, each deep in private thought as they watched families plod along the busy road searching for a place to start life over.

Brooke's mind reeled with disturbing thoughts. *Those poor people! All they have left is what they can carry. Their homes and farms are gone—wiped out! They had nothing to do with causing the war, yet their lives were destroyed. It seems no family has been unscathed by the ugliness of war.* She thought of her own family. *Will there be anyone left?* She wiped a single tear.

Barrett uttered a silent prayer asking God to prepare them for what was ahead. *God give us the strength to deal with what we are about to face.*

Neither knew what they would find when they reached Annalise, they were both fearful.

Brooke had no idea if her father was alive, and she had not heard from Charles. Her heart raced as the carriage drew closer to Annalise.

Nearing the family cemetery, still in silence, she reached for Barrett's hand.

When the carriage came to a stop, the couple sat quietly for a few minutes, trying to muster the strength they needed. With heavy hearts, they proceeded on foot to the old burial ground.

Brooke started trembling when she noticed several new tombstones. Nausea came over her as she walked slowly to the first mound of fresh dirt. She wasn't sure she had the strength to look at the names on the markers.

Barrett held her quivering hand.

She stood in front of the first tombstone, paralyzed with fear of the unknown, eyes closed. After a deep breath, she forced her eyes open, heart pounding in her chest. The tombstone's inscription only had the name— *Rory Fortner.* Her heart sank as she recalled what Barrett told her about her youngest, rebellious brother.

She cautiously moved down the line of graves, fighting to stay in control of her emotions.

Samuel Fortner... died in battle-1863
Reba Fortner... wife of Samuel-1864
Beatrice Fortner... daughter of Samuel and Reba-1864
Timothy Fortner... son of Samuel and Reba-1864

She fought back a sob as she wrapped her arms around Barrett. "Samuel's entire family has died. All of them gone. I can't look anymore. Is Father's grave here?"

Barrett scanned the small cemetery. "No, my love, I don't see any more new graves."

A sigh of relief came to her. Now she was ready to continue their journey.

Brooke was as prepared as she could be to view her childhood home. She resolved herself to the possibility that the house would be ruble, the barns, and manufacturing plant burned to the ground.

When they came up the last hill, overlooking the valley below, Brooke gasped, "I can't believe it, Annalise is still here. It is not as green and

colorful as it once was, but the house and outbuildings are still intact!"
Tears of relief streamed down her face.

Approaching the house, she saw a number of workers tending to what
few crops remained.

One of them glanced up and shouted, "It's Miss Brooke... she come
home! Praise be!"

All the workers stopped what they were doing and rushed toward them.

"William, stop here... I want to greet them," Brooke shrieked.

Barrett stepped out and helped his wife to the ground. "Prisse, please
take care of Nathan."

"Yes, Massa Barrett."

Brooke slowly spun around, her eyes fixed on her home. After a brief
time, she bent down and touched the dirt. "Annalise is still here. My home
has been spared! God has answered our prayers!"

By then the excited workers had surrounded them, all offering
welcoming hugs. "Miss Brooke and Massa Barrett, it is good to see ya,"
one excitedly yelled.

"Well I be... there William and Prisse, too," another added.

Brooke glanced up and saw two men rushing out of the house.

"Daddy! Charles!" she cried, running to them.

Alton bounded down the steps of the porch and embraced his daughter.

Barrett smiled, watching the reunion. *Thank you, Lord! Thank you!*

"Charles, it's good to see you." Barrett extended his hand to his
brother-in-law.

"It's sure nice to have you home." Then, much to Barrett's surprise,
Charles wrapped his arms around him in a genuine hug.

When the carriage caught up to the joyful family, Prisse stepped out,
holding a squirming Nathan. Smiling, she quickly handed the baby to
Brooke.

"Father, here is your new grandson, Nathan." She placed him in her
father's arms.

It took a moment until Alton could speak. Finally, he got out the words,
"The past few years, I have buried so much family. Now, we can start
living again. God is good!"

The cheerful homecoming continued; family and friends caught up on
the happenings of the last five years.

"Father, I need to know something." Brooke looked directly into his
eyes. "Just about everything else in this state was destroyed. Why was
Annalise spared?"

"Well, my daughter, let's all sit on the porch because I have a wild tale
to tell you. Sylvia, will you get everyone some of your orange tea?"

"Yes, suh, Massa Alton. Brennan, I need your help."

"I is comin. My word, Sylvia, you treat me like a slave."

The group roared with laughter.

There was sufficient seating on the large porch and everyone hurried to get comfortable. A few children perched themselves on the wooden railing. Even the dog, Arminius, sprawled out by his master's feet.

Alton cleared his throat. "When I last saw Barrett…." Alton looked at his son-in-law. "Son, I never expected to see you again. I didn't know what happened to you. Right after you left that day, a company of Southern soldiers came by to get Rory. I was despondent at that time. If it wasn't for Sylvia and Brennan, and the rest of you… well, I don't know what would have happened."

Alton continued. "Getting back to the story… I told them they were too late, Rory had already left. Then they gave me the devastating news about Samuel. To make matters worse, they suspected that Charles might also be a war casualty. The soldiers were on their way to Savannah to prepare for Sherman and his forces. They said that if Sherman came to Savannah, he would hit a brick wall." Alton began to laugh. "Some brick wall!"

Alton shifted his eyes past everyone, staring in the distance, obviously reliving the past. "Sherman and his troops were marching through the South leaving everything in shambles, and there was nothing and no one who could stop him. Several times in November and December, different people came and warned us to pack up and get out while we could… Sherman was coming! I was not budging. You know how stubborn I can be—I refused to leave. This was my home, and I was not going to be forced out by thugs. Finally, right before Christmas, George here…." Alton messed the hair of one of the black children sitting next to him, making the lad giggle. "This young man has been my spy. He ran up to me one morning and told me there were hundreds of Bluecoats on horseback heading toward Annalise."

He paused. "So I took my rocker from inside the house and set it right here on the porch. If I was going to die, I was going to do so in the comfort of my old chair with my trusted dog by my side. I left my shotgun inside though. Just sat here, drinking a glass of orange tea, and waited."

Alton began his story.

December 1864

Three of Sherman's soldiers sat on horseback at the top of the ridge, surveying the Fortner Mansion.

"Good for the pickin', I reckon," the corporal shot an evil grin. "Bet there's plenty of loot down there."

"We don't have time, not with Uncle Billy breathing down our necks," a man with sergeant's stripes retorted. "Remember... we have our orders."

"What General Sherman don't know won't hurt him," the corporal let out a huff of breath.

The trio observed the flurry of dozens of black people surrounding the house, holding what appeared to be weapons.

The sergeant snickered, "Well... well... well, what do we have here?"

"Are them thar rifles?" the third rider asked.

Watching through a spyglass, the corporal replied, "Looks like we are about to see a rebellion, Smitty! The slaves have armed themselves with pitchforks and shovels. Looks like their master is about to get some of his own medicine," he laughed scathingly, handing the spyglass to the sergeant.

Meanwhile, Brennan and Sylvia strutted over to take their stand next to Alton on the porch.

"They not hurt Annalise, boss, we not let 'em... this be our home, too." Brennan patted Alton on his shoulder.

Arminius stood on the porch watching the riders, teeth bared, growling.

"I'm going to go give Sherman's men what for." George picked up a handful of rocks and ran towards the men. A couple of his friends followed.

"George, be careful," Alton warned.

"Don't worry 'bout me. I be all right." George waved.

Alton watched as the boys darted up the hill.

When the youngsters reached the riders, George raised his arm in a threatening manner. "This is private property, turn 'round and leave. Now!"

The horsemen looked at George, and then at each other, chuckling.

Undeterred, George shouted, "If you try and touch our home, you have to get through us, and my momma and papa, and all our friends."

The irritated corporal, spoke, "Got a real live one here! Hey, Smitty, want to show him what for?"

"You boys are a nuisance." Smitty removed his gun from the holster, pointing it at George and his friends.

Alton noticed the man pull his gun. "Brennan, get ready to get my shotgun. If they shoot George or his buddies, they will have a real battle on their hands."

"Yes, suh, boss."

Looking through the spyglass, the sergeant chided his men, "You two boneheads... I thought you said they were going to rebel. Looks to me like they are defending the place." He shook his head.

"With pitch forks? You got to be kidding," the corporal stated.

Just then, another rider on a white horse rode up to the soldiers and barked a command, "Put that pistol away. We are not going to shoot any children."

"He is threatening us, sir," Smitty griped.

"We're the ones doing the threatening. Now put that pistol away, or I will put you in chains. I'm not going to have a bloodbath here."

The soldier reluctantly shoved his gun in its holster, keeping his eyes on the boys the entire time.

The man on the white horse dismounted and stood in front of the young lads. "Good morning, boys."

"What you want here, mister," George inquired.

"You know who I am?"

"No, suh, but don't much care. Just know if you come to burn this place, you have to go through us," George's voice cracked.

"See, sir, the boys are crazy," the corporal insisted.

"Silence! I will take care of this." He redirected his attention to George. "What's your name, son?"

The boy hesitated, but finally stated, "My name's George, suh."

"Well, George, I'm General Sherman. Whose place is this?"

"Massa Alton Fortner," George responded.

"Not sure who that is... an important man I bet."

"His daughter is married to Barrett von Weber, and when Massa Barrett get hold of you, he will tan your hide. He's the best fighter and shooter in the world," George boasted.

"Von Weber, you say?" Sherman's tone changed. He looked down at the mansion. "Who is that sitting in the rocker?"

"That be Massa Alton." George mustered a small grin.

Sherman stared into the valley where dozens of men, women, and children surrounded the large home. Each of them was holding a pitchfork, axe, shovel, or whatever they could get their hands on. "I would like to talk with your master... lead the way."

The general mounted his horse. "Sergeant, come with me, the rest of you stay put. And, keep your guns holstered. Let's end this peacefully."

Sherman and the sergeant followed the boys down the hill, toward the house.

The boys excitedly ran to the porch and stood next to Alton.

George blurted, "The general wants to talk with you, suh."

"He does, does he?" Calmly, Alton looked at George. "Think they want to surrender?"

George smiled.

Sherman and the sergeant halted their horses at the porch.

The protective employees, holding their makeshift weapons, immediately flocked around the intruders.

A small grin came to Sherman's face. The general dismounted, took his hat off, and wiped the sweat from his brow with his sleeve. Then he hit his hat on his legs, knocking the Georgia dust from his uniform. He looked up, put his hat back on, and straightened it, taking an inordinate amount of time. Slowly, he walked up the porch steps. The well-known general made his way to the chair next to Alton.

"May I?" Sherman said, pointing to the chair.

"Suit yourself." Alton shot back, still rocking.

The general sat down.

Arminius sat directly in front of the general, never taking his eyes off him, growling every so often.

"Should I shoot the dog, sir?" the sergeant said, fingering his gun.

"You shoot my dog and you will wish you had been killed in battle." Alton's eyebrows hunched together.

Sherman noticed a half dozen people step closer to the soldier on horseback. "Stand down, Sergeant. That's an order."

"Yes, sir." He slowly took his hand off the revolver.

Facing Alton, the general stated, "Good morning, sir. My name is General William Sherman."

"I know who you are... your reputation has preceded you. Have you come to kill me and burn my home to the ground?" Alton droned, peering straight ahead, not making eye contact with the general.

"I haven't come to kill you. You could leave, just walk away."

"So could you," Alton responded matter-of-factly.

Sherman grinned. "Yes, I could." He looked into the open door of the large home. "Is anyone else here?"

"You mean any women, so your men can rape them? I have heard of your exploits." Alton finally scrutinized the general.

"Not mine, but I do know some of my men are guilty of such things."

"Have they been dealt with?"

Sherman looked away.

"I suspected as much. Turned your head the other direction, didn't you?"

Not answering the question, Sherman eyed the large dog sitting in front of him. He shifted his attention to the three boys, each holding a number of rocks, arms positioned to throw them, if need be. "George here told me that Barrett von Weber is your son-in-law. Is that true?"

"Yes, sir, he is. Alton Fortner is my name."

"Do you have any weapons here, sir?"

"Only what the workers carry. Got a shotgun in the house, but Confederate soldiers took everything else... weapons, horses, saddles... everything. Said my country needed them. As if I didn't!"

Sherman peered around. "All I see are workers carrying pitchforks and shovels."

"Those are their weapons. Ever see a man's head after it has been split open with a shovel?"

"No, sir, I have not, but I suspect it don't look pretty." Sherman hesitated. "What do you do here, sir? Looks like a manufacturing plant of some type."

"At one time, I made clothing. Now I just sit here on this porch and drink tea... and wait."

"Wait for what?"

"Wait for my family to come home. Oh, my, where are my manners? Would you care for a cup of the best tea in the South?"

"As a matter of fact, I would love to wash the dust from my throat."

Alton raised his glass. "Sylvia, pour the man a drink. Let us show him some Southern hospitality."

The stern black woman filled a glass and handed it to the general, staring him down the entire time.

Sherman smiled, but Sylvia's look of disapproval remained. "Thank you." He took a sip. "This is quite the best tea I have ever tasted." He shifted his attention to Sylvia.

Alton watched every move the general made. "Thank you, but don't bother asking for the recipe because Sylvia will never give it to you. I've been asking for years. So have others."

A small grin crossed the general's face. "What family members are you waiting for?"

Alton sighed. "Before the war, I had three sons and a daughter, two daughters-in-law, one-son-in-law, and five grandchildren."

"And now?"

"Now?" Alton pointed up the hill. "Did you notice the cemetery up yonder?"

"Yes, sir, I remember passing it."

"I have buried two sons who were killed in the war. My other son is... well, I do not know if he is alive or not. My daughter, I pray she is safe. One of my daughters-in-law and three of my grandchildren died of typhoid last spring... hit us with a vengeance. My other daughter-in-law went crazy when she heard her husband was missing and presumed dead. She walked out the door one morning and has never been seen since. And my son-in-law, only God knows if he survived the war."

The general took a deep breath, "Sir, I am sorry for your loss." Sherman took a sip of tea and continued, "I have a dilemma here. I am supposed to destroy your business and home."

"Good luck with that, there is no business left, and why would you want to destroy my home? Why would you want to destroy Annalise?"

"Annalise?" he questioned.

"We Southerners give our homes names. We named this place Annalise after my grandfather's youngest daughter."

"I see. Well, Mr. Fortner, it is war. That is all I can say. We all know war is hell." Sherman's voice faded away.

"Destroying a person's home is not war, it's harassment, barbaric, and unethical. And it's not just my home, it's their home." Alton pointed to the dozens of black people, still clutching their makeshift weapons.

"But they are free... Lincoln freed them." He looked directly at Brennan. "Do you know you are free?"

"We always been free, suh." Massa Fortner bought all of us and set us free. He good man. Gave us all jobs—with pay, too. He built us homes, school, and a church. We Christians. We sing Massa von Weber's songs in our church."

The general looked around. "Then, why are you still here?"

"Still here?" Brennan looked at the general, confused. "I just told you suh, this our home. This our children's home. Where we work, go to school, and church. Why we want to leave our home? Why you want to destroy our home?"

"I have orders to." His answer was swift.

Brennan stepped back and raised his shovel.

The sergeant drew his revolver.

Sherman raised his hand. "Stop! Put that gun away, soldier!"

The sergeant holstered his pistol, but kept his hand close.

"You try, suh, and we fight. We protect our home with our lives," Brennan said without backing down.

General Sherman took his hat off, wiped more sweat from his brow, and took another swig of tea.

"Certainly is good tea. You know if my wife ever found out that I burned down the Hymnist's home, let's just say, this war would be nothing compared to her wrath." He looked at his empty glass. "Sylvia, I'll make you a deal. You give me the recipe for your tea, and I will pass by Annalise. Not a stone will be touched on this property."

Sylvia glared at him and then turned to Alton. Without saying a word, she disappeared. A minute later, she returned with a piece of paper. "The secret is in the orange peel." She handed the paper to the general.

General Sherman looked at the scribbling on the paper, smiling. He folded the paper and tucked it in his coat pocket. "Thank you, ma'am." He stood and put his hat on. Reaching his hand out to Alton, he said, "Mr. Fortner, any word on your son-in-law? Have you seen him?"

"Why would you ask that, sir?" Alton said, shaking the well-known general's hand.

"I know he came south looking for Lee's army."

"Did he find it?" Alton blinked.

"I heard he did. I believe he saved many lives... both Blue and Graycoats."

"That sounds like my son-in-law."

"Thanks for the tea." Sherman shifted his attention to Sylvia. "And, ma'am, thank you for the recipe. My wife will be grateful. And Brennan… it is Brennan, right?"

"Yes, suh." He still had his shovel raised over his head.

"You can put down the shovel. There will be no battle here. Last thing I want to do is destroy your home."

Brennan lowered his shovel and stepped back.

"Good day." Sherman tipped his hat, walked down the stairs, and grabbed the reins of his horse.

Alton walked to the railing. "General?"

"Yes, sir."

"The war is over, is it not?"

"Yes, sir, it is. Problem is the South will not accept it. We have a long ways to go."

The famous general mounted his horse and tipped his hat one more time. He rode to the top of the hill and motioned for his men to turn around and leave.

The crowd sat motionless, entranced by the story.

A big smile came to Alton's face. "General William Sherman kept his word—not a single stone was overturned at Annalise."

When he was finished, Brooke was the first to speak. "Oh, Daddy, I am so grateful that Annalise was spared." She hugged him.

"I thank the Lord for what happened that day." Alton continued, "Annalise was spared because of the good people that work here. And because of you, Barrett." He thought a moment and then added, "Son, how do you know General Sherman?"

"I saw him only once. He was present when General Grant asked me to find Lee's army. He only said a couple words to me. As I was leaving, he nodded his head and said, 'Godspeed, son.'"

"You have met General Grant?" Alton's eyes widened.

"Yes, sir, I did."

"What kind of man is he?" Charles chimed in.

"A man who knew what he was doing. History will decide what kind of leader he really was. I cannot answer it objectively."

"Enough talk. Let's go celebrate your homecoming with a big family dinner." Alton's smile covered his face.

The couple stayed several weeks at Annalise, renewing their relationships with family and friends.

Alton was especially thankful to spend time with his grandson, Nathan.

One cool fall morning Brooke and Barrett rode their horses to Annalise's Lair.

Sitting by the waterfall, Barrett reached for his wife's hand, his expression solemn. "Honey, I must leave for a week or so."

"Why?"

"Something I must do… visit an old friend."

"Will you be able to find him?"

"I hope so."

"Then you must go." Brooke realized her husband had unfinished business—the result of his military service. She would not stand in his way.

The next morning before sunrise, Titus stood in front of the mansion, holding the reins of Annapurna. The impressive stallion was saddled, ready to go.

Barrett bounded out the front door.

Brennan walked up to him carrying a heavy object wrapped in a white cloth. "Here it is, Massa Barrett... just like you wanted. I carved it myself!" Barrett helped Brennan place the object carefully into the leather bag strapped behind the saddle.

"Thank you, sir," the worker's eyes showed his sincerity.

"For what?"

The black man patted the object. "For taking the time to do this."

"It's the least I can do... he saved my life."

Barrett mounted Annapurna and looked down sadly at his wife and son. They had already said their private goodbyes. He hated to leave them, but knew he had to take care of his unfinished business. He smiled, tipped his hat, and sped off.

"Come back to us, my love," Brooke whispered, caressing her baby's head and watching until her husband was out of sight.

Barrett had a vague recollection of how to get to his destination, but the landscape looked different because of the vast destruction. Since Sherman's army had destroyed everything in sight, no longer were trees or buildings indicators of direction.

He hoped the little he remembered about the area would be enough.

Finally, he stopped in a small town, which looked familiar.

He noticed three teenage boys kicking a can in the street. "Hello, boys! What are your names?"

"The oldest boy responded, "I'm Tommy. These are my brothers—Johnny and Kenny."

"Good to meet you." Barrett tipped his hat.

"That's a beautiful horse, mister. Are you a general, or something?" Tommy asked.

"No, just a man looking for information."

"Like what?" Tommy's eyes widened.

Barrett took a coin from his pocket and flipped it to him. "I am looking for a certain place."

The boys' faces beamed when they saw the gold coin. "Yes, sir, what place you looking for?"

I am looking for a gigantic oak tree, near a creek. If I recall there was a grove of Sycamore trees next to the water. It looked like a perfect place for a swimming hole."

"You lookin' for a place to swim, mister?" Johnny asked.

The older lad jabbed him in the side with his elbow.

"Ouch! What you do that for, Tommy?"

"I'm oldest, I ask the questions," Tommy snarled. "Was it the biggest tree in the forest?" he asked.

Barrett nodded. "Seemed like it at the time."

Tommy turned to his brothers. "Bet that's the tree by our swimmin' hole."

"Yup." They all agreed.

"That there swimmin' hole is our big secret. What do we get if we show you?" Tommy probed.

"I'll tell you what, how about I give a gold piece to each of you?"

"For each of us?" Tommy asked, his excitement evident.

"Yes, each of you."

"That's a lot of money, mister. What you wanna go there for?" Johnny asked.

"Shut up, Johnny." Tommy pushed his brother.

"Well, it just seems strange to be paid to show a man a tree. Reckon there may be some buried treasure by it," Johnny whispered to his siblings.

"He just wants us to show him the tree." Kenny, the boy with bright red hair and a face full of freckles, added.

"We'll show you, mister," Tommy stated. "Just follow us... and try to keep up."

Barrett smiled. "I will try my best."

They took off running.

Barrett followed on horseback, easily matching the speed of the lads.

Thirty minutes later, the boys stopped at the base of a large oak tree. A rope was attached to one of the sturdy branches that hung over the water.

"Is this the place, mister?" Tommy asked.

Barrett looked around, smiling. "This is the place."

Von Weber reached in his pocket and flipped each of the boys a small gold coin. "Thank you, fellows."

Their mouths dropped when they caught their coins. "Thank you, mister!"

"You don't have any buried treasure around here, do you?" Johnny asked.

"Shut up, Johnny. You want to get us killed or something?" Tommy whispered to Johnny, loud enough that Barrett overheard it and grinned.

The lads turned and ran off, but not before Johnny shouted, "If you need anything else, you know where to find us."

Barrett waved. "I'll remember that."

The boys ran off a short distance. Once safely hidden in the forest, Johnny turned around and peeked through some trees.

"Johnny, what are you doing?" Tommy whispered.

"I want to see what that man is gonna do."

"Uh… I don't think this is a good idea," Kenny protested nervously.

"He might be digging up a bunch of gold coins," Johnny added. "Like these." He held up the coin the stranger had given him.

The boys quietly moved closer to Barrett, watching from the bushes.

The man knelt by the tree and lowered his head. They could not hear what he was saying, but they could see his lips moving.

"Looks like he's crazy," Johnny whispered.

"Shh!" Tommy warned, "He'll hear you!"

Barrett strode over to his horse and grabbed a shovel.

"Told you it's a buried treasure," Johnny boasted.

After a few minutes of digging, Barrett put the shovel down and walked over to his horse. He grabbed the object from the leather bag strapped to his saddle.

The boys could tell it was heavy when the stranger lifted it with both arms.

"It's a bag of gold," Johnny alleged, still watching

Barrett carried the item to the hole he had dug. Carefully, he put it on the ground and unwrapped it. He dropped it in the hole and patted dirt around it with the shovel. Von Weber stood, held his hat to his chest, and bowed his head. Then he looked at the sky and nodded. Not saying a word, he put on his hat, snapped to attention, and saluted.

The boys watched the stranger walk back to his horse and put the shovel in the saddlebag. Then he mounted his white stallion and rode off.

The brothers stayed hidden until the man was out of sight. Then they hurried over to where he had dug the hole.

"That man's crazy I tell you," Johnny insisted.

When the boys looked down, they realized they were standing on a grave, and jumped back.

"Someone's buried here," Johnny muttered.

"Right, Johnny. Some buried treasure! The man brought a tombstone with him." Tommy read the inscription:

Sgt. Jerry Roundtree
A trusted friend who died a free man
I Will Meet the Son at the End of My Journey

"What do you s'pose that means?" Kenny blinked.

"It means he's going to meet Jesus. What ya think it means?" Tommy answered sarcastically.

"I don't know. Sounds strange to me. How can you die a free man. Don't make no sense," Kenny admitted.

"Maybe not, but I do know that whoever that man is, he must be a real friend," Johnny added.

They glanced in the direction where Barrett rode off and then back at the grave. The brothers removed their hats.

"You know what? I think we should take care of this grave," Johnny stated.

"Yup. We need to plant some grass and flowers," Tommy concurred.

"That would be good," Kenny agreed.

Silence filled the air.

Johnny broke the quiet. "Do you think he was a Bluecoat or Graycoat?"

"What does it matter? He was an American," Tommy replied bluntly.

"Yep… and he was free," Johnny added.

Chapter Forty-Seven

Charleston, South Carolina
August 1868

The classy new steamship from Germany cruised into port at the Charleston Harbor early in the morning. The sun shone brightly, welcoming the passengers to America.

The port city was no longer in ruins. Buildings were being erected at a fast pace. The docks were being rebuilt to accommodate the large clipper ships, as well as the new steamers arriving from Europe. Most ships carried needed supplies, while passengers were the chief payload of others.

Alton and Charles Fortner waited eagerly to greet some special passengers aboard this particular steamer. Brooke, Barrett, and their three children—Nathan, Ludwig, and Amalia were returning from their three year stay in Germany.

Finally, the travelers began filing down the gangplank.

Alton beamed with joy when he saw his daughter step onto the shore. She wore a striking outfit—a tailored navy blue suit with a wide skirt that fluttered with every step she took. *For goodness sake, she's still the spitting image of her mother. Marriage and motherhood must agree with her.* She held the corner of her skirt up with one hand so she wouldn't trip, and cuddled a baby in her other arm.

Prisse was carrying Ludwig, who had recently turned two.

Barrett held the hand of their eldest son, Nathan, who was dressed in a suit and tie, just like his father.

"Brooke, my dear," Alton greeted his daughter with a long, welcoming hug.

"Barrett, it's good to see you." Alton peered down at the four-year-old standing next to his father. "And who is this fine-looking young man?"

"Nathan von Weber, sir." The young voice spoke loud and clear as he shook his grandfather's hand.

Alton beamed. "My, what a strong handshake!"

William and Prisse were standing in the background watching the reunion.

Turning to William, Alton added, "And William, my friend, you never seem to age."

"I sure feel like I do, Massa Alton." William grinned, white teeth gleaming.

The senior Fortner continued his greetings, "And Prisse, how are you?"

"Fine, suh."

"How was the trip?" Alton asked with arms stretched out to take the youngest member of the family.

"Long and tiring," Brooke said, handing the sleeping baby to him.

The proud grandfather gave Amalia a soft kiss on the forehead and stared for a long moment into the face of his granddaughter. "She is beautiful... like her mother."

Realizing it was past time to eat breakfast, Alton asked, "Are you hungry?"

"I'm famished. The food on the ship started off good, but by the end it was pretty tasteless." Brooke went on, "Daddy, I sure do miss good Southern cooking, especially Sylvia's fried chicken."

"That for sure, Miss Brooke. That for sure," Prisse agreed.

"Well, you will have to wait a bit longer for that fried chicken, but we can go get a hearty breakfast. I know of a fine establishment nearby. "

Walking into town, Barrett noticed new storefronts and businesses were thriving; the owners were hoping for a brighter future. "The city seems to be flourishing since the war."

"Yes. Charleston and Savannah have led the way in rebuilding the South. We have had plenty of problems. Many businessmen from the North came down and helped themselves to what little we had left. They charged us outrageous prices for goods and services."

"And Annalise?" Barrett asked.

"Still in operation. But, with the theft of my gold, and Confederate money being worthless... let's just say, I'm glad I saved so many greenbacks." Alton grinned.

Brooke joined in, "Daddy, you mean our textile business is back up and running?"

"Yes... we have a few contracts. The one that has really helped was a sizable contract from Europe." He turned to Barrett. "Son, I know that was because of you. Thank you."

"No thanks needed. We are family, anything I can do to help, I will. In fact, I brought a boatload of wine from the von Weber Winery. With the money we get from that sale, you can continue to rebuild the factory."

Alton paused. "I can never repay you for that, son."

"No need to, sir. Like I said, we are family."

They reached the place that Alton suggested, a new, family-owned restaurant. After a friendly greeting from the proprietor, they were seated at a large, quiet table in the corner.

After a lengthy conversation, getting caught up on the happenings of the last few years, and a tasty breakfast, Brooke asked Barrett, "Honey, would you mind taking care of the children for a while? I would like to do a little shopping."

"Sure, we will watch them. I am sure grandpa would love to spend more time with his grandchildren."

As Brooke wrapped her shawl around her shoulders, Barrett added, "Remember honey, we still have a thousand miles to travel. William and I do not want to carry a lot of extra merchandise." He smiled.

Brooke strolled down the sidewalks of Charleston, mostly window-shopping. She noticed a number of finely dressed matrons attended by their equally well-dressed spouses.

A large clock on a tower in the center of town sounded twelve bells, signifying that it was noon.

At the same time, a variety of unusual sounds echoed from a nearby store. Glancing up at the sign that hung above the door, she read aloud, "The Clock Shop."

She peered in the opened doorway and saw a wide array of clocks, each striking twelve o'clock in its distinctive way. "Oh, how lovely," Brooke whispered, noticing a couple cuckoo clocks with birds popping out of a door, making their appearance at the noon hour.

Her gaze shifted to a clock on the wall that had a carved ornate castle. She stepped into the cozy shop to get a closer look at the work of art that caught her attention. When the doors of the castle on the clock opened, colorful Bavarian dancers rotated around the balcony. *Oh, how beautiful! It's playing Beethoven's Ode to Joy.* Its workmanship, the intricate details of the castle, mesmerized her.

"Good afternoon, ma'am," a bearded man with a strong German accent greeted her. "I am sorry I kept you waiting, but we were about ready to close for lunch. May I help you?"

"Good afternoon, sir. I would like to get something special for my husband. He has always had an interest in Black Forest Clocks. This is one, isn't it?" she said, pointing to the masterpiece.

"Yes, ma'am, that is correct. Unfortunately, that clock is not for sale."

"That castle looks like one I have seen before." She looked at him with keen interest.

"It was a castle from the old country. I carved it from memory."

"You have a unique talent." She gave a warm smile of approval.

"May I show you another one you may like?"

"I don't want to keep you from lunch. Why don't I come back later?"

"My lunch can wait... a sale cannot." The German chuckled.

"In that case, please show me what you have."

"I believe you like the clocks with the figurines." He pointed to another one nearby.

"Oh, yes," she said, still smiling. "I do like that, but not as much as the one on the wall." She studied the clock he was trying to sell her. "You know, I am sure my husband would love it. But sir, we have a long way to travel. Can I get it wrapped and delivered before we leave town?"

"Of course. Where do you want it delivered?"

She looked out the front window and pointed down the street. "See that carriage in front of the restaurant."

"Yes."

"The gentleman feeding the horses is William. You can give it to him."

"I will see to it that it is wrapped carefully and is delivered. But ma'am, you didn't even ask the price." He smiled at her as he picked up a pen and paper.

"My husband has always told me if I like something, get it, and don't haggle over the price."

The German smiled. "And your name?"

"Mrs. von Weber."

Startled, the man stopped writing and looked up at her. "Von Weber? Any relation to Barrett von Weber?"

"Yes, I am his wife." Her eyes sparkled.

"You must be Brooke." He spoke with certainty, grinning broadly.

Bewildered, she asked, "How do you know that?" She stared at the German, noticing his eyes were watering.

Not saying another word, he walked over to the wall and took down the large clock that she had first admired. He brought it back, placed it on the counter in front of her, and began to wrap it carefully.

Confused by his actions, Brooke commented, "I thought you said that clock was not for sale, but you are wrapping it."

"It is not for sale. I made it for the man who saved my life. You said that castle looked familiar and it should... it is the von Weber castle in Germany."

A gigantic smile spread across her face. "Why it is. I knew it looked familiar." She laughed. "How do you know my husband?"

"During the war, I was captured by some Union troops. They were after stolen weapons they thought I had. They would have killed me if your husband had not showed up." He hesitated for a moment and looked at Brooke. "He never stopped talking about you."

"Of course, you must be Oscar the clockmaker. Barrett speaks of you often. In fact, while we were in Germany, he paid a visit to your kinfolk."

"He did?" A wide grin filled his face.

Just then, the door opened and Barrett entered, holding Nathan's hand.

Looking at Brooke, he announced, "There you are. We have been looking for you. When I saw this clock shop I wanted to look at all the...." Barrett stopped talking when he noticed the man behind the counter. "Oscar, is that you?"

"Yes, sir, it is."

Oscar greeted Barrett with a friendly hug.

"I can't believe it. After all these years, I never expected to see you again. It is such a big world," Barrett struggled to keep his emotions controlled.

Barrett faced Brooke. "This man saved my life."

"Do not believe a word he says. It is he who saved my life."

Turning to Barrett, the clockmaker asked, "Did you ever find the stolen rifles?"

"I did. Unfortunately, the outcome was not what I wanted."

"Did you ever catch up to the leader? What was his name... Gibbons?"

"No, I never have. However, I will never give up looking—until I find him."

Barrett paused. "I notice that your English has improved."

"It took a while, but I finally put the effort into learning not only to speak in my new language, but to read and write it, too."

"That's great! Is your business a success?" Barrett asked, glancing around at the display of clocks.

"Yes, it is. I ship clocks all over the country. I have my three boys helping me. Still very young, but their small hands can do much that mine cannot."

The friends shared highlights of the last four years.

Barrett tried to pay for the clock, but Oscar insisted it was a gift.

Von Weber thanked him and they were on their way.

Brooke was unable to contain her excitement when she saw Annalise for the first time in over three years.

Holding her new baby, she spoke to her. "Amalia, this was my home. I hope it will be again someday."

Barrett overheard her. "You really love it here, don't you?"

"Oh yes, I have so many fond memories." The expression on her face radiated joy.

Barrett watched her thoughtfully.

For a few seconds, Brooke said nothing. Then her eyes seemed to see deeper, past her heart and into her soul. She took in a slow, cleansing breath. "Here, boys can be boys. They can hunt and fish whenever they want. Yes, I love it here. I have missed it immensely. More than I thought I would."

Barrett watched Alton holding Ludwig. He gave a weak smile and looked back at Brooke. "You know, I see no reason why we can't move down here after we sell our house in Connecticut."

"But that house has memories, too... memories of you and your family."

"This is my family now. Furthermore, we should not keep Grandpa Alton from seeing his grandchildren every day. Besides, Cornelius has been eyeing my property for years; he wants my lake."

She smiled and threw her arms around him. "Oh, I love you! Thank you, thank you. How soon can we move?"

"Just as soon as I get everything in order."

"There is plenty of room in my house until you build your own place," Alton added with a huge approving smile.

"We can build our house close to the river and have a special room for you and your piano, so you can write your hymns." Brooke's big, dark eyes danced with anticipation.

Barrett looked at his children and sighed. "I hope one of these three will follow in my footsteps. One will surely become a concert pianist."

"I am voting on Amalia. Look how long and slender her fingers are." Brooke gently lifted her daughter's tiny hand.

"She will have to break into a man's world," Barrett cautioned.

"She can do it. She's a von Weber," Brooke said without an ounce of doubt.

"She's also a Fortner. They never give up," Alton boasted.

The von Weber family spent two weeks at Annalise before they were on their way again. The weary travelers would have to change trains many times in the next ten days. It was not an easy trip to New Haven, Connecticut.

One afternoon on the train, when Brooke was reading to the children, Barrett struck up a conversation with a boisterous gentleman from New York.

Barrett shifted his position. "This sure is a dilapidated train, isn't it?"

"You will notice a big difference in the trains when you reach West Virginia. It will get better!"

"Is there not a more direct route?" Barrett inquired.

"Yes, but it would actually take longer because so many sections of the rails are being rebuilt. Almost the entire train system in the South was destroyed in the war. It was outdated in the first place... at least, compared to the North."

The gentleman shook von Weber's hand. "My name is Albert. I sell parts for carriages and wagons."

"Glad to meet you, Albert. I am Barrett, and this is my wife, Brooke."

The man courteously tipped his hat to the lady. "We have to make a stop in a town in North Carolina, close to the Virginia line. Marauders hit many of the towns along the border, including that one. I stop there to give them my business, besides the people are very friendly. There is a nice hotel with a great eating establishment next door."

Brooke sighed. "Not another stop. Will we ever get home?"

"I know how you feel. I sometimes wonder if I spend more time on the train than selling anything." He smiled at Brooke.

The train's loud whistle and grinding brakes told the passengers they were coming to a stop.

Brooke gazed out the window. Most of the buildings were still in the framing stage. "Well, this looks like an exciting place!" she said, rolling her eyes.

Albert laughed. "Well, at least there are no saloons, or houses of ill repute here. This town was totally destroyed near the end of the war, like so many others. First thing the citizens did was rebuild the church. I think you'll like it here."

"Sounds like my kind of town," Barrett said, smiling at his wife.

She shook her head as she cradled Amalia in her arms. "I just yearn to be home." Brooke stared out the window.

The check-in at the hotel was quick and the accommodations more than adequate.

Even though the people in the town had lost most everything during the war, they were friendly and grateful to have an opportunity to rebuild their town, as well as their lives.

The cozy restaurant added to the von Weber's enjoyment; the tantalizing aroma of the food made everyone hungrier. A woman pianist entertained the customers as they dined.

Brooke noticed an attractive girl bring food to an elderly couple at a nearby table.

"Hey, Pastor. What you preaching on this week?" A man at a table across the room shouted.

A man cooking on a fire behind the counter replied kiddingly, "Gluttony. Something you need to hear."

The diners broke out laughing, including Barrett who was playfully chatting with Nathan.

The waitress glanced up and noticed Brooke looking her way.

Making brief eye contact, the two smiled at each other.

The hard worker made her way toward the kitchen, walking by the von Weber's table. She smiled at Brooke and then looked directly at Barrett, who was still bantering with his son. A look of curiosity appeared on her face.

Brooke noticed it and quietly teased her handsome husband, "Looks like you have a young lady who fancies you."

Barrett glanced up at the girl and politely smiled. Her long brown hair and dark eyes were striking. However, the expression on her face confused him. He watched her take beverages to a couple close to them, but her eyes kept tracking back to Barrett.

"Looks like she is smitten by you! Sorry, girl... he's taken," Brooke said loud enough for only her husband's ears. She continued to watch the waitress, curious about the girl's behavior.

Feeling her penetrating eyes, Barrett glanced at the mysterious waitress again.

All of a sudden, the worker's arms went limp and her tray of dishes came crashing to the floor.

All eyes in the restaurant turned to the clatter.

Then, without warning, the girl ran to Barrett and threw her arms around him, sobbing.

Bewildered, Barrett stood and cautiously put his arms around her, patting her on the shoulder. *She is upset about something and wants my help. Maybe she recognizes me.*

The woman at the piano stopped playing.

A young man who had been helping wash dishes, stepped from behind the counter, staring at the unfolding scene. Drying his wet hands on his apron, he strode toward Barrett.

When Barrett noticed the young man, memories flooded his mind. *Could it be?* He stammered, "Emmitt?" Then he glanced down at the girl still clinging to him and whispered, "Chastity?"

"Sir, is that really you?" Emmitt asked.

A huge smile came to Barrett's face. "Yes. It's really me!"

Emmitt rushed toward Barrett and joined in the embrace.

Barrett had his arms around both of them when he finally spoke to his confused wife. "Remember the story I told you about the abandoned town and the boy and girl we found there. This is them!"

Brooke's stunned look turned to one of pity as she recalled what the youngsters had gone through.

"Are you doing all right?" Barrett asked.

"Pretty good. Chastity has never gotten over her ordeal. She is extremely shy, doesn't talk much."

Barrett gently brushed the hair from the face of the crying girl, remembering the day he helped rescue her from the food cellar.

Emmitt stepped back, grinning. "So glad to see you made it through the war, sir."

Barrett turned his head and motioned toward his family. "This is my wife, Brooke, and my children—Nathan, Ludwig, and the baby—Amalia."

Chastity hugged Brooke, who responded by putting her arms gently around the once-battered girl.

"Sir, did you ever find the men who did the terrible things to my sister and killed everyone in our town?" Emmitt unintentionally clenched his fist.

Barrett replied honestly, "I have found all but one, and each of them has paid the ultimate price."

"So, justice is being served... like you promised." Emmitt let out a slow, cleansing breath. "You say there is still one of them out there?" The lad pressed for answers.

He shrugged. "He could have died during the war. Nevertheless, you can be sure I will continue looking for him. I know his name, and his rank in the Union Army. He headed north with a lot of gold. I'll ask questions when I get back home to Connecticut. I plan to file a formal complaint with the Justice Department. I spent almost a year in a Confederate prison camp, so I have taken a leave of absence the last few years. We are returning home from Germany, but I won't give up."

The lad stammered, "I guess that war cost us all a lot. Even today, when I see a Union soldier, I want to kill him. But I try to remember your promise—that you would see justice done."

"And I will try my best to see it to its conclusion."

"We are thankful you brought us to this town. Pastor Jeff and his wife helped us out a lot. They taught us to look at the good in people, not the bad."

"Did they survive the war?"

"Yes, sir. Pastor, come over here. I want you to see someone." Emmitt waved the cook over.

Pastor Jeff had been watching from behind the counter. He rushed over and von Weber reached his hand out to greet him.

"I never thought I would see you again," Jeff said, smiling broadly.

The woman at the piano joined the pastor, who introduced her to Barrett. "This is my wife, Lori."

Barrett spoke to the woman. "Glad to meet you. I have enjoyed your piano playing."

"Thank you, that means a lot coming from you!"

Barrett peered over at the empty piano. He paused as he reminisced about the day four years ago when the pastor said he hoped to hear him in concert someday. The Hymnist pointed to the piano, "May I?"

"Oh, yes, please do," the pastor and his wife, chorused in unison.

The restaurant became silent when von Weber took his place at the piano.

Jeff took his wife's hand and led her to an empty table. Together, along with the rest of the patrons in the room, they listened to the Hymnist make the piano come alive, in a way that only he could do.

The pastor squeezed his wife's hand and whispered, "This must be sort of what heaven is like." He closed his eyes and uttered a silent prayer of thanksgiving.

Chapter Forty-Eight

October 1868
Lexington Virginia

Virginia was one of the hardest hit states during the Civil War. Now, it was booming with the establishment of new towns and the reconstruction of the rail system.

It was almost eight in the morning when the train pulled into the station at Lexington, Virginia. The uniformed conductor walked through each car making the announcement: "We will have a four hour layover here. Tracks ahead are being repaired. You can stay on the train or visit the town."

"Honey, will we ever make it home?" Brooke asked, trying not to whine as she stroked her youngest son's head.

Barrett sighed. "It is a long trip, but we will make it. I am going to take a walk into town. I heard there is a great school here—Washington College."

"Well, don't miss the train!" She smiled, batting her long lashes.

"Don't worry. I'll be back in plenty of time." Barrett winked.

He put on his hat and grabbed his cane, which he used frequently since his side never healed properly from his war injury. He also was susceptible to pneumonia since his time in Andersonville, and his near death experience on the *Sultana*. Although, he never complained. He was grateful to be alive and tried to remember that each day was a gift from God. He planned to live life to its fullest.

While roaming through the town, he noticed a large crowd gathering in front of a restaurant. Curious, he sauntered over to investigate. He managed to catch a glimpse of an older man sitting at a table drinking a cup of coffee, interacting with a small group of college students.

"Excuse me, what is going on here?" Barrett asked a student next to him.

"President Lee is having his morning coffee. Every weekday morning he challenges his students to a debate."

"President Lee?" Barrett asked, confused.

"Yes, of the college... President Robert E. Lee."

Barrett was thankful his extra height gave him the advantage of looking over most of the crowd. He watched the man using hand gestures, apparently deep in conversation with a couple boisterous students. Finally, everyone broke out laughing.

"We have to get to class," one of the young people announced loudly to his peers.

With that, the students dispersed.

The gentleman was left alone, holding his coffee mug.

Barrett recalled the last time he saw Lee. *He looks much older, but I know war does that to a man.*

Walking closer, Barrett asked, "How is the coffee, sir?"

Lee glanced up, tipping his mouth slightly, "Hot." He studied von Weber. "How are you this fine morning?" the general set down his hot brew.

Barrett walked a few steps closer. "Splendid, thank you."

Lee took special interest in the man's cane and slight limp. "A war injury?"

"Yes, sir. Most of the time I don't notice it, but on these damp mornings...."

"I know how you feel. North or South?"

"Excuse me?"

"What side were you on? North or South?" Lee cocked his head.

"North, sir, but I am married to a Savannah girl."

"Happily married, I hope."

"Yes, sir. Extremely happy."

"Good." Lee paused. "I am Robert E. Lee. I do not think we have met. I hope I was not responsible for your war injury."

Barrett grinned. "No, sir, you were not. But we have met... twice."

Lee folded his arms. "Jog my memory."

"First time we met was at Harpers Ferry. One of your lieutenants tried to horsewhip one of my wife's employees. I didn't like that!" Barrett frowned as he thought of the unpleasant incident.

Lee scratched his beard. "Oh, yes, I remember you now. You had him pinned to the ground." He laughed. "As I recall I made a comment about the pistol you had, and you said something that has stuck in my mind ever since."

"And what was that?" Barrett blinked.

"It is hard to bring the future to men who are stuck in the past." He picked up his coffee and sipped slowly.

"I do remember saying that."

"The war showed that to be very true. You are Barrett von Weber, aren't you?"

"Yes, sir."

"You said we had met twice." He raised his coffee to his lips.

"Well, not really met. Actually, I saw you from a distance. You were about to take a drink of fresh coffee, like now."

He thought for a second and pushed his chair back. "Ah, yes, von Weber... the marksman... the scout... the bear." A grin took over Lee's face. He stood, facing Barrett. "I always said I wanted to shake the hand of the man who fired that shot. That was the finest rifle shot I had ever seen... or felt. It stung my hand a bit. I still itch from the burn mark on my wrist." He rubbed his hand recalling the incident.

"Sorry about that, sir."

Lee extended his hand to von Weber.

Barrett wasted no time in reciprocating with a firm handshake. "I am deeply honored to finally meet you face-to-face, General Lee."

"The honor is mine. You know, I still have that cup you shot. It's on my fireplace mantle and serves as a reminder of how one shot can alter a man's life."

"And change history," von Weber added.

"Such is war."

"Yes, such is war." Barrett nodded slightly.

"I often wondered why you never took the shot. You might have been able to end the war sooner."

"Not likely, sir. Your troops respected you. It would have been just a matter of time until they found out who fired the shot, and my life would not have been worth a plugged nickel. Furthermore, the outcome of the war would have been the same. Only difference... you would have been dead, your soldiers would have rallied, and ultimately more men would have died. And I would have spent the rest of my life looking over my shoulder."

"I suppose you are right. Do you have time to sit and chat with me a while longer? Can I get you a cup of coffee? "

"I would be honored."

"Before we do, Mr. von Weber, if you are carrying a firearm, please don't aim it at my coffee cup. I love coffee too much to see it go to waste." Lee laughed heartily.

"Well, sir, I always carry a weapon, but you don't have to worry. I'll keep it holstered. I too, enjoy a good cup of coffee."

Barrett sat across from Lee and the two chatted like old friends. When it was time to leave and catch the train, they shook hands.

"Mr. von Weber."

"Please call me Barrett, sir."

"All right. Barrett, if you happen to see my nemesis, Grant… give him my regards."

Barrett snickered. "I'll do that, sir."

He snapped to attention and saluted the old general.

Robert E. Lee returned the salute, and then watched the Hymnist walk out of sight.

Chapter Forty-Nine

March 1869
Washington, D.C.

A gusty March wind caught Brooke by surprise, but an alert Barrett caught her bonnet before it blew out of the carriage.

Here she was at the White House again, but this time Barrett accompanied her. He was performing at the Inaugural Ball before the newly elected President Ulysses S. Grant.

Brooke studied the impressive building in front of her, mind reeling with thoughts of the last time she had visited the White House, especially her talk with President Lincoln. *He certainly was honest, and he cared about the soldiers, both North and South, willing to help any way he could. Why would anyone kill such a great man?*

Sorrow filled her heart as she thought about his heartbreaking assassination. She had heard the president's widow wasn't doing well since that traumatic event, and whispered a prayer for her.

Arriving early, their carriage waited in line with dozens of others— each one carrying politicians and high-ranking officials, or perhaps elite representatives from the business world.

Waiting for their turn to unload, Brooke asked her husband excitedly, "What was President Grant like when you met him?"

Barrett laughed. "The first thing I noticed was his smell."

"He stunk?" She wrinkled her nose; a mannerism Barrett thought was adorable.

"Cigar smoke—he loves his cigars."

"As a person, I mean, what was he like?"

"He was a man on a mission—to end the war."

"Anything else?"

"I don't know much more because I only talked with him for a few minutes. I respected the man. He was a man who delegated responsibility and trusted that the job would be done right."

"Do you think he trusted you?"

"Most certainly. I have been thinking about that meeting since I knew we were coming here today. You see—I did not exactly obey his orders."

"Which were…?" Brooke's interest heightened.

"He wanted me to use my skills to do something I morally could not do... and I refused."

"You refused a direct order? I find that hard to believe." Her right eyebrow raised high.

"Well, it was not actually a direct order. It's hard to explain. I think we had a mutual respect for each other. I understood why he would ask me to do such a thing, and he understood why I could not do it." Barrett's thoughts lingered on that day.

Brooke was silent for a moment. She knew when to stop questioning her husband and had reached that point.

She changed the subject. "Are you excited to play before the president?"

"I look forward to it. I consider it my mission field. It is where I can express my heart, my feelings, and my faith."

When the carriage finally came to a stop, an attendant opened the door and helped them down.

Brooke slipped her arm through her husband's and they walked up the sidewalk on the perfectly landscaped grounds. "I still feel uncomfortable going to these things."

Barrett noticed a number of soldiers strategically located around the building.

"You will be the most beautiful woman here." He led her up the steps and through the large, ornate, wooden doors.

Von Weber scanned the room and noticed several armed guards, each keenly aware of every move of the visitors.

"Sure different than when I visited President Lincoln," she said softly. "Guards are everywhere now."

"I noticed that." Barrett surveyed the scene again, something he did instinctively.

The attendant at the door greeted them, "Name, please." He studied the paper in his hand, face solemn, waiting for the Hymnist's reply.

"I am Barrett von Weber, and this is my wife, Brooke," Barrett responded in his typical upbeat tone.

"Good evening, Mr. von Weber," the attendant said, sounding a bit more cordial.

"Lieutenant, why all the security?" Barrett asked, trying to make conversation.

"The new president was the General of the Army and he made a lot of enemies, both North and South. We are just taking all necessary precautions." He checked the couple's names off the list and gestured for them to move forward.

"There goes our trust in mankind," Barrett whispered as he took his wife's hand and stepped around the lieutenant.

As a stringed ensemble played in the background, the couple chatted with a few friends they had not seen since before the war.

Before entering the massive ballroom, Barrett heard a familiar voice call out his name. When he turned toward the front door, a big smile encompassed his face. "Cornelius!" He rushed over to greet his friend with a handshake and hug. "I'm surprised to see you."

"Well, it just so happens, I have a surprise...."

The harsh voice of the lieutenant attending the door caught their attention. In a stern voice he spoke to a new guest, "Turn around and leave before I have you put in irons and hauled off to jail."

"Don't talk to my friend like that," another guest snapped.

The crowd gathering at the door had blocked their view, but Barrett and Cornelius kept listening.

The attendant shouted, "Sergeant! Arrest this man!"

Cornelius groaned, "Oh, no! I should have stayed with them." He rushed to the door, leaving Barrett dumfounded.

"What do you mean?" Barrett asked, following his friend through the maze of people. Finally, he could see the security guards at the door talking to a couple men. He drew closer and could not believe his eyes—at the center of the disturbance were Wheaty and Moccasin!

"Arrest these troublemakers... haul them away!" the lieutenant hollered.

A guard wearing sergeant stripes pushed Moccasin to the ground, pointing his pistol at him. "Make one move and you are a dead Indian!"

Another guard stood with a rifle aimed at Wheaty.

Barrett rushed over. From the side, he grabbed the man's arm, disarming the sergeant who was threatening his Indian friend. Then he shoved the guard into the crowd, shouting, "You will do no such thing!" His voice reflected his anger. Immediately, he aimed the pistol point blank at the other guard's head and bellowed, "Drop it! Step back!"

"What do you think you are doing? I'll have you put in irons with them, I don't care who you are." the defiant lieutenant snarled at the Hymnist.

Quickly assessing the scene, Cornelius spoke loud enough for all to hear. "You have no right to treat these men like this." He pointed to Moccasin and Wheaty. "They are true heroes. It was because of them the war ended when it did."

"He's an Indian... and there is no such thing as a good Indian," the guard holding the rifle hissed.

The lieutenant summoned another guard, "Private, get the colonel, now!"

The soldier rushed to find the officer who was in charge of security.

The guard still holding the rifle, looked away for a split-second, and when he did, Wheaty disarmed him.

Barrett ordered the stunned guard to back up with hands raised. Without hesitation, the furious guard did as ordered.

Wheaty quickly spun around and locked the door before any more armed guards could enter.

Von Weber smiled at his former comrades. "Quick thinking, Wheaty! Am I glad to see you." He enveloped them both in a bear hug. "I see you made it back safely."

"Yes, we did, none too soon. We had just given Grant the message, so he sent the Union Army to battle the Rebels at Spotsylvania. It was bloody, but successful. If we would not have given him the whereabouts of Lee, a different story may have been written," Wheaty reported.

"What about Jack and Alex?" Barrett asked.

"We never saw them again. We have no idea what happened to them."

Barrett lowered his head. "They were good men."

"Yes. And good friends."

Von Weber nodded.

"General Custer was happy... he got his horse back," Wheaty snickered.

Just then, three officers in full military attire, rushed over to investigate.

"Everyone step back. What is going on?" one inquired.

The lieutenant attending the door answered, "Colonel, these two men were trying to get into the ballroom." He pointed to the Indian and Wheaty. "And this man... he disarmed your guard with some fancy movement." He glared at Barrett.

Sizing them up, the colonel noticed that two of them weren't in formal wear, like the other guests. Wheaty wore a suit, one appropriate for a Sunday morning church service. Moccasin's attire was his oversized Union dress jacket, military trousers, and a top hat.

"You know that is not going to happen," the colonel said directly, certain the unlikely guests would not be permitted to join the festivities.

Barrett fixed him with a glare. "These men are my guests. If they leave... I leave."

"And me, also," Cornelius agreed.

The colonel tried to intimidate Barrett with a long, cold stare. "And just who are you?"

"Barrett von Weber."

"Barrett von Weber?" He hesitated. "You look familiar. Have we met?"

Before Barrett could respond, a fully bearded man, followed by a dozen others, hurried over to investigate. "What's all the commotion about?"

The lieutenant replied, "General, I mean Mr. President... these uninvited men are trying to attend your Inaugural Ball. This gentleman says they are his guests." He gestured to Barrett.

Grant paused, taking a long drag on his cigar, studying the situation. Suddenly, a broad smile replaced his frown. "Well, I'll be... if it isn't Major von Weber." President Grant reached his hand out to Barrett who readily accepted it. "It is good to see you. I have been keeping tabs on you."

"What do you mean?" Barrett handed the guard's pistol to the president.

"I heard about your capture and am glad you survived Andersonville. I was glad I didn't have to keep my promise."

"What promise was that, Mr. President?"

"The one I made at Brandy Station... to tell your wife the bad news if you didn't return."

Barrett nodded, remembering, "I'm glad you didn't have to either, sir."

"Did you enjoy your stay in Europe?"

"Very much so. However, I am glad to be back. Europe has its own problems."

"Yes, I have heard. War is breaking out all over. Why can't people get along?"

Barrett knew there was no answer to the question.

President Grant shifted his gaze to Wheaty and Moccasin. "I remember you two. Come on in, you are my guests," he spoke with authority.

The new president addressed the guests who had gathered around them. "Gentlemen and ladies... it is because of these men that Lee was stopped. I was about to go a different direction when they showed up at Brandy Station and gave me the location of Lee and his Confederate Army. I am honored to have them here as my guests. They deserve a medal for their bravery."

"The men who deserve the medals are the ones who never came home... those who gave their lives." Barrett let out a huff of breath.

Grant nodded in agreement and then turned to the officer in charge. "Colonel Gibbons, I know you are in charge of security, and I appreciate what you do, but I will vouch for these men." His comment left no room for debate.

Gibbons? Barrett's body stiffened at the mention of the colonel's name. *Could this be the man I have been searching for?*

"Yes, sir, Mr. President," the colonel responded, turning to greet von Weber. He reached his hand out and uttered, "Like I said, you look familiar. I have the knack of never forgetting a face." He smiled at Barrett.

The expression on Barrett's face was hard, no hint of a smile. "What about the back of a man's head?" Von Weber never forgot the man he had found years ago, face down in the grass, shot through the back of the head.

"Pardon me?" Gibbons asked, confused.

Barrett took Gibbons' hand, gripping it tight, staring into the soldier's dark eyes.

The colonel's smile faded.

Grant boasted, "Colonel Gibbons had the distinct honor of serving under Lee at Harpers Ferry, and also under my command for a while."

"Gibbons?" Barrett's voice grew louder, still gripping the man's hand.

For a minute, an awkward silence filled the air.

"Have you heard of me?" Gibbons spouted arrogantly.

"I'm not sure. Were you ever in Southern Virginia?" Barrett sliced him with a glare.

"As a matter of fact I was. My men fought many battles in that area."

Barrett tightened his grasp, continuing his questions.

"Then, you probably know Lieutenant Rice?"

"Rice? Oh yes, the horse thief who stole General Custer's horse. We finally caught up to him. He was killed in a battle."

Barrett's vice-like grip began to cut off the circulation in the colonel's hand.

"Sir, you are hurting my hand!" Gibbons voice sounded somewhat panicky.

"Shooting somebody in the back of the head does not constitute a battle." Barrett pushed for the truth.

From a short distance, Brooke watched her husband, concern mounting. She had rarely seen him so angry.

"What are you talking about?" Gibbons shot back.

"You and Rice. Your evil deeds are well known in the South... going into a town and killing everyone."

Gibbons looked down at his white knuckles, but von Weber tightened his hold even more. "It was war, they tried to kill us." He tried to pull his hand away, unsuccessfully.

Barrett's face grew red with rage. "Tried to kill you... who did?"

"The Rebels in the towns."

"Towns like South Wales? There were no Rebels in that town, only women and children. The men were off fighting a war... defending their country."

Gibbons said nothing, sweat beading on his forehead. Again, he tried to pull his hand away, but Barrett wouldn't let go.

"I saw firsthand what you and your men did. All of it ordered by you." Barrett's tone suggested the worst was yet to come.

"It was war!" Gibbons yelled out in pain.

"Sir, let go of the man's hand," one of the officers in the crowd ordered.

Barrett felt the heat rising in his cheeks, his heart racing. "To rape and kill young girls? That is war?"

"The Rebels did that, we gave the people food and water," Gibbons hissed, extreme pain overtaking him.

The lieutenant tried to pull von Weber off Gibbons, but Barrett shoved him away with his other hand so forcefully that he fell into the crowd. "This is between the two of us," he stated harshly.

Barrett continued gripping Gibbons' hand so hard that the officer fell to his knees—helpless!

A sudden thought hit von Weber when he saw Gibbons on his knees with his left eye nervously twitching. A night, nine years prior, surfaced in his mind—a night he would never forget. *Is this the man who whipped William the night John Brown attacked Harpers Ferry?* He studied him closer. Barrett turned pale, realizing that the man he confronted at Harpers Ferry was the same man as the notorious soldier he had been trying to find—Gibbons.

Barrett gritted his teeth. "Now I know you. I never forget a face either. You are the man who struck down William at Harpers Ferry. You were going to shoot him and me. You said that he was standing in the way of military business. Do you remember?"

The crowd around them had hushed, everyone wondering what details would be revealed.

Barrett continued without giving Gibbons a chance to reply, "I came into one of the towns you had visited in '64. I saw the bodies of the women and children you butchered. I know you were there and I can prove it!"

"You sayin' this man was responsible for murdering all those people in South Wales?" Wheaty interrupted.

"Yes, he is."

"I just followed orders," Gibbons cried out.

"Followed orders?" Barrett shouted.

"Yes. We were told to destroy everything in our path, to cause havoc in the South. Now someone, get this madman off me," Gibbons screamed, fear written all over his face.

"Not to kill women and children. Those are orders a man never follows, no matter who orders it." Barrett's eyes spit fire.

Grant stepped closer, speaking calmly, "Barrett, surely you are mistaken. This man is a war hero. Please let go of his hand."

Another security guard neared von Weber and pointed a gun directly at his chest.

Wheaty stepped between them. "Put your gun away. Stay out of this!"

"Yes, let the man do a little interrogation," Cornelius growled to the guard who reluctantly lowered his pistol.

"I saw the dead and mutilated bodies you had thrown into the well," Barrett shouted, bending Gibbon's hand backwards. "The survivors I found gave me a clear description of you and your thugs. Poor girl was just thirteen and had been raped repeatedly by you and your men."

"You have no proof," Gibbons spit the words out.

"That's where you are wrong. I have two witnesses. One of them said the leader had a sword with a snake on it. He saw him push that sword through a teenage boy's body." Barrett grabbed Gibbons' saber with his free hand, pulled it from its sheath, and held it up. "Well, well... something you don't see very day... a saber with a snake!"

"I had nothing to do with that. The men were out of control." By now, Gibbons was in so much pain, he could hardly speak.

"I made a promise to that sweet girl and her brother... I would personally see that the men responsible for those hideous crimes would pay. I ran into five of your men a few days later. Good leader you are... you abandoned them, so you could go after the gold. Let's just say, all your buddies paid the ultimate price for their deeds."

"Let go of my arm!" Gibbons screamed through clenched teeth.

Von Weber bent the colonel's hand back to his wrist, forcing him to writhe in pain. Then he raised the sword and placed the point of it on the back of Gibbons' neck.

"Please stop! Stop hurting my husband!" a woman cried, stepping out of the crowd.

"I demand you release Colonel Gibbons," one of the officers yelled.

"Leave them alone," Wheaty said to the officer, "they have unfinished business."

Von Weber shifted his focus to the man's wife. "Judging by the clothes you wear, ma'am, you are pretty well-to-do. Let me tell you where your husband got his money. It was from the blood of nearly a hundred Union soldiers, an untold number of Rebel soldiers, and many innocent civilians. In one town, he and his group took all the young girls and raped them before stabbing them. That is what the person you sleep with every night did."

Barrett glared at the military leaders standing close. "You think this man is a good leader. Not likely... he knowingly sent his own men to their deaths and even shot his fellow soldier, traitor that he was, Sergeant Hornsby, in the back—over gold. Gold that he received by selling stolen weapons to the South. Weapons, which these two men and I were sent to recover."

"Gibbons was responsible for the weapons theft?" Grant looked stunned.

"Not for the actual theft... that was Lieutenant Rice and Sergeant Hornsby," Barrett replied. "Gibbons and his cavalry unit were sent to retrieve General Custer's horse that Rice had stolen."

"Why would Rice steal the general's horse?" President Grant questioned.

Barrett continued, "Rice had planned the whole thing with Hornsby. But, Hornsby got greedy and secretly moved the plan ahead, which resulted in the death of many Union soldiers. All for gold!" He shook his head, sadly. "When Gibbons found Rice, they concocted their own plan and went after Hornsby and the gold."

Barrett paused, "This man here thought he had all his tracks covered. Even went as far as sending those who helped him to their graves. Then he killed the only man left that could identify him—Lieutenant Rice. I found him shot in the back of the head, close to where Hornsby was murdered."

"Of course! When I heard about the theft of the rifles—I read the report. Lieutenant Rice signed it. I should have known he was involved." Grant groaned, as the truth became evident.

Barrett continued, "The theft was supposed to take place at Brandy Station, but three other men decided to do it themselves. Split the gold three ways instead of four."

"You need a witness to these outrageous accusations, sir," an officer in the crowd shouted out.

Wheaty insisted boldly, "There are three of them right here. Major Barrett, Moccasin, and I were all there. We saw what they did."

"But did you see Colonel Gibbons actually commit a crime? You need a witness who was there," the same officer protested.

Barrett bellowed, "I will bring forth the witnesses to see that this man is punished. He disgraced his unit, his country, and his family. And, if justice is not served by a court of law, then this is not the country that I love."

Von Weber shoved Gibbons to the ground. "I leave him in your hands. Like I said before, I made a promise to a girl and her brother—I would find the guilty soldiers and make sure justice was served. You are the last one! My job is finished!" He rubbed his palms together, signifying his work was done.

Von Weber handed Gibbon's saber to the lieutenant and spun around. He reached for Brooke's hand.

She had tears streaming down her face. She pitied those Gibbons hurt, but she beamed with pride for the way her husband stood up for what was right.

Watching them walk toward the door, Gibbons struggled to his feet. He tilted his jaw upward in a gesture of defiance and shouted, "They were Rebel scum. They didn't deserve to live."

Von Weber released his wife's hand and strode back to Gibbons. With one punch, Barrett knocked him to the ground. Standing over him, he shouted, "My wife is from the South. I have friends in the South and they are more American than you will ever be."

President Grant watched, holding a drink in one hand and a cigar in the other—speechless.

Barrett turned to the president, "Sir, I suggest you check out more thoroughly who you promote from now on. If not, you will be open to scandals in your administration. As for this... this... man, I demand you arrest him now! If you don't, then you are not the leader I thought you to be. I will bring forth the witnesses needed to have him hanged. If you do not see that justice is done, I will, and that is a promise, not a threat. You sent Major Wirz to the gallows because of trumped up charges. This man is a hundred times worse."

He tipped his hat. "Good day, gentlemen." With that, von Weber and his wife stormed out of the White House.

Cornelius, Wheaty, and Moccasin followed.

A few people attended to Gibbons, as his wife watched from a distance, tears filling her eyes.

"Sorry about this, sir, we will order the immediate arrest of von Weber," an officer spouted to Grant.

President Grant didn't move, staring into space. He cleared his throat and finally spoke, "I have known von Weber only a short time, but I know he is an honest man, a man of integrity. I believe he can produce the witnesses, and I am sure he will see that justice is done."

He scowled at Gibbons. "I believe you are guilty of the crimes he accused you of. Arrest this man!" the president thundered.

"On what charges, sir?" one of the politicians nearby asked.

"War crimes!"

The same man continued, "War crimes? Against the South? Sir, it was war… you know that bad things happen in war. Look how inhumane they treated our soldiers at Andersonville." He crossed his arms, seemingly proud of his rebuttal.

Grant stared him down. "That is a stupid argument, Senator. Andersonville had nothing to do with killing innocent women and children. However, it's even more reason I have to see this through. If von Weber produces the witnesses, and I think he will, we have no choice. As he said, our courts sent Wirz to the gallows, and we can do no less to Gibbons. Arrest him!"

The guards whisked the prisoner away.

Grant walked outside and stood on the veranda of the White House. Sipping his brandy, he watched Barrett's carriage leave in a cloud of dust.

Vice President Schuler Colfax joined him. "That von Weber would make a great politician," he stated, rubbing his beard.

"He would make a lousy politician," Grant spoke with certainty. "There is no compromise with him. Everything is either right or wrong."

Grant faced Colfax, reminiscing aloud, "You know, the first time I met Barrett von Weber, I gave him an order, and he refused to obey it."

"Refused an order? That would be grounds for a court martial."

"One would think so." The president lit another cigar and took a long drag.

"What did you ask him to do?"

"I implied that he should assassinate General Lee."

"He disobeyed that?"

"He is a righteous man. He could never shoot an innocent, unarmed man."

Colfax suppressed a snicker. "You're right. He would never make a good politician."

They watched the von Weber carriage continue down Pennsylvania Avenue.

"Now a Supreme Court judge, that is a different story," Colfax added.

Grant smiled as the vice-president strolled back into the White House.

The president took one last glimpse at the carriage that was almost out of sight. "You, Barrett von Weber, are the bravest man I have ever met."

Grant raised his glass into the air. "I toast you for that, and for your honesty and commitment to your country." He took another drink and then walked back into the home where he would reside the next eight years. He had guests to entertain.

Chapter Fifty

The Rest of the Story

Historical Characters

John Brown (Isaac Smith) 1800-1859

John Brown was tried for treason against the Commonwealth of Virginia for his attack on Harpers Ferry. Tried also for the murder of five men, and inciting a slave insurrection, Brown was found guilty on all counts. He was hanged on December 2, 1859 at age fifty-nine. It is believed that John Wilkes Booth, the man that assassinated President Lincoln, stole a Union uniform and gained access to the hanging. Today some consider Brown a hero; others say he was a madman, traitor—America's first domestic terrorist.

Robert E. Lee 1807-1870

Lee commanded the Marines when they captured John Brown at Harpers Ferry. He was against secession, but when his native state of Virginia joined the South, he was committed to serve in the Confederacy. He became the General of the Army of Northern Virginia. Even though outmanned and outgunned, many of his war tactics helped prolong the war. The men who followed him into battle loved and respected him. After the war, he became President of Washington University, which later became Washington and Lee University. Union troops occupied his home, and his property was turned into a military cemetery, known today as Arlington National Cemetery. The Proclamation of Amnesty and Reconstruction Act of 1865 gave most Confederates their American citizenship back. Somehow, a mistake in the wording of the bill omitted Lee. On July 4, 1973, over a hundred years after his death, President

Gerald Ford signed a bill returning Robert E. Lee's citizenship. He died of a probable stroke at age sixty-three and was buried at Washington and Lee University in Lexington, Virginia.

Ulysses S. Grant 1822-1885

Grant was the General of the Union Army. He served as President of the United States from 1869 to 1877. His eight years in office were plagued with scandals by men in his administration. Grant has been credited with the help of rebuilding the South, and passing the Fifteenth Amendment, which gave voting rights to black Americans. His picture remains on the fifty-dollar bill. He died July 23, 1885 at the age of sixty-three.

Abraham Lincoln 1809-1865

Lincoln served only one full-term as the 16th President of the United States. His assassination on April 15, 1865, was only a month into his second term. He was sixty-three years old. Considered by many historians to be America's greatest president, Lincoln was known for ending slavery with the Emancipation Proclamation in 1863. He pushed through Congress the Thirteenth Amendment to the United States Constitution, outlawing slavery. President Lincoln is known for delivering one of America's greatest speeches—the Gettysburg Address, which focused on principles of equal rights, liberty, and democracy.

Mary Todd Lincoln 1818-1882

Mrs. Lincoln suffered from severe migraines and many other illnesses throughout her life. She and her husband, Abraham, had four sons. Sadly, three of her children died at an early age. She was holding Abraham's hand at Ford's Theatre, when John Wilkes Booth assassinated the president. Mary suffered from severe depression and was institutionalized for a short time. She died July 16, 1882 at age sixty-three.

George Armstrong Custer 1839-1876

Custer graduated last in his class at West Point, but because of the raging Civil War, and his influential military friends, he had the opportunity to rise quickly in the ranks. He became the youngest army general at age twenty-three. His troops played a decisive role in Lee's surrender and were on hand at Appomattox when Lee surrendered. Despite his achievement during the Civil War, he is most known for the Battle of

Little Big Horn. There, Indians led by Crazy Horse and Sitting Bull, killed Custer and the three companies of men he commanded. Interestingly, many of the Indians carried Henry rifles, the type that Barrett von Weber was sent to retrieve. Custer died on June 26, 1876 at only thirty-six years of age.

General William Tecumseh Sherman 1802-1871

Sherman, known as "Uncle Billy" to his troops, had a long military career. His *Scorched Earth* policy and *March to the Sea* are well known throughout the world. Many historians believe Sherman's defeat of Confederate General John Bell Hood, and the fall of Atlanta, caused the Presidential election of 1864 to swing in Abraham Lincoln's favor. Sherman's victory came at the perfect time because if Lincoln would have lost the election, the Confederacy may have won the war, and the history of the United States would have been different. Sherman died February 14, 1871 at sixty-nine.

Father Whelan 1802-1871

Peter Whelan, a Catholic priest, came to Andersonville in June of 1864. As a former prisoner of war, he understood what it was like living in the camps—the suffering and hardship. The priest ministered to the men in the hospital, as well as in the camp itself, during the hottest time of the year. He raised donations of sixteen thousand dollars in Confederate money, which he used to buy flour to make bread for the Andersonville prisoners. Letters from prisoners often mentioned him favorably. Whelan was a key witness for the defense of Major Wirz at his military tribunal. He died February 6, 1871 at the age of sixty-nine.

Dorence Atwater 1845-1910

Atwater was among the first Union prisoners to be taken to the new prison—Andersonville. When Captain Wirz discovered Atwater could read and write, he was enlisted to record all the fatalities in the camp. He made a list for the Confederacy and one for the Union. However, Atwater did not trust the Confederates to give the copy to the United States Government, so he made another list for himself. Upon being released, he smuggled his copy out in his laundry. He delivered it to Washington where the government confiscated it and told him the names would be released to the public. Months later, the list was still not released. Atwater became friends with Clara Barton, who founded the Red Cross, and together they retrieved his list. Along with Barton, and a number of stone carvers, he returned to Andersonville to erect thousands of headstones in the cemetery. Of the thirteen thousand, seven hundred and fourteen graves, thanks to Atwater, only nine hundred and twenty-one are unknown. He was court-martialed for the theft of his own list, stripped of rank, marched through the streets of Washington in chains, and sentenced to life imprisonment. President Andrew Johnson pardoned him after a plea from Barton. Atwater died November 26, 1910 at age sixty-five. He kept his original list of the dead at Andersonville in his home in San Francisco, but it was unfortunately lost in the fires from the great earthquake of 1906.

Major Heinrich Hartmann Wirz 1823-1865

Wirz, a medical doctor, was born in Switzerland. In 1849, distraught over his wife's death, he moved to America. He enlisted as a private in the Confederate States Army in May 1861. Wounded in the Battle of Seven Pines, he lost the use of his right arm. After returning to his unit in 1862, he was promoted to captain. In April 1864, Wirz took command of Camp Sumter, where he remained for over a year. Shortly before the end of the war, he was promoted to major. Under his command at Camp Sumter, better known as Andersonville Prison, nearly thirteen thousand men died. After the war, Federal troops arrested him at his residence outside the prison walls and took him to Washington D.C. to stand trial. Tried for treason and murder, he was found guilty. Many historians believe his trial was for show—someone had to pay for the atrocities at the prison. He was hanged at the old capitol building, which today is the location of the United States Supreme Court. Eleven days after his death, authorities discovered that the star witness for the prosecution was not who he said he was. In fact, he was a deserter, a fraud. The United Daughters of the Confederacy erected a tall monument in honor of Wirz, just outside of Andersonville Prison, in 1908. In 1981, Sons of the Confederate Veterans awarded Major Wirz the Confederate Medal of Honor.

Fictional Characters

Colonel Gibbons

Gibbons was arrested and tried for the murders of the citizens of South Wales. Chastity and Emmitt both took the witness stand and testified against him, implicating him as the leader directly in charge of the massacre. He never made it to the gallows—he committed suicide a day before sentencing.

Barrett and Brooke von Weber

The von Webers moved back to Annalise to reconnect with family and help rebuild the South. Barrett and Brooke had five children. Their sons, Nathan and Otto, remained at Annalise and took over the family textile business. Ludwig moved back to Germany to operate The von Weber Winery. Their youngest son, Conrad, became a minister of the gospel. Amalia, their only daughter, followed in her father's footsteps as a well-known concert pianist. Alton Fortner, died in his sleep in 1876.

Barrett suffered from bouts of pneumonia after Andersonville, further complicated by his time in the frigid water during the sinking of the *Sultana*. The same disease took his life twenty-eight years to the day after that fateful night. The Hymnist took his final breath on April 27, 1893. Shortly before he died, he penned his greatest musical composition. It was not another hymn, but a patriotic classic. He entitled it—*America, God's Country*. There was a big place in his heart for his ancestral country of Germany, but how he loved America!

Brooke never remarried, although she had several proposals. She had loved a godly man, who loved her with all his heart. Every night before Brooke von Weber went to sleep, she picked up a picture of her beloved Barrett, kissed it, and then placed it back on the stand beside her bed. Early in the year of 1917, just days before World War I, she picked up the picture, kissed it, and clutched it close to her heart. She went to sleep peacefully, but never awakened. At her funeral, officiated by her son, Conrad, he said, "God took her because He knew, she could not bear to see her beloved country at war again, especially against her husband's ancestral country, Germany."

Today, just a few miles outside Savannah, Georgia, one can still climb that hill at Annalise and visit the old, but well-kept circular cemetery. Although the names on the tombstones are faded, they can still be read. Brooke von Weber is buried next to Barrett von Weber, near her mother and father. Each day, a member of the family places a fresh rose on the graves of Brooke and her mother. Barrett had arranged for the tradition to continue until the Lord's return.

History

New Haven Arms Company

New Haven Arms operated for only a few years, but the company made some of the finest rifles of that era. If either the Union or the Confederate Army had supplied all of their soldiers with the Henry repeating rifle, a new chapter in the history books could have been written. The outcome may have been different. Maybe more men would have lost their lives, or perhaps the powerful weapons would have ended the war sooner with fewer men killed. Maybe even the South would have won the war. We will never know. In 1866, New Haven Arms was reorganized and the name changed to Winchester Repeating Arms Company. The Henry rifle evolved into the Winchester rifle and became known as "The Gun That Won the West."

Andersonville Prison/ Camp Sumter

Andersonville National Historic Site now stands where the infamous prison once confined over thirty-two thousand prisoners. The walls, buildings, and pigeon roosts are gone. Time has erased the stench, groans, disease, suffering, and death. The now-pure brook, Providence Spring, and the cemetery with its thirteen thousand, seven hundred and fourteen graves, are the only remnants of what once was. Looking at the peaceful landscape, one could almost forget the horror that endured one hundred and fifty years ago; however, survivors could never forget! Today the site serves as a memorial to all American prisoners of war throughout our nation's history, and houses the National Prisoner of War Museum.

Andersonville Prison Camp is known for its deplorable conditions and inhumane treatment of captured Union soldiers. However, the prisons operated by both the North and the South, were guilty of allowing many thousands of men to die a slow, agonizing death from dysentery, starvation, pneumonia, and countless other diseases. Heat exhaustion claimed lives of prisoners in the South, while tens of thousands of Confederate soldiers in the North died horrible deaths from the freezing temperatures because they had no shoes, coat, or a blanket. The Civil War brought out the worst of mankind on both sides, often pitting father against son, brother against brother, American against American. Unfortunately, when it came to the prison camps, there was no end to the inhumanity.

The Sultana

It has been a hundred and fifty years since that ill-fated night claimed the lives of the returning prisoners on the Mississippi River. The sinking of the *Sultana* was one of the worst maritime disasters in the world, certainly more costly in lives than even the Titanic, yet rarely mentioned. April 1865, was an eventful time in America's history. The surrender of Lee and the Confederate Army at Appomattox, the assassination of President Lincoln, and the search for his assassin—John Wilkes Booth, all occurred in that month. Adding the fact that the *Sultana* disaster occurred in the South, where few people cared about the fate of Northern soldiers. The *Sultana* disaster simply got lost in the country's chaos.

The Mississippi has changed its path many times since that night. Today the *Sultana* rests below the ground in a field near Marion, Arkansas.

The stories about that night are still passed down to the people who live by the Mississippi River. Many locals say that on any cold, foggy night, if you listen closely, you can still hear the swishing of the paddles of that famous steamboat, the S.S. *Sultana*, as it makes its quest toward home. You can also hear the voices of almost two thousand, three hundred men singing about freedom as the paddleboat chugs to its final destination—home. They are singing one of Barrett von Weber's hymns…

I'm going home. I'm going home.
Thank you Jesus, I'm going home.

ABOUT THE AUTHOR

J. L. Rothdiener was born in Syracuse, New York. Raised in Lakewood Colorado, he and his wife of thirty-eight years now reside in Bolivar, Missouri. They have two sons, and three wonderful grandchildren.

Rothdiener has had a lifelong passion for writing and began submitting articles to magazines and newspapers for publishing at an early age. He believes that God has given him the ability to write stories which can help change lives.

OTHER BOOKS
BY J. L. ROTHDIENER

The Quest for Forgiveness

From orphan to superstar...

Singer-songwriter Brianna Bays rose from obscurity to the center spotlight. She had everything... fame, talent, beauty, and one of the most successful music careers in history. The world was her stage, but the screaming adulation of her fans could not fill the hole in her heart. Her past was shrouded in shadows, some of her own making, and some of which she was trying desperately to pierce.

No amount of success could bring her the one thing she needed most... forgiveness...

ISBN: 0983416877

A Quest for Skye

Doctors Morgan and Tammy Hamilton take a vacation from their pediatric clinic in Saint Paul, Minnesota to board a cruise ship for the Caribbean. Among the passengers is Skye, a nine-year old girl with an irrepressible spirit, and a passion for living that touches everyone around her. Infused with hope and a belief in a loving God, Skye becomes the daughter that the Hamiltons could never have.

But despite her open and honest nature, Skye is surrounded by ominous questions. As everything they value begins slipping away from them, these hardnosed and pragmatic doctors suddenly find themselves praying for a miracle.

But Skye has been praying too...

ISBN: 0985252332

The Quest for Freedom

Six American soldiers still held as prisoners of war, four decades after the fall of Saigon... When the last US troops withdrew from Vietnam in August of 1973, a handful of men were left behind. Penned like animals in the bamboo cages of their captors, they have long since lost track of the hours, the weeks, and even the years. For these men, the war is not over. They continue to fight it every day, as they are beaten and tormented in retaliation for battles that have all but faded from memory. But in the squalid darkness of their cells, they forge a brotherhood of shared suffering, reinforced by the struggle to maintain their faith in a God who seems to have forsaken them.

In this place of unending misery, a tiny flame still flickers in their hearts. Freedom...

ISBN: 194039791X

You can purchase these books on **www.Navigator-Books.com**.

www.ingramcontent.com/pod-product-compliance
Lightning Source LLC
Chambersburg PA
CBHW020633020726
47494CB00001B/170